THE FELLING CUT

FINAL GIRLS

BOOK ONE

R. L. RANDOLPH

Cover image: *Mount Corcoran* by **Albert Bierstadt** (c. 1876-1877)

Chapter break image: *Axe* by **Hal Blakeley** (c. 1935/1942)

Images sourced from the National Gallery of Art

Editing by: DerpyWickedFox Editorial

A NOTE

This book contains sensitive content.
You can view the content warnings in the back matter.

Playlist

Much of this manuscript wouldn't have been possible without music and the artists that provided it. Like Nick and Evie, I sought inspiration and solace in song as I wrote this novel. I've included my playlist for *The Felling Cut* below, but many of these songs also make an appearance in text throughout the novel.

1. ***Use Somebody*** by Kings of Leon
2. ***Uptown Girl*** by Billy Joel
3. ***Carry On Wayward Son*** by Kansas
4. ***Burnin' For You*** by Blue Öyster Cult
5. ***Barracuda*** by Heart
6. ***Bad Moon Rising*** by Creedence Clearwater Revival
7. ***Drift Away*** by Dobie Gray
8. ***Oogum Boogum Song*** by Brenton Wood
9. ***Roxanne*** by The Police
10. ***Wanted Dead or Alive*** by Bon Jovi

11. *Walk This Way* by Aerosmith
12. *(Don't Fear) The Reaper* by Blue Öyster Cult
13. *Can't Help Falling in Love* by Elvis Presley
14. *Closer* by Kings of Leon
15. *Safe and Sound (Taylor's Version)* by Taylor Swift featuring Joy Williams and John Paul White
16. *Wicked Game* by Chris Isaak
17. *Sweet Nothing* by Taylor Swift
18. *Believer* by SYML
19. *Abstract (Psychopomp)* by Hozier
20. *tiny things* by Tiny Habits
21. *Two* by Sleeping At Last

For the bookworms who prefer to be lost in pages instead of dealing with reality.
You are stronger than you think.

May your axe strike true.

"Patience, he thought. So much of this was patience - waiting, and thinking and doing things right. So much of all this, so much of all living was patience and thinking."

Gary Paulsen, *Hatchet**

∿ ∿

*EVIE RECOMMENDS THIS BOOK TO EVERY TEEN SHE can. Her favorite review was a student who came into the library, read it in one sitting, then handed it back to her and said, "Miss Morgen, this fucking rocked. Are there more?"

She gave him book two.

FOREWORD

In logging, three precise cuts are required to fell a tree.

The first two are sharp and quick on the face side, with the logger's axe burrowing deep into the wood to establish a breaking point. The third cut is the most important, and dangerous — the felling cut.

The felling cut should be made at the opposite side of the first two. It must be exact, because if not, the tree will fall into the loggers' safe territory, endangering the lives of the entire crew.

NOVEMBER

CHAPTER ONE

I SHOULD BE ALONE.

That was Evelyn Morgen's first thought after a soft thump from the hallway jarred her focus from the precariously stacked books beside her. An old paperback copy of *Hatchet* crinkled in her hand as she looked away from the returns cart toward the closed double-doors.

Evie was no stranger to working in Hawthorne's school library at odd hours. She came in before the sun rose and left far after it had set. The old building's quirks were intimately familiar after thirteen years of her own childhood education. There were stairs that creaked, venting that rattled, and doors that no longer opened — but none of the everyday noises made the hair stand at the back of her neck as it was now.

A primal part of her brain registered the threat before she did. *Something was wrong.*

Her lips parted, brows furrowing as she abandoned the book on the cart, the cover's illustration of a wolf watching her. Occasionally other staff lingered after hours, but it was almost

Thanksgiving break. The teachers were as eager as the kids for the end of the school semester.

Someone grunted in pain.

Evie stopped short, waiting for another sound, but nothing came. Chancing a small inhale, she strode toward the doors, her hand going to the handle to scold whomever was here this late.

If this is another senior prank — I swear —

At the last second, Evie thought better of bursting into the hall and glanced out of the reinforced glass window.

Even with the rise of school shootings across America, she'd never worried for her safety. Hawthorne was different — small, sleepy, and not prone to violence.

The glass chilled her nose as her gasp fogged the window.

Of the two bodies locked together in the hallway, only one was recognizable. The new math teacher, Ben Harriett, was so red in the face that it blended into his vibrant hair. His shirt sleeves bunched around his elbows, exposing pale freckled forearms as he grappled with an unfamiliar man.

She couldn't see the other man's face; he was bent, his long body folded almost in half as he wrapped an arm around Ben's torso. Ben struggled to surge forward, separating his back from the man's chest for half a second, only for the other man to overpower him.

None of their locked and awkward wrestling made any sense until the fluorescents glinted off black and silver — a gun. Ben twisted, but it was no use. The gun appeared and disappeared in a blink as the stranger pressed it into Ben's stomach. The other man's head bowed to Ben's ear, but the whispered words were lost in the sound of the gunshot.

Evie flinched, fumbling to hold onto the door and look away at the same time, but she was too slow. Ben's body crumbled and she could only watch as her new colleague landed on the scuffed linoleum.

The stranger rose to his full height, so white he looked nearly spectral, with blond shaggy curls on the top of his head. *He looks like Miss Ann's dog.* Evie blinked at the random memory of her childhood neighbor's Golden Retriever. Spit collected at the edges of the stranger's lips as he sneered down at the blood coming from Ben's stomach.

He pointed the gun at Ben and fired again and again and *again.*

Each gunshot made Evie jump, until the man was pointing an empty gun at Ben's lifeless body, the click of the vacant chamber echoing down the hall. Fighting back a scream, Evie jolted away from the window, looking at the open space of the library behind her — the only phone nearby was her cell, in her office behind the front desk across the room.

She glanced out again, watching the stranger's chest heave as the gun came to rest at his side. His face splattered with blood twisted as he reached into his pocket and pressed a button at the same time, the empty cartridge dropping into the pool of blood. The stranger pulled out a new cartridge and slotted it into the gun.

Bile rose in her throat as she took in the gore splattering his white shirt and the empty expression on the stranger's face like he hadn't murdered another person in cold blood. Bullet wounds mutilated Ben's body, rendering him near unrecognizable.

The emergency button. Her brain worked faster than her body. Every building in the Hawthorne school system was newly equipped with heavy, spring-loaded doors, shutters for exposed windows, and red buttons that set off the school's interconnected security system.

Evie took a step back, holding in a sobbed scream as her

focus split between keeping the doors in view and stumbling toward the office.

Her hip collided with a book display, sending piles scattering onto the floor and around her feet. Her head whipped down to them and then to the doors, expecting the man to have his face pressed against the glass, grinning like *The Shining*.

Instead, heavy, slow footsteps shattered the deafening silence in the hall.

Fuck this. Evie stepped on books as she fled, barely rounding the side of the circulation desk before she threw herself under it, curling into a ball at the back corner.

The hinges on the library doors creaked.

Evie clasped a sweaty palm over her mouth, looking ahead at the door to her office, mere feet away. The circulation desk didn't *feel* safe — not when she could see Ben's bullet-ridden body behind her eyelids every time she blinked.

The footsteps slowed. She turned her head, watching loafers come into view, shiny with specks of blood. The stranger kicked a copy of *The Bad Beginning*, sending it skittering across the carpet-tiled floor.

"I know you're in here."

His voice cut the silence like a razor wire.

Evie kept her breaths shallow and quiet as his feet turned in a circle. She knew what he was seeing — the construction paper leaves she'd cut out a month ago and taped to the walls. The far display was full of tiny hand-shaped turkeys that the kindergarteners made for her in art class.

His feet shifted, and then carried him away, toward the middle aisle of bookcases.

"If you come out, we can talk about this. I'm open to negotiation if you are. A librarian's salary can't be that well-paid." The sound of a book shifting on a shelf made her skin prickle, like he was perusing the children's reading material for himself.

You know I'm here. But you don't know where to look first. Evie closed her eyes, forcing herself to be *quiet*, as quiet as she hissed at the children who giggled during study hour. Blood pounded in her ears as she squeezed her hands into fists. They shook, but she ignored the tremor as she eased onto all fours, poised like a cat ready to leap.

The stranger's loafers disappeared around one of the bookcases.

The cracked office door in front of her simultaneously felt like it was mere feet away and a football field length from her. There was a copy of an old Webster's dictionary propping it open — because it auto-locked when it shut and she'd left her keys inside, like always.

Evie *leapt.*

She pushed herself forward in a half-crawl, half-jolt. Her body hit the floor, knocking into the rolling office chair behind the desk as she plunged forward, taking her chance as she heard the footsteps quicken behind her. As she reached for the door-knob, she glanced back, watching the stranger round the corner of the stacks, meeting her eyes across the empty space.

Her shoulder collided with the door, forcing the heavy hinge open before flinging her body through the narrow gap and immediately shoving it back to auto-lock behind her.

The door clicked the same moment his gun fired.

A spiderweb crack appeared, spreading across the glass inches from her face. Evie stared at the man as she reached over, flipped open the plastic cover, and slammed her hand down on the alert button.

Up close, she could see his features better, and her mind catalogued them in snapshots. He was sharp in every way, with a jawline angled toward his ears and an unnaturally cool look as he surveyed her — as if he didn't have a smoking gun still raised, barrel pointed at her face.

The alarm blared, red lights flashing overhead. His eyes narrowed, lips tightening at the edges. With a final feral look in her direction, his snarl returned as he turned to quickly make his leave.

All the air left Evie's lungs as she stumbled back. Her wobbly knees hit the back of her office chair and she collapsed into it, her body humming with adrenaline, hands shaking and heart beating nearly out of her chest.

She was alive. But all she could think was, *this isn't over.*

CHAPTER TWO

SHE FELT LIKE A FROZEN BURRITO SITTING IN THE precinct.

The blanket they gave her on arrival was one of those mylar blankets designed to help shock victims. She didn't *feel* shocked, she felt ready to be microwaved for two and a half minutes.

It crinkled around Evie's shoulders like a dog toy as she watched Sheriff Marlon Wyatt pace. The only other two cops in town deferred to him, but the old white man was as directionless as he was twenty minutes ago, waiting for *The Feds*.

He said *The Feds* like it was a primetime TV show airing at nine each Thursday night. He said it like she was supposed to know what that meant other than "*this is so much more than a man with a gun*" and so much more than the body already headed to the city morgue and so much *more* than what she expected when she went into work twelve hours ago.

Her mind looped the same confusing events that led her to this point.

Wake up. Breakfast. Water half-dead plant. Go to work. Lunch. Disinfect books.

Run from a murderer?

She couldn't comprehend how she'd ended up in the stagnant precinct when she was supposed to be home already, eating leftovers and watching cozy British mysteries.

Maybe she *was* in shock — just a little.

She glanced at the cup of coffee next to her seat. The hard plastic chair they left her in only had a thin and flattened piece of foam for a cushion with a layer of peeling faux leather covering it. She'd already sat for hours, waiting and watching and expecting *the Feds* to show up on their mysterious timetable.

Marlon stopped, looking over at Evie again as her entire body groaned. She was just lucky he hadn't called her parents. Even being an adult now, she was certain Marlon still saw her as the little girl that asked her father for a pet trout every Sunday fishing trip — or the renegade teenager he picked up time and time again after breaking apart parties in the woods. She'd only thrown up *once* in the backseat of his squad car, but he'd never let her forget it.

Evie broke eye contact with the sheriff to look at the precinct's door. Road salt remnants stuck to the glass around the decal that specified this one random storefront in a strip mall was the town's only underfunded police station.

The street was silent with no reflection of passing headlights. Hawthorne, Vermont was a ghost town after seven in the evening. Evie was pretty sure the town's elders rolled up the sidewalks each night and stored them in their garages until the next morning, and nothing was open — save for the liquor store that closed at ten.

Evie turned her head sharply when Marlon cleared his throat. His light blue uniform was rolled up at the sleeves and she stared at his pale forearms. The bloody white skin of the man in the library flashed in her mind, so different from Marlon's mottled and wrinkled arms.

"Can I refresh you, honey?"

"No thank you."

Marlon was silent before he gripped the back of a chair from a nearby desk and pulled it over. The legs tangled on the carpet squares and it stuttered once before he turned it around to sit in front of her.

"I was thinking maybe you could tell me about that man again and what happened to Ben."

Evie's jaw twitched. She'd told him *three* times — in fact, there was already a witness statement on record, taken as soon as Marlon showed up at the school. There was no further story and she was tired of being wrung out like a half-dry sponge for information she didn't have. Evie couldn't forget the vivid details of the attack. Every time she blinked, she was reminded in technicolor snapshots.

"I don't know anything else." She tried to keep the words from snapping at his outstretched hand, but they caught skin anyway. Evie bit her tongue as he shot her a reproachful look, half in response and half in fear of what would come out of her mouth next. *He doesn't deserve your ire. He's not the people wasting your time, making you wait here.*

With a deep breath, she channeled the voice she used on the kids who used random items as bookmarks — old receipts, greasy napkins, *a piece of cheese.* "I told you everything, Marlon. I was cleaning up after the school day and heard a noise in the hall — and — when I looked out, Ben was fighting with a man I've never seen before."

Marlon nodded, his head bobbing for a moment before his eyes flickered past her.

The bell above the door jingled, and Evie flinched. Marlon

didn't look alarmed, but that didn't stop her muscles from tensing. She expected to hear a voice go, *"there you are"* or *"got you"* like this entire thing was a bad horror movie.

Instead, Marlon rose, extending a hand. Evie turned, her eyes going from Marlon's outstretched hand to a Black man in a crisp suit.

He was tall and lean with a handsome smile on his serious face. It was like he was already trying to lighten the dark mood. For that, Evie was grateful, but she wondered if he knew from looking at her with the creased blanket around her shoulders, to her red-rimmed eyes — that she was the mess he had to talk to.

"Agent Anthony Wilson." He shook Marlon's hand once, up and down in a quick motion. With a nod, Agent Wilson looked toward a white man behind him. "That's my partner, Agent Harvey Beck." They both, separately, but in sync, flashed badges. It was all very *Law & Order*.

Dun dun. The music sting hummed in the back of her mind as she shifted her weight.

A pit in her stomach gaped wider and wider when the agents' attention shifted to her. She was going to be sick — but there was nothing to throw up except stale coffee and the remnants of her peanut butter sandwich from lunch.

All she really wanted was her leftover pasta, and to not feel like bursting into tears.

"Nice to meet you boys." Marlon's voice drawled. Evie's brain grasped at straws to distract itself because she suddenly remembered that he grew up in Kentucky and had only moved to Vermont when she was in middle school. He'd taken over for the beloved old sheriff and the town had questioned for three weeks if anyone *good* could ever replace him.

And now they were about to do the same with Marlon in six months.

Agent Wilson reached into his pocket and Evie felt her spine tighten. But all he did was pull out a peppermint, popping it into his mouth. At her look, he dug into his trousers again and held one out to her in offering.

"You can call me Andy if you want, but we need to talk."

Evie glanced from his hand to him before taking the peppermint. After unwrapping it, she pulled the blanket closer, nodding her head as her gaze flickered to Andy's partner, then back to Andy himself. "Okay."

The moment the word left her lips, the other agent, Agent Beck, headed toward the back office. After Andy beckoned her to follow them, she rose, shuffling with the blanket around her shoulders to the only enclosed office in the building. The walls were covered in a variety of fishing trophies emblazoned with MARLON WYATT under their various accolades. Interspersed were postcards from his grandkids. Evie was ushered inside and made to sit in another chair just like the one she'd just left.

Marlon lingered in the doorway. Andy didn't even look up as he cleared his throat. "We'll be a minute. We need to take a statement and talk to Miss Morgen, Sheriff."

Marlon started to open his mouth, but Agent Beck gave him a "*just a minute*" smile and shut the door in his face.

Evie's shoulders sank. This room was quiet. The lights weren't as harsh as the overheads in the booking area, and the two men in front of her didn't know her from — well — Eve.

"I know this will be —"

Evie cut Andy off, looking up sharply. "I gave a statement to Marlon, but I'm going to tell you the *entire* thing from the top again because I don't think they heard half of what I told them."

She kept thinking of the blond man's wicked snarl, the way his eyes cut through her — cut through glass like he could cut through her skin too. Whoever he was, she didn't want to see him ever again. She would rather eat her own legs than be in the same room.

Andy glanced back at Agent Beck before nodding. The other agent pressed a button on a recorder lying on the desk and Andy turned back to Evie. "From the top, then?"

"I was shelving books." Evie cleared her throat, looking up at the ceiling as she pictured her routine. "I was working on the ones that were returned this week — it's just me in the library so sometimes it takes me a couple days to get them back on the shelves. And I heard..."

She trailed off, thinking of what alerted her to the fight in the beginning. The adrenaline had long worn off and she was tired, but she distinctly remembered the thump.

"I heard what sounded like a bed, like when you're tired and you just let yourself free fall onto the mattress. It was such a loud *thump* that I jumped a little." She found Andy's eyes again, a deep brown, clearly listening even as he noted things down on a small pad of paper. Evie swallowed the burn of bile tinged with bitterness, wishing she'd never touched the instant coffee Marlon pushed into her hands an hour ago.

"When I went over to the library doors I saw two men fighting." Andy scratched another note onto the paper. "One of the men was Ben Harriet, our new math teacher, and the other was a man I'd never seen before."

"Can you describe the man to me?"

A chill crawled down Evie's spine. It felt like a snake coiling around her bones as she pulled the blanket closer for its flimsy protection. "I didn't see him at first. I didn't really see any part of him except for a white shirt. But he was young — maybe the same age as Ben or me." She watched as Andy's left hand moved his pen. "I'm twenty-eight, so I think he could be that age."

The man's curly hair and bloodied pale skin flashed in her mind and she flinched, sucking in a deep breath.

Andy looked up instantly, his hand stopping. At her expression, he shifted forward and reached out a hand, hovering it over her knee. "Hey, take your time."

Evie bobbed her head, forcing herself to exhale. "I'm okay. I saw the man's face after he shot Ben. They were fighting and he pulled a gun and pressed it into Ben's stomach." Her own churned as she uttered the words. "And he shot him." She pulled a hand free from the blanket, pressing it into her own soft flesh through her sweater. "Right here."

Andy's voice was gentle as he asked, "And then what?"

"He watched as Ben fell and then shot him again." Evie looked away, licking her lips. "He shot Ben over and over again. I don't know what he did after that. He was covered in blood and I moved away from the door to hide because I didn't know what to do."

"Okay." Andy shushed her, stopping her from spiraling. "But you saw the man's face?"

"Yes," Evie whispered, "he was white, with blond, curly hair, maybe six feet, lean, really angular." She spat out each descriptor, her eyes watering. "He had an expression on his face like he was waiting in the check-out line at the grocery store. It was just another Wednesday to him."

A sound from Agent Beck made her look up. He shuffled a file in his hands. Evie looked back at Andy. "And I turned because I wanted to press the emergency button they just installed in the library — in case there's a school shooting?"

Andy's full attention was on her and for some reason, Evie felt like it helped organize her jumbled thoughts. His eyes gave her something to focus on as the memories flashed in the forefront of her mind. "But I ran into a table and he heard me."

Her tongue felt loose, like it was going to fall out if she

didn't get the rest of the story out *right now*. Every detail spewed forth and when she finished, she leaned back in the hard chair, her shoulders slumping like she'd run a marathon.

It was only then that Agent Andy Wilson spoke again.

"We need you to take a look at a photo, Miss Morgen."

"You can call me Evie," she responded on instinct, her voice soft. Agent Beck approached her with the file outstretched. She reached for it, letting the blanket fall off one shoulder as she took the thin pieces of paper from his hands.

A white printed crime sheet stared up at her. Evie's focus flickered over murder and tax evasion among a long list of other mostly petty crimes. When she turned the page over, her eye caught on a photo paper-clipped to the upper left side.

It was *him*.

She thrust the papers back at the agents, feeling the panic rise in her chest at the mere sight.

"That's him." Her throat tightened. "That's who killed Ben, that's who did it."

The two agents exchanged a look and Agent Beck took the papers, shuffling them before turning another photo toward her. In it, the man from the library was standing in a grass field, fitted in a black suit, surrounded by tombstones.

"That man?" Andy asked, glancing between her and the photo.

She didn't care how many photos they showed her. She was certain. "It was him."

Agent Beck clasped the folder shut and inhaled deeply as Andy reached behind him to stop the recorder. The soft click echoed in the room as Andy's eyes found hers again.

"I'm so sorry, Miss Morgen. This was what we were afraid of."

The pit in her stomach sank lower, gaping wide as her mouth opened, trying to form words — but a soft ringing came from Andy's pocket. She watched him pull a phone out, then take the call. His serious, but kind, expression closed off — like he'd cut the lights and drawn the blinds to prevent anyone from reading his features.

"What do you mean they found him?"

Chapter Three

THE BLACK SUV THE TWO AGENTS DROVE WAS SLEEK and quiet on the road to the next town.

The draw of Hawthorne was that it was smack dab in the middle of nowhere, chock full of all the small-town charm that *Hallmark* movies made millions from. Despite its rural nature, it did have access to larger towns if you were willing to drive fifty-five minutes to get to them. As Evie sat in the backseat, she found herself wondering what the agents did on long drives — if they ever listened to audiobooks, or if they chattered exclusively about cases. Maybe they didn't talk at all. They certainly weren't now.

Marlon's beet red face lingered in the rearview as Andy and Beck whisked Evie away. She assumed they were just going to the next town over because Beck promised she'd be home soon, but *soon* was vague enough that she wasn't entirely confident in her presumptions. The caveat was that the case was now under FBI jurisdiction — meaning Marlon would have to wait for updates via official channels, no longer privy to the goings-on of the investigation, or where the key witness was being taken. Evie was secretly glad the old man couldn't immediately go blabbing to her parents every detail of the night's events.

Maybe I am an extra in Marlon's The Feds? *But I wouldn't last past the first five minutes.* She paused in her musings, frowning at the all-black car interior. *But I did survive tonight, maybe I'd make it to the climax before dying.*

As they neared the highway exit, Agent Beck turned around to eye her. "We should tell you —" He glanced over at Andy, then sighed. "They found the guy during a roadblock trying to leave the area. We need your positive identification of him. If you get in the room and you're not sure — *you have to tell us.*" He stressed the words, eyes serious. "I know tonight's been a lot, but if you can't make this positive identification, then we have to book him on something else. His lawyers are sharks. They're the whole reason he's never been booked and *kept* before now."

Evie nodded slowly. "Okay." *No pressure, Atlas can hold the sky, I can identify a murderer.* Though this felt perilously closer to Prometheus — however there might not be much of her liver left to consume after her teenage years.

In minutes they were downtown, pulling into a parking garage next to a building that housed the city's police force. Agent Beck opened the back door for her and Evie clambered out, with only herself and her cell phone in her pocket. She couldn't remember where her purse was as she stood, waiting to be told where to go like a lost puppy.

Andy motioned for her to follow him and Evie quickly moved to match the man's long stride. Agent Beck lingered behind them as she entered the building. A short elevator ride up to the fifth floor led to a bustling area full of cops and detectives and *men* everywhere. Evie scanned the room as Andy directed her around desks toward a side room.

Once the door was shut, it was blissfully silent, almost unnaturally so.

It really did feel like the set of *CSI* or *Law & Order*. Through a window, she could see a wall with printed heights, denoting where heads were.

She stared at the one marking six feet — the same height as her father.

She couldn't hear it, but she saw the door swing open on the other side. Andy guided her by the arm to the center of their room.

"They're going to file some people in. You take as long as you need before you tell us which one you saw tonight. There's no right or wrong answer, you just need to be certain."

Evie nodded, licking her dry lips as she wished for chapstick and a hug. Something comforting — that was all she wanted in this mess of an evening with guns and blood and men with dark eyes and bolts of fear shooting down her spine.

Five men entered in a single file line.

The first man was white, but he was short, his head barely reaching the five foot five marker. Evie immediately looked past him and his grubby fingers holding the sign for *one*. He wasn't even close to the man she'd seen. Number two was a taller white man, but his hair was a dirty brown and his nose was crooked. Number three was the wrong ethnicity — he might have been Filipino, but honestly Evie couldn't tell. He wasn't the blond, pale-skinned man that had stalked her through the library.

She stopped short at number four. He looked so unbothered as he held his number and stared directly ahead. She knew the window was mirrored on the other side, but Evie swore his eyes were boring into her.

They were the same black holes attached to a sneer, holding a smoking gun and watching the glass crack.

Evie sucked in a breath. Andy's hand came down on her arm as she rocked forward — a grip, but not a harsh one

"Hey, whoa."

Every muscle in her body coiled, tightening with the adrenaline racing through her veins. The fourth man moved his head, tilting it as he stared. His curly blond hair was ruffled and he looked a volatile mix of angry and bored.

"I —" Evie stuttered, eyes locked on the man, waiting for him to pull a gun and point it at the window again. "It's number four. It's four."

Agent Beck turned, eyes flickering between her and the suspect. Andy eased his hand off her arm, like he was certain she wouldn't bolt at this very second — but he stayed close.

"You're sure?"

Evie took a step forward, then another, taking herself to the very edge of the window, past the line that said she was too close — past the point where the mirror would work to conceal her features on the other side.

She didn't care. She wanted the man on the other side of the glass to see her lips move as she said, "*Yes.*"

The other room was a flurry of activity. The five suspects were taken out immediately and Andy pulled her back, annoyed but curious. Evie was tired, she was upset, and she wanted to go home and forget this day ever happened, but instead she looked back up and said, "What now?"

A female officer entered the room and guided her to another office where she sat down and was handed a stack of paper. It was a transcript of the recording she'd done for Andy and Agent Beck. She read through every line once, before returning to the top. Her mind echoed with reminders from her great uncle advising her to read everything twice and never sign before she was sure. She had just been applying to her first job at a coffee shop when she asked him to look over the contract — being the only lawyer in the family. His caution rang like alarm bells in the foreground as she picked up the pen and signed the witness line under her sworn testimony.

The agent left and Andy entered the room again. He looked softer around the edges this time and as he leaned against whoever's desk it was, he offered her a water bottle.

"Well."

Evie took it, raising an eyebrow. "Well?"

Am I done? Did I get a good grade in murderer identification today?

"Evelyn Morgen." Andy smacked his lips together, giving her an unreadable look. "How would you feel about being a key witness in an FBI trial?"

Evie stopped in the middle of trying to unscrew the lid. "Excuse me?"

Andy inhaled slowly, then held his water bottle down by his side. "The man you identified tonight — the one who killed Ben Harriet — his name is Jonathan Murphy and I've been trying to nail his family down ever since I joined the Bureau."

Evie twisted the plastic top again, feeling the seal snap in her hands. She took a long drink, then stared back at Andy. "Why?"

He ran his free hand over his short black hair. There were lines beside his eyes, the kind that you only got from laughing or smiling too much at too many people — but he wasn't smiling now. He looked torn on how to answer.

"Can I level with you?" He leaned forward, head tilted. "I'm going to do my best to keep you safe through this whole thing, but the Murphy family has been a thorn in the lion's paw of the FBI for years. Jonathan — the one who you saw tonight — his father died five months ago. And ever since we've been running around with our tails between our legs trying to figure out what Jonathan Murphy is going to do to fill his daddy's big shoes. So far we've had some light larceny, no crime that we could pin on him — not until tonight. Not until Ben Harriet. My bosses have been *up my ass* about it. This is a huge break in the case. We might actually be able to put him behind bars and cut his family off at the legs."

Evie sat forward in her chair, looking at Andy. His white shirt was rolled up at the sleeves, exposing the dark skin of his lean and muscular forearms. He had no wedding band on, but she figured that didn't mean much. He could have kept it off because of what he did for a job. The thing that got her was the way he tried to be relaxed and kept second-guessing himself — tension held in the micro twitches of his shoulders. She wondered just how much he was supposed to say.

"I just don't understand," she breathed out. "Why Ben? He was just a math teacher. We got coffee together every Tuesday for fuck's sake."

Andy grimaced. "He wasn't just a teacher; he was an undercover cop."

"Ben?" Evie flailed, her mind scrambling. "The Ben who taught math to third graders... he was an undercover cop? Why?" Inappropriate as it was, her mind shot to *Kindergarten Cop*, but it didn't match up. None of it seemed to align.

Andy shrugged. "We picked him for the same reason you're sitting here questioning me. He was a good fit, unthreatening. And we heard a few rumors that Murphy might be moving his business from the west coast to Vermont."

Evie stared at the water bottle, shaking her head. "How bad is this man, Agent Wilson?"

"His entire family has ties to every major organized crime job in the last half century, with a father who had it in deep with some illegal gambling across borders. His uncle is in prison for money laundering. It was mostly white collar" — Andy took another drink — "until Jonathan stepped in and did his best impersonation of the *Godfather* and nixed the family members he couldn't stand and decided to take the business in a different direction. We have some rumors of human trafficking, but nothing is confirmed."

She laughed. The inappropriate noise startled them both as she stared at the tile floor, absolutely bewildered. "And he chose Vermont?"

"His mother apparently grew up there — moved to California as a teenager and got involved with the Murphy family. She died a decade and a half ago from cancer. I assume there's probably some mommy issues spurring that business decision. We figured Ben would be safe at the school and he'd alert us. We didn't hear from him this evening and —"

"And tonight you got the call he was dead." Evie's brain ran in tight circles, trying to remember if she'd seen Murphy in town before. In the past week she felt like she'd barely looked up from work. She'd gone on a couple walking visits to classrooms, plus she'd had afternoon reading classes with kindergarteners. The library stayed open extra hours, just in case any of the kids wanted to exchange their loans — or someone's parents were late. Honestly, it was the same life she'd been living for the last four years since college.

There hadn't been anyone creeping at the edge of her vision, setting her teeth on edge, or making the hair raise on the back of her neck. She didn't understand how or why Jonathan Murphy had suddenly appeared in her life and upended it in moments. It wasn't *fair*.

"And we got the call."

Evie slumped in the chair. Suddenly the exhaustion was too much to fight and she closed her eyes, letting the wave sweep her undertow. When she opened them, Andy looked half-pitying.

"Is there any way I could go home?" She shifted the water

bottle to her other hand, worried that he'd say no and she'd have to curl up in a corner.

"Actually." Andy rose from his leaned position. "You've done enough." He reached for the doorknob. "Stay here a sec while I handle the paperwork. I'll drive you back."

Time slowed as Evie waited, crunching the plastic bottle between her palms. By the time Andy returned, she had drained it completely and dropped it into a recycling bin as they walked out of the office. She followed him back to the parking garage and instead of shuffling into the back of the SUV, he motioned for her to get into the passenger side.

"No Agent Beck?"

"Nah." Andy grinned as he backed out. "Loser got stuck with grunt work." Every line by his eyes crinkled and Evie smiled as she turned to look out at the quiet city only just waking up.

"It seemed like you two were quiet. Has he been on this case with you the entire time?" Evie tried to keep herself awake, uncertain if she'd drool a puddle if she fell asleep in the car. That seemed like a safe enough question for the lighter mood.

"Yeah." Andy drummed on the steering wheel to a quiet 80s station in the background. "And no. Actually, he's not the only partner I've had on this case. He's relatively new to the whole '*bring down the Murphy empire*' goal we've been tossing around for years." Andy merged onto the highway. "I used to have another partner, but he got out of it pretty fast. He lives in Washington or some shit and became a lumberjack."

"A lumberjack?" Evie laughed lightly. "Interesting choice."

"Oh he *hated* the FBI," Andy agreed with a chuckle. "I'd trust him with my life though." The statement was fond and Evie decided that whoever Andy Wilson trusted with his life probably deserved her trust as well. The man next to her didn't seem like a bad judge of character at all.

The conversation lulled in and out for the bulk of the drive back. Every time Evie felt her eyes grow heavy, she'd quickly formulate a half-thought question and throw it at Andy. Occasionally her probes would stir him to ask a few questions of his own and she ended up feeling like they were old friends as he pulled into her driveway.

Evie stretched, glancing down at her watch. It was after five in the morning as she unlocked her front door. Andy followed her inside as she flipped lights on to her small ranch. It was simple, and had belonged to her grandparents, willed to her when she was in college. She liked its old charm — a lot of oak wood and a lingering, faint smell of mothballs.

"Can I get you a cup of coffee before you head back?" Evie was already headed to the kitchen as she shot the question to Andy. He stopped at a wall covered in framed family photos and hummed a confirmation. Evie filled up her old coffeemaker, doling out enough caffeine into the hopper to kill a man as she pressed start.

She was about to explain to him the story behind the photo of her as a toddler on her grandpa's knee at Christmas — ice cream all over her face — when Andy's phone rang.

A cold shiver ran down Evie's spine as she watched him answer it. The same closed expression covered Andy's face, smoothing away the kindness.

"Agent Wilson."

"No, I understand."

"I'll handle it."

Evie stared at the half-filled coffee pot, snippets of the conversation filtering through the haze in her mind. The black hole in her stomach opened wide, sucking the brief feeling that *maybe* this was all done as quickly as it happened.

Andy appeared in the doorway, his face drawn. "Evie, I'm sorry. We don't have time for coffee anymore."

Chapter Four

In a perfect world, Evie would have been standing in the kitchen with a white coffee mug when Andy delivered the news. It would have fallen gracefully from her hands and shattered in slow motion, splattering lukewarm coffee across her legs. There would have been shards and caffeine on her floor as she stuttered a shocked one-liner like they do in the movies.

But this was reality.

Andy leveled her with a look and said simply, "Murphy's guys broke him out and killed four officers on their way. He made sure to snag your file off of a desk before he left. He's seen your face, Evie. He knows you identified him. He'll want you dead."

He's seen your face, Evie.

Evie blinked.

He knows you identified him.

There was nothing in her hands to drop, no quips on her tongue.

He'll want you dead.

The words hung in the air like smoke until Evie heard the coffee pot click next to her, signaling the brew was done. She reached for her cabinet-full of thrifted mugs to exotic locations she'd never been. "The coffee is done."

"Evie, I need you to pack a bag." Andy's tone was gentle as he stepped toward her until they were nearly chest to chest. He laid a hand on her left shoulder. "I have to take you somewhere safe. The first thing Murphy will do is track you down. He doesn't leave loose ends."

This had to be some sugar-induced fever dream. Nothing else made sense as she nodded, letting Andy point her toward the hallway. She barely remembered pushing open her bedroom door and turning on the light, staring at the clothes in her closet half sleep-deprived, waiting for them to magically move themselves to a bag.

When they didn't *bibbidi bobbidi boo* themselves into one, she dragged her small weekender out. Her mother gifted it to her after college, and Evie attended precisely two concerts in New York before deciding that she didn't like to travel all that much. Thrifted mugs were one thing, public transit was another.

She pulled old scarves and tote bags out of it, leaving them on the floor. Footsteps in the hallway made her pause, until she heard Andy start talking and her front door close. Garbled voices trickled down the hallway like the background noise of someone else's memory.

Evie grabbed an obscene amount of underwear and threw them into the bag.

Did she need t-shirts? What about jackets or her thick wool scarf? She wanted to step out into the hallway and ask Andy if he could come help her, but the words stuck in the back of her throat as her eyes started to burn.

There was a rap on her door frame and Evie jumped, looking over her shoulder.

"All good in here?" Agent Beck's dark hair was rumpled and there was tension in his shoulders as Evie looked back at the old weekender, uncertain of her answer.

"If it helps, Andy said pack warm. Something comfy, I guess. You, uh —" He reached up, rubbing the back of his neck with a freckled hand. "Don't need anything fancy. You probably won't be getting out much. Our witness protection cases never do."

Witness protection. The words sent a shiver down Evie's spine as she shoved sweaters into the bottom of the bag before adding leggings and her warmest pajamas.

She wondered while she packed if Agent Wilson would be the one to stay with her until this was all over. She didn't know what qualified as over — maybe catching Murphy again? But then she'd still need to wait for the trial to take the stand. This wouldn't be over until Murphy was in federal prison somewhere — or dead.

Nausea burned at the back of her throat as she looked up, but Agent Beck was gone. She poked her head out of the doorway, just to see him talking with Andy in hushed tones.

If Murphy was coming after her, what did that mean for her parents? She paused with her hand on a sweater her mother gave her for Christmas last year. She went over to her parents' house weekly for family dinner. She drove her mother to doctor's appointments. She took her dad Christmas shopping every November before Thanksgiving and then helped him hide her mother's presents in Evie's house because her mom liked to snoop and shake boxes.

She pushed the sweater into the bag and then called down the hallway. "Andy?"

He looked up immediately, passing a phone to Agent Beck. "Yeah?"

Evie stood in her bedroom doorway, taking shallow breaths. "My parents? What's going to happen to them? I'm their only child now and there's never been anyone else in my life. I mean I know people in town — but I'm not *close* to anyone. Is he going to target them?"

Andy's expression softened. "Hey, it's okay. You're going to be okay. Why don't I drive you to their place before we head out? I just got the plane squared away for us. We're going to drive to DC and fly out from there. You can tell them goodbye and I'll keep an agent in town for a few days."

It sounded good in theory, but all Evie could think about was the way Ben's bullet-riddled body had buckled in on itself and fell to the floor.

Evie wrung her hands together. "Okay, I'm almost done."

Andy offered her a small smile. "Pack warm." She watched as he walked back to his partner before she finished shoving her bag full of random winter clothing. When her skincare items were packed and she was redressed in a warmer outfit, Evie stopped. She turned slowly, taking in her bedroom, wondering when she'd be back.

Then she shut the door behind her on the way out.

Agent Beck offered to load her small bag into the backseat of the SUV but Evie politely declined and sat it at her feet, holding her purse in her lap. The SUV pulled out as quickly as it could and Evie weighed her keys in the palm of her hand.

Dad can check on the house while I'm gone. Even if it's a few weeks, I don't want the pipes to freeze and burst without me being here.

"I heard from the director." Andy was talking in the front when she finally refocused. "Murphy is now classed as a wanted felon. We were keeping it quiet before but now we've put out a

BOLO for any agency to take his ass down if they see him. It's a murder charge and he has plenty of resources to flee the country if he really wants."

Andy hesitated, then continued, "We're sure he'll be keeping an eye out for you, Evie. Any jury who listens to you on the stand would put his ass behind bars for life."

Agent Beck snorted. "Or longer."

Out of the blue, the car felt warm, almost suffocating. "So I'm his target? And he's the FBI's."

"Exactly." Andy offered a half-smile in the rearview mirror. "Luckily for you, we're the good guys." Evie knew the smile should have comforted her, but it just made her insides twist.

"In any case, we can't put you at risk. You're our only eyewitness. You're being officially, but unofficially, put on a protection detail. No documents will be filed about your location in case Murphy has someone digging for information. Also Witness Protection is slower than molasses."

Evie loosened her grip on her keys, prepared to ask what that meant when Andy pulled into her parents' driveway. She was so focused on getting out of the car, she barely heard the front door open before her mother was shouting her name across the quiet yard.

Evie glanced up, feeling something in her chest shatter as she ran toward her mom and wrapped her arms around her. The moment Evie's arms touched her mother, she heard the other woman come undone. Evie glanced up to see her worried father before feeling him envelope them both in a hug.

"We were worried sick, where were you? Marlon called us this morning and said something happened? Why didn't you pick up the phone when we called? Who are these men?" Her mother spoke a thousand miles a minute and it took Evie several moments before she could extract herself enough to take a deep breath.

Andy and Agent Beck were already inside with them and had shut the front door to close off the family reunion — and goodbyes — from the rest of the neighborhood. Evie steeled herself before she launched into the abridged story, trying to skirt around the gory details of Ben's death. As Evie spoke, her mother sank into an armchair, gobsmacked and silent.

"I... oh, I don't understand, you have to leave town?" The words were almost comical. Evie stared at her mother and then glanced over her shoulder, catching Andy's eyes, pleading for him or Agent Beck to intervene.

Andy stepped forward and slipped his badge from his pocket. "Mrs. Morgen." His smile was gentle and Evie was grateful that in the moment she could move back and try not to fall over from the sheer exhaustion in her bones. The more Andy explained, the paler Evie's mother was until she was a specter in the chair. Evie's father touched his wife's shoulder and Evie thought his hand would go right through.

He looked over at Evie. "You have to leave now?"

Evie swallowed the lump in her throat and nodded. "I have to go. I saw too much." Evie wrapped her arms around herself, feeling small in front of the Adults in the room. They were Adults, with a capital A, all handling this far better than she could. What did Evie know other than children's books and quiet evenings in her house watching *Murder She Wrote*?

Her father stepped away from the chair and wrapped her in a deep and crushing hug. He shot the agents a look over her shoulder. "Take care of my daughter."

Tears overflowed as she hugged both her parents goodbye. Her father's motor oil scent mixed with her mother's cheap perfume, both familiar and overwhelming at the same time.

In less than twenty minutes, she was back in the SUV. Agent Beck told Andy goodbye as he stayed with her parents

— keeping Andy's promise. Her parents would be safe, but in order for that to happen, she had to go.

Andy was quiet until they were well out of the town limits, back to drumming his fingers on the steering wheel. Evie glanced over after wiping her face mostly clear of snot and tears, muttering, "I'm sorry about them."

"What, your parents?"

"Yeah." Evie turned to watch the morning commuters passing them on the highway. "They've been like that since I was in middle school. I..." Evie bit her tongue, willing the exhausted tears to stay in her eyes and off of her cheeks. "I had a brother. He died in high school after a drunk driving incident. He was the quarterback. It was a real town tragedy. They've never really let me out of their sight since — and I guess I never tried."

Dad rock from the 80s played over the radio and it reminded Evie of Saturday mornings listening to her father tinker in the garage as she passed one door upstairs, forever shut.

Finally, Andy whistled low. "I gotta give it to you, you're far more interesting than what I expected when we got a call that it was a children's librarian mixed up with all this."

She turned, catching the gentle tease. "Don't judge a book by its cover."

Andy laughed. The sound broke the rest of the tension into tiny pieces, letting them fall onto the floorboards. The car wasn't quiet after that, it was an ebb and flow again of questions and conversation. Andy told her about a scar he had just above his eyebrow from playing football, and then about the gunshot he'd taken in training.

"Isn't that... ironic, you've only been injured during training?" She was tired and maybe that was what made her laugh turn into a little half-drunk giggle as he rolled his eyes.

"Well, it taught me not to get in the way of a fucking gun again." Evie broke into louder laughter, watching him shake his head.

He pulled off just before entering DC, driving through a coffee place to get them two larges before the flight. He knocked his cup into the side of hers in cheers before taking a swig.

"I think you'll be fine during all of this. Just gotta keep laughing, keep looking forward, you know?" Andy stuck his cup into the center console and shot her a sidelong glance. "Worst thing you can do is let the bad thoughts win."

Evie blew out a breath, letting it coast along the top of her hot coffee. "I'm good at distractions. I think. Maybe not good enough for wherever we're going."

"It's the most remote place I can think of." Andy steered them off an exit. "And it's with someone who would take a bullet for you."

She frowned, not much caring for the idea of someone *needing* to do that for her. Evie turned herself in the seat to look at Andy fully. "Would someone I've never met really do that for me?"

Andy shrugged, a small smile on the edges of his lips. "He did it for me once." There was an air of fondness in the words that made her chest tighten.

Evie snorted, shifting back around. "Alright, I get one bullet. I guess."

Andy laughed. "Yeah just one." He turned the car toward signs for an airport. "Don't waste it or he'll be gone in the wind and relocate to Alaska or some shit."

CHAPTER FIVE

It took almost six hours to fly from DC to a small airfield outside of Seattle. Evie dozed while she could in the private plane the FBI chartered just to cart her across the country. If she had friends, she'd tell them how wild this was — but she really only spoke to coworkers. Actually, the closest person she'd known for a while was the budding friendship with Ben.

That thought was sobering.

When they landed, Andy guided Evie's sleepy body into the backseat of another black SUV and told her to lie down if she needed to.

She woke up in the middle of nowhere.

Trees sped past the car windows, an endless green blur that made her think of obscure quotes overlaid on aesthetic photos posted to social media. Where Vermont was shades of vibrant oranges and reds in autumn and barren branches in winter, Washington was all evergreens. She expected rain — but the fine mist over everything, inside and outside, was more beautiful than she imagined.

Evie wasn't certain how long it really took from the airfield to where they were now. It was long enough for her stomach to pang with hunger, a reminder of the last twenty-four hours and not enough snacks.

It was clear she'd missed civilization. The rural road consisted of cracked asphalt before transitioning seamlessly to gravel. She bounced in the backseat, looking down at her small bag, her phone long gone and left with another agent back at the airfield in DC. She didn't have any reason *not* to trust Andy, but he could have been taking her to the middle of the woods to drop her off *Hatchet*-style, and she didn't have the same tenacity or will to survive as a preteen boy. She was far too old and tired for that.

Her stomach churned, focusing on the car slowing instead of her own mortality. It rounded a bend in the road and then crested a hill. Andy eased the SUV to a stop and glanced at her in the rearview mirror.

Evie didn't notice him. Her gaze was too focused on the cabin.

She pushed the door to the backseat open and climbed out into the chilly November air, standing next to the car as she took in the hand-carved logs on the exterior and small porch with two rocking chairs.

It looked quaint, with a picture window behind the rocking chairs.

This is a safe house.

She didn't know if it was in the traditional '*James Bond*, too many spy movies' way — or if the rustic allure was drawing her in. Evie's muscles melted into jelly at the thought of going inside and reading in front of a crackling fire, maybe even nursing a cup of hot chocolate under a warm blanket.

Andy cleared his throat and motioned to her bag. "You want me to grab that?"

"Oh, no, I've got it." Evie turned, shaking away thoughts of sugar and sleep. As she shouldered it, she expected Andy to unlock the front door to the cabin, but instead they climbed the few stairs and stopped on the porch. Andy knocked mud off his boots and leaned against one of the posts.

Evie settled in one of the rocking chairs. There was nothing but trees as far as the eye could see. Little patches of gravel denoted paths that snaked up to the front door and then toward the side of the cabin. She spotted a small woodshed off to the right with a modest pile of wood against it. To its side was a stump with a wood axe embedded in it.

She twisted in the chair, peering through the picture window. Pleasant surprise hummed in her chest at the dark but home-y interior. She couldn't make out much, but it was enough to ease a bit of the anxiety in her stomach.

As she turned to ask Andy why they weren't going inside yet, he cleared his throat.

"I'm not going to leave you here until Nick comes along, don't worry." Andy offered her an easy smile. She frowned as he looked away again, lost in thought as she processed the fact that *he* wasn't staying.

They were silent, the sounds of the woods their only company until Evie heard an engine. Andy's hand moved to his hip where his gun rested, but when a blue truck came into view, he eased his hand away and smiled wide.

The truck rumbled up like a grumpy hound dog, stopping next to the SUV. The sky had grown darker and Evie couldn't make out who was in the cab as she sat on the edge of the rocking chair's seat, not wanting to appear too comfortable.

The rain shifted from a mist to a drizzle as the door to the cab opened.

A man in dark, faded blue jeans climbed out. His brown boots were caked with mud, which had traveled up, leaving little splatters on the hems of his jeans. Evie's eyes crawled up his body, taking in his dark maroon flannel, partially buttoned. It looked warm, worn, and soft to the touch, but it was stretched across his broad chest clad in a white t-shirt. The seams of his workman's jacket pulled around his wide shoulders as he rolled them back. Her gaze caught on his full beard, realizing the man's hair was long enough that it passed his ears, reaching toward his beard like they'd meet again.

As Evie's eyes met his, he faltered a step.

"Andy." His deep voice was smooth as he rubbed his pale hands together, blowing into them. "What brings you here?"

Andy nodded toward the other end of the porch. "You wouldn't be asking me that if you answered your damn phone once in a while, Nick." His easy smile fell as Evie stayed seated, fidgeting with her scarf.

She would cry if she had to leave. She just wanted a bed, a hot meal, and to be left to her own devices to process everything. She didn't think that was too much to ask for, and she didn't want to hear whatever discussion the two men were about to have.

Their voices carried from the other end of the porch anyway.

"Keep her safe, please. You're the only one I trust."

"I don't even work for the government anymore, Andy."

"It doesn't matter —" Andy sighed, clearly frustrated.

It took everything in Evie to keep her eyes on the evergreens and not look over at him. *Of course he's tired of babysitting.*

"This is me coming to you as a friend, Nick. I'm not begging, but I'll get on my knees if you need me to."

The other man — Nick — grumbled something that sounded like *"Not necessary."*

Evie looked up when Andy slowed to a stop in front of her.

Her eyes flickered over him and his slightly rumpled suit before they slid to the other man. They were about the same height, but where Andy looked like he was a distance runner, Nick was bulkier in a way that made her think of mountain men on the History channel that lived in the woods all by themselves and ate pine cones for dinner. His beard certainly fit the stereotype.

"Evelyn Morgen." Andy motioned to her, then waved a hand to the man next to him. "Nick Barber. Nick, this is Evie. Evie, this is Nick."

Evie pushed herself up from the rocking chair, unsure how she should greet him. This didn't seem like a handshake kind of situation, but Nick offered her his hand anyway. She took it, feeling the warmth from his palm engulf hers.

"Nice to meet you." The words came out softer than she really intended them to and she stepped back, pushing her hands back into her coat pockets.

Nick's eyes lingered on her. It wasn't exactly unnerving — but *intense*. Something Evie couldn't put her finger on made her heartbeat flutter. His blue eyes made her feel small though, like he was seeing too much. Her shoulders curved in on themselves as she looked down at the wooden boards beneath her boots.

"We should go inside." Nick fished out the smallest keyring she'd ever seen from his pocket. There was a key for his truck and a key to the front door — plus a cheap plastic keychain from a vacation spot. "Before any of us catch a cold."

Andy cleared his throat as Nick unlocked the front door. "I can't stay. Bosses need me back."

There it was.

Evie knew the words were coming at some point, but her blood ran cold all the same. She gave him a slightly panicked look, unsure if she wanted to be left alone with a man she'd only just met — no, she wasn't unsure. Evie was one hundred percent certain she didn't want that.

Andy stuck his hand into his pocket and pulled out a small cell phone. She couldn't help but gawk. It was *ancient* — like old Nokias from the 90s. There was no hinge or flip to it, no glass screen, only a plastic casing that looked like it was three decades old and didn't even have *snake* on it.

He pressed it into her hand, which had apparently come out of her jacket on its own because Evie was surprised when the cool plastic hit her palm.

"I will call you every week that I can. I'm the only one with the number and will update you about the case. But I have to ask you — don't call anyone from this. Don't call your parents, friends, coworkers — *anyone.*"

The words were redundant. She didn't have anyone to call, but she still wrapped her fingers around the phone and nodded dumbly. "Okay."

"Stay warm."

Andy stepped back and Evie watched him walk down the stairs, the last vestiges of anyone that she knew in miles leaving just like that. She wrapped her arms around herself, feeling something coil into her stomach. It was somehow worse than the pit feeling from before. This was thick, heavy, and sticky anxiety — coating her bones, lying in wait.

Andy waved a hand from the SUV, the movement just visible through the back window before he drove back down the drive. She just stared, standing on the front porch of a stranger until the man behind her cleared his throat.

"Why don't you come in?" The gruff words were almost identical to the ones before, but a little softer. "It's cold out here."

Evie picked up her bag, staring at the empty road one last

time before sucking in a breath and following Nick into the cabin.

He turned all the lights on and she felt a little better once she wasn't looking into a dark room. The dim lights, as they were, did their best to illuminate the deep wood tones everywhere — from floor to ceiling. They were soft and golden, offering warmth to the small space.

The floor was a seamless extension of the porch, the walls the same as the logs outside. In the small square of an entry space, Evie faced the U-shaped kitchen with a sink against the wall and the stove to the left, built into a counter. On the right, the fridge sat next to a small trash can, all sectioned off with linoleum.

Evie's eyes moved, taking in a small round table with three chairs next to the counter and a hallway. The hall was dark, but that didn't matter because her eyes were drawn to the left of the entry. On the far wall, which she hadn't seen when she'd taken a small peek through the darkened window, was a giant stone fireplace.

A small pine table sat in front, serving as a coffee table to an older and well-loved brown leather couch. There was a chair too, a slingback with wooden arms and the same leather covering the seat. Instead of a flattened cushion, it just looked well-squashed, like if she sat down she'd sink right down and never get up again.

Her gaze was focused on the side table next to the couch — which she was pretty certain had a small stack of books on it, when Nick walked into her view. She followed him with her eyes as he bent down on one knee in front of the fireplace and dutifully added three logs to a small pile of ashes and kindling before striking a match. There was no way her attempt to light a fire would be anywhere near as effortless. In the span of a couple minutes, it engulfed the logs and quietly crackled, filling the cabin with warmth.

Nick stood back up and Evie grasped her bag, watching as he ran a hand over his beard.

"There's —" He cleared his throat, glancing toward the hall. "There's not much to show, but I'll give you a tour. Come on."

After a tilt of his head, he turned toward the hallway and flipped the light on. He was right; there truly wasn't much to the cabin. He shoved the first door open as she hurried a couple steps to catch up to him.

The bathroom consisted of a decent-sized shower against the far wall for how small the cabin was. In the corner the washer and dryer were side by side in a linen closet with some storage. The mirror, sink, and toilet were all standard and sparkling white.

It struck Evie how clean it was. It was spotless, even though she was sure he hadn't been expecting company, let alone someone staying indefinitely.

Nick leaned back, glancing at her before moving forward. His voice was softer when he spoke again. "First door here, this can be your bedroom." He opened the door and then stepped back, giving her space.

Evie lingered at the threshold to look at the small bedroom. There was a wooden dresser and full-sized bed taking up most of the room. The wooden floor had no rug and she was grateful she'd thrown a couple extra pairs of socks into her bag. It was modest, but it was clean and smelled mostly fresh, except for a lingering tinge of stale air.

When she turned, Nick was closer in the tight hallway but clearly trying to keep his distance. She didn't know if he was sizing her up or if he was concerned about startling her. Evie didn't know if she was concerned about the stranger or grateful he had been kind so far.

"It doesn't get used much — well at all, really." He cleared his throat, motioning to the dresser. "You can unpack, there's nothing in there. Closet has a few boxes but if you need hangers, I can grab you extras." He looked tired and Evie remembered he'd just come home from work, but he spurred on before she could say anything. "I'm at the end of the hall. You know — case you need anything." Nick was a man of few words. When his eyes flickered to her bag, his expression softened. "I'll get you anything you need from the next town. I gotta go to the store soon anyway."

Evie stood in the spare room, holding her bag and frowning. "Oh — I don't — I mean maybe Andy can transfer you money for me but I was told not to bring —"

Nick cut her off. "Money's not an issue. You're not gonna pay for a thing while you're forced to stay here." A grimace settled over his features. "I'll make sure of that from the Bureau myself if I have to."

She thanked him softly, finally placing her bag on the end of the bed.

Nick lingered in the doorway. "Well, I'm starved. I'm gonna get out of these clothes and warm up some leftovers. There's plenty if you'd like some." He didn't wait for her response before disappearing.

Evie heard his door shut with a firm click as her stomach grumbled. She unzipped her bag, focused on pulling out pajamas as Nick's door opened again. He passed her open door and she saw him hesitate before shaking his head and continuing on. It was only after she heard the fridge opening and cabinets closing that she slowly walked back out to see Nick had a pot of stew on the stove already warming. Two bowls sat on the counter next to it.

"No dietary restrictions?"

"Oh!" Evie wrapped her arms around herself, shaking her head. "No, I'm good."

"Good." It was the first time Nick smiled at her and the gentle tilt of his lips made the tension in her shoulders unwind as she sank into a wooden chair at the round table.

She watched him fill both bowls and open the fridge again, calling over his shoulder, "What do you want to drink?" He listed off a few options and Evie went with water, praying it was the simple option. Nick pulled back and grabbed two glasses from an overhead cabinet.

Evie pushed to stand, assuming the bowl left on the counter was for her, but Nick shot her a look that made her freeze in place. He placed a bowl in front of her and laid a napkin and spoon next to it. His voice was gentle, but stern. "Be careful, it's hot."

Evie sank back down in her chair. Her throat felt unnaturally tight as she looked up at him. "Thank you."

Nick shrugged with a gentle smile, grabbing his bowl and water before taking the seat catty-corner to her. There were only three chairs so he wasn't directly across, but he also wasn't sitting right next to her.

Evie decided she was okay with that.

They talked about blissful nothing over the bowls of stew. Nick mumbled something about the weather always being rainy or snowy here, then apologized that he didn't have a television. Evie brushed it off — she didn't watch *that* much TV at home, but she *was* excited for the rain.

When she could see the bottom of her bowl and her stomach finally felt full for the first time in hours, an intense wave of exhaustion rolled over her. Pushing back in the chair slightly, she yawned, trying to cover it up with her hand and turning her head. "I'm just going to —"

"Leave the bowl." Nick nodded toward the guest room, no nonsense. "Make yourself at home."

Evie hesitated in the hallway, eyelids drooping as a sense of weighted silence hung between them. She licked her lips before she looked over at him, murmuring, "Thank you, Nick Barber."

He smiled, making the lines around his blue eyes crease. "You're welcome, Evelyn Morgen."

CHAPTER SIX

WHITE SHEETS COVERED EVERY PIECE OF FURNITURE, loose edges lightly flapping in a breeze from the open windows. Jonathan Murphy walked slowly through the mansion, taking in the half-packed fineries. He entered the office, looking ahead at the wide expanse of glass perfectly framing the Pacific.

He was in the middle of relocating — though it seemed like a pin had been temporarily put in that plan as he sank into a familiar leather chair and the memories of his father's lectures that came with it. The warm leather and dark walnut desk were a stark contrast from the rest of the modern house, but each piece was an antique. Hundreds of Murphy men had worked from this space, and now it was his turn.

The files scattered across the desktop were copies of various ones he'd paid or bribed to get. There was one on the agent heading the case against him — Agent Anthony Wilson, FBI — and a partially redacted case file on Jonathan Murphy, himself.

They didn't know much. The case was built on a foundation of playing cards. One swift blow from Murphy and they'd be back to ground zero.

Well, they *had* nothing, until the events of the last few days. Now, the FBI had a little librarian.

She was a sweet thing. The photo attached to her file must have been pulled from social media because she was clearly leaned up against someone cropped out. Her round face bore a large smile, a stark contrast to the terror he'd seen and caused. She was on the shorter side — maybe around five-five — the thought made Murphy picture the same face behind cracked glass in Vermont.

She'd worked for Hawthorne for the last four years, making Evelyn the sole librarian of an entire school system of bright, budding young minds.

The FBI file was benign. She didn't have any significant others, just parents who Murphy, honestly, didn't give two shits about. A brother died years ago — Murphy could relate to that one — and she didn't even have a *pet* for god's sake. She was the perfect civilian casualty if he hadn't fucked it all up.

His focus drew back to the smiling photo. The little brunette with brows drawn together and determination in her eyes as she hit the alarm had ruined all his plans.

Murphy felt so obscenely stupid for killing Ben Harriet — but once he saw the soft features of the undercover agent, he couldn't contain himself. The gun fell into his hand and pressed itself into Ben's stomach.

The five shots into the body afterwards, however, that was all Murphy.

It was personal. Ben Harriet used to be Ben Young and Ben Young used to work in the Murphy household as security. He was bright eyed just a few days ago when Murphy entered the school to say hello to his old friend. The FBI's image of Ben on file was an older version — Murphy remembered a younger face from years ago when he met Ben for the first time during a mandatory family meeting.

And then he'd learned Ben was a cop. A dirty, lying, filthy pig who'd walked into his house and gotten a few secrets from Murphy's liquor-loosened lips.

And Murphy was furious.

He shuffled the files, staring down at the information on Evelyn Morgen. According to the people he'd bribed back in DC, she left with that agent, Wilson. But she'd surface. He'd give it a few weeks, keep his head down and ear to the ground, but he'd find her.

And he couldn't wait to press his gun to her stomach and ask her to smile for him as he emptied his clip into her.

Murphy picked up an abandoned whiskey glass, taking a swig as he looked up at the sound of footsteps. Two men entered the office — the first was his father's previous head of security. The second was Will Bryant.

Murphy didn't bother to stand as Bryant stopped near a bookshelf and leaned against it. The head of security took position near the windows, the evening breeze ruffling the sheer curtains.

"I need you to find someone for me, Will." Murphy put his whiskey down after he felt the burn hit his throat. He slid Evie's smiling face across the desk. "Take care of her for me."

Bryant stepped over, sliding the photo off of the edge of the desk with a single finger. He flipped it over and saw Evelyn Morgen's name listed with a few others from the FBI and nodded. "Timeline? Anything I need to know?"

Murphy wrapped his fingers around the glass again as he clicked his tongue. "It's important to me she's dead before the end of the year." It was November; that wasn't a tough ask.

Normally, Murphy wouldn't immediately call someone else to clean up his own mess, but this was a *special* circumstance.

Bryant was the best for a reason — he was ruthless and didn't leave a trail. Murphy needed that right now.

It was also *Will*, the same Will that knew Murphy more often as *Jonathan* and though they didn't cross paths intimately anymore, the desires lingered, as they were oft to do. Murphy could sit behind the desk in the shadows of his father's fathers pretending, but he was still just a boy at heart that trusted the one in front of him with some of his deepest secrets.

If this case went to court — everything he'd worked so hard to get would crumble. The thought of being stuck in a cell for the rest of his life made his fingers itch, twitching for a gun and the control to end it himself before the time ever came for bookings or trials.

From the corner of the room, the head of security snorted. "If only you'd been more careful about that undercover cop and not tried to move our entire operation to bum-fuck Vermont."

At the mention of *Ben*, Murphy's fingers tightened on the whiskey glass. *Ben* was his own problem. He was proof that Murphy needed to remember his place, that letting undue feelings crawl under his skin was the wrong course of action in a plan so tangled, spiders couldn't navigate the web.

Murphy looked at the older man over the edge of the glass. He sat it down and, in one smooth motion, drew a gun. The older man wasn't even looking when Murphy pulled the trigger.

The man's head exploded, spraying the sheer curtains with a mess of blood and brain. The body fell with a thud and Murphy turned his gaze back to Bryant, raising an eyebrow.

"She's out of state. One of the cops I paid in Hawthorne said she was taken somewhere by the agent heading the case, Anthony Wilson."

Bryant flexed his hands, sighing. "Right." He looked over at

Murphy, and for the barest of moments Murphy watched questions flash across the other man's face. They were gone before Bryant verbalized them. "I'll make some calls, get on the road for you." Bryant turned toward the door. "You've got my number if anything changes."

Murphy cleared his throat, effectively stopping the other man in the doorway. When Bryant turned to acknowledge him, Murphy looked over at the body and then back at Bryant. "Do this for me and you might finally stop freelancing, Will."

CHAPTER SEVEN

NICK'S TRUCK TIRES KICKED GRAVEL AS HE TURNED the old monstrosity around. Evie wrapped her arms around herself on the porch, staring at his hand in the rearview, bidding her goodbye.

She raised hers back.

When his tail lights disappeared, Evie shut the cabin door and locked it firmly, leaving her staring at the empty room. A chill crawled up her spine despite the fire Nick left roaring.

She'd wanted to shower last night and crawl into her own bed. Instead, she barely had enough energy to pull off her travel clothes and put on a pair of pajamas. The bed in the spare room had a semi-comfortable mattress, but it didn't feel like home. None of the wooden walls and quiet sounds of the forest outside did anything to help her relax. She was on edge, but not at the same time, a weird mixture of apprehensive and wired.

Fitful sleep finally hit sometime early morning, and she stirred easily when she heard Nick head down the hall at the signs of first morning light through the window. Evie had dragged herself up and pulled on a cardigan that covered her from her neck almost to mid-thigh, before she poked her head out into the hallway just as Nick headed into the living room.

He made a pot of coffee and when she walked toward the table, he offered her a mug. The man looked a little rushed as he pulled on his work boots from the night before.

"Gotta go back to the logging site." He'd left his mug in the sink after downing the coffee in one gulp. "I'll be back later — but it's three hours away from the cabin. If Andy'd just *called* —"

She'd told him to go, barely half a sip out of her own mug. He was an adult with a job and she was in the middle of the woods. It seemed to be stressing him out though, because the pleasant and quiet man from last night was gone.

Nick gave her a pained look as he climbed into his truck and said he'd be back as soon as he could, but not before making sure her burner phone was sitting on the kitchen table.

Even though Andy left her with the explicit instructions not to call out — Nick told her to dial *him* first and left a scrawled phone number on a piece of scrap paper.

She assured him that it would be fine. But now here she was with a near-full mug of coffee, an empty cabin, and her own thoughts as her only company.

Evie walked back over to the table and sat down, taking a sip from her lukewarm mug. The coffee was a little bitter, but she didn't feel like getting up to look for sweetener. She just... felt like sitting there, staring down at the rippling brown liquid.

She frowned, wondering what her parents were doing at this very moment. The burner phone was still on the table, still resting next to the scrap of paper. She looked up at the clock hanging on the wall just above the fridge. It was barely seven in the morning, making it almost ten in Vermont. Evie guessed they were already up. Her father was retired and Evie's mother only did odd jobs here and there.

There was no need for her parents to work after the settlement from her brother's death.

She pushed the mug away and grumbled, standing up to walk over to the sink. Dutifully, she focused on washing both her mug and Nick's abandoned one until they were sparkling. Pulling open a drawer near the sink, she found kitchen towels and laid one out on the counter, placing both mugs on it to let them air dry. Then she took a step back and turned in a small circle in the kitchen.

"I shouldn't snoop." She whispered the words to the empty cabin and then bit her lip.

Evie started with the cabinets lining the far wall. Inside was a variety of canned and dry goods. She twisted soup cans around, reading the labels for benign options, all traditional American pantry fare. If nothing else, she could eat chicken soup until spring and probably survive out here by herself.

The next cabinet had stacked plates and bowls, a grand total of four each. She guessed Nick didn't have a need to host dinner parties, but the stark small amount made her think of her grandmother's china she had stored in her upper cabinets back home. She had two full sets and never used them. When did she have a chance to pull down silver-inlaid sets of dishware?

The thought made her pause.

She *wanted* to host a dinner party. When this was all over, she was pulling down both sets. She was going to invite not only her parents, but Andy and Agent Beck too. Maybe even all the neighbors up and down the street. She'd call it a celebration of life — a celebration of *her* life not being ended by a murderer.

The next cabinet had two bottles in it. One was whiskey

and Evie laughed a little, pulling it down to look at the familiar label. Her father used to drink with Marlon on every Sunday fishing trip. He tried to pretend it wasn't what clanked in the back of his car every time they headed to the lake on the weekends, but Evie knew better. She never really cared for drinking, not before her brother, but certainly not after unless it was to numb the pain. The backseat clinking stopped pretty soon after his death in her father's case.

Evie bent down to look in the bottom cabinets. She found some supplies for s'mores and snorted, unable to imagine Nick making a roaring fire just to roast some marshmallows for himself, but maybe it was how he kept himself entertained alone in the wilderness.

The fridge was balefully empty, with a half gallon of milk, root beer, and real beer. There was a single bowl of stew left and Evie assumed that would be her lunch.

Nick seemed so *boring* for an ex-FBI agent.

There was a final cabinet, across from the fridge. She expected some cleaning supplies when she pulled the handle, but instead, on the back of the cabinet door, there was a leather sling cradling a handgun. Evie recoiled almost immediately, staring at the shiny black weapon.

She shut the cabinet door carefully and glanced around the cabin, wondering for a moment if Nick had guns stored in the walls.

"This is definitely a sign that I'm losing it." She whispered to herself again, walking toward the leather couch. It looked like it had been in the cabin for a while, but she'd gotten the impression Nick hadn't owned the place for very long. The dichotomy made her think that he'd just kept whatever furniture was here when he moved in.

Next to it was the small console table and Evie crouched

down with a smile, finding the books that she'd seen the night before.

There were eight and she dragged every single one out, plopping them onto the cool wooden floor.

The first book was a well-worn copy of *Wuthering Heights* from the 70s. It had a slightly bent cover, and her fingers ran over it, staring at the very dramatic illustration of Heathcliff standing on the moors next to a spindly, leafless tree.

The book under it in the stack was *Pride and Prejudice*. Evie pushed it to the side and found herself laughing as she stared down at three almost identical books. The first had a bright blue cover with bold white letters reading '*FISHING IN*', then an illustration of Washington State under it, a star at the heart of the state. The second and third books covered hiking and foraging, respectively.

Evie shook her head, she supposed if she got truly and utterly desperate she could completely lose her mind and learn about all the different species of fish in Washington. Maybe she'd learn how to pick mushrooms. Or maybe she'd meet vampires or werewolves in the woods since this was getting dangerously close to the plot of a paranormal young adult novel.

The last three books, Evie wasn't familiar with. She pushed one to the side that had a lonely cabin on the front cover, the title in a slanted and stylized font to look like smoke drifting away above the cabin. *ALONE* seemed like the kind of thriller you'd read in a cabin if you were a true masochist and weren't terrified of the nightmares that would follow after finishing it.

Left with just two books, Evie picked the first of the mass market paperbacks, staring at a woman on the front cover with half a boob out, draped in a vaguely plaid patterned blanket and leaning onto a shirtless man who looked like he'd never smiled a day in his life. The title was *phenomenal* and made Evie burst into little giggles as she whispered, "Hello *you*."

The Highlander Barbarian's Wife's Sister had a generic photo of the Scottish highlands on the back cover, with a couple author blurbs from romance writers she'd never heard of. The first one specified that it "made her nonexistent kilt burst into flames" while the second author wrote about how she adored that the author spent "at least three paragraphs per page on Angus' abs."

Evie flipped it open to skim page one with a little laugh, in awe that Nick had this just *sitting* in his little cabin. Her eyes skimmed some vague informational paragraph setting the scene before she glanced over at the last novel, which was another romance but this one was a little more chaste, something vaguely western.

She picked up the rest of the books and stacked them carefully, leaving out *Wuthering Heights* and *The Highlander Barbarian's Wife's Sister*. She wasn't sure if she wanted to be sucked into the messy drama of two interconnected families in the English moors, or to be wooed by a constantly half-naked man in a kilt. She could decide later.

Evie stretched as she stood back up. A shower was necessary — and taking one while Nick was out of the cabin made her feel a little better.

She hadn't known what to expect. Andy had given her enough assurance that he wanted her safe from Murphy, but being dropped *here* was confusingly unexpected.

Nick was kind, quiet, and left her to her own devices all night. It was slightly nerve-wracking being left alone in the wilderness, but the other alternative was showering in a strange man's house with him two feet away from her in the kitchen.

Evie grabbed her packed toiletries and shuffled down the

hallway, feeling like a middle school camper getting naked in the public showers for the first time.

With the light flipped on, the bathroom was peaceful. There was a small window in the shower area, looking out on the trees and back side of the cabin. The tub was a clawfoot. It looked old and like it'd been in the cabin for a while — like a lot of the rest of the decor around. Above the tub, a shower head that was slightly more modern had been installed, with a rack for a shower curtain.

Evie pulled out her moisturizer, toothbrush, and face wash, placing them carefully on the edge of the sink just to watch them fall into it. There were no cabinets other than the ones next to the laundry. She hesitantly stepped over, opening one to find six towels neatly folded with some washcloths and hand towels. Everything was a deep navy color, almost black, and they were the biggest, fluffiest things she'd ever seen.

She tugged a towel and washcloth out, opening the other cabinets just to peek. Inside one was cleaning supplies — a bucket with some spray, room freshener, and spot cleaner. Next to it was an extra gallon of laundry detergent. The cabinet above contained a small collection of toiletries.

Evie reached in and pulled out a body wash in a black bottle with a name in French she didn't recognize. She didn't have shampoo or conditioner with her, and she hoped Nick wasn't a three-in-one kind of guy. When she flipped the lid open, she was assaulted by the heady, warm scent of fir and mint. It was like walking past a fresh evergreen tree right after it rained and it made her toes curl as she carefully put it back into the cabinet.

She figured out the shower with a little cursing, leaning in to fix the knobs and water until it came out lukewarm and slowly got hotter. Beside the window to the outside was a small shelf with a partially used bottle of the same body wash and its two friends, a mint scented shampoo and then a matching conditioner. Bizarrely, all the labels were in English and French.

Evie took her time under the steaming water, letting it run over her and squeezing a small amount of the shampoo into her hands. She tried to relax, but the idea that someone could be in the cabin made her rush through the process of soaping up and rinsing off.

When she stepped out onto a little gray rug, she toweled off and dressed in a pair of fleece-lined leggings and a loose sweater. She'd never really been gifted in the chest department, solidly middle of the road, and she hoped it was loose enough she wouldn't have to put on a bra when Nick came back. Being isolated *and* forced to wear underwire for months seemed like a fate worse than death. At least she had an IUD and no period — small miracles.

She scrubbed her teeth, feeling a little more human with every act. Leaving her face wash next to the shampoo on the shower shelf felt strange. It didn't take up too much room, but if Nick needed her to, she'd keep all her things in the bedroom. She didn't want her presence to feel like a slow infection into his quiet and simple life.

Evie's skin crawled as she put her dirty clothes into a small pile in the corner of her room. A couple more days and she could justify using Nick's detergent to run a load.

She found herself back in the living room, wishing for a TV she could turn on or quiet music to fill the echoing silence, instead she picked up *Wuthering Heights* and flipped to page one, sinking herself into a story she'd read easily fifty times.

It was hard to concentrate between wondering when Nick would be back and if Andy would eventually call her. The black phone sat on the kitchen table, but when Evie glanced at it, it stayed as still and quiet as the rest of the damn cabin.

After thirty minutes of fidgeting, she got up, poked around

in the kitchen again, and ate the leftover stew. She flipped all the lights on when it began to get dark. Then she found herself in front of the fireplace, prodding at the crackling fire with one of the pokers, then nudging the damper chain. Evie paced back and forth and reminded herself if something happened and Nick truly didn't return, she could at least call 911.

The clock above the fridge said it was nearly eight by the time she heard tires on gravel. Evie's head shot up from her position on the couch. The last few pages of the book in her hands fluttered shut as she held it with one hand and watched Nick's truck come into view. She stood, then sat back down, not wanting to appear too eager like she'd been waiting for him to come back all day. With a frantic flick of her fingers, Evie reopened the book and forced her attention on the pages as the front door unlocked.

Evie tried to even her breathing — to appear normal — before she finally let herself look up, trying to stay casual as Nick strode past the back of the couch with a tired smile and dropped a greasy brown paper bag onto the kitchen counter.

"Bought dinner for us, figured you'd be hungry." He cleared his throat, unlacing his boots. "Sorry I don't have much in the fridge — actually, I hope you had that stew. That was the best thing in there." He stood back up, kicking off his boots next to the door.

Evie watched him go back and forth, like she was following a tennis match.

"I'm a shitty host." Nick stood behind the couch, looking down at her with a frown before nodding over to the bag. "But I brought burgers and fries as a peace offering."

A smile tugged on her lips, unbidden. There was something utterly charming about him when his long and floppy hair was mussed. She shut the book gently. "You're not a shitty host. Thank you for the food."

She couldn't tell if it was just the dim lighting or if the tips of Nick's ears darkened. He grumbled something under his breath before heading toward the hall and shouting over his shoulder. "Don't wait for me! I'm running through the shower!"

The bathroom door clicked shut as Evie turned to lay the book on the side table, mulling over the fact there was a small smile playing on the edges of her lips and a warmth in her own cheeks. She shook her head, grabbing two plates and placing them on the table. In the other room the shower started up and she paused with her hand on the brown paper bag, her mind drifting to the fact he was just one wall away, shedding his work clothes, stepping into the shower...

She pulled the bag open sharply, muttering under her breath, "Holy shit, no more romance novels."

When Nick reappeared just as she sat out two root beers, her heart missed a beat. His long, wet hair was plastered to his cheek as he ran a towel over it roughly. The hallway was doing nothing to keep the warm smell of his body wash, the same that she'd used earlier, from drifting toward the kitchen table.

The man across from her dropped into his seat and unwrapped the burger in front of him, dunking a fry into ketchup. His pajama pants were a blue plaid and it made her glance over at the side table with the highlander romance still sitting out and proud.

"What'd you do today?"

Evie looked up after a bite of her own hamburger. "I read, showered, and tried to not think about how someone's out to kill me." She dipped a fry in ketchup and pointed it at him. "Did you chop logs all day?"

Nick gave her a wry smile, bright blue eyes twinkling. "I did *not*. It's the end of the season, it starts to get too icy for the work to be safe up in the mountains. I'm actually finished for a while, so lucky you — you'll get me full-time in the cabin."

Evie didn't know why her stomach flipped.

They ate in a comfortable silence for a few minutes before she caught Nick glancing over at the side table. He grinned slowly. "This place was a rental, someone left the bodice ripper."

Evie couldn't contain her giggles as she held her root beer by its neck and peered at him. "Have you read it?" It was her curiosity as a librarian — she'd seen stranger people taking out odder genres.

Nick's lips lifted into a smirk around the lip of his bottle. "Maybe."

CHAPTER EIGHT

THE DAYS BLURRED TOGETHER IN THE CABIN.

A full week hadn't even passed, but time seemed to both fly and crawl in the middle of nowhere, making Evie question her own sanity — and wonder why Andy had still yet to call.

She woke up one morning and found Nick ready with two mugs of coffee. They'd already settled into an almost routine. He was an early riser and had her a cup by the time she dragged herself out from the warm quilts on her bed.

"Gotta chop some wood today." He took a swig from his coffee and looked out the front window. Her eyes followed, watching the snow flurries. When Nick finished his mug, he sat it in the sink and stretched his arms out over his shoulders. "So you and I don't freeze into popsicles in a couple weeks when December hits."

She decided right there that it would be good for her to get out of the house too. Which is how she found herself seated in one of the rocking chairs with her scarf around her neck, a cardigan *and* a jacket *and* a blanket from the hall closet.

Nick insisted on the last one.

Evie chalked it up to the fact that it would probably annoy Andy if she ended up with a cold or the flu while she was trying to isolate from a killer. Still, Evie unwound her scarf, letting it hang over the edge of the rocking chair. Her cheeks felt warm and she wasn't sure if it was the book in her hands or the man she was currently watching in the snow-flecked yard.

Nick was dressed in a pair of dark jeans and had a white t-shirt under a brown flannel. On top was a brown coat. He heaved the wood axe over his shoulder again and brought it down with a sharp crack, splitting another log.

Evie sucked on her teeth and glanced back down at *The Highlander Barbarian's Wife's Sister* open in her lap. The beginning didn't make much logical sense — after the wife's sister was forced to don mourning colors, she was also apparently isolated to her sister's husband's castle in the Scottish highlands. Well, *"isolated"* was the word the author used, but the love interest had *definitely* kidnapped her. Evie decided that it could be overlooked, romance novel logic wasn't real-life logic.

Besides, she was having a good time with it. The back cover review was right, Angus' abs were discussed *frequently*.

Evie glanced over the edge of the book to watch as Nick shed his jacket. He slung it over the edge of the wheelbarrow full of wood next to him. When he shifted, he turned toward the forest and squinted at the sun, rolling up the sleeve on his left arm, repeating the process on the right.

Her mouth went dry.

Look away. She couldn't already be eyeing him like a piece of meat.

Nick ran a hand over his shaggy hair and then grasped the handle of the wood axe, thick fingers wrapping around it as he pulled it out of the stump and set up another log.

Evie slapped the paperback shut with a huff and glared at

the cover. In a way, it was and wasn't the root of all her problems — and she'd blame the rush of emotions on the book because she really didn't have anything else to take her anger, boredom, or frustration out on.

"Hey." Nick's sharp voice startled her as she snapped her head up. He stood in the middle of the yard, axe on the ground as he used the handle to balance in a slight lean. A small, teasing smile pulled at his beard as he raised an eyebrow. "Don't destroy my copy."

Evie raised an eyebrow right back. "Your copy?" She lifted the offending romance novel and waved it at him. "Of *The Highlander Barbarian's Wife's Sister*?"

"Yes, Evelyn, it's a classic." He scoffed — but Evie could see the tiny smile grow to lift the edges of his lips and his beard.

She groaned and dropped it onto the table next to the rocker. "I'm sorry, *sir*. I'm just..." She glanced at the wooden roof, staring at the open slats and sighing heavily. "I don't know what I am. I don't know what I'm doing, or what I should be doing."

Evie dragged her gaze away and hesitantly looked at Nick. His grip had loosened slightly on the axe and the way he was staring slack-jawed at her made her pause.

She frowned, pushing up. "Sorry — who am I to complain? You gave up your peace and quiet as a favor for Andy at the last minute."

"Hey." This time the word was quieter.

Evie's hand gripped the blanket as she tried to ignore him.

It didn't work.

"Hey, look at me."

She cringed, forcing herself to leave the blanket in the rocker before turning.

Nick glanced at his watch. "It's too late for us to go to town today — the road will be too icy on the way back after all this light junk." He motioned to the flurries dusting his jacket. "But I'll take you tomorrow if you want to get out for a while."

The instant relief that blossomed in Evie's chest was almost too much to bear. She gave him a hopeful look and whispered, "Really?"

"Really." Nick heaved the axe before dropping it solidly to embed it into the stump, motioning to her. "Come out here."

Evie glanced at the blanket and book before wrapping her arms around herself and trudging down the couple steps. The gravel crunched softly under her boots as she passed his truck. The pile of wood in the wheelbarrow looked like it would last years — but keeping the cabin warm probably took far more than what he'd done today.

She slowed to a stop in front of Nick and lifted her chin. "Yes?"

A small smile played on the edges of his lips as he looked down at her. Evie's eyes flickered away from his, landing on the axe. "Are you going to teach me a life lesson with wood chopping? A little lumberjack word of wisdom to take home to Vermont? I can't embroider, so don't expect me to put the words on a pillow or anything."

"Absolutely not." Nick's voice was gruff and she laughed as she looked back at his slightly annoyed expression. "I am not putting an axe in your hands."

"That feels sexist," Evie muttered, half-joking as she looked at the heavy, red metallic weapon in the stump. "I bet I could do it."

"I know you could."

The words stopped her in her tracks as she realized how close he was — closer than they'd really been except for occasional brushes in the hallway.

"But" — Nick amended — "you have noodle-y little

librarian arms and I'd have to at least get you weight lifting before I was confident you could swing and not miss."

Evie's lips twitched. "Well, one: *rude.* Two, you're not wrong. I don't go to the gym, I shelve books for a living."

Nick's smile lit up his face. "And I'm sure you do it well. Save the axe-wielding for me."

She made a face at him, her nose scrunching. "That's what you say now — one more month of me and you'll be begging me to Cinderella your little cabin into shape. Or you'll just stick me outside and tell me to shut up when I run out of books."

He shook his head. "I think that goes against protecting you, especially if you freeze your toes off, but that's an entirely different conversation."

His smile was such a bright spot in the yard, Evie couldn't think. She just smiled back — this man, so willing to help — really did feel like the best and safest option.

"I want to show you something."

Nick's stance shifted and he reached up and slowly put his hands on each of her shoulders. Evie started, looking up in alarm as Nick swiveled her toward the forest. They walked a few steps before she stood right at the tree line. The pressure of his hands left her shoulders and she watched him as he came to stand next to her.

Nick clenched his hands into fists at his sides, balling them tight enough his knuckles turned white before he faced the forest and let out a scream that echoed and rattled the trees in front of him. The sudden noise made Evie jump, staring in shock until Nick cut himself off and grinned.

"Now you try."

"Are you *insane?*" She spat the question out, her mouth gaping. "People will come running to see who made the giant mountain man scream bloody murder."

Nick pressed a hand against his chest as he bent backwards. The laugh that came out of him moved his entire body, shaking it with mirth. "No one is coming up here. There's not a single soul for miles. Now scream. You'll feel better."

"Oh my *god*." She muttered the words under her breath, turning away from him to stare at the evergreens and underbrush. There was just a wall of foliage in front of her. Her mind twisted and flipped, running over if this would really help — if something could even help the mental gymnastics she fought with each night.

"Scream, Evie."

Nick said her name; not Evelyn — *Evie*.

She inhaled sharply before setting her shoulders and letting out an ear-piercing scream. She screamed at the trees for being in front of her and the cabin for trapping her. She screamed at Murphy who was out there in the world with a gun and a vendetta. Evie screamed because she hadn't spoken to her parents in a week. She screamed because Andy hadn't called with an update. She screamed because she was tired. She screamed because she missed the monotony of her life, her work, her kids who asked her what books they should read next.

She screamed for herself.

The yell died in a sad warble. The muscle spasmed as she clenched her shaking hands and stared at the trees. The adrenaline in her veins made tremble, ready to run inside — but Nick sucked in and screamed again.

Evie glared at the forest before clearing her throat and letting out a hoarse yell. It echoed with Nick's and Evie stomped her foot, stepping forward and screaming louder. They both yelled at nothing and everything until their vocal cords gave out.

Nick's voice rasped, "Better?"

She wrapped her arms around herself, eyes lingering on the forest before turning back toward the cabin. "A little." She caught his small smile as he walked with her back up the porch and grabbed the book and blanket off the chair. Evie snatched her scarf up, the gentle knit of her mother's hand the only reminder she had of her parents as Nick opened the door and headed straight to the kitchen to start the coffee pot.

"You know —" He dumped the grounds in the chamber, never looking up. "When I moved up here that's all I did for a month." Evie stood in the entry, watching him as he filled the chamber with water and watched it drip coffee. "I felt fucking crazy when I made the decision to move here. Like I'd lost my damn mind or something, giving up the FBI, my job, the agent position —" He fell quiet, hands on the countertop.

The set of his shoulders made his muscles stand out in the flannel, pulling it tight across his back as he sighed and hung his head. "I'm gonna be honest with you, this shit will not be easy." His eyes met hers, freezing her in place. "This will never be easy, but it doesn't have to be all bad. You may not know me or trust me yet and we may have had a very weird first meeting, but... you ever need to scream at the trees again and I'll be there with you, Evie Morgen."

She inhaled softly as she took in the man almost too big for the tiny cabin kitchen. He was every inch of someone else's dreamy lumberjack fantasy — from his wind-bitten pink cheeks to the beard taking up the lower part of his face.

"Thank you, Nick Barber."

He shrugged, smiling lopsided. "It's a great way to get some quick relief. It does get boring here —"

"It's really not boring." Evie felt a little silly as she looked at the small stack of books she left on the coffee table. "It's peaceful here. I just miss my creature comforts, I guess? I don't know and I'm sorry for being rude or insinuating —"

"You didn't insinuate anything." Nick cut her off, pointing with a mug as he pulled two down from the cabinet. "I'd say you're handling being dropped off in the woods with a total stranger like a champ."

Evie huffed, kicking her boots into a pile by the front door and peeling off her coat, tired of feeling like a marshmallow. "You aren't a total stranger." She threw her coat onto the rack near the door and then hung her scarf over it. "Andy told me two things about you before he dropped me off on your stoop like a rejected child at summer camp."

Nick cackled, his shoulders shaking and she watched him lean back and touch his chest with the motion. She realized with a little start that the full-body movement meant he was *really* laughing, not just a wry smile or a sideways glance. The joy was so immense it overtook his entire body.

With a grin up at the ceiling, he shook his head. "So what are they?"

"What are what?" Evie filled their mugs. "What did Andy tell me about you?"

"No." Nick lounged against the counter. "What are your creature comforts?"

Evie stood with the glass coffee pot in her hand like an idiot. "Oh."

Nick raised an eyebrow, waiting.

She slotted the pot back into its place to collect the last drips and picked up her own mug, using it as an excuse to focus on anything but his gaze.

Evie blew on it, frowning. "At home?" She took a scalding sip. If her tongue burnt, she wouldn't have to admit how boring she was. "Well, I like to do chores and make sure everything's in order on my weekends so my weeks run smoothly. If I have spare time I sit and read —" Evie paused. "I guess I'm just a librarian stereotype."

Nick hid his soft smile with his coffee mug. "Sorry I don't have better book options for you."

The plain mug in her hands was *so* interesting. She took another sip to kill the quiet seconds before shrugging her shoulders. "It's really okay. I just like... soft music, nice books, warm drinks." Evie avoided his eyes. "I don't need much, but I am missing the music a little."

Movement in front of her made her finally look away from the coffee. Nick shifted and placed his mug on the counter. "You know, I'm pretty sure this place had a stereo that I shoved into a closet. Let me find it, set it up. We'll get some CDs — off the grid but not total silence."

Evie's heart clenched. "Really?"

Nick toyed with the handle of his mug, pushing it back and forth. The coffee sloshed up on the sides but never quite breached the lip. Finally, he picked it up again and took another drink. "I'm really trying not to be the worst host in the world, here." He grimaced. "I think I'm failing though."

This time Evie smiled. "I don't think you are. You're great." She shifted past him, not quite a reach but close in the small kitchen as she placed her mug into the sink.

He smelled warm — oak and pine, with hints of fancy French soap.

The smell of him in close proximity was a lot to form a thought around and she leaned back just as quick, playing it off as adjusting her sweater as she pivoted toward the hall. She paused at the threshold, looking back at Nick. "I'll wash our mugs tonight before dinner."

As she turned away, Nick had to pry his fingers from his mug. Evie lingered in the hallway just long enough to hear Nick let out a long breath — while both of them stared at the empty space in the doorway where she'd been.

CHAPTER NINE

"THE SEASON'S OVER — CONDITIONS GET TOO ICY and dangerous once the trees are heavy with snow. It's bad enough in the mountains during summer. The higher we're up, the harder it is to get the big ones down."

Evie hummed in the passenger seat, glancing out the truck window as they bounced down the mountain road. The trees blurred into vaguely green blobs, but she'd already spotted an eagle and a fox darting back from the side of the road.

She tried to keep it light, but she *was* painfully curious about Nick's work. Which led them to a conversation about the logistics of logging, including its terminology and how teams worked. It was fascinating — and it made her want to spend hours finding books to research the topic.

Looking away from the window, she surveyed him. "How many trees do you cut down daily?"

Nick raised an eyebrow, grinning. "I thought we were switching who asked questions?"

"Oops," Evie laughed, biting her tongue. The truck cab was chilly this morning when they got in, an uncomfortable silence settling. When they both opened their mouths at the same time, Nick suggested maybe they just needed to take turns. They hadn't exactly cornered each other to ask the questions swirling between them.

Evie wanted to know the man she was suddenly stuck with. She knew he was curious about her too — though she imagined Andy'd already filled him in on the basics. It didn't make her uncomfortable, she just wanted to level the playing field.

"So." Nick glanced over as he drove down the familiar road. "That means it's *my* turn to ask you something."

A disgruntled sound came out of Evie's mouth as she crossed her arms. "Fine, but that's my next question."

He went quiet for a moment before asking, "If you could eat one thing right now, what would it be?"

"That's easy." Evie felt a small smile creep up onto her face. "Hawthorne has this Christmas... market? Festival? It's a parade too. Listen, it's a lot of things. It starts December twelfth and goes for a whole week. The kids get off school and the town gets decorated and..." She sighed, smiling wistfully as she relaxed her arms. "A lot of people run their own booths and bring holiday treats to sell. The last two years I've bought peanut brittle from the woman down the street from me and I swear, I eat it all in one sitting."

Her eyes fell onto Nick again as he laughed softly. His eyes flickered away from the road and caught hers. "The whole tin?"

"The *whole* tin." Evie pressed a hand against her cheek, laughing at herself. "It's meant for an entire family, it's like the size of a bucket of kettle corn!" She giggled, leaning back in the seat as the truck bounced. "I love it. I also love that there's always a hot chocolate booth, but" — she turned back to him excitedly, waving her hand — "it's not just something powdered from a packet, it's *French*, Nick."

"*French?*" He raised an eyebrow, his mouth dropping open in faux surprise.

"Well, it's not *authentic*. There aren't many French immigrants moving to the middle of nowhere, Vermont, but it's like drinking five liquefied chocolate bars with some marshmallows on top for posterity's sake."

Nick nodded slowly, unable to keep the smile off his face. "That does sound pretty good."

His words were lost on her as she stared at the small town suddenly emerging out of the trees. She must have dozed off in the back of the SUV when Andy brought her through because Evie definitely would have remembered the quaint town that Nick was navigating now. Everything was laid out like a capital T, with rows of stores on either side that led to a larger building at the crosshair that had *WELLS CREEK TOWN HALL* on a sign made from timber and brick.

They drove past a post office and diner to the left, with a grocery store and a hiking store across the street. Then there was a park that seemed closed for the winter. As they neared the town hall, Evie spotted a florist's shop to the right of it, but Nick veered the truck left and pulled into a small parking lot in front of a converted house.

The sign outside the small house was partially hidden by some bushes, but she could still make out *WELLS CREEK LIBRARY* in all caps. *I guess they all got their signage from the same place.* As banal as the downtown was, being at a library again made her want to fling herself from the truck cab and race through the doors.

Nick smiled gently. "I need to double-back to the market to pick up a few things so neither of us starve over the next week. You can come with me or stay here. Or I can stay here." He waved a hand before reaching down and fishing a leather wallet from his pocket. "Whatever you want."

Evie blinked as he held a plastic card out to her. When she finally took it, he muttered, "I don't think Stephen will give you any trouble, but there's *my* library card if he does. Get books out, use it — like I said — whatever you want."

She glanced down at the small gray card. On the back, Nick's signature was in cursive, far less messy than her own. With a little smile, Evie looked back up at him with her hand on the truck's door. "Thank you." As she went to open it, she felt the warm touch of his fingers on her arm and froze.

"Do you — I mean, *would* you like me to come in with you?"

The truck was quiet for a moment as Evie shook her head. "No, I want to be okay. I *will* be okay." She swallowed a lump in her throat before sliding out.

Nick leaned over the bench seat, pointing barely two blocks away. "I will be right over there. You could scream and I'd hear you."

Evie grinned, tilting her head up to look at him. "I'll be okay, Nick. Whatever I want, right?"

"Right." His voice sounded unnaturally thick as they stared at each other for a heartbeat. After a moment, she climbed out of the truck. Nick waved her up the library stairs and once she was situated out of the cold, he finally backed the truck out of the parking spot and turned it around. She eyed him as he circled the lot and pulled back onto the main road, parking in a parallel spot in front of the market.

It was laughable, and he was right — Evie could shout right now and he'd hear her. Instead, she raised a hand in a wave as Nick got out of his truck and pointed to the grocery with huge, exaggerated movements that he'd be just inside.

Her heart felt warm as she turned and grasped the handle to the library door, sucking in a happy little gasp as she tugged it open, a bell chiming above her head.

The smell of old books and electric heating hit her immediately.

She was right — the building was clearly a converted old house. To the right of the foyer was a set of stairs leading up with a rope strung across them. Directly in front of her was a small desk with a computer on it and a door behind it. Evie glanced from one side to the other, taking in an old dining room filled with shelves at different heights and packed with books. To the right, a smaller room led to the back. She leaned over, peering to catch a glimpse of a brightly painted wall and a few children's books.

"I'm coming!" a voice shouted from the back. Evie grasped Nick's card tightly in her hand, wondering if the disembodied voice was Stephen.

The door swung open on a double-hinge, clicking back into place as an older gentleman, not much taller than she was, stepped out with books in his hands. He had a shock of white hair and bright green eyes when he finally looked up to see who was in his library.

"Well, you're new." He grinned, putting the books down. "What can I do for you?"

Evie laughed, pushing her hair back as she stepped forward. "I'm in town for a while... visiting a friend." It seemed like the best excuse on short notice and flimsy as it was, she barreled forward. "He said I could use his card, but I'd really like my own if that's all right? I don't want him on the hook for any of my loans." She placed Nick's card on the desk and slid it closer to the librarian, her only proof that her story wasn't a complete lie.

The man looked down at the card, then slid it off the desk and hummed as he typed something into his computer. "Nick Barber, hm?" He slid the library card back over.

Evie felt like her cheeks were on fire as she pocketed it. "Yes, he's an old friend." She stuttered over the lie, aware this was already not going well, but she spurred forward anyway. "I'm a librarian too — actually, a children's one — for an elementary school. Well, actually, the school is from elementary through high, but I cover it all." She flailed for a moment as she fought to fill the silence. "I've just wanted a book so much since I've been here. There's really not many at the cabin and I'm dying a little."

The older man looked up, a smile playing at the edges of his lips. "Well, let's fix that for you." He bent down and pulled out a blank card from a drawer, scanning it before sliding it across the desk with a pen. "Sign your name here."

Evie stared down at the card, uncertain but picking up the pen anyway. With a little flourish, she signed *Evelyn Morgen*, the flick of the pen on the last *n* sliding off the signature line.

He picked up the card and typed something before holding it out to her. "Well, let me be the first to welcome you to Wells Creek, Evelyn. I'm Stephen and it's nice to meet you."

She took the card, smiling back gently. "It's nice to meet you too."

His answering smile made his eyes crinkle kindly. He motioned toward each of the rooms. "Browse, pick whatever you'd like. The library is yours." With a wink, he turned toward the door behind the counter. "Shout if you need help finding anything, fiction is to the right, nonfiction starts on the left. This place makes a giant circle, you won't miss a thing."

Evie waited until he was behind the door before she threw herself to the right, starting at the first section of fiction novels and running her hands over the spines. Up close she could smell the old paper and ink, looking around to see familiar titles she'd shelved herself. There were others too, new releases and old, but it didn't matter. The only thing she cared about was being in the presence of the books she often found comfort in.

She walked straight past the thrillers and mysteries, unsure when she'd be able to pick up one of those again — maybe not for a while. Instead Evie started in historical fiction, with literary novels about women in world war II, ending up in historical romance. She perused the titles, sliding books out to read their back covers before landing on two paperbacks that sounded nice, stashing them under one arm as she circled the rows, moving into the next room.

It looked like the room used to be part of a kitchen or maybe a study, but now it was painted a cool green with illustrations of trees and forest animals on the walls. Evie walked past a painted moose to look at the middle grade books, plucking a worn paperback of *Charlotte's Web* off the shelf and smiling as she put it with her other finds.

She walked past biographies, town histories, a small row of CD audiobooks, circling back to the front desk. Stephen stood behind it again as she slid her finds onto the counter. He hummed over each title as he scanned them and Evie proudly handed over her new library card, grinning as he slid it back to her on top of her stack.

"I'll see you soon, I hope?"

"Oh, sooner than you'd expect." Evie beamed, tucking her library card into her pocket and pulling the books to her chest. "I'll make Nick bring me back."

Stephen chuckled, shaking his head. "Good, he needs to get out of that cabin sometimes. You make him bring you to town. Don't let yourself go stir crazy up there."

Evie felt another blush creep up her neck, promising softly that she would as she gave Stephen a last smile before walking outside. The air was brisk and she hugged the books tighter to her chest, walking down to the sidewalk. It was quiet, with barely any foot traffic, so she picked the section of sidewalk that passed in front of the town hall, walking slowly as she glanced over to make sure Nick's truck hadn't moved.

As she shuffled the books around, Evie missed the tote bag she kept stashed in her car for times like these. She wanted the comfort of sliding her finds into it and treating herself to a semi-burnt coffee at the local cafe just down from the school.

"It's not *that* many books," she muttered to herself as she crossed the road.

She came to *HIKER'S PARADISE* first, a strange name for a dark green shop with backpacks and quick-ignite fire packs in the windows. She wasn't sure it was much of a paradise to hike through the mountains, so she ignored it in favor of walking toward Nick's truck.

A prickle went up Evie's spine and she slowed. There was no one around, just a few cars passing through. Even the diner across the street looked mostly empty.

By all accounts, Wells Creek was the perfect, sleepy town for her to hide in. A flash of uncertainty twisted Evie's stomach as she put her head down and pushed the door open to the small market, craving the security of four walls and the man inside.

Market was a generous term. It was clear that the four aisles in the center of the store had the basics only. There was a row for snacks, a row for canned goods, a couple baskets of fruit near a cash register with a teenager standing behind it.

The aisles were so short, she spotted Nick immediately, his entire torso visible as he mulled over two loaves of bread. Evie shifted the books under one arm and sidled up next to him.

Nick glanced over, his face breaking into a soft smile. "I see you found a few."

"Well —" Evie shifted the books around just to hold up one with a slightly different half-naked Scottish man on the cover. "I had to find out what happened to..." She glanced over at the title. "*The Scottish Royal's Cousin's Aunt.*"

Nick's grin was wide as he chuckled, shifting the basket on his arm to pull out a tote bag. After shaking the plain canvas out, Evie could see it had gray and green text printed on the front.

ALL'S WELL THAT ENDS WELL IN WELLS CREEK, WASHINGTON

He held it out to her. "For your books."

Evie didn't know what to do. Her heart crawled into her throat as she took the tote, clutching it as she asked, "Really?"

Nick's laugh was softer, a little cautious. "Yeah, well... I thought you'd come out with more. I had every intent of showing up at the library so you didn't have to walk back through the cold alone. But you're here now, so... here." He pried the tote from her fingers gently and opened it up. "Put 'em in here."

The three books slotted into the tote snugly. Evie reached for the straps in Nick's hands, her skin brushing his for the barest of moments. A spark skittered up her arm as she cleared her throat, pulling the tote up onto her shoulder and looking over at the bread. Her body felt warm as she pointed at a random loaf. "That one looks fresh. I'll eat a few PB and H's on it."

He reached for the bread, giving her a side-long glance. "H?"

"Honey," Evie said simply, shrugging her shoulders. "I don't really like jelly."

Nick reached around her and plucked something off the shelf. His arm brushed her shoulder as she watched him plop a bear-shaped bottle of honey into his basket. "Anything else?"

They wandered the aisles one last time before Nick sidled up to the checkout. He dropped the basket back into a stack of its friends next to the register as the teenager bagged everything in brown paper sacks. Evie shifted the tote bag on her shoulder, reaching up to pick up the sack with the heavier things but Nick deftly switched the bags' positions, pushing the one with the bread and honey into her hand.

"Thank you for the food." Evie looked up at him as they walked out. "And the tote bag — and bringing me into town. Sorry for interrupting your normal routine."

Nick unlocked the truck and deposited the sacks on the floorboard. When he looked back up, he pointed the truck key at her. "No more apologizing."

Evie gave him a wry smile as she climbed in. "Sorry."

He shot her a withering look as he pulled out of the parking spot, making her giggle. She expected him to turn back in the direction of the cabin, but instead Nick went past the florist, weaving down side roads as Evie glanced out.

"Where are we —"

The words died in her throat as he pulled in front of a small windowless brick building with a neon sign reading *ADAM'S* mounted above the door on the blue roof.

"I thought we could get something to eat before heading back." There was something hesitant in his expression. "If you're up for it."

ADAM'S parking lot was mostly empty and Evie glanced around it before she gave him a slight nod. "Yeah, I'm okay with that." She shivered as she climbed out of the truck, following Nick as he pulled the door open, letting her step inside first.

The bar was exactly what she expected from the exterior. It was one large open room with a dark wood bar-top against the far wall. The flooring matched the bar, save for the small area that contained a dance floor near a jukebox. She imagined it was probably often packed in the evenings with the amount of booths lined the left wall, four or five by her quick count. A singular TV hung behind the bar and from the entrance Evie didn't care to look long enough to tell what sport was on. Nick raised his hand and caught the attention of the man behind the bar.

The bartender threw his hands up in a *"What are* you *doing here"* gesture before slinging a towel over his shoulder and stepping out. Nick met him halfway, clasping him in a hug.

Evie glanced between them, trying to puzzle out their relationship. They were clearly comfortable with one another and the other man had dark brown hair like Nick's. He was also at least a decade older, but it barely showed with how bright his eyes were.

"Look what the cat dragged in." The bartender grinned, his eyes falling on Evie. He let Nick go and rubbed his hands on the towel slung over his shoulder, offering her a hand. "Chuck."

"Evie." She smiled softly as the door to the back opened. A lean and muscular girl with long black hair walked out, glancing up to find no one manning the bar, her head swiveling.

"Nick!" the girl cried out happily, rushing to throw her arms around him with a wide smile. "I thought you'd never come back." Closer, Evie could tell she was younger than them all. Where Chuck's skin was pale, the girl was tanned, with angular brown eyes. She turned toward Evie, her smile growing wider. "Hi! I'm Hope."

Evie smiled back, but a wave of discomfort settled on her shoulders. Nick clearly hadn't been here in a while — because of her? Or was it something else? Had she completely derailed his life and he'd just been polite thus far to not mention it?

Nick gave Hope a side hug and then let her go, motioning

to Evie. "Evie's a friend staying with me for a bit. Evie, this is Chuck, the owner of Adam's and his daughter, Hope."

Evie's back bristled with the creek of the door, turning sharply just to see an older couple walk in and give Chuck and Hope a cheerful wave before making their way to a booth. Evie turned her head back to the group, shifting closer to Nick.

Nick's hand moved, brushing against her arm as he nodded toward one of the open booths. "You wanna sit? We'll grab some dinner."

"Just shout when you're ready! I'll be right over." Hope grinned, already bouncing toward the couple who had seated themselves. Evie watched her go, trying to wrap her head around the dynamic between Nick, Chuck, and Hope.

Nick led Evie to one of the booths after a patron snagged Chuck's attention. She chose the side that put her back to the kitchen, leaving her a view of the front doors.

Nick took the opposite seat and pulled paper menus out from between a pair of salt and pepper shakers. As he slid a menu over, he said, "I normally get the burger, but everything is good and fresh. Hope's taken over making the soup in the mornings since she's back from college — I don't know what today's is — probably potato."

Her eyes cast down at the menu for a moment, the hairs on the back of her neck still raised. Evie stared at the words, but nothing really registered. There was a small selection of sand-wiches, a burger, then some chicken strips. Even though her stomach grumbled, she only ordered a bowl of soup when Hope suddenly appeared.

"Do you want to leave?"

Nick's question drew her eyes from distractedly scanning the bar to him. Evie forced a smile and shook her head. "No? Why would we need to leave?"

His eyebrow slowly arched as he steepled his fingers, elbows resting on the table. There were a thousand words unspoken in the glance.

Evie just kept her sunny smile up. "We haven't even gotten our food."

Nick stared until Evie shoved the menu against the wall, looking away sharply.

"Seriously, it's fine."

The more he didn't speak, the more Evie wanted to compensate. She took a drink of water and glanced over at the TV. She'd never been interested in sports a day in her life, but she still rambled out, "Oh who's playing?"

Nick was *still* staring. Evie didn't know if it was maddening that he wouldn't take the bait, or a sign that he really never should have left the FBI. By the time Hope returned with their food, Evie was squirming in the booth.

"Please stop." She looked up at him, picking up her spoon. "Please."

Nick relented, looking down at his burger before sighing. "Don't pretend with me."

Evie's gaze snapped to him, watching as he picked up his burger. Nick took a bite, chewed thoughtfully, then sat it back down and caught her eyes again in an inescapable snare. "It's one thing for you to be uncomfortable, but don't tell me you aren't just because of some bullshit social rule you think you have to follow."

She pressed her lips together, feeling her jaw tighten. "I'm not uncomfortable."

"You're stubborn," Nick muttered, eating a french fry before swiveling his plate so she could reach them too. "Now eat more than just that tiny ass cup of soup."

Around them, the bar slowly filled. She fought a flinch every time the front door opened, double-checking every new person wasn't blond, tall, covered in blood —

Nick pushed his plate back, fishing his wallet out. "I'm going to go pay before Chuck gets swamped." He stood and then rested a hand on the table. "Are you okay if I step over there?"

Evie didn't want to dignify him with a response, but she pushed her untouched food back anyway and nodded. "Yeah, I could scream and you'd hear me." She echoed his words from before, a half-attempted wry smile lifting the edges of her lips.

He frowned, mouth opening before he just shook his head and stepped away.

The doors to Adam's banged open as a group of men burst into the bar. They were all young guys, shifting backpacks as they laughed and headed toward the only free bar table left. Evie felt her spine straighten, scanning the large group.

She only let out a breath when there wasn't a blond man in sight.

Turning her head, she folded her napkin, laying it on the table before she felt eyes on her. Evie slowly looked up, scanning the bar again. It was busy — sure — but not busy enough that she couldn't see most of the tables and people. She'd sworn she'd looked at every single one as they entered. None of the floating tables near the jukebox were paying any attention to her.

She turned her head, looking down the barstools before her eyes froze.

At the far end, a man in a white shirt sat, pale hands wrapped around a glass. His back was angled away, but he had a crop of unruly blond hair at the top of his head.

Evie's stomach plummeted.

She was so focused on the man's profile that she jumped when Nick reappeared next to the table. He was in the middle of pocketing his wallet and pulling his keys out when his eyes scanned her face. Nick reached out, breaking Evie's concentration for the barest of moments and she watched his hand near hers. When she turned sharply to look up at him, Nick's hand stopped moving.

"What is it?" Nick's voice rolled over her, deep and rough, *commanding*.

She opened her mouth, words caught as she glanced around him, but the man at the bar was in a conversation with Chuck. He had a hooked nose and crinkles around his eyes and a wedding ring on his hand.

It wasn't Murphy.

Her stomach uncoiled and a wave of nausea took its place, rushing in to fill the void. Evie pushed up from the booth, bile on her tongue. "It's nothing. Are we ready?"

Nick stepped to the side, giving her room to stand before his body angled close, shielding her from the rest of the bar. His hand hovered near her back, warmth radiating from it, but never touching. Then he leaned down and muttered, "Yeah, we're ready. Let's get out of here."

CHAPTER TEN

SHE WAS EXPOSED.

The doors were at her back — but they had to be, right? She was trying to make it through the shelves to the office door. If she just made it, then she would be safe.

Evie lunged, but her body collided with a table. Books toppled, the table rocking back and forth and she tripped. She fell for ages, her hands clamoring to get over the multiplying books steadily turning themselves into a mountain. That was when *he* appeared.

"*Hello, Evelyn.*"

No one ever called her Evelyn — except her father when he was tired. But even then it was asking her to be quiet, to move along for the night — it wasn't in the way *he* said it.

Evie backed up on the rough carpet. The blond man glided like the flooring wasn't shitty, cheap carpet squares. He looked like he was only made of right angles and sharp corners. He was tall. He was covered in *blood*.

She finally slammed against a bookcase and jolted upright.

The office door looked so much farther away. She ran, rocketing past him. Did he have a gun? He did, didn't he?

Her eyes dared to dart back and there it was, a shiny, black thing in his hand. Maybe it was silver. She didn't know because she banged into another table — where were all these tables coming from? She waded through books toward the circulation desk. She could curl up in a ball — no. She needed to get to the office door.

Evie let out a cry of surprise as he appeared in front of her again.

"*Where are you going, Evelyn?*"

She knocked into him, her shoulder coming away bloody. Evie gasped, reaching up, unsure if it was her blood — his blood — the blood of Ben. She looked over her shoulder and the doors to the library were wide open. There was Ben's body, in a mangled heap in the corridor. His legs were bent at awkward angles, his eyes open.

"*Why?*" he asked, the rasp echoing.

Evie reached for the doorknob. She had to feel the cool metal to know she was safe.

In the most maudlin of ways, her fingers did manage to grasp it. She shoved the door open with all her might when there was a loud *BANG*.

She looked down, letting go of the handle.

The door fell away, she fell away. Her stomach bled. Her insides were ripped open, spilling out. She saw Murphy standing to the side, the gun still raised as he shrugged.

Evie let out an ear-piercing scream.

Her room was pitch black as Evie lunged upright in the bed. In her panic, the quilts fell off the bed, but she scrambled, desperate to press her chilled hands against her warm stomach under the old t-shirt she slept in.

She barely had a second to register her smooth skin before

she heard rapid footsteps in the hallway. Her door flew open and Evie jumped again, staring at the gun in Nick's hands as he scanned the room and entered.

He lowered it immediately when he met her wide, terrified eyes. Nick made a sound in the back of his throat — half tired, half pained as he flicked the safety back on and left the gun on top of the dresser right next to the bedroom door.

"Evie?" He was across the room in two long strides and she found herself pressing her hands against her stomach harder, trying to regulate the gasping breaths that were taking over her entire body.

"*Evie*. Shh." There was so little light coming through the plaid curtains near the headboard that all she could see was the sharp curve of his jawline as he knelt shirtless by her bedside, rasping voice cooing at her. "*Hey*." His hands rose, floundering before resting one on her forearm. "Look here, Evie. Eyes on me. You're safe. It was a dream."

She shivered, taking a shuddering breath. With the quilts gone, she felt a chill crawl up her spine and take root in the sweaty cluster of hair at the nape of her neck. How long had she been in the nightmare's clutches? How long had she tossed and turned?

Her legs ached — that much she did know — and her stomach roiled at the thought of her fighting the quilts, plunging herself toward nothing in this strange bed in a stranger's cabin, one wall away from the stranger in front of her.

She couldn't wrap her head around any of it. She couldn't fathom that only a week and a half ago she was at home at this time of night, sleeping peacefully in her bed, unaware of the Murphy family or her new co-worker being an undercover cop.

"What can I do?" Nick sat back on his haunches. His rough fingers shifted slightly and she looked down at his hand as it slid toward her wrist. Her hands grasped her stomach and Nick slowly eased one away, then the other. Which was probably for the best, because she could see little half-moon indentations her nails left in the soft skin.

Evie stared down at their hands in her lap. She shook her head, clenching her hands into fists, hyper-aware of Nick's eyes on her. "Nothing." The silence engulfed the room like a yawn. She blinked slowly then unclenched her hands before whispering hoarsely, "Why now?"

Nick shifted and she watched him as he fixed the askew blankets. He pulled them up from the floor, arranging them back over her lap. When he was done, Nick's voice was careful, quiet. "Maybe it finally sank in."

Evie blinked, half to keep the sudden tears at bay and half because she was having a hard time focusing on his face when his hands were lingering so near. They were the same hands that lifted a wood-axe into the air and brought it down with startling precision. The very same hands that toyed with his drink hours ago in the bar. And they were the exact same hands that had just touched her arms, trying desperately to soothe her sticky, sweaty nightmare-tinged skin.

What had he just asked her?

Eyes on me.

Her lips parted as she tilted her head, staring blatantly. After a moment, she rasped, "Why me?"

Nick sighed, a quiet and resigned sound that wasn't put-out, just sad. He rose from his crouch and sat on the very end of the bed, putting his elbows on his knees as he hung his head.

"I can't begin to understand what you went through that night."

Evie's nausea ebbed at the cadence of his voice alone. It was like turning on an audiobook and realizing the narration was the perfect speed. It made her brain feel like there were tiny shocks lighting her up from the inside out.

"I noticed you start to distance yourself at the bar. I saw the way your body tensed. I'm not blind to these things, but I didn't feel like it was my place — we're — I mean —" He let out a frustrated noise that sounded vaguely like a softly muttered "*fuck*" before clearing his throat.

"Evie." The way he said her name felt reverent in the dark. He shifted, twisting toward her. "This isn't going to go away. It won't just be one nightmare. What you went through" — he corrected himself — "what you're *going* through is not fixed by one trip to the library or a night out at a bar and I'm sorry."

"Why are you apologizing?" She wrung her hands together in her lap. "I'm the one who woke you up screaming bloody murder."

Nick's slight smile was visible in the dark as he chuckled. "I'm apologizing because I can carry the gun, I can look over your shoulder, and I can keep you in this place that no one else knows of — but I can't stop *this*." At that, he leaned forward and tapped the edge of her temple. "And sometimes that's the worst enemy you have to fight."

Evie's eyes fluttered the moment his finger touched her temple, unable to formulate a response. It was the most the two of them had spoken since the truck ride home and she felt silly that he was on the edge of her bed, talking her down from the things that went bump in the night.

"Thank you." She landed on the words awkwardly, shaking a little as she pulled the quilts closer. "Go back to bed, I'll see you in the morning for coffee." Evie tried to end on a light-hearted note, but it fell flat in the dark. He needed to get out of the room. She needed to be alone again — to breathe, to process, to reconcile.

Nick stood up, taking her dismissal as what it was, and

then paused. He turned toward her and — whether because it was dark, or because it was the middle of the night — he bent down and smoothed her hair away from her forehead, a simple touch before pulling back and retrieving the gun from the top of the dresser. He lingered in the doorway, clearing his throat. "I'm just down the hallway if you need anything."

"I know." Evie's heart crept into her throat, strangling her. "Thank you, Nick."

He pulled the door shut when he left and Evie stared, wishing he was still there, silhouetted in the hallway light, taking up every inch of space with his broad chest.

As she slid back down in the bed, turning to one side, then the other, Evie was thankful he was only two steps down the hallway — ready and on alert in case something happened.

She just wished he didn't have to be.

CHAPTER ELEVEN

GENTLE BIRDSONG AND THE BEGINNINGS OF daylight streamed through the curtains above her head just before she drifted off. If anyone had asked, Evie would have sworn that the only reason she fell asleep was because of the comfort of making it through the night, not the fact that she heard Nick wake up — pause for a few seconds outside her door to check on her — before moving to the kitchen.

Her nap was fitful, dragging in and out of consciousness before Evie finally got up and wrapped herself in a quilt. She watched Nick dawdle in the kitchen for a moment from the hallway before shuffling over to the counter and picking up the white mug he'd left next to the coffee pot. When he turned around, he took note of her disheveled appearance before nodding toward the front of the cabin.

"You should go see what's outside."

Evie grumbled as she poured her coffee, lifting her head and then freezing at the stark white lawn, visible through the windows. Letting the quilt drag behind her, she stopped in front of the window, looking past the two rocking chairs and porch to stare at the white-dusted evergreens and Nick's truck covered in a layer of snow.

"Oh my *god*."

Vermont wasn't exactly a stranger to snow — but it was slushy and thick and often more of a headache than it was worth. Snow in Vermont meant bundling up and reminding herself that she did have to feed herself — thus she *had* to go into work on the days school was open and trudge through the thickly packed sidewalks.

This was different.

This was snow outside of a remote cabin, covering every surface, untouched and undisturbed. She felt cocooned by it. There was no reason for her to go out — there were no kids, no tasks, and no bills.

She just had a stack of library books and a warm fire and a mug of coffee.

Nick quietly came to stand next to her and stared out the window before a small smile lifted his beard. "Guess you're glad we got our errands done yesterday."

"Yeah," Evie whispered, unable to tear her eyes away. "It's beautiful."

"It is nice when it does this. It's a pretty place." He turned his head, glancing over at her and then nodded toward the crackling fire. "But let's hope it melts enough for me to drag in the rest of that wood I chopped."

Evie finally looked at him and then paused, feeling her lips quirk at the sight of his pajamas. She hadn't paid attention to them in the kitchen because he'd been facing away from her — and he certainly hadn't worn the shirt last night, because if he *had* that would have changed the tone of their conversation entirely.

The pants were fine, they were a dark blue plaid fleece... but the shirt was something else. Evie covered her mouth as she felt laughter bubble up, uninhibited in her throat. It burst out around her hand as she stared at his torso, reading the words on the gray shirt.

KISS ME, I'M A FED

Nick's eyes flickered down. When they glanced back up, there was a lightness to them, a sparkle in the blue as he waited for her to say something, a wry smile on his lips.

Evie burst into laughter instead, unable to stop it from escaping as she stared from him to the shirt and then back again.

He made a show of spinning in a slow circle. "I know, I know. Get it out. Andy actually bought this for me, don't be rude."

She pressed her lips together, trying to hide her smile, and failing completely. "Sorry, it just caught me off guard."

Nick's smile was so wide the edges of his eyes crinkled with the effort. "S'alright, I know it's a very tempting shirt."

Evie felt her chest and neck flush, clearing her throat as she looked away and made her way back to her mug of coffee. She just needed a reason not to be standing so near — so aware of his tall body and reminded of his warm hands touching hers in the dead of night.

She took a long drink as Nick stretched. "Looks like we'll have to head to town next week for a few staples. Might end up in the next town over for supplies before the snow hits us really." He stepped over to the kitchen and Evie watched as he refilled his mug with fresh coffee.

"Also, I have something for you."

"What?" Evie paused with her lips on the rim of her mug and a heavy dose of skepticism in her heart. When students said they had a '*surprise*' for her, it normally consisted of a bug, or trash, or sometimes even a dead animal.

Nick grinned as he sat his mug down, eyes alight with mischief. "Wait right here."

She turned, watching him disappear down the hall, his door opening — but not shutting. He said *wait*, not *don't look*. Evie leaned to the side, catching a glimpse of a wood-paneled room. Nick cursed as something fell and Evie jerked away, not wanting to be caught peeking. The sound of him lumbering down the hallway made her bite her lip in anticipation.

Nick reappeared and her jaw dropped.

"Shut the *fuck* up."

He burst into laughter, making a little wiggling motion with his fingers on his left hand as he heaved a huge, early 2000s stereo in his arms. Nick walked it over to the wall next to the fireplace and when he sat it down, it nearly came to his hip. Evie gawked as he plugged it in and the digital display lit up vibrant green.

Nick turned with a flourish. "You should have seen your face."

If last night was a nightmare, this was a dream. She stopped in front of the stereo, staring at the old neon-tech monstrosity and gasped, "I love it."

He beamed as he bounced on the balls of his feet. "I knew this place had one when I bought it — I swear it was right here in the listing photos too. But then I couldn't remember where I stashed it. I looked last night and it was in the back of my damn closet. Who keeps a stereo like this?" He waved a hand. "It doesn't matter, because I also found *this*." He stuck a hand in the pocket of his flannel pants, then produced a chunky CD sleeve case.

Evie shook her head, staring at Nick as he unzipped the case slowly, letting the CDs glimmer as he fanned them in front of her face. "Pick your poison, Evie — looks like we have all the greatest hits from the Stones to Elvis."

She snatched the case from his fingers in a flash, holding the CDs in her hand gleefully as she flipped through the options. Nick was right — there were a lot of oldies, ranging from the 60s to early 90s. Her fingers brushed a green CD emblazoned with *NOW THAT'S WHAT I CALL THE 80S* and pulled it from its protective sleeve.

Nick took it from her fingers carefully and bent down, pressing a button before slotting the CD in. Static noise made Evie's shoulders jolt, then a painful skipping sound reverberated out of the speakers that sent her back to her childhood of holding portable CD players at *just* the right angle so they didn't scratch her beloved CDs.

He jabbed the button again and the digital display jumped from the staticky track one immediately to track two.

Music blared out and Evie took a step back, laughing loudly as the opening notes to *Uptown Girl* by Billy Joel weaved themselves through the cabin.

Nick turned, the smile on his face threatening to split it as he pointed a finger at her and started to sing along. Evie laughed as she leaned forward to turn the knob down, but Nick grabbed her hand and spun her in a circle, shouting the lyrics as he pulled her forward, dancing around the coffee table.

"Don't you dare touch the sound! You wanted music, we've got it!"

She laughed gleefully, threading her fingers through the warmth of his as he spun the quilt right off her shoulders. It fell into a heap on the floor as she threw her head back and danced with him, shimmying her hips. Memories flickered through her mind like a catalogue of film, snippets of riding in the backseat of her older brother's car as he switched stations between every song, trying to curate the perfect playlist on the fly.

Nick pushed her away suddenly, spinning her out. Evie stared at the empty hallway for a second before she was tugged back, her body spinning in tight as she landed on two feet, a little breathless, a little flushed. Her hand came down to rest on his upper arm, steadying herself as the song ended, the room filling with the sounds of *Wham!* They stared at each other, chests heaving, but Evie knew the wide smile on Nick's face was reflected on her own.

He opened his mouth, but from across the room, the little black burner phone started to ring. Evie stared at it, wide-eyed before she jolted, leaving the warmth of Nick's hands. She nearly slipped on the quilt as she snatched the phone and answered the call breathlessly.

"Hello?"

"Evie, hey —" There was some rustling on the other end and the connection wasn't the greatest when Andy spoke. "Sorry for not calling sooner but it's been all quiet here in Virginia. I hope Nick's been treating you all right."

At the mention of the only other person in the room, Evie glanced up, her eyes finding Nick standing right where she'd left him, his hands in the pockets of his pajama pants. He wasn't making any attempt to not listen to the conversation and something about how casually he stood made Evie smile as she turned her attention back to Andy.

"Yeah, it's been really good." The next lie came easy. "I've been in the cabin every second except for a brief reprieve to watch Nick chop some wood." She wasn't sure why she felt the need to hide their trip into town from Andy, but like a guilty child, she didn't want her privileges being revoked before she got to enjoy the full scope of them.

Andy snorted. "God, I'm sorry to subject you to that. We'll catch Murphy as soon as possible."

Evie couldn't hold back the laugh as she glanced over at Nick, who was gesturing to the stereo and threatening to put his fingers on the knob to raise the sound. She side-eyed him and turned away.

"So, there's nothing?"

"Sorry, Evie." Andy sounded genuinely apologetic. "I've pulled as many strings as I can but my bosses are starting to get irritated that I'm not working on other cases. I promise, we're working on it. Hang tight. I didn't feel right not calling. I wanted to check up on you as a friend."

"I appreciate it." She wrapped her free arm around her torso, worrying her lower lip between her teeth. "Will you tell my parents that I'm okay? And that I love them?"

The sound of a door creaking on the other end of the line reminded her of the time difference.

"Of course. I gotta go, I'll call as soon as I hear anything — but hey" — Andy cleared his throat — "no news from me is good news, okay? I'll call if there's ever any reason for alarm."

Evie stared at the cabin's kitchen, already so familiar, so comfortable. But this wasn't a place for her to feel settled — she needed to remember to be scared.

"I know, thanks Andy."

"Tell Nick I said thanks."

The line clicked and Evie pulled the little phone away from her ear. It was thin and black, made out of cheap plastic and a sim card that could be removed and crushed if needed. She felt like a Bond girl, trapped in an isolated cabin waiting for 007 to rush in and whisk her away.

The issue was she wasn't sure she *wanted* to be whisked away.

"All good?"

Nick had moved a little closer. She set the phone back on the kitchen counter and nodded. "Yeah, no news, I don't know what else I expected." She gave a half-hearted laugh and then looked down at the wooden floor. "Maybe for this to all be wrapped up in a few days and to be able to go back to my life?"

Nick made a noise of sympathy in the back of his throat before he touched her shoulder. His fingers lingered for a moment, strong and grounding. "I'm going to grab my book from my room. My plan for the day is my ass, that couch —" He hooked his thumb over his shoulder to gesture to it. "And, unfortunately for you, you've got all my spare attention."

Evie's lips quirked at the edges. "Poor me."

Nick grinned before he disappeared down the hallway and into his bedroom.

Evie busied herself by grabbing the fallen quilt from the floor. The CD was already nearing the end and she rifled through the case until she found a random instrumental album shoved in one of the back sleeves. She switched the CDs, leaving the case on top of the stereo before walking over to the couch to arrange herself on one end.

The side table still had her books stacked. She'd finished *The Highlander Barbarian's Wife's Sister* a couple days ago, which is what prompted her to pick up the aptly named sequel — *The Scottish Royal's Cousin's Aunt*, which she was almost 100% sure was about the first main character's best friend. But then again, the familial lines started to get murky with all the descriptors.

Evie curled her legs up underneath herself, thumbing through the library book until she found where she'd stopped at the first page of chapter two. Nick came down the hallway, whistling *Uptown Girl* under his breath and going straight to the kitchen. She glanced up when he reappeared in front of her with both of their mugs.

"This is mine..." He trailed off, putting his full mug of refreshed coffee on the coffee table, then shifting around to place one next to her. "And here's yours." He had a well-worn copy of *Fahrenheit 451* in his other hand. As he plopped down on the other end of the couch, Evie glanced at the book with a little smile.

"Were you holding out on me?"

"Oh, yeah." Nick grinned. "This is mine though, the rest were just kind of here when I moved in. I like this book." He wiggled the floppy cover at her. "I think I read it for the first time in college — hated it, then picked it up again when I was training. Something about it..." He trailed off, a wry smile on his face. "Well — whatever it was, I like it now."

She smiled, pulling the quilt back over her feet. They settled into a quiet, filled with the ambient noise of the fireplace popping and the stereo looping. Evie kept shifting, trying to find a comfortable spot on the couch.

It ended with her leaning back against one of the arms, her legs outstretched with her socked feet almost touching Nick's thigh as he rested against the opposite arm, head propped up as he thumbed through worn pages. Evie's chest constricted when his blue eyes rose to meet hers for the barest of seconds, a hint of a smile on his lips.

She didn't have the heart to tell Andy that it was okay if things took a little longer than they originally planned. Washington wasn't a bad place to be stuck, at all.

Chapter Twelve

There was something magical about shitty motels.

He rubbed his hands on his jeans, sighing at the old and dingy vending machine. It looked like it had been beaten and battered by Colorado weather — but as he shoved a couple quarters in and snagged his bag of potato chips, he decided it would do to provide an early dinner.

In his pocket, his cell phone vibrated. He only had the one and very few people had his number, so he shuffled the chips around to fish it out. He ripped open the bag while he pressed it to his ear. As he popped a chip in his mouth, he muttered a quick, "Hello."

"I expected more back and forth, Will."

Will Bryant rolled his eyes and chewed loudly as he walked toward his room. "I'm on break. You didn't give me enough time to actually get you the information."

"And how was I supposed to know this?" Murphy sounded put out. *Normal Thursday.*

Bryant unlocked his room. As he closed the door, a low moan echoed in the dark.

"Hold on." He shifted the phone from one hand to the one with the bag of chips. Walking over to the side table, Bryant flipped the lamp on. A small-town motel didn't look twice at its residents and didn't ask many questions.

Still, he'd been very careful to draw the curtains and tape the edges so no one could see in. It was for his own personal comfort, but also he just found people broke incredibly fast when they were subjected to extended lengths of total darkness.

The man in the folding chair groaned again, his head moving sluggishly back and forth. There was blood caked in various places where Bryant had taken his time, carving and slicing and enjoying himself as he peppered the agent with questions.

"Okay, back." He kicked the agent's leg. "Say hi."

The other man grunted and Bryant turned the phone so Murphy could hear it. He surveyed the man. He'd give him... one, two days max before he bled out. But Bryant didn't really intend to let him make it that long.

"I'd love to sit and chat, Jonathan." Bryant finished his chips, crumpled the bag, and chucked it into the corner. "But I gotta see an agent about a girl, you know how it is. This pig just isn't... *squealing* as much as I like."

Murphy's voice was dry. "Might have to poke him again."

Bryant grinned. "Maybe."

He dropped his phone onto the bed, rubbing the salt and grease on his jeans. "So, are we going to talk now? Or do you want to keep this little back and forth flirting thing we've got going on?"

Agent Harvey Beck raised his head, spitting blood onto the already stained carpet. His voice was raw as his lip curled. "Fuck you, you're not getting shit from me."

"That's kind of the problem, I *need*" — Bryant grabbed a butter knife and ran his thumb over the dull side — "something, or this all happened for no reason. And I'm good at my job, I don't do shit for nothing." Bryant moved in a flash, lunging forward to drive the dull butter knife into the other man's thigh with pure, brutal force.

Beck howled, his head dropping back as he strained against his bindings. Bryant was well aware the noises coming from his room would cause concern sooner rather than later. This was tiresome — and his well of information had clearly run dry.

Bryant watched the other man squirm and curse, blood pumping through his veins in a rush that made his head spin. His pants even tightened at the front — just a bit. It always made him hard watching someone in pain. "Now, where the fuck is she?"

"You're —" Beck wheezed out a laugh as he slowly looked up at Bryant. "You're never going to find her. We made sure of that. Murphy is going to rot in fucking hell."

Bryant sighed, shaking his head. Every torture session was the same these days. Too many Hollywood movies made men feel like this was *their* moment to shine. But they all broke eventually.

He leaned closer before fisting a clump of Beck's hair in his hands. He held the other man's head back, uncaring if he ripped a chunk of scalp out. A lot of people *could* tolerate the pain, which was why Bryant always opted to break the brain first.

"So she's with someone your partner trusts?" He purred the words, then dropped Beck's head, a few pieces of hair fluttering with it. Bryant sucked his teeth, then clicked his tongue. "Well, there's very few people Agent Anthony Wilson deigns to trust and he's got no friends... except..."

The feral smile that lifted the edges of Will Bryant's lips made Harvey Beck's face drop.

"What about that ex-partner of Wilson's? The Barber guy?"

Beck stared, lips pursed.

"That's what I thought. Why didn't I think of him before?"

Twenty minutes later, Will Bryant walked out of the dirty bathroom and wiped his hands on his trousers. He swung his duffel bag onto his shoulder and fished his phone out of his pocket to send a text.

Murphy didn't exactly *like* texts, but Bryant figured he could deal with it as he walked past the crumpled chip bag and the body. God, he'd hate to be room service.

"We cannot tell the precise moment when friendship is formed. As in filling a vessel drop by drop, there is at last a drop which makes it run over; so in a series of kindnesses there is at last one which makes the heart run over."

Ray Bradbury, *Fahrenheit 451**

*ON THE WEEKENDS, NICK TRAVELED FROM THE FBI training grounds with a group into town. While the other guys used the phone signal to call home, take a load off at the bar, or mess around, Nick often found himself in a bookstore.

He picked up a copy of *Fahrenheit 451* on a whim. The book became his constant companion during training, dog-eared and well loved.

This is the only quote Nick Barber has ever and will ever underline in a book.

DECEMBER

CHAPTER THIRTEEN

THE PHONE WAS RINGING AND VIBRATING ON THE edge of the kitchen counter when Evie rounded the corner, still wringing water from her hair with a towel. She'd thought she'd heard something while in the shower, but honestly — she wasn't expecting Andy's call this soon.

She picked it up as she ruffled her hair. "Hello?"

"Evelyn."

An alarm went off in her mind.

Andy's voice broke from the bad connection. "Is Nick around?"

Evie looked at Nick's closed door. The days had begun to blur together — same early mornings, Evie showering, Nick rustling in the kitchen when he finally emerged from his room. For whatever reason, neither of them had rushed to make coffee this morning and Evie's shower ran late because the hot water felt so nice. She'd not seen Nick since last night.

"I can get him." She held the towel loosely in her hand as she walked down the hallway. Lingering for half a second in front of his door, Evie chewed on her lip before she knocked and called out, "Nick?"

"Put me on speaker." Andy's words jarred her as she heard movement.

Nick's door swung open, revealing him half-dressed with only a pair of sweats on and no shirt. He looked alarmed to see her standing so close as Evie hit the speakerphone button.

Andy's voice rang out. "You there?"

"Yes," Nick cleared his throat, still thick with sleep and disuse, looking down at the phone in her hand with a furrowed brow. "What's going on?"

Andy started to speak, but had to pause, a hoarseness in his tone that made Evie's stomach churn. "Harvey is dead. We found his body in Colorado." His voice shattered. "He was on vacation with his *wife*."

Evie stared down at the phone. Her body felt weird, like she wasn't really seeing it, or standing in the hallway anymore. Agent Beck, the one who'd stood behind her in her bedroom as she packed, the one who'd spoken to her parents — dead.

Before she could register it, Nick's hand wrapped around the phone. She watched him, almost in a trance, as he turned it off speaker. He asked Andy what happened, but Evie was already taking a step back, watching Nick's body turn to the side as he spoke harshly into the phone. Her mind couldn't comprehend what was being said, but Nick's tone was furious and chastising.

She didn't *want* to hear.

She dropped her used towel into the basket in the bathroom before walking past the dining table and the couch. Her hands were on the doorknob before she could really think to grab her coat, only shoving her bare feet into her boots as she opened the front door, walking outside.

The silly paper calendar Nick had on the fridge had been

flipped to December this morning. As Evie stared out at the slush-covered grass, all she could think about was watching Nick hang it up two mornings ago, saying maybe it would help her keep track of the days — help them both not get lost in the isolation.

She was lost anyway.

Evie inhaled, but her lungs felt frozen. Pressing a hand against her breastbone, she tried to breathe again, swearing she could feel her heartbeat stutter and start again as it echoed in her ears. A layer of slushy snow covered Nick's woodshed, remnants dripping off the tin roof. Her eyes flickered past it to the trees around the cabin.

Evie's tongue felt fat. It was a mass in her mouth, making it hard to swallow as she stared out at the familiar sights — over grass and snow and slush and Nick's truck.

He's dead, he's dead, he's dead. It's your fault.

She laid her hand on the post next to the stairs, wondering if Nick would understand if she started screaming.

Before she got the chance to choke out a yell around her tongue, the door opened behind her. Nick's heavy boots appeared in her peripheral as she looked down at the icy porch.

"Hey." His voice was soft — the verbal equivalent of a hand, palm out, trying not to spook her. "It's cold out here, you wanna come back inside?"

She liked how he offered it as an option, when she knew that between them both, his will would win over hers and she'd go inside regardless. It was the only place to go.

Evie tipped her head up, staring at the slush. Wet hair plastered itself, half-frozen, to her cheek. "What did Andy say?"

"Let's talk inside." She saw his hand move before it landed on her bare arm, turning her toward him so they were chest to chest. "You're going to catch a cold." Nick's mouth dipped down, brows furrowing as his warm fingers slid up the goose-bumps on her forearm.

"Yeah." Evie cleared her throat, pulling back to wrap her arms around herself. With one last look at the muddy snow, she walked back into the warmth of the cabin. Nick shut the front door as she kicked her boots off. She ignored the couch in lieu of crashing into the chair closer to the fireplace.

It was just as soft as she assumed it would be. The cushion quietly hissed out the air as her body curled up into it. Nick deadbolted the front door and Evie watched him kick his own boots to the corner and then shrug his jacket off. He must have thrown it on the moment he got off the phone because he was still shirtless underneath it.

He hesitated before muttering, "Don't move, I'm going to put a shirt on."

Evie didn't know if she should feel offended, but it didn't stop her from staring at the corded muscles on his back as he walked down the hallway and into his room. He didn't even bother to swing the door shut. She sat in the chair and watched him tug a t-shirt over his head.

She couldn't make excuses for herself. Any of these conversations would be a thousand times easier with Nick shirtless — which is why her throat felt glued shut as he went straight into the kitchen and got them water, bypassing the empty coffee pot. He placed a glass on the coffee table in front of her chair and then sat himself at the end of the couch closest to her.

"Beck disappeared on Friday." Nick sighed, but his eyes didn't waver as he stared at her. "He was in Colorado with his wife visiting family. The wife said he left one afternoon to run an errand — never came back."

Evie's stomach roiled. "Murphy?"

Nick went quiet. She could practically see his thoughts spinning, trying to come up with the right thing to say. His shoulders shifted back, spine straightening before he finally nodded.

"Most likely. They found Beck at a motel three blocks away. There were signs of torture, but he was ultimately strangled to death."

The pit in her stomach opened up like a vacuum as her entire body reacted. Nausea shot up her throat and wrapped its hand around it, cutting off her ability to say anything as she fumbled to stand. Nick jolted up from the couch, but all Evie could do was suck in a wheezing breath, hands flying to her chest, pressing against her shirt, trying and failing to make her lungs work properly.

It was simultaneously like her body wanted to dry-heave and cease breathing. Her fingers shook as her breathing grew ragged, sawing in and out in uncoordinated gasps. Faintly she registered footsteps retreating from her. Leaning over, her eyes screwed shut and for a moment she wished she *would* just throw up — in the middle of this stupid wooden cage of a living room.

But nothing came up — because there was nothing in her stomach in the first place.

Hunched forward, her sides ached as Nick suddenly reappeared. There wasn't an ounce of hesitation in his movements as he crouched partially, putting his face in front of hers. Evie pulled her head back to stare up at him, expecting *something*, anything to come from his lips.

Instead all he did was press a cool washcloth to her forehead. The shock of the frigid fabric was enough to make her blink *hard*. His blue eyes bore into her. "This isn't your fault."

The fabric scratched over her skin as Nick stepped closer, using his body to support hers. One of his hands reached around, bracing carefully against the small of her back.

"It is," Evie rasped weakly, reaching up to touch the washcloth as they stared at each other. Nick's hand brushed hers to keep it in place as she grimaced, glancing away. "It *really* is."

Nick talked over the end of her self-pity, interrupting her. "It's not, Evie." His tone was harsh and she jerked, put off by the anger in his voice. Nick's face twisted in a scowl as he pulled his hand back. "It's the work of a twisted fucking man who does twisted fucking things. You didn't kill Harvey Beck. You didn't kill that undercover cop — Murphy did. And if you start blaming yourself for every action of a madman, you'll never be able to sleep again."

She didn't have the heart to tell him that she already wasn't.

Ever since her first nightmare, the dam had broken in her body. She woke up in cold sweats after thirty minutes of sleep. She always jerked awake in the middle of being chased through her library, the cabin, her *house*, by Murphy — just before he pulled the trigger and killed her. Now she could barely breathe, a bone-deep panic that she hadn't felt in *years* — not since her brother went out one night and never came back.

"It's all because of me. It's *me* that brought Beck into this mess."

Nick leveled her with a look so harsh that her mouth snapped shut without another word.

"Listen to me. Harvey Beck was a grown man who knew the risks of being an FBI agent."

Was.

"And does Andy?" She broke, spitting back at Nick. "Have *you* thought about the risks of being here with me?"

Nick shifted, putting his chest against hers. He smelled like laundry detergent and cedar wood. The scent coupled with the way he was the only thing keeping her upright made her chest flutter.

"I am not going to let anything happen to you."

End of sentence.

She pulled the washcloth off her forehead finally, clutching it in her palm as his breath puffed against the side of her forehead. One lean and his lips would be touching her bare skin. But he didn't move. He was unwavering in his support.

Evie squeezed the damp washcloth. "I know." Her skin burned under his gaze. "I know you wouldn't."

That's what scared her the most.

Chapter Fourteen

Their infrequent trips into town weren't enough to keep the cabinets stocked and Nick said as much to her. It was decided they would drive an hour and a half away, to the next town, and grab what staples they could fit into the truck cab, just to last through the snow.

She didn't mind endless cans of soup, peanut butter and honey sandwiches, or the random stews that Nick threw together — but she felt guilty. He was being far *too* considerate cooking multiple times a day, food shopping, chopping wood, *and* dealing with her neuroses.

Evie did do the dishes though. And that seemed to be enough for the man on the other end of the truck bench.

Soft rock crooned from the radio, or what Evie called *dad rock*, a very specific genre for middle-aged divorcees sobbing on their way to the hardware store. It wasn't unpleasant, just a little amusing as Nick drummed his fingers on the steering wheel to the sounds of Creedence Clearwater Revival.

Evie couldn't judge much, it wasn't like she didn't know nearly every artist that had played so far.

"I need some water for the storage room and extra logs for the fireplace." Nick spoke over the music. "And whatever you want, chuck it into the cart. Wells Creek isn't exactly stocked with all the latest and greatest."

Evie leaned back in the seat, smiling tightly. "I don't need much."

"I *know*." Nick rolled his eyes, looking back at the road. They'd been on a highway for the past thirty minutes. "I mean," he amended, voice softening, "just grab something if you want it. That's why we're going."

She fell silent as the radio changed to the next song. When they'd gotten into the truck cab she'd fiddled with the dial, listening to the scattered sounds of NPR and country music until Nick batted her hand away and moved it with a twist of his wrist to this station. She guessed if her options were between The Police and Alan Jackson, she'd take *Roxanne* any day.

"Okay?"

"Okay," Evie grumbled, pulling her jacket closer. "Maybe I'll look at a pack of t-shirts or leggings, I'm kind of tired of wearing the same three things to bed."

Nick smiled but didn't say anything as he picked a spot in the wide parking lot. There were a lot of cars around, lined up and down in diagonal spots leading up to the door. If she had to guess, about seventy percent of them were filled, with a few larger spots for RVs and buses taken up at the back. It was the busiest place she'd been in *weeks*.

Normally the mass of people wouldn't have bothered her, but the moment Evie's boots hit pavement, she felt the need to suction herself to Nick's side like she was made of velcro. He came around the side of the truck and fell into step beside her, talking over the list in his head as they walked to the front doors and through them. She stuck close as he grabbed a cart and followed him like a puppy over to the groceries.

It was only as he was looking through the produce that Nick glanced up and frowned. "You want me to go to the clothes with you?"

"Oh." Evie shifted from one foot to the other. "No, no it's okay. I'll be right back."

"I don't mind. I can head over with you," Nick hummed, holding up a bag of apples. "Would you help me eat these?"

She nodded, taking a step back. "It's okay. I'll just... be over there." Evie ducked her head, feeling strangely discombobulated as she walked toward the center of the store where all the clothes were split into sections. She breezed through the kids' section, eyeing the women's and looking for a pack of leggings, or anything that she could lounge around the cabin in.

Just as she came across a three-pack of leggings, her eyes caught on a display of coats. Of course the one she had on was nice. It was the one she wore most-frequently back home, but some of the coats looked fuzzier and like she could sink herself into them and never come out. Near the coat rack were a selection of cheaply made scarves. Evie turned and touched one, thinking of the hand-knitted one that was sitting on the seat in Nick's truck out in the parking lot.

As she rubbed the fabric between her fingers, the hair on the back of her neck prickled. Evie sucked in a breath, feeling a pang of white-hot panic jolt through her like electricity.

Not again.

She'd tried in vain to suppress the memory of Nick so close, both the night of her first nightmare and after Andy's call. It was *embarrassing*.

She'd never had this feeling before so frequently. Anxiety wasn't an emotion she lived with daily — just snippets of memories after her brother died, waking up in a jolt praying it had been a dream. This hollow panic in her chest was as unfamiliar as it was startling, the same shaking feeling she'd had in Adam's when she'd caught a glimpse of the blond man at the bar.

Evie slowly raised her head, scanning the women's section. There weren't very many people around; most of the carts were headed to the Christmas displays at the back of the store. There were trees, ornaments, lights — hell, she'd even seen inflatables towering over the aisles when she and Nick entered.

The emptiness made it easy to catch sight of a mother with two young children, trying to corral them toward the cart as she picked up a pair of pajamas.

Evie exhaled, clutching the pack of leggings tightly before taking a step back, easing away from the coats and scarves. She didn't need them, hers were perfectly warm and she'd be back in Hawthorne before it got any colder — she turned on a dime, suddenly wanting to be near Nick. Evie wove through clothing racks, finding herself in the men's section.

As she weaved between the aisles, she spotted a few flannels, then a pack of men's t-shirts. She hesitated, wondering if she should pick a few up to sleep in — she really *wasn't* lying to Nick when she said she was getting tired of her same pajamas. It wasn't like she had that many different pairs at home, but she kept waking up in cold sweats, her shirt stuck to her chest and back. It was making laundry hellish having to cycle how many times she wore her clothes and then throw in extra loads every time she deigned to have a nightmare.

In the span of time it took Evie to hesitate, she looked up and locked eyes with a bulky man with grizzled features, arms as thick as tree branches. She froze.

He barely glanced at her as he grabbed a pack of 3XL t-shirts, muttering, "Pardon me, hon."

She flinched, bumping into a clothing rack, then she

tucked tail and *ran*. Bursting out onto the aisle, she squeaked out, "sorry!" to a startled woman, dodging her cart as she raced, breathless, to the other side of the store.

The freezer aisles were barren — save for a group of people fighting over frozen sacks of corn and peas. Evie passed the bread and taco shells, then the snacks, before she finally skidded into the opening of an aisle lined with soup cans.

Nick was at the very end, standing in front of a display of crackers.

It felt like someone had a hand wrapped around her heart, forcing her organ not to break free of her chest as she clutched the plastic wrapping of the leggings and almost broke out into a sprint to get to the end of the aisle.

Nick looked up just as she got within arms' reach, his face twisting in confusion as she chucked the leggings into the cart next to a few cans of tomato soup. He frowned, reaching out for her, bending down and curving his torso toward her. "Evie? Are you all right?" When she shifted closer, he gripped her arms. "What happened?"

Evie shook her head rapidly, trying to curb the rising panic clawing its way out of the pit in her stomach. The damned pit that seemed to open every time she thought of Murphy, or the shining black gun, or the way Ben fell to his knees and then his body was just *there* —

"Hey." Nick's voice brought her back to the aisle, the moment they were standing in. His left hand slid down her arm and touched her hand, before slowly picking it up. "Hey, look at me."

She tilted her head up, their foreheads almost colliding as his warm skin pressed against hers. She felt clammy and stricken — like the sheer terror of losing your parent in a grocery store when you were only a kid.

Nick kept his eyes trained on hers as his right hand

repeated the process to pick up her other hand. "There you are." He squeezed both her hands at the same time, a firm but gentle gesture. "Squeeze them back for me."

Evie swallowed thickly, squeezing his hands as she sucked in stuttering breaths.

"That's good," Nick whispered. With her hands locked in his, he pulled her a step closer and pressed his head against hers, filling up her vision with just his calm features. "Take a deep breath with me, slowly inhale through the nose, out through the mouth, come on."

She blindly followed his instructions, the inhale stuttered, but the exhale smooth. She wasn't worried about what she looked like to the other people in the aisle on the random Tuesday afternoon. She could only focus on Nick's unwavering blue eyes, a singular anchor among the sea of panic that threatened to drag her under.

Evie let the panic go, and with it went the rest of her energy, the adrenaline crashing out of her body as quickly as it had arrived.

She moved toward his warmth on instinct, stumbling to land against his chest, pressing her face into his shirt. He released her hands only to wrap his arms around her fully in a hug. Nick's entire body was solid — the kind of solid that they used to describe trees that weathered record storms. He smelled like pine too — fresh pine and fancy soap and smoke.

He held her, his breath fanning the hair at the crown of her head as he whispered, "I'm right here. Just breathe."

It was like the other embrace, but this time she actually let herself relax into him.

Evie stood there, wrapped tightly in his arms with her hands almost folded across her chest until her breathing evened out. She didn't feel trapped, she just felt *held*. The moment she started to move, Nick's grip loosened until they were barely brushing. She tilted her head up, her voice raw. "Thank you."

He didn't ask her what happened, instead, he pressed a hand against the small of her back and guided her toward the soup. "Pick three." The next aisle they went down — he did the same, making her pick three different snacks to take back to the cabin. The trend continued until they were at the perishables, where Nick picked up some shredded cheese and eggs.

Once it was all in the cart, Evie turned to walk toward the front, but Nick went the other direction. She fell into step beside him, confused until they reached the electronics at the back of the store.

Nick pulled the cart up next to a giant discounted bin of CDs. "Go wild."

"What?" She looked at the CDs, then at him. "Are you sure?"

He waved a hand. "I'm not going to force you to listen to whatever they left in that case at the cabin — we might get so desperate we put in Kidz Bop. No one wants that."

Evie let out a half-laugh, half-gasp before digging in. A lot of the CDs were collections of oldies or best hits, but her hands roamed across them anyway. She sorted a small pile for herself, hands lingering on a CD full of 70s hits like *Drift Away* by Dobie Grey. It also had the *Oogum Boogum Song*. She slid it into a stack with a decade old Kings of Leon album.

Nick's eyebrow rose. "You sure that's all you want?"

Evie gave the bin one last glance before her eyes fell on a display of brand-new CDs across from it. When she stepped around the discount section and picked up a copy of Taylor Swift's latest, she expected to hear Nick scoff behind her.

Instead, when she turned around, he flashed her a smile. "Yeah get that one too, I haven't heard it yet. She's a great lyricist."

She slid the three CDs into the cart and walked beside him to the check-out, where Nick did the majority of getting every-thing onto the belt. He nudged her to pick out a drink from the cold case next to the cash register, then one of the snacks from the other side — picking out a bottle of water and a bag of pretzels for himself. She grabbed a bag of red licorice and a water bottle, adding them both to the pile.

Once all the bags were settled safely in the truck cab, Evie found herself pulling her legs up into the seat after buckling, the floor mostly full of bags, save for the eggs on the bench beside them.

Nick cranked up the heat as the truck roared to life, rubbing his hands together before motioning to the bag with the CDs in it. "Pick one out for us."

Evie grabbed the Kings of Leon CD, welcoming memories of high school as she ripped off the thin plastic and fed the CD into the truck's dash.

Nick reached past her, fiddling with the knobs until the first song drifted out of the speakers, low and heady. Evie sat back, wringing the trash in her hands before letting it drop into one of the bags.

As Nick pulled out of the parking lot, her fingers twitched. She reached over the eggs between them and held onto the edge of Nick's coat, exhaling softly after touching the familiar fabric. The truck eased to a stop at a light and Nick grabbed the carton of eggs, settling them precariously in the floorboard before tugging her across the bench so her body could fall against the side of his.

Evie didn't care about the seat belt cutting into her hip. Her head dropped to his shoulder, closing her eyes just to listen to the music as Nick's hand squeezed her arm before returning to the steering wheel. Neither of them said a word on the drive back.

Chapter Fifteen

Nick was right — the calendar on the fridge did serve as a great reminder of how time bled out in the solitude of the cabin, leaving productivity to die a slow death.

Thirty straight days of living in the same five outfits she'd chosen in her bedroom, picking up a routine of coffee in the mornings and books in the afternoon with Nick — then the occasional trip to Wells Creek for another library book and to grab a few things at the market.

All of this to say — she missed home, and she didn't want to be here anymore, looking over her shoulder for a boogeyman ready to kill her the moment he found her.

"Hope keeps asking when we're going back to Adam's." Nick leaned against the counter as he sipped his coffee. Evie's eyes rose from her seat at the kitchen table to take him in.

When she didn't say anything, he spurred forward. "I just think it might be a good thing for us to go do. It's December, it'll start getting too snowy... We could get out of this cabin before we both go stir crazy and blow off a little steam."

She bit her tongue and looked back down at the book in

her hands. She'd borrowed it from Stephen last Saturday — the day after the fateful trip into the other town. Neither she nor Nick really wanted to go back into an open area after it, but her library books were due and Nick needed some actual gear to help get them, and the cabin, through winter.

Evie was constantly reminded of nature documentaries they showed the high schoolers of prey animals. Rabbits with twitching noses and deer with necks on a swivel, watching and waiting because an attack wasn't an if, it was a when.

Still, Evie found herself in the truck twenty minutes later, with her arms crossed as she watched the foliage blur. She readjusted, giving Nick the cold shoulder for dragging her out again. It was both infuriating and a little validating to simmer in the anxiety and anger that kept her up at night. Half of her bad mood was probably due to the fact she wasn't sleeping, but she didn't care — she just *wanted* to be angry.

Nick fiddled with the radio dials in her peripheral. The 70s CD she'd gotten last week filled the cab with the opening notes of *Drift Away*.

"Come on." He smiled. "You can't be mad when *Drift Away* is playing."

The original recording crackled as Nick crooned along, partially off-key. His voice wasn't entirely awful, and Evie fought a small smile as Nick really got into the chorus and *ohs*.

"You can't just sing to me and make me feel better." Her attempt at firmness fell flat the moment she remembered the way he grinned and heaved the stereo out to the living room for her.

Nick grinned. "I definitely can."

He hummed louder, mixing up the words into a veritable salad and only getting about every third one right. Evie rolled her eyes and dropped her head back to the seat, laughing as he mumbled through the verses, then belted the chorus, full-throttle, as they rumbled down the road.

He threw his head back, howling along to the final round of the chorus, bobbing his head as he drummed his hands on the steering wheel. He actually knew the final few lines, yelling them out with Dobie Grey as the guitar played them out.

The track faded. In the seconds between the CD switching songs, quiet overtook the cab. Then the *Oogum Boogum Song* started up.

A grin broke Evie's features as she giggled, thinking of the yearly Halloween party. It didn't matter how many years she was a librarian, there was something about seeing the kindergartners dressed as little yellow and black bees, or the handful of superheroes with their capes and spandex, that just made the Halloween season the best part of the fall semester.

Evie caught Nick's gaze on her, a quiet *something* settling between the two of them.

"This song reminds me of work." She picked at her sweater. "We're pretty small, it's all the grades — so the little first and second graders get to trick or treat in classrooms with their siblings. I always decorate the library, really go all out."

Evie fisted her hands. If she kept pulling her sweater, it would completely unravel and leave her in the worst bra she owned for a cold evening at the only bar in town.

"I did a Scooby-Doo theme this year. It was... the bootleg version." She laughed at herself. "I had to do a lot of the art and details myself, even if it was a little low-budget, I transformed the entire place into a mystery for the kids to solve. A lot of them do trick or treat in the neighborhoods," Evie stuttered, then blew out a breath. "I mean Hawthorne is a really safe place normally."

"Did the kids like it?"

Evie smiled fondly, feeling her throat tighten. "Yeah, they'll probably be a little sad I'm not there to decorate the library as the North Pole and to do story times. I've read *The Lion, The Witch, and The Wardrobe* every year I've worked there. Some of the high schoolers come back to listen if they can get out of class."

As Nick pulled into a parking spot near the front door of Adam's, Evie's words hung in the air for a moment, like they were unsure if they were going to fall or float away into the night. She missed work. She wanted to work there for years — long enough that she saw her kids start in kindergarten and walk the stage as seniors.

A soft expression crossed his face, indecipherable in the dim light. "You gonna be okay tonight?"

Evie glanced at the other cars. It would be busy inside — busier than she was used to. But this was Adam's — Chuck and Hope were inside. And Nick was here.

"Will you stay next to me?" Her voice was soft as she held herself back from asking for more, memories of his hands on her, grounding her. That was a last ditch effort, a hail Mary, and she didn't want to overstep.

Nick's gaze burned the side of her face as her fingers touched the door. His response was a deep rasp over her skin. "Always."

They walked into the bar together, and Evie stopped short at the size of the crowd. She wouldn't have been surprised if they took census of Wells Creek and found that the majority of the townspeople were here. Almost every table was full, with people standing around the jukebox, drinking and chatting.

From behind the bar, Chuck looked up, pointing to a booth that was half-cleared in the back. Nick weaved them through the crowd just as Hope spotted them, making a beeline to grab the couple dishes and beer mugs left.

"Busy night?" Nick looked up, chuckling.

"*Ugh.*" Hope made a noise of pure discontent, waving toward the group of older men all lingering around the juke-box. "Motorcycle rally. I don't know if they're headed home or headed out — it's the crew that goes to the local children's hospital, though. Which I think is super sweet." She shuffled the dishes around in her hands, rambling, "They always stop here and they always tip well so it's not *that* big of a deal, you know?"

Evie glanced around Hope at the jovial men. Some of them had large mugs of beer, while others had shallower glasses with either clear or amber colored liquid.

"I'll be right back to get your orders. You want food? We probably have something left, but it's been so busy that I haven't made more soup. Dad won't hire another chef either — cheap bastard."

"I'll get us some drinks at the bar, Hope, it's fine," Nick laughed and waved her off, nodding over to Evie. "Unless you're hungry?"

"No, I'm okay." Evie offered the girl a small smile. "I appreciate it though."

"Just let me know!" She was off in a flash and Evie watched her beam at a redhead sitting at the bar. When the girl smiled back, Hope blushed bright pink.

Nick nodded toward Chuck. "What do you want to drink?"

Evie fiddled with the sleeve of her jacket before shrugging out of it, partially to give herself more time to think as she mulled over Nick's question. She didn't want to think — but the only time that had happened was when she'd gotten plastered in high school. It was her first party that friends dragged her to after her brother died — no one wanted to party with the girl whose brother was killed by a drunk driver. When one of the asshole stoners suggested she leave because she was bringing the whole vibe down, she'd grabbed a bottle of tequila and pounded half of it in one go. It worked — she was numb and no one gave her pitying looks — but she'd vowed she wouldn't do it again with her head hanging over her best friend's toilet at 3am. That only lasted as long as the next party, and the next, nights blurring into hungover mornings.

"A whiskey." Evie finally looked up at Nick. "Neat."

Nick raised an eyebrow, hands on the table, primed to push up and go to the bar.

"It's been a week." She leveled him with a look, daring him to argue. So she never drank anything more expensive than watered down liquor as a teen — it would be fine. "I used to drink on my dad's fishing trips." Two sips definitely counted, though she remembered spitting them back out. She was rambling now, desperate to not sound ridiculous as she muttered, "Don't give me that look."

He shrugged. "Wasn't giving you a look."

Evie watched him slide up to the bar where Chuck was. The two men spoke and Chuck's eyes flickered over. Her skin felt too tight, an itchy, unfamiliar feeling that she didn't like at all.

Nick returned a moment later, sitting a beer on his side of the table and a small glass of whiskey in front of her. As he sank back into his seat, Evie stared at the drink. She didn't want to be here. She didn't want to look at a drink her father used to down in the days after her brother died. She didn't want to be reminded of the way Marlon asked her to please stay out of trouble — for her parents' sakes — every time he drove her home.

The funk settled, pressing her down deeper as Evie scowled at the glass. She sloshed it around with one hand before lifting it up to her lips.

The moment the whiskey touched her throat, she coughed.

It wasn't a quiet sound. It was a knee-jerk reaction to the fire going down her throat, a blaze that cleared her senses in an instant. She dropped the glass back to the table with a half-fumbled clank and avoided Nick's eyes as she tried to clear her throat and swallow back the nausea the alcohol had brought up.

When Evie finally blinked back the burn in her eyes, nose, and throat, Nick spoke.

"Are we just going to sit here tonight, or are we going to actually talk to each other?"

Evie swished her glass back and forth, shrugging. "You're the one who brought us here." The moment the words left her lips, she cringed, reprimanding herself for acting like a sulking teenager. "Sorry." Her eyes flickered up to meet Nick's, frowning. "I don't think I should drink this." She pushed it a safe distance away.

"Do you want to leave?" His untouched beer dripped condensation onto the vinyl tabletop as Nick stared. "Because going home is also an option, Evie."

Home.

Each of his words struck her. He would take her back to the cabin — back *home.* Because even though home was Vermont, home was also now the little cabin in the woods out past Wells Creek. It was the crackling fireplace, the mugs of coffee in the morning, and the shouts down the hall if the washer and dryer were empty.

Evie knew that home could be a lot of things. Home could be people too, but it was like Nick had suddenly activated the part in her brain that realized that the cabin was just as much of a home, a safe place, for her, as her little house in Hawthorne.

"No." She fumbled out quickly as she tried to gather herself. "No, it's okay. Let's just enjoy ourselves, okay? Chuck and Hope want to see you, I'm sure you have other friends to go talk to, or acquaintances to nod at — we should stay."

Nick's right eyebrow rose just a hair, then his lips twitched. "Do you think I have a lot of people I need to go nod at? Make appearances for?"

"Well." Evie looked down at the glass of whiskey because it was her literal only escape from his blue eyes. "I don't know what you did before I got here — go do *that*."

He ran his fingers over the neck of his beer bottle, gliding his thumb up the side and collecting the condensation, eyebrow still raised. "Do you think I did *a lot* before you?"

Evie suddenly wished she had a jug of water in front of her, not a bad decision in a glass tumbler. Her throat felt sandpaper dry, her mind desperately trying to process the drop in his tone and the shift of his body to lean over the table toward her.

"Because I didn't," he whispered. "I don't have anyone to smile at, or to nod at, or make appearances for. I'm pretty sure I warned you two weeks ago that you have my undivided attention."

Discomfort crawled under her skin, twisting her stomach as she sucked in a breath. "I just don't want to stop you from going to talk to someone — or —"

Nick took a swig of his beer and her words died in the air, falling flat, transfixed on the way his neck moved when he swallowed.

Jesus Christ, he's hot.

Her head jerked, eyes finding the jukebox to stare at instead of the man in front of her. The muscled motorcyclists were mingling but all she could think was, *For god's sake, get it together.*

The familiar notes of *Barracuda* by Heart drifted through the din of the crowd, adding to the dingy, smoky atmosphere.

She glanced back over at Nick to see his eyes on her. They

were pinched at the corners, his familiar laugh lines deep in thought instead of cracking with the next smile. The sudden tone shift made her antsy, and she spat out the first thing that came to mind.

"I like this song." It was a lame recovery. "It reminds me of my mom."

The lines next to Nick's eyes crinkled, pinching into something familiar, unable to stay off his face as he offered her a small smile and took another sip of his beer.

"Do you want to dance?"

"What?" She had to make sure she heard him right, fingers paused on her glass. "Now?"

"Yeah." Nick's smile grew a little wider. "Like we did the other day."

She didn't have the chance to respond before he was sliding out of the booth. Nick shifted around the table to stand close to her, making Evie feel a little dizzy and she craned her neck up to watch him extend a hand. When she took it, he pulled her out of the booth, dragging her toward the jukebox and the small area where the motorcycle club mingled and an older couple danced to something just between the two of them.

Barracuda ended almost as soon as they reached the expanse of floor. Evie began to leave when the familiar sound of *Roxanne* by the Police filled the empty air. She turned slowly, feeling the grin spread across her face as she held Nick's hand and laughed.

"I really, *really* love this song!" she shouted over the music. The heady, electro-pop was something she'd always loved blasting in her car when she was a teenager, rifling through the CDs in her parents' house and stealing the ones she actually enjoyed.

Nick started to laugh as Evie moved her hips back and forth, singing aloud and forgetting every single lyric except for the occasional wail of *"red light"* — but it didn't matter, because for a moment she felt entirely safe to be stupid with her hand in his.

The drums and beat made her want to dance and she grabbed Nick's other hand, forcing him to two-step awkwardly with her. There was an unreadable expression on Nick's face as she sang off-key, smiling and dancing in a little circle.

The next song was *Wanted Dead or Alive* by Bon Jovi, which finally got Nick moving. A few other bar patrons filtered onto the small dance floor and Evie found herself grinning at one of the bikers as they both screamed the lyrics and shimmied.

Adam's probably didn't normally get this kind of song and dance, but at the same time, Evie didn't *care*. There was something so nice about being able to mess up the lyrics, better than the freeing release of shrieking at the trees outside the cabin.

Sure, screaming at the cabin had felt a certain level of nice, especially after she first arrived. There wasn't a soul anywhere around that would have come running, but here — at Adam's it was socially acceptable for her to be a little stupid, to grip the hands of the man who had been forced to take her in, and ignore the flipping in her stomach as she beamed up at him.

Aerosmith filtered through the speakers and Evie tapped out as she stumbled away from Nick toward their booth. He was right behind her as she dropped into the seat and looked up at him, inhaling sharply.

"Are you all right?" He boxed her into her seat. With his hands braced on the booth-back blocking the only exit, there was nowhere for her to go as he bent down. Evie tried to steady her racing heart as he huffed. "You need water." Nick glanced away, catching Chuck's eye.

The question tumbled out before she could stop herself. "Why are you single?"

Nick did a double-take. His eyes were slightly wider, his mouth partially open as he stared at her in stunned silence. Evie paused as she realized with glee that this was the first time she'd ever seen him truly caught off guard.

In response to the question, he pushed the glass of unfinished whiskey out of her reach and thanked Hope when she sat down two glasses and a jug of water for them. Nick dropped down into his seat across from Evie, pouring her water and pushing it across the table.

"I never thought it was right to force anyone to relocate to the middle of fucking nowhere." He cleared his throat, entirely too focused on pouring his own water. "Especially once I decided I didn't want to be an agent anymore."

"So..." Evie trailed off, taking a drink of the cool water and making a face. "That's it then? You just shot everyone down?"

"Why are *you* single?" Nick's eyes finally rose, and the weight behind them pinned her.

Evie's mouth snapped shut, her jaw working as her mind spun. Why was she? She just couldn't tolerate the history everyone knew about her in Hawthorne. She was the younger sister of a brother killed in a terrible drunk driving accident. She was the one who'd been driven home one too many times by the sheriff. She was the sweet librarian with a wild past for a small town and that was all she was. Ben had been the first person new to town who'd given her a second look and he'd been a fucking undercover cop trying to make his cover story a little stronger.

Her stomach twisted as she looked around the bar and finally muttered, "Well, I'm currently being hunted by a murderer, so I guess that's why."

"Good thing that doesn't deter me."

Evie's eyes rose, staring at Nick, ready to rake him back over the coals for an answer to what *that* meant — when the emergency phone in her jacket pocket began to vibrate. She shot up, grabbing at it with her hand and looking over at Nick. He was out of the booth in a second and she fought her way around the crowd to burst out into the night, a prayer forming in her mind as she hit answer.

All her breath left her lungs as she answered, twisting in the cold night air like wisps of smoke.

"Andy?"

Andy's voice was tinged with exhaustion. "We got the coroner's report back — it wasn't much. My bosses are pissed because we can't say that Murphy had anything to do with Beck's murder. There's no evidence or ties to him."

The tiny flame of hope was snuffed in an instant.

Andy barreled forward unknowingly. "Murphy's been lying so fucking low — listen, Evie." He sighed. "You can't be home for Christmas this year. It's just not safe."

Bile burned her nose as she sucked in a harsh breath and stared at Nick in front of her. She made some sort of noise of agreement, told Andy she appreciated the call, then heard the dial tone as he hung up first.

By Nick's expression, she didn't need to reiterate the conversation.

"Let's go home." He was gentle as he touched her shoulder, steering her toward his truck. She got in on autopilot, waiting to feel the warm air on her face as the engine roared to life and the radio automatically turned on.

Don't Fear the Reaper played on the classic rock station as Evie wrapped her coat around herself. She stared out the window, watching the trees blur as Nick drove them home, feeling the burn of his concerned glances every few minutes on the side of her face, but she couldn't bring herself to meet his gaze.

CHAPTER SIXTEEN

THE CABIN WAS A MAZE.

It was like she hadn't lived in it for a month. The rooms were *moving*. She could hear him, coming closer each time she opened up a door leading to nowhere. Nowhere to hide, nowhere to go, and the man behind her wanted her dead.

She grabbed onto a doorknob, throwing it open to a vaguely wooden bed frame and soft sheets. There was a quilt to one side of the bed and Evie wondered if she would be safe if she just dove under it and pulled it over her head.

"*Evelyn.*" The voice could be the man behind her, but it also could be her father.

But why would he be in the cabin?

Evie grabbed the blanket. If she couldn't see him, he couldn't see her, and she would be safe.

"*Oh, Evelyn, I think someone's trying to get to you.*" There was a sharp laugh and Evie clutched the blanket tighter, curling up on wooden the floor in a ball. She couldn't believe anything he said. It had to be a lie because Nick wouldn't be that stupid.

But yet —

There was a pained shout and Evie flung the blanket away and found herself in the hallway again. She started to run toward the living room, but everything elongated, like she was running in place.

Then he was there.

Murphy stood in the cabin's living room, in front of their couch, their fireplace. He had a gun to Nick's head and Evie opened her mouth to tell him she'd do anything, *just don't hurt him*.

But Murphy pulled the trigger anyway and Nick's brains splattered across the stone.

A bloodcurdling scream ripped from Evie's throat as she clawed at her sweat-soaked shirt. She sucked in a stuttered breath, listening for a beat before she heard footsteps in the hallway. Her door eased open and Nick was there, completely fine, in pajama pants with a bare torso. He had a shirt in his hand though. Evie glanced down at it, rasping, "Sorry."

He shook his head, pulling his shirt on as he stepped into the room. "It's okay, don't apologize." There was exhaustion laced with his words and Evie glanced over at the small clock on the nightstand, realizing they'd only been home from Adam's for a couple hours. If he'd been asleep at all, he'd just fallen into it.

"I —" Evie stuttered as Nick stepped over and flicked her nightstand lamp on.

"Scoot."

She startled, then scooted over at the motion of his hand, pulling the sheets to her chest as he sank down next to her.

"What are you —" She didn't have a chance to ask as he picked up the tattered copy of *The Highlander Barbarian's Wife's Sister* that she was in the middle of rereading.

Nick cleared his throat and then flipped it open to page one.

"*I never expected ta' see a man so tall, so shirtless, sitting in my home when I came back from the funeral.*" His Scottish accent was impressively terrible, lilting at the wrong moments and veering heavily into Irish, Welsh, Kiwi, and a little Russian — weirdly enough.

Evie's mouth dropped open as she tried to formulate a response to him reading the first line of the book to her. She finally found her brain long enough to gasp, "What are you *doing*?"

Nick looked at her over the book. "Well, I figured the only way to get your mind off of whatever happened in that nightmare would be to completely distract you with something so traumatizing that your brain has no other option but to fixate on this instead." He lifted the book, flopping its pages. "So here I am, traumatizing you."

She was speechless as they stared at each other in the dim light of the warm-toned lamp on the nightstand. She wasn't even sure he could see the page. His face was shrouded in shadow, but when he pulled the book away, she got the opportunity to see *him* and the creases at the edges of his eyes attempting to add some levity to the situation.

"You're going to read me that?" She looked down at the book, cautiously aware of the fact they were only inches away from each other in her bed. "Right now?"

"Yes." Nick nodded, taking a moment to readjust and lean back on her pillows. "So get comfortable. I'm going to do my best to narrate this as — who the fuck wrote this?" He flipped the cover over, glancing at the author's name that had been partially rubbed off. "I guess it doesn't matter. I'm going to do it justice."

There was something so disarmingly charming about Nick when he was clearly past exhausted. Evie settled in next to him, shifting closer to glance over his shoulder.

He tugged the book away, frowning. "No looking ahead."

"Nick." Evie tried to hide a laugh. "I've *read* it."

"Yeah, but you've not heard *me* narrate it." He gave her another look and then reached over, wrapping an arm around her shoulders to pull her into his side. "I guess I can make an exception just this once."

She laughed, finding herself falling against him. When she glanced up, he adjusted the book and looked down. Their eyes met and Evie couldn't help the little flip her stomach did, turning her head to rest it on his shoulder, muttering, "All right, traumatize me."

Evie didn't have to look up to know he was smiling.

"*I never expected ta' see a man so tall, so shirtless, sitting in my home when I came back from the funeral. I really never expected the man to be my sister's husband, waiting for me to come back from burying his wife. He hadn't been at the funeral, as we buried Ginni next to Pa and the rest of our ken at the small church in the windy Scottish highlands. Mum was beside herself, but she insisted she be there.*"

Nick's accent flickered in and out and Evie shifted, reaching up to thumb at the pages. "This is the sad part, skip forward."

He snorted as he batted her hand away and flipped a couple pages in. "Sorry, you want this scene?"

Evie glanced up as Nick's brow furrowed as he *growled* from deep in his chest.

"*Ach, your sister was a good lass, but you cannae expect me to go home to my castle, my people, without a wife. I'll miss her as the day is long, but ya' are comin' with me lass.*"

The giggle that bubbled up in the back of her throat was unmistakable as Evie leaned back against Nick's shoulder and let it loose, laughing at the gruff and cartoonish way Nick was trying to sound brutal and commanding. It fell so flat from the man who'd been nothing but endlessly kind to her — the man who was sitting next to her at this very moment reading to her from a cheesy romance novel about a Laird kidnapping his dead wife's sister.

Nick's chest started to shake as he tried to talk around his laughter. "Shit, I'm losing my place —" He put a finger on the page. "*Yer coming with me lass. Don't ya' dare pack anything black either, I'll get ya' a new kit in my tartan.*"

Evie let out another peal of laughter, rolling off of him to land on the pillow. "I don't think that's how *any* of this works."

Nick dropped the book slightly, smiling as he watched her laugh. "Probably not, I've never researched any of the intricacies of this specific plot."

She looked up at him, shaking her head. "I can't believe you read this."

"Listen —" Nick's smile grew. "This cabin was *very* quiet when I moved in, and while I wanted a retreat, I wasn't exactly enjoying myself doing nothing before I got the logging job. And who could say no to this cover?"

He flopped the book closed, flashing the cover at her. Nick's thumb rested near the woman's boob, artfully tipping out of the tartan draping over her.

Evie rolled her eyes. "I mean I can't fault her, she gets action on page twenty-seven, what a woman." The moment the words left her mouth, she felt a blush blossom across her chest and creep up her neck. "I mean — that's fast for a romance novel."

Nick's eyebrow quirked, his smile shifting into a smirk. It was a dangerous one too — the kind of look that made Evie think about the bar before Andy's call and the way Nick's fingers had roamed over the neck of his beer bottle.

"Would you call this romance?" He flipped the book over,

looking at the genres listed above bar code. "Ah no, it says right here *romance / erotica*." His eyes flickered back up. "I think the scene on page twenty-seven classifies it as the latter."

She sucked in a breath. "I mean it definitely has to do with the skirts line."

"The skirts line?" Nick looked back at the book. "I don't remember *that*."

"Oh, come *on*." She sat up, letting the sheets fall down to her waist as she plucked the book from his hands and fanned the pages out, finding it on page twenty-two, when the main character was already on horseback riding with her past brother-in-law and future husband.

"*We were approachin' an inn*." Evie cleared her throat, not even attempting an accent and instead reading softly in her own voice. "*I couldn't remember the last inn I'd stayed in, other than the few trips Mum, Ginni, and I had made to Edinburgh for the seasons, we didn't travel much out of the home. But this one looked like the kind of inns that travelers stayed at who didn't have carriages or all the fancy things the English women did when they passed through the country*."

Evie glanced up to find Nick's attention rapt. "Sorry, that was early, it's... here."

"*We're not staying in one room.*" *I was insistent on that. I wasn't about to compromise myself and my future for this man who forced me on horseback with a knife to my back.*

"*Suit yourself, hope ye' find someone downstairs to take ye' in instead of me.*" *Angus had a small smile on his face, the kind of smile that meant he was daring me to do it, and I was just stubborn enough that I might.*

But then he unpinned his McTarynn brooch from the tartan slung over his torso and shoulders, exposing the white shirt that was plastered to his body with a thin layer of sweat from us riding all night. Angus wasn't looking at me anymore. He was

*too busy tugging the shirt up over his head with practiced ease
and tossing it over a wooden chair in the corner, his boots echoing
on the wooden floor as he stomped over to the water basin to wash
his face.*

*His body caught in the firelight, all rippling abdominal
muscles, sheened with a fine layer of sweat and dust, but deeply
cut and scarred in some places. This was a man who'd
seen war.*

*Something about the way his body moved, the way his back
arched as he ran the water over his face and beard, letting it drip
down his torso, made ideas awaken under my skirts."*

Evie lowered the book as she licked her lips. "I mean, any
woman who ogles her dead sister's husband is pretty bold. And
then the author *had* to make sure there was only one bed left at
the inn just so they could have an excuse to sleep together — I
mean I guess they didn't *have* to do anything other than liter-
ally sleep but the tension was already building and he *was*
already half naked..."

She trailed off, a slow dying of her thought process as she
stared at Nick in mild horror at her own loose tongue. If he
hadn't put a shirt on, this would be *the exact same scenario.*

Her room felt small. Where before Evie had sworn the
space was cozy with its wooden walls and full-size bed with a
soft quilt and a few pillows, now it felt stuffy. She was too close
to the man leaning against her pillow with dark, lidded eyes
staring at her in the dim lamplight.

"Guess so." Nick exhaled. "I do remember her talking
about his abs a lot. Do women really notice them that much?"

Evie didn't know what to say. Had she noticed *his* the
morning Andy called to tell them Harvey Beck was dead? Yes.
Had she noticed them tonight when he stood in the doorway?
Yes.

"I..." She trailed off, trying to think of an appropriate

response and coming up blank. Finally she landed on non-commitment. "I think some women do."

The room went silent. Evie swore there was an unspoken question in the way Nick looked at her, asking '*do you?*'

She suddenly wished the book on her nightstand had been anything but *The Highlander Barbarian's Wife's Sister* — she should have been reading the fishing or hiking guides instead. Those would have at least been a distraction, if not put her to sleep. This was something else entirely. The air simmered like a pot threatening to boil over.

Finally, Nick broke the tension with a tight smile. "Well, that author apparently loves them." He shrugged, adjusting the pillows with a yawn and sliding down in her bed. "And if you don't kick me out, I think I might end up here for the night."

Evie reached over him, ignoring the way his eyes snapped open to watch her drop the book on the nightstand and flick the lamp off. Things felt both better and worse in the dark, and before her eyes could adjust, Evie retreated to her side of the bed.

"That's fine," she said softly, curling her legs up. "I feel bad for keeping you awake all the time. Not only did you have to bring a stranger into your home, but apparently she shrieks like a deranged lunatic every night."

The bed shifted and Evie watched as Nick's face came into focus, all dark features, a slightly furrowed brow, and a slightly misshapen beard from how his head was resting on the pillow. His hair fanned out and Evie was sure she'd never seen him so unkempt.

"I want you to be able to rest. I want you to feel safe."

The words hung in the air until Evie threw them to the side and leaned in, dropping to rest her forehead against his chest, breathing in the scent of the laundry detergent and his shampoo. She'd thought about touching him, hugging him, ever since the day in the grocery store and the dark room gave her permission to finally do it.

Nick's left hand moved slow enough that Evie could gauge where it would go before it did — right to her side, chastely touching her waist and holding her gently as she whispered, "I do feel safe. You make me feel safe."

CHAPTER SEVENTEEN

EVIE HAD NEVER PAID MORE ATTENTION TO A POT OF coffee in her entire life.

She meticulously measured the freeze-dried grounds. She walked slowly so she didn't spill a drop of water as she filled the reservoir. She clicked the lid into place with a firm press, then flicked the switch hard because it occasionally jammed.

And now she watched it, her eyes following the drip as it collected and dropped down into the glass pot.

All of this to avoid looking at the man sitting at the kitchen table with his copy of *Fahrenheit 451* loosely hanging from his fingertips. Evie didn't know until this morning that Nick wore glasses. She had no idea until he'd come out of his room after awkwardly leaving hers and walked past her to go to the bathroom.

There he was, with a pair of black frames on the bridge of his nose, one finger alternating between resting on his lips and flipping the page.

It was librarian porn. She'd fallen into her own version of

librarian porn, except *she* was the target audience and *he* was the reason she was starting to feel faint and hyper-focusing on making a mediocre pot of coffee.

The pot dinged and she jolted, pulling out two white mugs from the upper cabinet on autopilot. She filled them both up and walked them over to the table, putting Nick's down in front of him before sinking into her own seat and taking a cautious sip.

He looked at her over the edge of his book and gave her a soft smile, whispering a husky, "Thank you." His morning voice still hadn't worn off and Evie didn't know what was worse, knowing he had one and knowing what it sounded like — or knowing that he'd never spoken to her with it before *now*.

She brought her mug to her lips again, wishing the hot coffee would burn off whatever was infecting her emotions. She could *not* stay in this cabin; she'd either combust or drop dead in the hallway from the stress, anxiety, and sheer gall of it all.

"I think we should go into town," she blurted out and looked up to see Nick staring in mild alarm. "I have books to return to Stephen and we should go before it gets too snowy. Didn't the radio say the weather was about to take a turn for the worse before Christmas?"

Nick slowly lowered his mug then glanced toward the front window. "It is a clear day, we could probably pick up a few things in town in case we get snowed in."

"Great! I'll be ready in a bit!" Grabbing her coffee mug, Evie nearly spilled it in her rush to get down the hall. The moment she was inside her room, her heart lurched.

She was a pretty even-keel person. There were very few things that ruffled her, all things considered, other than murderers hunting her down.

But, looking at her rumpled bed with the imprint of Nick on the side she normally slept on — that ruffled her. She'd woken lying chest to chest with him in her small bed, painfully aware of his hands on the small of her back and the fact she'd not had a single nightmare after falling asleep with her nose against his chest.

Evie turned away from the bed, focused on dressing warm for the drive into Wells Creek. She wasn't lying, she did have a few library books to return, waiting in the tote bag Nick had bought her, but it wasn't like Stephen would charge her late fees.

She slid the tote onto her shoulder, dressed in a pair of leggings and a fitted turtleneck. Overtop of it, she'd layered a thick cardigan.

When she stepped out into the hallway, Evie saw Nick's closed door and exhaled in relief as she moved into the empty living room to clean up the last dredges of the coffee and chuck the used grounds into the compost bucket. She'd watched Nick trudge through the snow to dump their fresh food waste at the farthest property line where the yard met the forest for the last two weeks. They hadn't had any issues with wild animals near the cabin yet, so Evie just followed his lead.

Nick emerged from the hall, running a hand over his beard. He'd *trimmed* it.

She stopped in the middle of washing her hands, taking a second to process the neater shape of it before wiping them on a kitchen towel.

"You ready?" Nick moved around the counter and she felt his warmth at her back as he reached around her to grab the bucket. "I'll empty this if you start the truck for us."

She turned in the small space, nearly chest to chest with him again as she held her hand out and Nick dropped his keyring into her palm. There was the truck key, next to a faded *VIVA LAS VEGAS* keychain that was chipping around the edges, then finally the house key.

Evie nodded, caught for a moment between him and the sink as Nick smiled. "You better think of something to put on the grocery list, I'm not going up and down every aisle."

She scoffed, "Poor you, traversing all four aisles must be such an arduous task."

Nick glanced at her over his shoulder, grinning. "Put your coat on."

"Yes, *sir*." Evie rolled her eyes and breezed past him.

The truck's heater was blasting by the time Nick pulled open the driver's side door and climbed up to join her in the cab. She'd already fiddled with the radio until she could barely get a signal for a pop station and shot him a pleading glance when Nick's hand crept toward the radio to fix it back to the 80s station.

"Please, five minutes."

"If you want to listen to music through a tin can I'll let you."

Evie grinned in victory, but even she had to admit it was terrible. They weren't even off the cabin's road before she switched it back to the clearest station — unhappily tolerating the end of *Don't Stop Believin'* which reminded her of shitty network shows from a decade ago.

Nick drummed his fingers on the steering wheel, glancing at her. She'd pulled her scarf off in the heat of the truck and was rubbing her neck, the tag on the cardigan bothering her. Evie pulled her hand away and frowned.

"What?"

He shook his head, looking back out at the road. "Nothing."

She adjusted in the seat. "Nick." At the sound of his name, his eyes flickered over. He'd left his glasses at the cabin and Evie wondered if he only wore contacts out and she'd just never realized.

In the grand scheme of things it didn't matter — but it felt like information she should know.

After a beat of silence, Nick spoke. "Do you want to grab a bite at the diner?"

Evie swore there was a light flush to his neck and the tops of his ears.

"Oh." She fiddled with her scarf again. "Yeah, that sounds nice."

Their eyes met before Nick nodded once and offered her a small smile. "Good."

The rest of the ride was silent and Evie wasn't sure if she should break it or not. By the time she found her misplaced courage, they were on the main road. She didn't know what to think — the diner wasn't a place they'd ever been together.

Sure, there were other stores in town — she'd briefly walked behind him in the hiking store and wandered through the market — but this was the *diner*. This was where the rest of the town gathered to eat if they weren't at Adam's.

She tugged at her cardigan, the low neckline showing her turtleneck under it. It was an outfit she'd worn on many fall and wintery days to wander through the library, shelving books for the kids or planning out her next themed table display.

Nick pulled into a diagonal spot in front of the diner, an older brick building with a simple sign that matched the rest of the town.

WELLS CREEK DINER was just one long room when they walked inside. The faded brown tile on the floors almost matched the worn tan booths lining one wall. Behind a register, a woman raised her hand in greeting to Nick before nodding to him to pick a table.

He steered Evie to a booth, taking the seat that gave him a view of the front door and the street while Evie sat with her back to them. She felt a prickle of fear at the back of her neck as she sat down, but it was eased almost immediately by the motion of Nick looking up and scanning the room before he took his own seat.

Nick wouldn't let anyone hurt her.

The same woman from behind the counter approached their table. Up close Evie could see she was mid-40s, with soft wavy blonde hair and a sweet smile.

"Well, hello there." She sat two menus down, looking at Nick. "You know, Jared was just saying that the season was done and we probably shouldn't expect to see you out of that cabin until spring."

Nick smiled. "You can tell Jared if he keeps telling people I hibernate like a bear then I'm not covering for his late ass next year."

"Well." The woman laughed and turned her attention to Evie. "I'm Carol. I hope he isn't bothering you too much. He is a little grumpy, like a bear." She gave Evie a conspiratorial smile. "What can I get you to drink?"

Evie opened her mouth to order, but Nick cleared his throat, pushing the menus away as his eyes cut over to her. There was a small twinkle in them as he grinned. "Two coffees — she likes hers black — and add a splash of cream for me, Carol." Nick rubbed his beard. "And do two specials, pop the yolks on mine and leave hers soft."

Carol wrote down the order on her pad with a flourish then grabbed the menus. "You got it."

She was gone in a flash. Evie stared at Nick, her lips slightly parted as she tried — and failed — to ignore the question at the forefront of her mind.

"Is this a date?"

Nick's head tilted slightly and something in the way his lips twitched up at the edges into a little smile made her heart flutter. "It's brunch."

Evie didn't know what to say. Something hung in the air that neither of them had the guts — or the confidence, in her case — to actually verbalize.

Carol came back with their coffees. Evie's was so bitter that her toes curled in her boots, but the warmth of it was comforting and reminded her of Nick sitting at the table and flipping through his book.

"Why *Fahrenheit 451*?"

Nick took a drink. "Like I said, I like it. Reminds me of the times in training that didn't suck. Reminds me of a lot of moments with Andy, or flipping through the book trying to find a reason to stay in the position I was forced into."

She nodded slowly, a comfortable quiet falling over their table. It didn't take long for the food to come out — the specials were two eggs, a piece of toast, three slices of bacon, and a side of the crispiest hash browns Evie had ever seen. She ate every single bite while the conversation flowed back to what he was picking up at the market and if she was going to take out anything specific from the library today.

When they were done, Evie watched Nick fish his brown wallet out of his jacket pocket and throw down a couple bills. She stood up and his arm easily encircled her waist, guiding her back out into the balmy cold.

It barely took five minutes to pull into the library lot, but in that span of time Evie was certain — it had been a date.

"I'll be over there." Nick nodded toward the market as she

climbed out of the cab. "Don't rush. When I'm done I'll head back over here, okay?"

She looked up at him with a tiny smile. "You'll hear me scream if I need anything."

He gave her a soft smile back. "I'll come running."

There was both a strange lightness and a weight in her chest as Evie pulled open the door to the library. She waved at Nick one last time before stepping inside and seeing Stephen.

Pulling out her stack of read books, they chatted for a few minutes as Evie pushed her hair behind her ears and then leaned over slightly. "Did you get a few new things in? I know you said you might last week."

Stephen leaned closer to her, his voice dropping like it was a secret. "I did. They're over there." He nodded toward a small stack on one of the shelves. "Grab a couple before my other regulars pillage them."

"You're the best, Stephen." Evie shot him a giddy grin, already heading toward the new arrivals.

"I'll be in the back!" Stephen called after her, "I need to finish up these donation boxes I got and see if anything's worth keeping." Evie glanced back, but the older man was already disappearing into the office.

With her empty tote on her shoulder, she ran her fingers over the new books. There was one historical fiction, which wasn't her favorite — but in the center there were a couple of books she'd been waiting months for release.

Even though a large chunk of what she read was kid lit or children's fiction — she still really enjoyed all genres. There was an adult fiction about a magical island here in the Pacific Northwest, then a romance about two engineers from NASA.

As she slipped them into her tote bag to check out later, she walked slowly along the mismatched shelves, fingers sliding over the variances between the metal and the old wooden ones pressed against the walls. This wasn't a traditional library, but she'd been in it a few times since her first visit and there was just something comforting about being here — being present in a place that was always her happiness, even from a young age.

She was rounding the corner, pointed toward the romance section when she froze.

There had been a sound, just a small one, that made every hair on the back of Evie's neck stand tall. She scanned the shelves hurriedly. Normally she would disregard the occasional creak, but Stephen was in the back and it had sounded like footsteps.

Her eyes cast over the shelves, looking between them as she felt her heart rise in her throat. She took a step forward and walked over to the romance section, her back to a wall as she stared at the familiar titles. Holding her breath, her ears strained .

The floor creaked.

She pulled her tote bag closer with shaking hands, eyes flickering behind her to look at the children's section, then over to the front door. There hadn't been any other cars in the parking lot. She should have been the only person in here except for the other librarian.

"Stephen?" The man's name was barely a whisper. Evie wasn't sure she could make herself speak any louder unless she forced it from her lungs. She walked along the wall, keeping her back protected with eyes trained on the shelves, then flickered to look at the archway and front door.

She reached the foyer and planted herself in front of the desk. "Stephen!"

The door swung open. "Oh, sorry, Evie, were you waiting?"

She pulled both books out of her bag quickly, feeling like there were eyes on her. "No, sorry, just wanted to make sure you heard me. I thought…" She trailed off, shaking her head. "It's just us in here?"

Stephen shot her an odd look as he scanned her library card. "Far as I know." He snorted. "Well, maybe the ghost of my ex-wife. She's not dead, but she's probably still haunting this place. She used to call it my mistress."

Evie forced a half smile at the joke, sucking in a breath as the bell behind her jingled.

"Well, well, well." Stephen looked up. "If it isn't Nick Barber."

As quickly as the tension coiled, it released. She turned sharply to see Nick in the doorway, with her scarf hanging from his hand. "You left this in the truck."

Before she could stop herself, Evie's eyes scanned the other room — the nonfiction section that she'd never wandered into — and paused for half a second on a shadow. But it had to be nothing — Stephen had said it himself there was no one here.

Nick caught the shift, stepping fully into the library and filling the small foyer with ease. There was something about the set of his broad shoulders and the stern look on his face that made Evie want to rush to him and tuck herself against his chest.

He was *safe*.

"Ready to go?" His voice was firmer, the lightness long gone as he shot Stephen a quick smile. "Hope you've been well, but you know how these roads get if we leave the ice to freeze."

Stephen waved them off, rolling his eyes. "Go on." His hand was on the door to the office as he looked back at Evie. "Don't rush back to return those copies, the other residents can wait. You savor those books, Evie."

She smiled back at Stephen, stepping closer to Nick. The office door shut and the library was quiet for a moment before Nick rested a hand on her arm. "Are you —"

"Can we just go?" Anxiety swirled in her stomach. "I really just want to go home."

He nodded sharply, frowning as he shifted so she was walking in front of him out of the library. The moment Evie breathed in the outside air, the anxiety eased.

She'd let her mind run away again.

But as Nick drove them home, something dark settled in her stomach — an acidic awareness that something felt *wrong*.

CHAPTER EIGHTEEN

SHE WASN'T AT ALL WHAT HE'D EXPECTED.

There was a folded photo of her in his jean pocket. The female who was standing in the foyer didn't carry herself the same way he thought she would. She was a little shorter than he'd imagined, or maybe that was because she was standing between a man his equal and the old coot who ran this place.

Her dark brown hair was the same color of her panicked eyes. Bryant really liked how her soft, rounded cheeks flushed a just-fucked pink and her lips parted in alarm.

She was so fucking *scared*. He bet if he was closer he could hear her little bird heart fluttering against her breastbone under all those layers of sweater.

She looked like a tight little thing, he'd give her that.

The old man called her by her nickname before he disappeared into his office. He'd been in the back when Bryant entered the library this morning, no idea he wasn't alone.

Bryant watched their whole exchange — before he followed the female as she picked up her silly little books and slid them into her stupid kitschy tote bag. This place was old, and his boots scuffed on the floor. He paused just in time to see her head shoot up.

She was like a startled deer from that point onward; aware of danger, but unsure why.

It was *far* too early for him to step out and kill her, even if Jonathan would have been reckless enough to command it. There was a reason Bryant was the one in this shitty little town in cold as fuck Washington.

He needed to see the way she moved. She *was* cautious. He'd planned to sit in the library for a week or two if need be. Because where else would a librarian end up, if not the small-town library for a familiar haunt?

In forty-eight hours he's already gathered so much information. The singular bar in town was owned by a friend of Nicholas Barber, who was a retired FBI meathead with a shiny record and an even shinier family history of do-gooder men who liked to play with guns — and maternal ties that rivaled Murphy's. The Barber family was *interesting*, but he wasn't Bryant's focus.

It was little Evelyn Morgen, often seen but not heard in this town. Though he'd gleaned from a bored teenager at the local grocery store that, *"Yeah there's some new woman hanging around with the weird guy who lives in the woods."*

That was really all the information Bryant needed.

He would take this slow, savor it. He'd been all over the fucking south expecting Evie to be holed up with some of Andy's family or friends in Memphis or Charleston. It hadn't even occurred to him that she would be with a *Barber* of all people.

Bryant wasn't foolish enough *not* to keep Jonathan updated. But tracking down Nick Barber was more difficult than either of them intended, and Bryant had yet to make the call that Wells Creek was where the librarian had temporarily settled. He didn't want to move too fast, that was always Murphy's fatal flaw. Bryant preferred a more measured solution.

If Jonathan Murphy was Achilles, William Bryant was Patroclus.

Bryant had to wonder though — was Nick Barber getting any of the added benefits of having to babysit this female day in and day out? Bryant would. He would have her screaming if it was up to him — weren't the quiet ones always freaks?

He waited a good fifteen minutes before he pushed the door open to jingle the bell and then turned with his hands shoved in his coat pockets to walk toward the front desk, watching as the door to the back office opened and the old librarian walked out.

"Oh." The man looked up, a friendly smile on his face. "Haven't seen you here before. What can I do you for?"

"Just passing through." Bryant smiled. "My girl loves books and I wondered if you let visitors get cards here? This would be a great hiking place for us."

"Oh absolutely, even if it's just a few days, I can write her a temporary pass." The old man's hands were wrinkled as he pulled out a little form and slid it across the desk. "You can even take this home to her if you'd like."

Bryant took the paper. "Thank you so much. This town just seems so great, I stopped at the diner this morning and it was good — good food, good people, you know?"

The older man hummed softly. "Oh this town is full of people who care about each other. You don't find them like Wells Creek anymore." He moved a couple books behind the desk, then glanced up. "Anything else I can do for you?"

Bryant felt his smile flicker as he nodded. "Yeah, I was just curious if there were any new faces in town? I don't want us to stick out like a sore thumb."

The older man's skin tightened around his eyes. "We get a lot of tourists. Not a problem to be a new face in town."

"I noticed the bar." Bryant leaned forward, trying to smile a little better — be a little more convincing. "My girl, she hates bars, but I hoped there was a younger crowd she might feel a little more comfortable with. Saw that pretty little waitress but not very many others."

The librarian's face was no longer friendly. "I'm sure your girlfriend would be comfortable enough there." He pointedly looked away at the computer. "You have a good day now."

Bryant's smile fell entirely, seeing no point in it anymore as he chuckled. "Yeah." As he turned to walk out, he caught the older man glancing at his side profile.

Bryant had a feeling if he didn't work at an appropriate pace, his chance to strike at Evie Morgen would pass him by. People in small towns talked too much.

CHAPTER NINETEEN

"DID YOU KNOW CHRISTMAS IS THIS WEEK?"

Evie was standing in the kitchen, staring at the damn calendar again as Nick walked back and forth behind her, cleaning up their breakfast. She'd offered — but he'd said it was fine.

He'd been doing that for the last three days since they went into town.

"I did." His voice sounded closer before he nudged her to the side so that he could open the fridge and put the butter back from the toast they'd both eaten. When he was done, he glanced down at her and then over to the calendar. "I didn't know if you'd noticed."

Evie scowled. "It's just so soon."

"Well, do you want to celebrate?"

The question was so simple, but Evie felt like she'd been handed a loaded gun. Ironic — considering the reason she was even dreading the holiday in the first place.

Every year since she'd gone to college, then subsequently moved into her grandparents' old home — she would spend the night with her parents on Christmas Eve. Magically overnight, her mother would drag out all the presents from their hiding spots and scatter them around the tree, as if Santa had visited. There was never much for their small family of three — but it was the thought that counted. Even if Evie had opened a kitchen appliance, or a new set of sheets the last couple of years — it was the thought of her mother walking through the store and going *"Oh, Evie needs that"* that made it special.

Her stomach twisted. "I don't know if I can."

He frowned, his eyes softening as he touched her shoulder. "I didn't ask to upset you." He faced her, bending his head down so they were closer. "I'm sorry. I can't imagine what it feels like to know you can't talk to your parents during all of this. Maybe Andy will pull a small miracle out of his ass — or..." Nick trailed off, then glanced out the windows, a line appearing between his brows. "We'll go into the next town, find a pay phone and you can call from that. Murphy's good, but he's not tapping every phone line across America."

"You'd do that?" Her voice broke. "For me?"

"Do you see anyone else in this kitchen?"

Her eyes burned as she shook her head, unable to speak, too agonizingly sad, but grateful. "I appreciate that more than I think I can say." Evie looked away, blinking rapidly. "I'm... I'll be right back." She stepped out of the kitchen quickly, refusing to look back at him, just needing one second to breathe, to think, without being subjected to the way his body called out to hers.

Ever since that day in the grocery store she'd been unable to stop reaching for him.

Evie scrubbed a hand over her face, exhaling. There was no point in holing up in her room — it wasn't like it didn't hold its own memories. The nightmares had lessened, and were mere fragments of their former selves since he'd been in here.

The front door opened then shut as she pulled a cardigan she'd been using as a house coat. The cabin wasn't cold enough to warrant it, but there was a level of comfort to pulling it tight and tucking her arms around herself.

When she stepped back out into the hallway, the living room was quiet. Nick's boots were missing from their usual spot by the front door. As she walked over to the front window, she passed the stereo, which had been turned on but the CD removed from it. The little sleeve was open, like Nick had started to rifle through it before leaving.

Evie stopped in front of the window, realizing *why*.

Nick held the wood axe over his shoulder as he trudged toward the forest, coat haphazardly slung on. He slowed to a stop near the new growth and underbrush at the edge, before he looked around and walked toward the side. Evie watched as he rustled a small fir tree, which barely came to his chest. A couple of needles fell off, but nothing else jumped from the sparse branches.

He tugged the wood axe off his shoulder and then brought it down close to the ground, felling the thin truck in only two strokes, letting the tree tip into his hand. When he looked up, his eyes swung back to the cabin, catching hers. Even from inside, Evie could see his grin as he picked the tree up and headed back.

She rushed away from the window and threw the door open to the brisk air, staring at Nick as he dropped the axe off and hauled the little tree inside.

"Ta-da." He smiled wide, nodding toward the empty corner next to the fireplace and window. "Wanna help me get this set up there? Go find a basket we can prop it up in."

Evie darted to the bathroom where there was a large wicker

laundry basket — it was empty and it would do. She snatched it and rushed back to the living room, helping Nick sit the trunk down. Evie grabbed a few of the logs near the fireplace, stacking them sideways and leaning them just *so* until the little tree was mostly upright.

When she stepped back, she was covered in a few pine needles and her hands smelled like sap, but it was the greatest thing she'd ever seen.

"I don't think I have ornaments." Nick shrugged off his coat. "Or lights, but it's something."

"It's *perfect*." She wanted to thank him, to say the right thing to convey the rush of emotions at the fact he'd trudged out into the half-frozen ground and cut a tree down for *her* just because she wanted to celebrate a stupid holiday — but nothing came out. Her throat felt tight as Nick's eyes landed on hers.

His lips tilted. "Maybe there's a Christmas CD in the case, something festive. I think I could whip up some hot chocolate."

Evie's lip trembled, just a little. "You don't know how much I..." She looked away, staring at the stupid tree, one red ornament away from being the spitting image of Charlie Brown's.

Nick's hand squeezed her shoulder, his eyes kind. "Merry Christmas, Evie."

She threw her arms around his neck, standing on her toes to embrace him. His warm arms wrapped around her as she hugged him tightly, muttering, "Thank you, Nick. Just... thank you."

The ideal December, Evie thought as they slowly parted, would be decorating on the first with her mother — starting with her parents' home, then moving to her own living room. This, somehow, was almost better. The small tree was a little crooked and there was nothing to hang on it, just the light scent of pine in the air and a genuine knowledge that the only reason it was inside the cabin was because Nick *cared*.

"I'll help you make the hot chocolate." She pulled away, hating to let him go. "If you'd like."

Nick nodded toward the kitchen. "Go on, I'm going to wash the tree off my hands."

As Nick ventured back down the hallway, Evie found a Christmas album with all the classics. She turned it up, letting the music fill the living room as she grabbed all the ingredients. Chocolate bars shoved in a cabinet next to the fridge, a little milk to melt them, and two mugs. Evie laid everything out, putting a shallow pot on the stove.

Nick rounded the corner, the sleeves of his flannel pushed up past his forearms. "You found music."

She nodded, roughly chopping the chocolate so it would melt a little faster. The process was meditative and when her mind wandered, she found herself thinking again of the small Christmas market in Hawthorne. As the days grew darker and the school rushed toward break, Evie always watched the city decorators hang snowflakes on the light poles just outside her office windows.

"Bing Crosby is always festive." She glanced up at Nick as he lingered on the other side of the counter, catching his smile as she scraped the chocolate into the pan. "I thought I'd make it this way. I'll try not to scald it — I normally just get mine from the market at home." The words fell out unbidden as she picked up a spatula and started to move the chocolate around in the pan, making sure it was on low.

He shifted his position, bending down to lean his head on his hand as he watched her. "Is this the one with the peanut brittle? What's it like?"

Of course he remembered her telling him about the stupid

peanut brittle. "Well... Hawthorne isn't very big, really." She kept her eyes on the chocolate, a good enough excuse to not meet his. His gaze on her was both unnerving and solidifying — his attention felt like a privilege.

She swirled the chocolate, then added a splash of milk. "Hawthorne is a lot like Wells Creek, I guess. There's a little park in front of the town hall and vendors set up in rows. It's mostly locals who sell homemade ornaments, or wreaths, but..." She flicked the stove off, daring to dart her eyes up to his as she grabbed the mugs. "There's a woman in town, her name is Anne."

Nick's lips twitched. "And she makes hot chocolate?"

Evie nodded vigorously, grinning as she poured half of the thick, molten chocolate into a mug — more chocolate than milk. "It's turned into a tradition, her and her husband and their kids always serve fresh French hot chocolate. I don't think she's *actually* French, but I don't question when someone hands me a mug of molten sugar."

She pulled the pan away and sat it back on the stove, watching Nick walk around the counter. He moved behind her and she paused for a moment, trapped between him and the stove as his hand brushed her side. He leaned over her, opening the upper cabinet and pulling down a bag of mini marsh-mallows.

"Can't forget these." He flashed her a smile, then sprinkled a few on top of each of the mugs. "This market sounds great, have you always lived in Hawthorne?"

She turned, their personal space intermingling as Evie stared, letting out a small breath. "Yeah, I grew up there with my parents and my brother."

Nick paused, his brows drawing together. "You have a brother?"

"I don't, not anymore." Evie glanced away, staring at their

mugs. "When I think about the Christmas market, I think about dragging my older brother around as a kid." Steam rose from the hot chocolate as she grimaced. "And then I think about my parents — losing another kid but not really. And then I start to think about how suffocating life has been for *years* and —" She didn't know where all the words were coming from, but they all poured out until she choked.

"I'm sorry."

She turned her head, staring at him in the close quarters. Nick's lips pulled down into a gentle frown, making his beard sag. "I'm an only child, you know?" He lifted a hand, pushing it through his hair. "I always thought life would be easier with someone else to catch my parents' attention, and it's not the same, but —" His eyes flickered away and she watched the furrow deepened in his brow. "Maybe it is? Maybe we were both the sole focus for too long and it makes holidays a little harder. You want to reach out because they're family, but you also want to be able to exist during the holidays without the burden of someone else's grief or expectations."

It felt like he'd sucked all the air from her lungs.

"And —" Nick gave her a chagrined glance. "I'm close to my cousin who didn't have the best go of things. She had a wild few years — and I think of her a lot this time of year. I see the snow and think, '*Fuck*, I hope she's staying sober,' and then I have to stop myself and remember she's an adult, she got through rehab, but..." He trailed off. "It's those memories that aren't even scarred, they've just got these fucking scabs you have to try not to pick at when it's late at night and your brain won't turn off."

Evie swallowed hard, forcing herself to clear the lump in her throat as they stared at each other. "It sounds like we both need a little more than hot chocolate to get through this week."

Nick chuckled. "Yeah, well, I've got a couple bottles of

whiskey we could probably break into. Seems like the occasion."

She laughed softly, leaning back. Nick's hand shot out and he grabbed her side, just a hair's breadth above her hip bone. "Careful of the stove, sweetheart." She jerked away on instinct, putting herself against his chest.

They stood there for a moment, his hand touching her waist and their breathing shallow and Evie wondered if this was all a terrible idea — if she needed Andy to pull her out and drop her with some unnamed agent until Murphy was found.

But then Nick pulled his hand away with a lopsided smile. "We should drink our hot chocolate before it solidifies in our only coffee mugs."

And with one teasing statement, the tension faded. Evie ignored the pang in her chest, and the way his eyes lingered as they sat on the couch the rest of the night. They drank hot chocolate until they were both sick from the sugar, and talked quietly, letting the raw wounds of old memories breathe for a moment in the safety of the cabin's living room and each other's company.

Chapter Twenty

Evie wanted silent snowfall. She wanted crackling fires and quiet evenings.

Unfortunately, Washington's winter thunderstorms were wicked. The last week had been plagued by echoing explosions of thunder and flashes of lightning, interrupting her already tenuous relationship with sleep.

It was a clap of thunder that finally made her drag herself out of bed. It had been days since she and Nick spent the evening talking with hot chocolate. Every time Evie walked out of her room she could only think of the way they'd gotten so close, but still nothing happened.

She wondered if she was imagining things, if the isolation in the cabin had finally cracked her. Maybe he was just being kind — between being unable to see her parents and the way her skin crawled last week in the library, she worried maybe the anxiety *had* finally broken her.

Regardless, the storm wasn't letting her sleep, and ironically, the clock over the stove told her it was officially Christmas.

"I wonder if Santa will skip the cabin," she muttered to herself as she walked around the counter and into the kitchen. She used to tell the kids during reading hour that if they were quiet and listened well, then she'd put in a good word — at least the ones young enough to still believe. Putting a word in was really just Evie's code for catching their parents during pick-up and giving them a little incentive to get that toy the child had talked nonstop about and slip it under the tree.

An ache settled, forming a rock in the pit of her stomach as she pulled a glass out of the cabinet. She *missed* work. She missed seeing the kids and the way they often ran to her to show off a loose tooth, or a new growth spurt — or her favorite, when they asked if she had a book recommendation.

Her little bookworms were her favorite.

She loved seeing a regular come in with a stack and leave with an even larger one. She loved parent nights when they'd drag their guardians into the library just so she could meet them and have to explain that yes — she was the one who gave them so many books, but fostering that love of reading was *so* important.

Evie missed *being* there — for the parent-teacher night, the Christmas market with her hands warmed around a paper cup of molten chocolate. The little tree in the corner of the living room made her heart pang because though this place felt like *home*, she had to constantly remind herself it wasn't.

This was a cabin with a man who couldn't say no when she was dropped on his doorstep — there was nothing else. *This* was nothing else.

She turned the sink on, sighing as she filled up the glass. There was no point thinking about home, work — anything but the current situation, which was a lot of '*hurry up and wait*' from Andy and a sincere awareness of the pitfalls of the American justice system.

Evie leaned against the counter, lifting the glass up to take a sip when the cabin lit up like it was the middle of the afternoon. The flash of lightning was enough to startle her, but the thunderclap that came after made Evie flinch.

The glass tumbled from her hands and crashed to the hardwood floor, breaking into thousands of shards — and embedding one in the top of her foot.

Evie screamed, partially from the storm and partially from the glass as she jumped back, pain radiating through her foot as her head jerked at the sound of a door in the hallway crashing open.

Nick was there in less than a minute. The only thing she could comprehend was that he was shirtless, in only a pair of boxers, hair tousled from sleep and eyes only on her face. He rounded the corner and Evie jolted back, gasping out, "There's glass everywhere, be careful."

He let out a frustrated sound, barefoot like she was, before he pivoted and shoved his feet into his work boots. He crossed the glass like it was nothing and Evie's head shot up in alarm as he grasped her by the hips, large hands encircling her thighs and extending around to her ass. Wordlessly, Nick lifted her and sat her on the counter, giving her a deadly look.

"Don't you dare move." His voice was gruff and still laced with sleep as she winced. Nothing happened when he flipped the light switch and Nick's face twisted in barely contained annoyance. "God — *fuck* —" He muttered small curses as he crouched and violently threw open the cabinet under the sink.

"Nick —"

"*No.*" His voice cut through the dark as he snatched something out of the cabinet, the glass crunching under his boots. A flashlight suddenly flicked on. "Evie you're *hurt.*" He picked up her leg with one hand as he held the light with the other.

Even she had to admit it looked bad — but that was only

because the top of both feet were scattered with tiny cuts. It didn't hurt, but there was a small piece, about the size of her thumbnail, embedded upright in her foot.

He sat the flashlight on its end, casting the light up. Evie watched as Nick stepped partially away, hand still on her leg, opening the far cabinet where the handgun was strapped to the inside. He reappeared with a white box, sliding it onto the counter next to her, a myriad of first aid supplies neatly organized inside.

"Come here." His voice was softer this time as he shifted her on the counter so she could raise each foot. The beds of her feet were fine, it was just the tops and sides that had taken damage from the shards ricocheting off the floor.

Evie watched him as he bent down, shifting the flashlight so it was closer. He picked up a pair of tweezers from the first aid kit and carefully pulled the shard out of her foot. She winced, but in seconds Nick had it wiped down with an alcohol swab, antibiotic cream on it, and bandaged it.

The rest of the scratches barely needed wiping off.

"Thank you." She tilted her head at him, frowning. "I'm really sorry I woke you up."

"It's okay." Nick was within the reach of her fingers, but she stayed still as he packed the first aid kit up and stashed it away, washing his hands off. He fixed her with another look. "Now *don't move* until I get all this cleaned up."

"Yes, sir." She muttered the words unthinkingly with a roll of her eyes. Both of them froze. Heat rose to her cheeks as Nick paused. His eyes locked on her for a heartbeat before he started cleaning.

Evie felt ridiculous sitting on the kitchen counter in nothing but an old t-shirt and a pair of underwear. She'd expected her trip to the kitchen to be quick and now she was desperately trying to not look suspicious as she pulled the fabric down to cover the curve of her ass.

All it did was further exacerbate the fact that she was on the counter and Nick was stooped over the garbage can, dumping shards of glass into the trash.

She dropped her legs off the counter, resting her palms before pushing up. Nick's hand came down on her hip, cupping the side of her thigh as he stopped her short.

"Wait." His eyes pinched at the edges. "Let me make sure I didn't miss anything."

Evie hesitated as Nick lingered for a breath. Then he let her hip go, seemingly satisfied that she wasn't going anywhere. She watched him get down on one knee, running his hands over the linoleum floor, palms skimming to make sure no shards remained.

When he was assured, he rose back up. All she could think about was getting herself back into her bedroom, shame coating her tongue at the fact that she'd — yet again — roused him from a night of sleep.

Nick's hand cupped her hip, helping to ease her off the counter. As Evie's feet hit the floor, she winced slightly at the sting, looking down at her toes bumping up against his boots. When she raised her head again, his face was tilted down, staring at her. In the dissipated light of the flashlight, all Evie could really see was the yellow reflection in his blue eyes and the way they flickered away for a moment, then quickly returned to hers.

His lips parted, head angling just so.

She couldn't breathe, chest to chest with him as her tongue darted out to wet her lips.

Then he was gone.

Nick pulled away abruptly, making a noise in the back of his throat that sounded like a half-apology. She could see the tense curve of his back leading into the tops of his boxers, muscles taut.

It took him grabbing his jacket for her to finally take a step forward and garble out, "Nick?"

He didn't look back at her as he threw the coat on and pulled the door open to the raging storm outside. Rain lashed against the side of the cabin, blowing sideways and wetting the front porch. She caught the edge of the door, the cold cutting through her thin shirt.

"Where are you going?"

She was afraid her words would get carried away in the wind, but she knew he heard her. He pulled his jacket closer, his voice gruff.

"I can't be inside right now. Shut the door, Evie. Go back to bed."

Frigid air caused goosebumps to pebble on her exposed thighs. "But, why?"

Nick whirled on her and for half a second she considered stepping back, but then the fire in his eyes died in an instant.

"You're too damn much, that's why." All the air left her lungs. He barreled forward, standing two feet away from her on the porch with his jacket collar flipped up. "I can't fucking do this. You're too much. You're too... too fucking *soft*. I can't get you out of my mind and I don't even think I want to half the damn time, and that's not why you're here and when you're standing in front of me. I can't get it through my thick fucking skull that you're off limits."

Evie clutched the doorframe, needing something solid to keep her upright as his chest heaved. She opened her mouth, desperate for something to say.

The only thing that spilled out was, "I'm sorry."

Nick laughed, a pained, hollow sound. "No, *I'm* sorry, Evie. You've got no reason to be sorry. You don't have any reason to apologize to me or for my actions. They're mine alone and I just need to *think* for a second and I can't think when you're right *here*."

Evie didn't know if she should retreat inside like he'd asked or if she should reach for him. Her body moved without her mind, freezing the soles of her feet on the porch, but she didn't care as she grabbed Nick's hand, hanging limply at his side.

Her decision was made.

Evie wrapped her fingers around his, before turning and guiding him back inside. The lock clicked as she took him in. Rain speckled his jacket. She couldn't fathom making him take it off when they were so close again.

"I've never seen you this rattled." She cleared her throat, crossing her arms over her chest. His fingers twitched before he carded a hand through his hair.

Nick shrugged his jacket off and it took everything in her to keep her eyes on his face.

"Why the hell were you even out here?"

"I was getting water." Evie stood in front of the door, unmoving, even when he stepped closer and hung his jacket back up. "The storm woke me up, then the lightning and thunder startled me and that's when I dropped the glass."

He shook his head, shoulders shaking with another tired laugh. "The storm will pass."

Haunted blue eyes snared hers and for a heartbeat she was torn between slapping him and grabbing him to force him to listen to reason.

"And this?" she breathed out. "What's happening between us? Will that pass?"

His face twisted, mouth pressing into a firm line. "That'll pass too."

Evie swallowed back every bile-tainted anxious thought on

her tongue and instead whispered, "I don't want it to pass, Nick."

"Evie —" Her name hung in the air for barely a second before she snapped.

"What did you mean the other day? In the bar?" She took a step forward, hands balled into fists so he couldn't see the way she was trembling. "That a murderer can't deter you?"

He laughed again, another joyless thing instead of one with his hand on his chest and his head tipped back. "Isn't it obvious?" He took a step forward, meeting her halfway. "*Evie.*" Nick's voice lowered, turning pleading.

Don't push me away, a voice screamed as his fingers touched her cheek. Her eyes fluttered, waiting to hear the end of his sentence, waiting to *know*.

"I've fallen for you."

His face was stripped bare, the line gone between his brows.

"Oh."

Nick's lips twitched, the barest hint of real humor at her reaction. "Yeah, *oh*." He took another step and they were toe-to-toe again, chest brushing chest as his hand guided her head to tilt, forcing them to breathe the same air.

Then he dropped his chin and kissed her.

CHAPTER TWENTY-ONE

EVIE LIFTED HER ARMS TO WRAP THEM AROUND Nick's neck, fingers digging into his still-damp hair as he pulled her flush against his chest. His lips slanted against hers as she gasped, desperate to breathe air into her lungs but not willing to part yet.

His beard scratched her jaw as his lips fell to kiss the spot better, making their way across her skin as his hands grasped her hips. His palms were large against her thighs, coaxing her forward as she panted. If he didn't give her a moment, her heart was going to flutter out of her chest and get swept away by the storm.

Nick turned his head to the other side and mirrored the kisses as light fingertip brushes traveled up her leg. A half-strangled moan rose in the back of her throat as the rough pads of his fingers dug into the soft skin of her inner thighs.

She felt him smile as he held her tighter. "We don't have to —"

Evie tightened her grip on the hair at the nape of his neck.

"Nick." Her voice didn't sound like her own for a moment, hoarse and needy. "Shut up."

In the dim light of the cabin, his smile lines creased. Nick nodded before he drew her back to him. The second kiss was softer, their open mouths slanting as he walked backwards. She could barely keep up as he kicked off his boots, pulling her around the kitchen table.

Evie gripped the back of a chair, steadying herself as she tilted her head up and kissed his throat. Her heart rose to rest on her tongue. They were both nearly naked and his hands were so *warm* under her shirt.

"Look at me, sweetheart."

Her eyes met his. Nick's right hand shifted, lifting from her hip to touch her jaw, cupping her face as his thumb ghosted over her swollen lips.

"There you are." His voice was soft. "You tell me if this gets too much, okay?"

She didn't know it was possible to keep breathing with her heart in shards. Her chest felt tight as his thumb moved from stroking her lips to running over her jaw. It was her turn to nod.

Nick's eyes ran over her face before he smiled again. "Let go of the chair, Evelyn."

She looked at her hand white-knuckling the back of the wooden chair and let out a shaky laugh, loosening her grip. He grabbed her hand, fingers intertwining as he guided them toward the hallway.

It was darker back here, the sound of the heavy rain dim as it beat down. In the muffled darkness, Evie's heart rate kicked, stepping closer, squeezing his hand, and pulling him to a stop.

With a hand on his shoulder, she leaned up on her toes to kiss him. Evie pressed her palms against his bare chest, pushing him back until he hit the wall. His hands dropped to her ass, rucking up her t-shirt to ghost his fingers over her underwear.

Nick's moan was breathless against her lips. *"Fuck."*

She couldn't help but smirk.

In seconds, one of his hands rose and gripped the back of her neck. Evie gasped as she found herself pinned to the wall. Nick's mouth slanted, his tongue sliding past her lips while his other hand gripped the inside of her thigh.

He had her leg hitched in an instant. His hips aligned with hers and as she felt him through his boxers, her mind fogged. Her hips rolled forward against him, rubbing against his bulge with a soft whine.

It was her turn to struggle as she clawed at his shoulders for purchase. *"Nick.* Fuck, I —"

His hand on the back of her neck kept her stable as he pulled back, barely enough to give them breathing room.

"Is it okay if I touch you, Evie?" He spread her thighs wider, allowing him the room to rub against the seam of her underwear. "Is it okay if I make you scream?" His pupils were blown out as his gaze flickered down to watch them grind against each other. "I'm going to make you feel so fucking good while I do it, honey."

All she could do was nod as he cupped her through her underwear. Evie's head dropped back, fully supported by his hand as she forgot to breathe for a moment. His fingers slid over the fabric, circling before moving to her panty line, stroking her sensitive skin.

In a small, sharp motion, he had her exposed.

With her underwear pulled to the side, Nick's hand was free to roam. Evie didn't know if she wanted to fall back against the wall for support, or press herself into his touch as his fingers teased gently, sliding up and down.

She inhaled as his grip on her neck tightened. Her eyes fluttered, meeting his gaze in the dark, breathing out hard as he grazed her clit, muttering a litany of curses mixed with praise under his breath.

Her nails dug into his upper arms as his finger stroked her clit once, then twice, setting a rhythm. She bit down on her tongue, whining as Nick kissed her throat.

"I've been thinking about teasing this little clit for weeks, rubbing it, licking it, *sucking* it nice and good." Goosebumps erupted across her arms as he mirrored his words with his finger, toying with her. Another finger joined his index, rolling her clit between them.

Evie came off the wall in an arch. "*Nick*," she keened his name, the torturously slow movements making her heart race. "God, please, I..." She sobbed, no idea where the sentence was ending. She just knew he needed to do *something*.

"I know, sweetheart." His whisper was against her throat as he pulled his hand back, just holding her for a heartbeat. "I know you've wondered if I'm good with my hands and I'm more than ready to show off for you. Come on, honey."

She nodded, half-aware that her legs were moving as he pulled her toward his bedroom. She'd follow him anywhere as long as he didn't stop touching her.

Moonlight filtered in through two windows, letting her eyes adjust. She'd only caught glimpses of his room, and even those small slivers felt like a gross invasion of privacy. His bed was larger than hers, partially under a window on the back wall. The sheets were tousled and Evie was vaguely aware that she was the reason he leapt out of bed as he bent down to kiss her shoulder.

"Still okay?" His warmth surrounded her, expression as soft as his voice.

There was something so sweet about the way he kept checking in. Continually keeping her on edge, but also allowing space. She knew in her heart it was quick — but at the same time, it felt like everything must have been leading here from the start.

"I want this." She turned, pushing his hair back from his face. Her hand slid over his beard, feeling the scruff against her palm as she smiled. "I've *really* wanted this, Nick."

His face lit up, as he leaned into her touch, kissing her palm. Evie giggled as he grabbed her hip, bracing herself for him to push her down to the bed, but instead Nick scooped her up. She squealed, grabbing his bare shoulders as she wrapped her legs around his torso and tipped her head back, laughing as he plunged them both onto the bed.

As her back hit the sheets, Nick's face dipped down, kissing the column of her neck. Evie ran her fingers through his hair, untangling it as his lips skimmed her shirt collar.

"I'm taking this off." The hands on her thighs pushed the shirt up slowly. Evie dropped against the bed, staring as he inched the t-shirt over her stomach, exposing skin. Coaxing her arms up, he tugged the shirt off and sucked in a breath, staring down at her.

For the first time in her life, she didn't feel like she needed to hide her body, to shield him from seeing the way her chest flattened and hips spread. She'd always been so painfully average in build, not too small, but not curvy or particularly thick either.

Nick's eyes burned as he chucked her shirt to the floor and brought a hand to her stomach, running it down to hook a finger in the waistband of her underwear.

"I'm taking these too, Evie."

She bit her lip. "What about you?"

"I can wait." His voice was gruff as he bent over her, focused on her thighs as he rolled her underwear down. "I like waiting." One hand skimmed over her left calf, catching the fabric as he turned his attention to the other side. When they were gone, he held her by the knees, breathing hard.

His nostrils flared as he sank lower on the bed. "Sweetheart," Nick hummed and pressed a kiss to the little swell of her stomach. "I need to taste this pussy."

A low moan escaped as he spread her thighs, kissing the inner skin of each one before his head moved just a hair, tongue darting out to lick a stripe over her arousal. Her hips jerked toward him as he chuckled. "*Fuck*, you even taste sweet."

She slid a hand into his long hair, scratching his scalp as she groaned his name. His tongue was so warm and wet that Evie wanted to close her eyes and sink into the bed, but the sight of his broad shoulders pushing her legs apart as he buried his head in her pussy made her roll her hips up to meet his every touch.

Nick echoed her noises, a man possessed as he forced her legs wider.

Evie arched off the bed as his thumb found her clit. The sparks that shot through her body made her thighs tremble. She swore she could feel Nick smirk, but her eyes shut tight as her body succumbed to the movement of his fingers and tongue. The pressure was already starting to build as she squirmed, hiccuping out nonsensical sounds.

She wasn't used to this — to anyone putting her pleasure first.

The first few times Evie slept around in college were lackluster at best. Men or women — it didn't matter. The fumbled hook-ups of her past were more intent on getting themselves off than her. She knew it took her time to warm, to sink into the pleasure, and she'd accepted that.

Then she moved back to Hawthorne and was faced with the same pool of prospects she'd known and left behind from high school. No one was worth fooling around with, especially once she realized it would be the talk of the town. Fielding *"when are you getting married?"* questions with someone she just wanted to casually sleep with sounded like a fate worse than death — *especially* if they never made her come.

His lips wrapped around her clit and Evie squeaked as his thick finger pushed inside her, stretching in a way that made her thighs shake. "Oh — *fuck*."

"That's it, sweetheart, I want to hear you scream."

Evie saw stars as he curled his finger, thrusting it in tandem with his tongue on her clit. Clinging to him and the bed, she focused on the rush of building pleasure, and the way her heart felt like it was going to beat right out of her chest.

Nick growled, the sound making her toes curl as he let a second finger join the first. "This okay, sweetheart?" His head shifted far enough back that he could speak as she nodded, not caring as long as he kept going.

Evie's hips arched as she spasmed around the thickness of two fingers, feeling dizzy until he dropped her thigh and focused his tongue's attention on her clit.

"Fuck, I — oh my *god*." Evie writhed against the bed, tugging at his hair at the root as she felt his beard scratch her thighs. Every touch sent sparks through her as her core tightened, softly sobbing out, "Please don't stop. I — I might actually —"

"Oh you will." Nick didn't let up, his voice hoarse as he dove back between her thighs. "And you'll say my name when you do, Evie." His fingers curled, rubbing a spot she'd never reached herself, making her jaw drop open in shock as Nick looked up at her, hair a wreck and a giant grin on his face. "Scream my name as I make you come, honey. Give me that cum all over my beard as a reward for doing a good job."

The orgasm hit her like a fist to the chest, knocking the wind out of her.

His name left her throat in a rush, repeating it as she rode the high. She could hear the way his fingers slid into her, working her through the orgasm. The only thing that lessened slightly was his pressure on her clit as she twitched, her chest rising and falling rapidly until he finally slid his fingers out of her.

Her eyes were shut tight, blocking out everything as she felt Nick softly press a kiss to the inside of each thigh, beard scratching her oversensitive skin. The bed shifted as he moved and Evie peeled her eyes open in time to see his head dip, kissing just above her belly button. Nick glanced up, a smile on his lips. His hand cupped her hip, watching her chest rise and fall as her breathing evened out.

"Do you need a minute?"

Evie shook her head, the air leaving her lungs as Nick brought his hands down on either side of her head, bracing himself above her. His beard was slightly damp as he kissed her slowly, tasting herself as his body covered hers. She never wanted to kiss anyone except for Nick Barber.

Raising her limp arms, she pulled him closer, his body settling. With his chest against hers, she could hook a leg around him, rolling her hips against his boxers. She was still sensitive and the movement made them both moan as Nick deepened the kiss.

She nipped at his lower lip as her hand found his boxers. Evie shoved them down his thighs, relishing in the thick, muscled skin it exposed. Her fingers explored, cupping his ass and laughing as he grunted against her lips.

"Are you feeling me up?"

"I absolutely am." Evie squeezed his ass, her hands full. He burst into laughter, pressing his head against her throat as the rumble of his chest made her body shake under his, her laughter joining his.

She let him go after a moment, smiling as she tucked her

head into his shoulder and kissed the muscle there. With his arms on either side of her head, she'd never felt safer or more at home. As her lips grazed his throat, his laughter faded.

Nick turned his head, capturing her lips again as the length of him settled against her leg. Evie sucked in a breath, pulling back to glance between them, choking a little when she saw the sheer size of him.

He shifted to support himself with one hand over her head, cupping her jaw and stroking the side of her face with his thumb. "We don't have to do anything more tonight." His eyes locked on hers, forcing her to stay focused on him. "But I promise I'll go slow, sweetheart. All I want is to make you feel good."

Evie shivered, nodding against his hand. "I trust you."

"That's not something I take lightly." His eyes softened, the creases at the edges smoothing out as he leaned down and kissed her slowly. She could hear her heart in her ears, echoing thumps as the hand that was on her face slowly pulled away. Nick ran it down her neck and chest, lightly teasing her nipples. It continued traveling, spreading her open just to touch her clit and hum when she pushed against his fingers. One finger circled her opening and Evie whined as he pulled it back again.

Nick shifted back, breathing hard. "Do you want me to find a condom, honey? I... Fuck, I'm not sure I have one."

"Implant." Evie gasped the word, cupping the back of his head and pulling him into a harsh kiss. Her skin already felt like it was on fire again. Every touch made her head spin, her heart race, and any hesitations disappear. "*Nick*, I need you."

With their chests pressed together, Nick wrapped a hand around himself. His breathing sped up for a second as his hand jerked, breathing out harshly as he nodded to himself and then kissed her jaw slowly, rolling his hips forward until he was guiding his cock against her, rubbing her clit slowly with the tip.

As he pushed down, Evie rolled her hips up, gasping in soft breaths as he teased her entrance. He was big — and she was glad he'd prepped her with his fingers — but it was a burn that felt right as he sank into her slowly.

Inch by inch, he thrust in. They breathed almost in sync, foreheads together as Evie reached out, gripping his shoulders while biting her tongue.

Nick stopped, grunting softly. "You feel better than I imagined — *Christ*."

She took a second to adjust, her eyes rolling back into her head as Nick punched his hips forward one more time, bottoming out. She was so *fucking* full, surrounded by him.

His lips touched the shell of her ear, whispering gently, "Breathe, honey."

Evie sucked in a breath at the command, her nails digging into his shoulders. Their kiss was messy as Nick held onto her, pulling back before thrusting again. Evie arched, her back leaving the sheets as she made an inhuman sound. He was pulling them from her body effortlessly as she wrapped her other leg around his hips.

Nick held her in place, pushing her into the bed as he grunted, "Hold onto me, sweetheart. Just like that. *Fuck* —" He bit down on her lower lip and she shivered, goosebumps scattering across her skin as she met his slow, shallow thrusts.

She didn't care what else happened right now. The only thing she wanted was to feel Nick on every inch of her body. Their skin stuck together, the heat of him making her light-headed and driving her wild.

She moaned, not caring how it sounded as his teeth toyed with her lower lip, biting it and then sucking it into his mouth as his hips sped up.

Nick grabbed her chin, whispering, "Look at me, sweetheart."

Evie's eyes fluttered open, their breath mingling as he pulled out before slamming back into her. The movement made the bed frame shake as her mouth dropped open, screaming in pleasure.

Sex had never felt like she was drowning in the other person, but with Nick she was sinking deeper with each thrust, the stretch making her thighs shake, her muscles tensing already.

With one hand on her chin and the other on her hip, Nick guided her to match his rhythm, his eyes dark. "That's it — *fuck* — you feel me? You feel every inch of me? I never want you to forget how I feel inside you."

Evie's mind whirled, rambling, "Nick — I'm close, I can't —"

"You can. You will." He gripped her face, distracting her with a kiss so passionate her mind went blank. "Let go for me, Evie. I've got you, sweetheart. Let yourself feel good."

With another punch of his hips, Evie felt him bottom out again and dropped her head back, scrambling to hold onto something. One hand landed on his shoulder, the other grabbing his right hip and digging her nails into the side of his ass as her core tightened.

"Touch me, Nick. *Please*, touch me."

He dropped his hand from her face, palm flattening as he found her clit with two fingers, rolling and rubbing it at the same speed as his hips.

Evie let go.

Her body curled into his, her orgasm wracking her as she screamed with the release.

Nick drove into her, gasping, "Look at you, taking me so fucking well." The words sent a shiver down her spine as his fingers kept moving over her clit, prolonging her orgasm as he grunted. "I feel you coming — *fucking* tight like a little vise. Never gonna let me go, honey? You're just gonna keep me in this little pussy forever?"

Aftershocks sparked over her skin as Nick's thrusts became disjoined. With one more, he jolted, groaning her name as he came deep inside her.

Nick dropped, his arm shaking by her head as he tried to keep his full weight off her. As he kissed her breathlessly, she released her nails from his hip. It was like being covered with three weighted blankets, his large body engulfing hers.

"Don't want to crush you," he groaned as he pulled back, slipping from her. She followed him, unable to bear him leaving, even as he kissed her jaw and whispered, "Hold on, sweetheart, just one second. Be good for me and lie there."

Nick pushed up from the bed and Evie blinked as he stumbled out of the bedroom. The floorboards creaked underfoot before he came back with a washcloth, kneeling on the bed and gently running it between her thighs. Her throat tightened as he dropped it into his laundry basket and returned to her, wrapping her in his arms, her head coming to rest on his chest.

She turned her cheek, gazing up at him. Evie ran her hand over his pecs, moving her fingers up to tangle them in his beard. He was the most handsome man she'd ever seen — the kind of man that made heads turn when he entered a room.

And here she was, in his arms.

"What're you doing?" His voice was rough as he trailed his fingers over her bare shoulder.

Evie smiled. "I was just thinking about how handsome you are." Even in the darkness, she could see the way his cheeks darkened at the compliment. She wanted to be the only one who could fluster him that much. "Thank you."

Nick's hand cupped the back of her head. "You're the one who just called me handsome, shouldn't I be thanking you?"

"I'm not thanking you for that." It was easier to whisper the words with her eyes closed and her warm cheek against his chest. "I... I needed that." Her mind spun for a second, wondering how much was too much to say.

His fingers massaged the sweat-sticky skin at the nape of her neck. With a deep inhale, Nick's chest rose with her head on it, before he let out a deep, contented sigh. "Evie, I want you here and using me for whatever you need until I have nothing left to give. You hear me? It doesn't matter — just as long as you stay."

She laughed, burying her face in his chest. It was her turn to inhale, surrounded by the thick, musky smell of him. It was a mixture of his familiar shampoo and the smell of the pine trees outside. And — if she focused hard enough — she swore she could smell a hint of the hot chocolate they'd shared.

CHAPTER TWENTY-TWO

SOFT FINGERS STROKED THE HAIR AT THE CROWN OF Evie's head, applying gentle pressure to her scalp before dragging down to her shoulders, brushing her bare skin. She didn't dare move her head, or change her breathing pattern as he touched the wisps of new growth at the nape of her neck.

"Good morning," his voice rumbled.

She squinted at the hazy morning light filtering in through the open curtains, but found Nick smiling when she focused on him. The creases around his eyes deepened as he rubbed his beard, tilting his chin down and cupping her face.

Flashbacks peppered her mind as Evie shifted slightly, her legs tangled with his, his thick quilt tucked around her shoulders tightly like he'd covered her in the middle of the night.

With the way he was looking at her — she was certain he had.

"Hi." She gave him a sheepish smile, biting her lip.

The cabin was silent and the bed was warm and Evie felt *happy* as Nick cradled her head. His eyes ran over her features before he leaned in and murmured, "Merry Christmas," against her lips.

Her eyes widened as she leaned into the kiss. "Oh my god. It *is* Christmas!" Evie squealed, then sat up with a jolt only to throw her arms around him.

Nick's face lit up, laughing as he pulled her close. "Yeah, honey, it's Christmas."

Kissing him was like lighting the fireplace in the living room. Warmth flooded her body — filling her up with a bubbly kind of joy as he wrapped his other arm around her and tugged her halfway on top of his chest. In his arms she felt invincible.

"Let me run you a bath." Nick pecked her lips once, then twice. He peppered kisses all over her face, smiling as he did it. "I'll make it nice and hot, then maybe join you."

She *was* sore, just enough to make her body feel like she'd *done* something last night. The something being Nick, who was still kissing her temple and muttering sweet nothings against her forehead.

Ringing echoed down the hall, making them both freeze.

Evie's heart lurched — Andy's emergency cell — but before she could move, Nick was up in a flash. He didn't bother to find clothes to cover himself up, leaving Evie to stare in wide-eyed wonder as she got to look at his naked body for less than half a second before he darted down the hall.

His ass really was perky.

Bending over the side of the bed, Evie scanned the floor for her shirt from the night before. It was in a pile near the end of the bed and she crawled out from under the covers, tugging it over her head as she heard Nick speak.

"Yeah, Andy, she's right here." He grinned, making no move to hide the way his eyes lingered on her, licking his lips. "She'll love this. Thank you for calling."

Kneeling on the bed, Evie watched with a frown as Nick held the phone out to her.

"Andy?"

"Hey, Evie." She could hear the smile in Andy's voice. "Merry Christmas."

She laughed, glancing up at Nick as his hand brushed her hair back. The gesture was so soft it made her pause before she cleared her throat. "Merry Christmas to you too, surely I'm not important enough for you to call just to say that?"

Andy laughed. "No, I'm just the middle man. You're about to be patched through to your parents."

"What?" The air left her lungs as she nearly dropped the phone, fumbling to keep hold of it. Andy didn't say anything else and Evie opened her mouth to ask him if he was being serious when she heard the line connect.

A quiet voice on the other end whispered, "Evelyn?"

"*Mom?*" Evie's voice broke, the single word getting caught in her throat as tears welled at the first sound of her mother's voice in over a month. All this time she'd spent trying not to linger on the fear that kept her up at night — the fear for not only her own life, but fear for her parents who were completely unaware of the messiness of the situation their daughter had gotten herself into.

"Oh, Evie." Her mother's voice cracked and Evie choked back snot. "Your dad's right here, we're both right here. It's so good to hear your voice."

Nick's hand smoothed over Evie's shoulder, suddenly making her aware of his presence. He bent down and kissed her head, rubbing her back gently. Evie watched him step away to grab clothes from his dresser, sniffling back tears the entire time. He left the room, allowing her privacy as she crawled back to the head of the bed and pulled a pillow into her lap.

Evie rubbed her throat, finally calming down after a moment of blubbering.

"Are you okay?" Her father's voice came from the other line, sounding thick, but stable.

"Yeah." Evie sucked in a ragged breath, looking around Nick's room in the daylight. "Yeah, I'm —" She stopped herself before giving out anything identifying. "Andy... Did he say anything to you all?"

"He said he sent you somewhere safe," her mother supplied. "That's all we've known, and we knew we couldn't ask because what if someone found you? But we've been so worried. He's told us every time he's spoken to you but he said he had to call off hours most of the time, that everything is slow and his boss doesn't like when he calls us — oh, sweet-heart — it's different to *hear* you. We're so glad he could arrange this and that you're okay."

Evie scrubbed at the tears on her cheeks. "I promise I'm okay. I've been..." She tried to think of what she could say, wondering how long they had, and what she could divulge when it'd only been a month of her life that had slipped away in the cabin.

There was a painting of the Wells Creek town square on the far wall of Nick's room that her eyes lingered on. The artist had drawn it in watercolor, giving it the same dreamy quality that all vacation rental art had.

They were meant for a moment in time — not for life.

"Safe." She landed on the word. "I've been safe. I'm with someone Andy trusts and I trust him too."

She tried not to think of the pit in her stomach from the library, listening to the drizzling rain on the side of the cabin walls. Somehow it didn't surprise her that Washington couldn't spit out a few snowflakes to continue the magic from the night before — it felt baleful, like everything was one note off from the lyrics of a song.

Their questions were all variants of the same thing; more confirmations that she was okay, that she had what she needed — reminders that they missed her.

Evie's eyes rose to see Nick emerge from the bathroom, a pair of gray sweatpants on his hips. He was barefoot and shirtless as he walked back into his room, towel around his neck to catch the drips from his damp hair.

She expected him to grab a shirt and leave again, but he strode straight up to the side of the bed and leaned down on one knee, making the mattress sink as the smell of the water and the shower gel assaulted her senses. She didn't hear a word on the other side of the phone as he leaned in and kissed her temple, before moving to peck her cheek.

"Evie?"

Her mother's voice startled her. Nick was close enough that she knew he could hear it too.

"Yeah?"

"Is the man there? The one that Andy sent you to stay with?"

Evie's mouth was dry as she stared at Nick's face. "Yeah, he's right here."

Understatement of the century.

"Can we thank him? Do you think that would be okay?"

Nick sat down next to her, leaning back against the headboard as he took the phone. "Hello Mister and Missus Morgen."

Warmth radiated off his clean skin, and a wave of exhaustion hit her, a lethal combination of last night and the emotions catching up. She dropped her head to his shoulder, lying on him and pressing her nose into his throat. He smelled so nice, so *familiar*, it made her chest ache.

As he spoke to her parents, he stroked her hair. The conversation was barely five sentences, Nick assuring her parents that he would protect her and them thanking him profusely.

Nick passed the phone back to her and Evie held it to her ear, leaving her head on Nick's shoulder as she struggled with what to say.

"Merry Christmas." She settled on the well wishes, feeling a hollow ache in her chest as she said them. "I love you."

"We love you too." It was her father who spoke this time and Evie could hear sniffling in the background. "We'll see you soon."

Evie didn't have the heart to correct him before they hung up.

The phone was hot on her ear for a second too long before she dropped it in her lap as she leaned on Nick. She didn't just need his physical support — she needed the way he emotionally held her together. She felt thin, like the brittle clay vases the children made in art class that always shattered in the kiln.

His breath was slow and steady and Evie let her eyes slide shut as she whispered, "I don't know if that helped or made it worse."

She found herself pulled even closer, sinking into the full embrace of his arms. A few tears slipped out unbidden from her clenched eyes, aching as she clung to him.

"Come on." One of his hands touched her hair again and Evie pulled back enough to look up as he spoke. "Let's go into the living room and I'll make us Christmas brunch with those eggs that I think expired yesterday."

Her lips twitched.

Nick cocked an eyebrow. "I know I'm a romantic, you don't have to tell me."

Evie laughed softly, pausing as she reached up to touch his beard, cupping his face only to frown. "Are we... Are we okay?"

His hands splayed across her back. "Let me ask you — do you regret last night?"

She shook her head gently, running her thumb over his damp beard. "No, I'm just worried *you* do."

His eyes widened and Nick stared down at her with the comical look of a man who had never heard anything so stupid in his entire life. He opened his mouth, then closed it, only to open it again. "You think *I* regret last night? When I could have happily kept you in this damn bed for a solid twenty-four hours until you were *begging* to be left alone just for some sleep?"

Evie felt heat creep up her neck and reach her cheeks. She bit her tongue. "Well... when you put it *that* way."

He grunted, pulling her against his chest and then dipping his head to capture her lips with his own. The kiss was searing, spreading the heat on her cheeks throughout her entire body as she clung to him, half draped across his lap, the soft and well-worn fabric of his sweats brushing against her thighs as the shirt hiked up on her hips. Nick's hand slid down until he was cupping the back of her ass, muttering against her lips, "Don't question me."

"Yes, sir." Evie grinned against his lips, feeling the light bloom in her chest again at the feeling of him surrounding her.

The groan that left his throat made her shiver.

"Say it again."

Maybe a part of her knew all along that the teasing nick-name did it for him — but it made her giddy all the same to slide her fingers into his beard, tugging on it as she whispered, "Yes —" Evie looked up at him from under her lashes, power and desire thrumming in her stomach. "*Sir.*"

The words that rumbled out of Nick's throat were half-garbled as he pulled her into another passionate kiss, but she was pretty sure she heard him mutter "*what a woman.*" She giggled as she sank into his arms. He seemed satisfied to just hold her in his lap, brushing his lips over every inch of skin he could reach.

With his head buried in her throat, Nick whispered, "I need to give you your Christmas present. I need to feed you. Then I need to fuck you. Maybe not in that order."

In response, Evie's stomach grumbled.

He smiled, amending his list. "Food first."

She nodded, her eyes running over his features. His light blue eyes lit up the room, the gentle slope of his nose complimenting his strong jaw and all his *hair*. A part of her couldn't believe that it had been over thirty days here — but the other part was painfully aware it had been only a few short weeks.

Nick shifted to the edge of the bed with her in his lap. Before she could chase her spiraling thoughts, he was standing up with her legs wrapped around his waist.

She laughed, tilting her head back as she held onto his shoulders. "I have *legs*, Nick."

"Not when I'm around." He grinned, his eyes bright as one hand groped her bare ass. "Especially not when I know you're not wearing any underwear."

Evie buried her head in his shoulder, laughing as he felt her up and carried her out of the bedroom, down the hall, and plopped her down onto the couch. She landed with a soft bounce, turning her head to watch him as he walked into the kitchen and jerked open the fridge.

"So, I didn't *plan* much for today — I mean my half-ass tree should have been proof enough of that." Nick was talking into the fridge as he rummaged around. "But I'm happy to say the eggs actually expire tomorrow and we definitely have the ingredients for a full breakfast with some pancakes if you'd like it. Then we can have that hot bath that I promised."

She rested her arm across the back of the couch, perching

her chin on it with a smile. "That sounds good. What can I do to help?"

"Find us some music." He emerged from the fridge with a carton of eggs, milk, butter, and a pack of bacon. "Make it Christmas-y so we can get into the spirit of the season." Nick dropped the ingredients onto the counter as he hunted for a bowl for the pancake mix.

The CD case was full of random albums, but Evie found an Elvis CD that managed to have a few of his Christmas classics interspersed with other famous songs. Slotting it into the speakers, she turned the knob until the music drifted out, filling the air. She glanced up in time to catch Nick smiling at her and turned away, biting her lip and going to add another piece of wood to the fireplace.

As the smells of breakfast filtered out of the kitchen, Evie found herself leaning on the other side of the counter from Nick, watching as he spooned pancake batter into a pan. The silver-dollar shaped pancakes all landed on a plate, closely followed by strips of bacon and scrambled eggs. Her stomach grumbled again as she grabbed the coffee pot and fixed two mugs, carrying them over to the table.

Nick swept in behind her, arranging the plates around two chairs before he dipped down and kissed her on the cheek. "Sit down before the food gets cold."

Evie took the seat she always did, but squeaked when Nick reached under her and dragged the seat and her in it, until they were side-by-side. With only the music and the sound of their utensils, she felt the rest of the anxiety uncoil in her stomach, uneasiness settling over her shoulders. Unexpected guilt ate at her, that she hadn't focused enough on her parents, or worried as much as they'd clearly worried about her.

Nick added another pancake to her plate. "Are you okay?"

She cut the small pancake in half, wiping it through some

honey on her plate before sighing. "I just feel on edge. I feel like
I'm waiting for the other shoe to drop."

He frowned, setting his fork down. "Because of?"

Evie hesitated, then sat her own fork down. "In the library
— the other day — I swear I wasn't alone. I even asked Stephen
and he said it was just the two of us. But while he was in the
back..." She bit the inside of her cheek, trailing off. "I feel crazy,
Nick. I feel... untethered."

He covered her hand with his own. "I'm right here. I'm not
going to let anything or *anyone* hurt you. In your head or
otherwise — next time you feel that way, you tell me."

Evie frowned, snippets of the day at the grocery store flickered through her mind. She'd probably need therapy after all of
this, something she wasn't a stranger to after her brother died,
but all the same, she hated feeling out of control. The cabin
wasn't a prison, but there was a weight on her chest suggesting
otherwise.

"Evie."

"Yes, next time I'll tell you."

He nodded, brushing her hair off her forehead before he
leaned in and kissed it. "Do you want your present?"

"Only if I can give you yours."

It didn't take them long to clear the table, the scraps going
into the bucket that Nick tossed outside each evening, then the
pans being left in the sink for later. Evie would probably end
up cleaning them tonight, just as a distraction from the holiday
itself.

Returning to her room felt strange. Tugging on a pair of
leggings and a sweater, she snatched Nick's gift she'd been
working on for a week from her nightstand drawer.

As she stood next to her bed, she paused, realizing that even
if barely any time had passed, this place had rooted itself

enough that she was associating it as hers. These were her quilts, her clothes in the dresser, and her socks on the floor.

She found that didn't bother her as much as she thought it would.

When she stepped back into the living room, she found Nick standing near the speaker. "Do you want your gift first?"

"Mine to you is unwrapped." She held it tightly behind her back, feeling her cheeks flush as she approached him. "Let me just give it to you first. It's not —"

"Don't finish that sentence." He shot her a look and then shuffled something behind his back, holding out a hand only to wiggle his fingers. "Give it."

Evie laughed and pulled the copy of *The Barbarian Highlander's Wife's Sister* out from behind her back, placing it in his hand. Nick stared down at it in confusion before she stepped closer and flipped open the first few pages, showing him the various notes she'd left for him in the margins. She'd spent days underlining and highlighting scenes, adding her own commentary as she reread the silly book — knowing it was her only option, but hoping it would make him smile all the same.

Nick's face broke into a grin as he sat something out of view behind the stereo and then fanned through the pages.

"I'm sorry I couldn't do more —"

"It's perfect." He grabbed her by the chin, pulling her into a searing kiss as he muttered against her lips, "I love it. I'm about to flip to page twenty-seven and see what you wrote about *that* scene and then tonight, I'm going to do it to you." Evie giggled, clinging onto his arm as Nick continued, "And then we can move onto fifty-six — which I *hope* and *pray* you wrote something about that. Do you want me to sling a blanket around my shoulders like a kilt? Are you into that, honey?"

Evie's body shook with laughter as he kissed her jaw. "That's a definite yes, I think I have a plaid one somewhere."

He sat the book on top of the speakers, sliding something into Evie's free hand. When she looked down at it, her heart rose into the back of her throat.

The untreated wooden frame looked handmade, with a thin backing. When she flipped it over in her hand, she felt her throat close, staring down at a photo of herself in Nick's arms. The jukebox at Adam's was partially visible in the background and the photo was clearly taken at a distance, zoomed in, but it was the pair of them dancing. Nick had a huge smile on his face, his hands forced onto her waist by Evie as a grin split her face, their eyes only for each other.

"Hope took it. Chuck had the frame. I can't take all the credit." Nick's voice was soft, raw emotion undercutting his words as he pushed her hair off her neck. "If nothing else, it's a reminder you were here, in Wells Creek, and it wasn't all bad while you were."

"Nick." Evie's voice broke, before she leaned up and wrapped her arms around his neck, pressing their lips together.

As the music faded, Elvis' *Can't Help Falling in Love* filled the air. Nick took the frame from her and placed it on top of the book, wrapping his arms around her waist as he slowly started to sway them back and forth.

Evie's clay heart burst, shattering into pieces as she rested her forehead against his and closed her eyes, all too aware that the man in front of her had gone from being a stranger to her everything.

CHAPTER TWENTY-THREE

Wells Creek didn't have much going for it.

It was the same three roads, the same fifty people, and not much else. Especially during the off season — the weather was too temperamental for inexperienced tourist hikers, and anyone local seemed content to rot in an endless loop of nothingness.

Will Bryant longed for Los Angeles, and places *rarely* made him miss that shit hole.

But here he was, standing at the base of a hill and looking at the trees. Bryant tugged on the beanie he'd snatched from the hiking shop before it closed this afternoon with a resigned sigh.

Jonathan was mostly leaving him alone.

There'd been a terse phone call after killing the FBI agent, leaving Bryant to hunt for a drink in this shitty town only to end up at the lone bar — Adam's. Chuck Adams and Nick Barber went back to his short-lived FBI days. It didn't take Bryant long to nurse his drink, watch the pretty little Asian girl flit around the room to regulars, and catch a glare from her 'father' for doing it. Bryant couldn't catch a fucking break.

At least his recon amounted to something; Nick Barber's only friend in the town was a cool thirty-five minutes away — long enough for Bryant to get in, do his job, and get out.

He pushed a tree branch to the side, the weight of a gun on his hip. All he could think about was the way Evelyn's eyes had sought him out in the library. The female was such a little thing, nostrils flaring and neck twitching. The doe and the hunter.

She'd been in the grocery store one day and he'd watched through the windows as she'd flitted around. He hoped the poor bastard was getting some kind of compensation for tolerating her. She had a tote on her arm and was chattering a mile a fucking minute. The kind of conversation that had no end in sight.

Bryant could think of a thousand other ways to use her mouth.

As he stepped over a fallen tree, he smirked. There was a good chance he'd find the two of them in bed. What a good photo that would make for Murphy — both bodies riddled with bullets, covered in blood. He was a damn artist.

Will Bryant's first and only love was death.

It was finite, simple to understand, and never talked back. He'd lost count of all the missions he'd done, the lives he'd taken, and yet, every last one of them made him harder than fucking steel afterward. No better rush to take a life and still have his own.

The slope of the hill began to even out and with the reduced pressure on his thighs, Bryant's stride grew longer, able to eat up more of the distance between himself and the tiny cabin. The property records on this place had changed hands a thousand times, once being built as a retreat by a rich couple, then quickly turning into an ever-changing rental for hikers. But it was situated in a spot far away from the popular trails and to be honest, the forest around it was mediocre — no water features to draw out-of-towners to pick this place for their stay instead of more picturesque options.

The remoteness made it a perfect place for him though. They really couldn't have made their nest anywhere better.

His little sitting ducks must be readying themselves for bed. As Bryant approached the forest's edge, he could see the cabin in its clearing. It looked small, with the lights dim inside and a few puddles dotting the yard from the week's rain storms. He didn't see anyone cross the front windows, but the chimney was still putting off smoke and that was the only sign of life he needed.

There was a twig of a tree lying to the side of the cabin, like it had been chucked out the front door and then dragged off to the side. It was a pathetic thing and Bryant snorted at the sight of it. Christmas cheer hadn't even crossed his mind, too focused on preparing for this, though their deaths would make a great gift for Jonathan.

He wanted Nick Barber to watch as he killed Evelyn Morgen, but the smarter option was to shoot him first. He drew his gun, checking the cartridge. Bryant wasn't a stupid man. There was a reason he was the best at his job. There was a *reason* Jonathan called *him*.

With the silence of the forest at his back, he wondered for a moment if he should wait for them to sleep, but then his watch buzzed. The allotted ten minutes he'd given himself for the walk were over. The roads were remote, but he couldn't risk someone finding the stolen truck he'd abandoned.

With a heavy sigh, Bryant rolled his neck and approached the cabin.

Chapter Twenty-Four

"Are you coming to bed, or not?"

Evie looked down at the photo of herself and Nick dancing at Adam's — it had found a home on her nightstand, even though she'd barely been in her room the past few days. Nick was *very* persuasive in his reasonings why she should just move her things down the hall.

Rolling her eyes, she poked her head out of the door, seeing Nick doing the same.

"I'm just going to get a glass of water. Do you want one?"

"Nope." Nick grinned. "I want you to finish up all your routines so I can drag you to bed."

"*Nick.*" Evie laughed, adjusting the *KISS ME I'M A FED* shirt. All her clothes were in the laundry and she wished it wasn't that weird period after Christmas where all the stores were closed. She needed more clothes, though Nick was happy to share his.

The only issue was that he *loved* to take them off of her.

"You look great in that! I can't wait to kiss you!"

A stupid smile tugged on her lips as she walked down the

hallway. Give Nick Barber an inch and he loved to take a mile instead. She couldn't complain —

Evie stopped short at the entrance to the hall, turning her head to stare out the front windows. The forest was dark and peaceful, but she'd sworn she'd heard a soft *thud*. Her heart flipped, opening her mouth to call out to Nick.

Before she could get a word out, the cabin door shattered inward, shards of wood flying across the living room. Evie screamed as a man with dark brown hair and a wild smile stepped in.

"Hello Evelyn."

There was a gun in his hand, and he looked like every other man she'd seen walking around Wells Creek — loose jeans, button up over a plain shirt — but he *felt* different.

Evie stayed behind the kitchen table, raising her chin. "Who are you?"

He flashed his teeth. "Will Bryant, but you probably know my work." Bryant shifted then, waving his gun back and forth as he spoke. "A little job I did in Colorado comes to mind, Agent..." He paused, pursing his lips. "Berk?"

"Beck," Evie whispered, a chill crawling down her spine as the cool air from the outside flooded the once warm cabin. "You killed Agent Beck."

"I did. It was messy. He tried not to give you up." With a mocking frown, Bryant shook his head. "But it's my job to clean up Jonathan Murphy's biggest problems and..." He clicked his tongue. "You became a big problem — little old you."

Licking her lips, Evie felt the hairs on the back of her neck stand up at the sound of a door easing open in the hall behind her. Bryant's focus was on her — *for now* — but she knew if Nick was trying to gauge the danger, she was in his sightline.

Evie looked around for a weapon. The closest was Nick's

gun strapped to the kitchen cabinet, but she wasn't sure if she could get it out of the holster fast enough. She'd never shot a gun before and she suddenly felt very aware of how trapped she was. Bryant could raise his gun at any moment, even if he seemed content to just smile at her and toy around.

"Anyway." Bryant smiled. "Where's your boyfriend, Evelyn? Or do you prefer Evie? Honestly, I think you suit Evelyn, it's so old world. Really goes with that little cardigan outfit you wore to the library the other day."

Evie's eyes darted back to him.

Her gut had been right. There *was* someone else in the library with her and Stephen. She'd been stalked for *days*, she wasn't crazy —

Taking an abrupt step back, Evie watched as Bryant matched her movement, stepping forward in his heavy boots. Before either of them could make a move, the stereo between them blared to life, Elvis crooning at top volume.

Bryant flinched as Evie heard the door at the end of the hall behind her slam against the wall.

"Evie, get down!"

She dropped to the floor immediately, covering her head as Nick strode out of his room, gun in hand. He fired a shot, and, caught off guard, Bryant cursed loudly. Blood pooled at Bryant's side, slowly turning his shirt crimson.

"Go to your room, right now," Nick barked the orders and she scrambled back on her ass.

Bryant raised his gun and pulled the trigger.

Nick was suddenly on one knee next to her, the gun in his hand skittering across the floor. Evie gasped, reaching over to grab him on instinct. His leg bent at an odd angle as Nick held onto his calf, blood welling between his fingers, soaking his pajama pants in seconds. Bryant held his side with one hand, eyes murderous as Evie dropped Nick and plunged herself toward the fallen gun.

Scrambling, she reached forward, fingers sliding against the cool metal. *Point and shoot.* She could do that. It didn't matter what she hit —

Bryant's boot came down on her arm, pinning her in place as she let out a shriek at the pressure. Something cool pressed against her temple and Evie's heart stuttered.

"This was not how I wanted to do this. I had a fucking *plan* and you two ruined it."

From behind her, Nick snapped, "Don't shoot her. Shoot me first."

Bryant rolled his eyes and turned his head, looking at Nick on the floor. "I already shot you, Captain America."

"You did." Nick grimaced. "But this isn't my first time."

Bryant's focus wavered and Evie took her chance. She grabbed the barrel of the gun, shoving it hard to the side. Bryant pulled the trigger, firing it right next to her head. Ringing exploded in her ears, a stinging sensation lighting up her cheek as the bullet flew past her and embedded itself into one of the walls. She ignored it all as she tackled his legs.

The entire cabin teetered, righting itself in a snap as she slammed into Bryant, putting every ounce of force she could into throwing him to the ground. His knees buckled as he scrambled to keep a hand on his gun. She kicked her foot out, knocking it from his hand. Grabbing onto a chair to stay upright, Evie scrambled around the kitchen table, darting toward the kitchen.

Jerking open the cabinet door, she reached for Nick's other gun, pulling it clean from the holster. She raised it as Bryant rounded the corner, rage filling her body, squeezing the trigger.

It didn't budge.

Bryant laughed.

"Oh, Evelyn, the safety's on."

She threw the gun over the counter, hoping it landed near enough to Nick for him to grab it before whirling around and grabbing one of the kitchen knives from the block. Seeing red, Evie screamed — a sound so deep from her chest that she felt it rattle her bones. It was a noise she hadn't heard since that first week at the cabin, after shrieking at the trees.

In another second, she was lunging at Bryant again, startling the hell out of him as she brought the knife down, cutting his cheek and throwing her full weight against him. He fell back a step with a loud *oof* and she pulled the knife back, plunging it into his shoulder this time, feeling it bounce as it hit bone.

Bryant's scream echoed through the cabin.

"Move!" Nick shouted and she stumbled back in time to see him on his feet again, leaning heavily to the right. He didn't hesitate, pointing a gun at Bryant, shooting him in the stomach.

Bryant raised his gun, stumbling forward a step. Nick fired again, hitting Bryant again, causing his body to jerk, dropping down to his knees.

The gun slipped from Bryant's red-stained fingers. Blood dripped down Evie's own hand as she reached for the knife in Bryant's shoulder, jerking it free as he howled in pain. He looked up at her as his good arm searched the floor for the dropped firearm.

Evie nudged it with her foot, sending it skittering across the linoleum and out of reach.

Flashes of Murphy in the library assaulted her. The man had the *audacity* to send someone else to kill her? He had the *audacity* to send a man into her new home and shoot the man she — Evie couldn't think, the edges of her vision tinged with red, her head and heart pounding in sync.

Someone said her name, but Evie's lip curled as she met Bryant's eyes.

He didn't have time to shield himself.

She plunged the knife into the side of his neck.

A gurgle choked out of Bryant's mouth, followed by a dribble of blood as his eyes widened. Evie released the knife, recognition flooding her veins of what she'd just done. She stumbled back again, her hands shaking as his body fell forward. He twitched, face down, blood leaking out from his jugular in pulses.

Evie stared at him until his body stopped spasming.

She'd killed him.

"Evie!" Nick repeated her name. He limped forward, moving slowly as the sound of tires crunched over the gravel drive. She flinched, looking out to see a white truck flying toward the house.

Evie croaked out Nick's name, terrified that Bryant had reinforcements.

Instead, Chuck jumped from the driver's seat, gun in hand, breathing hard as he ran toward the cabin. He slowed when he neared the porch, his body filling up the doorway.

He stared at her and Nick before his eyes flickered down just as Evie felt something warm and wet touch her toes.

CHAPTER TWENTY-FIVE

"TURN, PLEASE."

The EMT stabilized her head gently, gloved hands wiping an alcohol swab across her left cheek. Evie sucked in a little breath at the sting, focusing on the badge on the woman's chest that read SARAH. She knew a Sarah at school, the girl really loved the *Warrior Cat* books.

She'd actually begged Evie to get the entire series after she devoured the first three. Evie vividly remembered going over her book budget for the year and realizing she didn't have enough to complete the *entire* series since there were an obscene number of them. But what Evie could do was contact the girl's parents to see if they'd be willing to make a donation.

The next week the library had the entire series, including the spin-offs, all thanks to the head of the town bank and Sarah's father.

"Ms. Morgen?"

Evie refocused.

"Were you injured anywhere else?"

The endless ring in her ears made her wince. "The gun..."

She didn't know why her voice sounded so rough, but as she touched her throat, she realized tears were dripping down her face.

"It just grazed you." Sarah soothed her. "I promise, the scratch isn't deep. It'll heal, maybe even without a scar. You were *very* lucky, Ms. Morgen."

She didn't feel lucky.

"Where's Nick?" She turned her head, the sounds muffled on one side, scanning the yard. She was sitting in the back of an ambulance and Nick hadn't come out of the cabin yet. Even though he was the one who was actually shot — he should be the one in the ambulance, not her.

"My colleague is taking a look at Agent Barber."

"He's not an agent," Evie snapped, pushing away from the gurney. "I —"

"Evie." Chuck spoke up as he strode across the lawn, running a hand over his beard. There was something about his expression that made her blood run cold.

"Is Nick okay?"

Chuck frowned. "Last time I checked, yeah." He glanced at the cabin. "I think he was talking the cops through the events again. I wanted to tell you that Andy's on his way."

Evie startled, her hand landing on the door to the ambulance. "He knows?"

"I called him." Chuck crossed his arms over his chest. He had a holster strapped to his hip with his gun safely tucked away.

The details were fuzzy.

She remembered Chuck walking into the cabin, shards of the broken door crunching under his boots, holstering his gun once he realized it was just Nick and Evie. She remembered catching Nick's arm as his knee buckled, Chuck helping her get Nick to one of the kitchen chairs. She remembered Nick holding her hands tightly, ignoring the blood on them as he whispered to her to just keep looking at him — that the cops and ambulance would be here soon. She remembered Chuck throwing a blanket over the body in the kitchen while muttering, *"Fuck the coroner, you shouldn't have to look at this."*

Evie stared at Chuck, his white shirt untarnished, completely unruffled by the evening's events.

"They'll want to talk to you." Chuck raised one eyebrow. "Do you understand?"

"I killed him."

"You did." Chuck didn't mince words. "It was self-defense, Evelyn. He was *sent* here to kill you both. He was in my fucking bar four days ago and I just thought he was passing through."

"You didn't know." Evie stared at Chuck's profile in the red of the ambulance's tail lights, "None of us knew."

"Nick would have known. He would have spotted that slimy fuck from a mile away."

She didn't want to admit that she'd known something was wrong too. How were they supposed to know who was safe and who wasn't anymore?

With a shiver, Evie wrapped her arms around herself, painfully aware she was still splattered with blood. Sarah had wiped Evie's hands off, but it wasn't like a couple wet wipes could take care of the oxidizing blood under her nails.

Evie nodded toward the porch. "I think I'm going to go sit down."

Chuck fell into step beside her, and next to him, she felt tiny. She eyed the two squad cars parked behind Nick and Chuck's trucks, then the ambulance catty-corner with the coroner's van as she took a seat in one of the rockers.

Nick's low and frustrated voice carried outside the hole where the cabin door used to stand.

Evie shivered again, glancing over her shoulder at the open door. Chuck stepped into the cabin, reemerging with a blanket. He tossed it over her, covering up the blood-splattered shirt and the pair of shorts she had on underneath. Evie pulled it closer as two coroners carried a body bag past her.

Nick appeared in the doorway, leaning heavily against it as two officers brushed past him. One of them lingered on the porch when he saw Evie in the rocking chair, but before he could say anything, the sound of tires on gravel made everyone's heads turn.

A black SUV skidded to a stop just behind the squad cars.

The other EMT stopped next to Nick. "We really should get you checked out in the ambulance. You might need to take a trip to the hospital."

Nick pushed up, using his height to tower over the EMT as his eyes narrowed. "I said it's fine, the slug barely grazed me."

"Nick, your calf is bleeding again." Chuck's deadpan brought all the eyes on the porch to the blood slowly soaking Nick's flannel pants. Nick heaved a sigh.

"Fine." He turned his attention to Evie, touching her hair. "Are you okay?" The touch alone made her heart flutter in her chest, the careful grip she had on her emotions faltering as she struggled to rein it in. Her head hurt, her ears felt unbalanced, like the left was filled with cotton.

She stared up at him, her heart in her throat as she nodded. "Go get patched up."

Nick's hand shifted, touching the bandage on her cheek with his thumb before he graced her with a small smile, nodding his head toward Andy who'd reached the bottom of the porch steps. "There's the man of the hour, come here, help me over to the ambulance."

"Agent Barber we can use the gurney —"

Nick's eyebrow rose at the EMT. "Not an agent, and not

needed. I've got Andy right here." He grinned, clapping Andy on the shoulder before grunting as he made his way down the two steps and onto the grass. Evie watched Andy support him, the EMT guiding them toward the ambulance and into the seat she'd just vacated.

It left her on the porch with Chuck. She turned and glanced at the older man, but his attention was on the busted door frame. "I could probably patch this. You don't want raccoons."

Evie stared at him, half in disbelief, half in realization that even though he could have left two hours ago, he'd lingered. It didn't matter if he'd done it for Nick or herself, what mattered was that he was here, gun on his side, standing in the freezing cold just because he could.

She threw her arms around his shoulders.

Chuck caught her, his entire body going stiff as she hugged his neck tightly.

"Evelyn."

"Sorry." She smiled up at him sheepishly, pulling away to rewrap the blanket around herself. "But also... thank you, Chuck. Thank you for being the only other person in this town who knows what's happening —"

He cut her off with the wave of a hand, his face twisting like he couldn't handle hearing it, but his cheeks were reddening in embarrassment. "I think about you and my stomach twists into knots thinking about something similar happening to Hope. Maybe that takes away some of your gratitude, but I have to think that someone would watch after my girl too."

Evie's heart melted. "Can I help with the door?"

"You can sit down." Chuck shook his head, looking at the frame. She would have felt bad about the gruff dismissal, but she could see the slight smile on the edges of his lips as he inspected the wood.

She sank back down into the rocker, watching as the coroner van shut its back doors. Andy stood at the end of the ambulance, his head tilted up as he faced Nick. Nick grimaced as he barked something at Andy. Evie imagined if it was anyone else, Andy would have them in handcuffs, but he just looked irritated as he ran a hand over his face. To the untrained eye, it almost looked like a lover's quarrel.

The sound of a phone ringing startled Evie. Chuck pulled his cell out, looking down at it and then sliding his finger across the screen. She heard Hope's voice filter out as Chuck answered, stepping into the cabin to take the call.

The front porch steps creaked.

Evie turned back around to see Andy pushing up his sleeves. He looked tired — she could see the worn lines around his eyes and dark circles making his under eyes gaunt as he leaned back against the post. Memories of her mother's words from Christmas trickled through her mind — something about his boss not allowing him the time to focus fully on her case.

"Are you okay?" Andy eyed her.

She pulled the blanket closer and sighed. "Well, I was just trying to go to bed and a man held a gun to my head. Not my relaxing evening plans, Andy."

He nodded his head slowly. "Yeah, I'd imagine that wouldn't be fun."

Shifting in the rocking chair, Evie glared. "Ask your questions."

He waved a hand. "I..." Andy's sigh was like a gust of wind. "Just tell me what happened. I got part of it from Nick but he said you were in the living room when the guy broke in."

Evie's cheeks hollowed out as she sucked in a breath,

recounting the details — omitting the fact she was returning to Nick's room, not her own. It wasn't that she didn't want to admit to Andy that something was happening, but it was fragile. She knew the moment it was no longer just between her and Nick, it would shatter.

She wished they could have stayed in the Christmas bubble a bit longer, where time seemed to just stop before New Year's. When she ended on Chuck helping Nick into the chair and the police arriving, Andy looked pensive.

"And you never saw this man around town?"

"No," she answered immediately, then paused. "Well..." Trailing off, Evie glanced over at the forest, frowning. "I thought someone was following me the other day. We ran into town to get groceries and I went to the library. It's normally just me and the librarian but... it felt different, Andy."

"You sure it's not just... anxiety? PTSD?"

"Are you really diagnosing me with hysteria?" Evie raised an eyebrow. "Gee, I don't know. I've been isolated in a cabin for over a month. It *surely* couldn't be those."

"Don't get snarky." He shifted, leveling her with a look. "What I'm asking is for proof that he's been in town. He's not tipped off Murphy as far as you know — we don't know this —"

She cut him off. "He said his name was Bryant — William Bryant. He monologued like a —" She hesitated, feeling the anger bubble in her chest again. Flashes of Bryant standing in the doorway, smirking at her, then down on his knees, blood bubbling out of his throat assaulted her.

Andy waited.

Evie's eyes locked with his. "He monologued like a fucking *Batman* villain, Andy. He was thrilled to be in the cabin, thrilled to *find me*. Murphy sent him, but no, I don't know if he told him. I can't prove that he's been in town or hanging around. Chuck said he was at the bar but I can't tell you if he rolled into town and found us or if he's been stalking me for days. So yeah, maybe it is anxiety or PTSD but how would I know? I'm here, isolating like you told me to, trying to not lose my fucking mind in the process."

Andy's expression softened slightly. "Okay, okay. I'm sorry." He lifted his hand and rubbed the bridge of his nose again, then paused, looking at her over the top of his hand.

The blanket had slipped off of her shoulders and Evie glanced down at herself. Blood stained the top of KISS ME crimson. Glancing up, she watched the realization dawn on Andy's face.

"Sir!"

Both their heads snapped to the side, watching as Nick strode across the lawn. Evie winced as he favored his uninjured leg, stomping up the porch and planting himself partially in front of her seat, staring Andy down.

"You got what you need yet?"

She didn't have proof of Murphy, but Andy had all the proof he needed to puzzle out Nick's protective behavior and Evie's current attire.

"*Fuck*. Really?"

She shrank back in the rocking chair, pulling the blanket up to her chin.

"*Really* what, Andy?"

"I don't know what's worse, you taking her into town where this asshole clearly saw her and stalked her back here, or that —"

"Don't finish that sentence." Nick's voice was barely above a whisper, his shoulders squared. "Don't."

The porch fell silent.

Andy licked his lips, clicking his tongue before he shook his head and nodded. "Right. Well, I have a shit ton of paperwork to do about... whatever happened tonight, and you both need to go to the hospital. I can't in good faith leave you in a cabin with the door off the hinges."

"I'm fixing it." Chuck emerged from the cabin next to Evie's rocker, causing her to jolt slightly. He glanced down at her and then looked back up at Andy and Nick. "Got Hope bringing me the tools now. I'll get it back on the hinges, clean up the kitchen too."

Nick wavered slightly and Evie stood up, sliding an arm around his torso to hold onto him. "I think you need to go to the hospital."

He made a low noise in the back of his throat. "It's fine."

She glanced up at him, her voice barely a whisper. "I'm not taking whatever replacement bodyguard they give me. It's you or I sit in the middle of the road and wait for Murphy to come find me himself."

Nick scowled down at her, but relented long enough for her to shuffle him forward and off the porch. Andy watched them, but didn't shift to follow until Evie had Nick walking back across the grass, toward the waiting ambulance. She didn't know what had crawled up his ass and died, but he could either help or get the hell out of her way.

Sarah and her partner helped load Nick into the back and Evie braced a hand on the door, preparing to hoist herself up when Andy's hand landed on her arm. She turned, pausing mid-motion to narrow her eyes at him.

"I'll omit what I can. I'm getting enough pressure from my bosses as it is." Andy's head tilted, his words barely audible as he leaned in. She was having trouble processing, and as she turned to the side, his voice became clearer on the right. "But I'm begging you not to compromise this. I know I dropped you off in the middle of fucking nowhere with him. I know I can't ask you not to form an attachment with the only person you've got — but you cannot distract him. That's how shit like tonight happens."

A bolt of white-hot anger shot through her veins.

Andy looked down at the shirt again. "Don't make me put in a request to transfer you. The Witness Protection guys aren't going to let you go to the library, Evie. They're going to sit you in a motel room until you can recite *Days of Our Lives* episodes in your sleep. And they certainly won't lend you their damn t-shirts."

"I don't know what you're talking about." She pulled herself up into the back of the ambulance, her knuckles white. "It was just laundry day, Andy."

CHAPTER TWENTY-SIX

BY THE TIME THE AMBULANCE PULLED INTO THE ER entrance of the hospital two towns over, Evie could barely keep her eyes open.

Nick squeezed her hand as Evie glanced over at him on the gurney. She was perched on the edge, and while he refused to lie down at first, he'd slowly sunk onto his back the longer the ambulance ride took. His left leg was extended. Sarah and the other EMT, Jackson, had cut back Nick's pant leg to fully access the bullet wound.

When Bryant pulled the trigger, he'd been a hair off, but the graze was far deeper than the one on Evie's cheek. She winced as they cleaned Nick's leg, wiping away oozing blood.

"We'll get you patched up in no time." Jackson grinned at Nick, then looked at Evie. "You coming with us?"

The back doors opened and Evie shifted to stand, clearing her throat. "No, it's okay." Her hand slipped from Nick's. "I should probably get cleaned up somewhere."

He frowned at her, turning his head as the gurney started to move. "You can come with me, Evie. It's okay."

She looked down at the blood caking her fingernails and made a face. "I'll find you in ten minutes. I just need to get this off of me." When she glanced back up, the line between his brows had eased slightly and she knew he understood.

She jumped out behind Nick's gurney, following Sarah and Jackson into the ER. A nurse was coming out of a side hallway and Evie cleared her throat, stopping the other woman in her tracks.

"Is there anywhere I can get cleaned up?"

The nurse took her in and sucked in a surprised breath. "Sure, are you with..."

She trailed off, her eyes widening at something behind Evie.

Evie's head whipped around to see the FBI flooding the quiet emergency room. The few people in seats looked up as the agents began to disperse. One followed Nick's gurney while another spotted her and started to approach.

"Yes," Evie said quickly, turning back to the nurse. "Please, just take me anywhere."

She suddenly didn't want to see if Andy was close. She didn't want to hear him berate her again, or remind her that he was well within his power to rip her away from Nick and Wells Creek and drop her in a motel somewhere with a rotating team of agents that didn't care if she was bored out of her mind — or terrified.

The nurse glanced between her and the agents before grabbing Evie's bare arm, plastering a wide smile on her face. "Come with me. Excuse me, sir —" The nurse whirled on the agent approaching them, her lightly Indian-accented voice stern. "*You* can wait out here."

The agent opened his mouth, then closed it again, baffled — but it was too late. The nurse whisked Evie past a set of double doors.

A half-strangled laugh bubbled up in the back of Evie's

throat as she was guided into a brightly lit hospital bathroom. The nurse whipped open cabinets and pulled out a few wash-cloths, turning the hot water on and sticking them under.

"When we got a call about a shooting and an FBI witness..."

Evie couldn't help but snort. "Yeah, that's me."

The nurse shook her head. She was older than Evie by a couple years, graying hair around her scalp tapering to a rich black that fell long and straight, pulled into a ponytail. The woman's eyes were a kind brown as she handed one of the washcloths over to Evie.

It felt like heaven as Evie wiped her neck, pulling it back to see blood.

"I'm Nikita." The nurse smiled, her eyes growing concerned. "Can I ask...?"

Evie knew she shouldn't explain too much, but it came out in a rush. "A man attacked the... place I was tonight." She stumbled over the words, trying to keep them vague.

Nikita stepped over and ran soap and warm water over Evie's arms, cleaning them off. The bathroom was quiet for a moment before Evie frowned at the other woman.

"The ambulance was there really fast. Did something else happen in Wells Creek?"

"You all were the second call. There were two on the way into town." Nikita busied herself wiping off the side of Evie's neck where she'd missed a spot. "We got a call earlier in the night that a man had a heart attack around eight in the library."

Evie's blood turned to ice in her veins.

"The library?" She pulled back. "Was it a man in his late seventies? Stephen Vogt?"

"Yes." Nikita blinked. "I take it you know him?"

"Yes," Evie whispered, grabbing the soap and scrubbing her

hands and nails again, plunging them under the burning hot water. "Can you take me to him? Can I see him?"

Evie was painfully aware the shirt and shorts weren't the best attire to wander around a hospital in, but she couldn't stand the thought of Stephen being so close and not going to see the man who had unintentionally become a part of all of this.

Nikita hesitated for the barest of moments before she looked over at Evie and gave one, sharp and quick nod. "I'll take you to him. At least let me check your cheek before we go. What did you say happened to you?"

"I didn't." With a swallow, Evie turned her head to the side, letting her remove the small tape and then clean the wound. Wincing, Evie sucked in a breath. "A gun went off next to me, grazed my cheek." She paused. "My ears are still ringing. It's been hours."

Nikita threw away the old bandage. "A handgun?"

Evie nodded.

The next words were muffled, but Evie knew they were coming.

"Firing a shot that close to your eardrum could cause lasting damage to your hearing."

She closed her eyes for a moment, before forcing a smile. "I wondered about that."

Nikita's eyes were softer, but she looked away fast, finishing up. "Let me take you to Stephen's room. He's stable, but tired."

Evie stepped out of the bathroom, and a gurney stopped her short.

Two men in white scrubs were guiding the white-sheet covered body to the elevators, chatting back and forth. At the end of the hall she could see the coroner's van, slush and mud still on its tires from Nick's front yard.

Nikita touched her arm. "Take a left."

Evie allowed herself to be guided away. The elevator doors dinged and even though she didn't watch, she could *feel* the moment Bryant's body was no longer behind her.

The emergency wing had a few nurses, but not a single suit. As Evie skirted around a nurse's cart, she caught a glimpse of agents lingering in the waiting room.

She wondered where Nick was — if he'd been patched up and let go already.

"Here we are."

Nikita stopped in front of a door. The sign next to it had ROOM 56 with the braille translation underneath. Slotted into a small clipboard mount was a sign that read STEPHEN VOGT.

Evie flexed her fingers, feeling the skin pull tight from the harsh soap as the nurse rapped lightly on the door and stepped in.

"Mr. Vogt, you have a visitor."

Fully conscious of how she looked, Evie paused just inside the room, steeling herself before stepping forward to see Stephen lying in the bed.

He looked small.

His already light skin was muted. A wire snaked from his wrist to the IV feeding him fluids. Stephen's eyes widened at the sight of her and Evie offered him a small half-smile as the nurse excused herself and pulled the door shut.

"Evie, what in the world are you doing here?"

Evie planted herself in the chair next to his bed and tilted her head at him. "What're the chances we both end up in the hospital the same night?"

"Evie, what *happened* to you?" Stephen coughed, shifting up in the bed as he did it. They both reached for his water jug

and he batted her hand away with a stern look, taking a long sip
and then looking over at her again. "Are you okay?"

She really wished people would stop asking her that.

"You should see the other guy." *American Pickers* played on
the TV at a barely audible tone, the two hosts walking through
some man's barn out in the middle of nowhere, finding old
metal signs to buy for a couple hundred bucks.

"What's going on, kid?"

Evie looked over at Stephen, her eyes running over his frail
body in the bed. Her brother had lain in a hospital bed for a
week, hooked up to multiple machines that breathed for him as
their parents knelt next to him, praying he'd wake up.

He lost brain function around day five and they pulled the
plug on the eighth.

Evie's lower lip trembled as she felt her throat close. "I'm in
trouble, Stephen, and I think I'm putting everyone else in
danger too."

He grabbed her hand, squeezing it tightly.

The words came out in a flood.

She started from the top, whispering about the library,
about how Murphy stalked her through her own place of work.
She couldn't meet Stephen's eyes as she described sitting in
police stations and then eventually being ferried to Nick
Barber's cabin in the middle of the woods. Choking back tears,
Evie lifted her free hand, wiping at her cheeks as she explained
the night's events.

The only thing she omitted was the way she plunged the
knife into Bryant's neck.

"And he said —" Evie stared at the acoustical ceiling tiles,
sucking in a shuddering breath. "He said he was *in* the library
and I think I caused that. I think I put you in danger and I
knew I would put Nick in danger and then he was *shot* tonight
—"

"Evie." Stephen's voice was quiet, gentle as he squeezed her hand. "Look at me. I'm old. I'm going to have a heart attack, it's an old man's rite of passage." Patting her hand, Stephen raised the hospital bed. "I know who you're talking about."

Evie's stomach churned.

"There was a man in the library not... two hours after you left the other week." Stephen glanced to the side and she watched the emotions play across his face. "He was asking too many questions about Wells Creek." Stephen turned his head back around and stared at Evie. "I should've told that bastard to get lost."

Evie licked her lips, sucking in another breath. "He was in town a while then." Glancing up at the door to the hospital room, she briefly wondered if she needed to burst out into the waiting room and drag an agent back here, to give Andy proof. But she knew the testimony of two people close to her didn't mean anything to the FBI. Bryant was dead and he didn't leave a neat trail leading right back to Murphy — he didn't preemptively do the FBI's job for them.

Stephen touched the back of Evie's hand again. "But he's dead?"

"He's dead," Evie confirmed softly.

"You just be careful." The lines by his eyes creased, his face wrinkled with worry. "You hear me, Evie? You be careful, you don't leave that boy's side again."

At the mention of Nick, she nodded, pulling her hand away from Stephen's before he could feel her start to shake. "I promise."

American Pickers filtered down from the mounted TV, broken by voices in the hall.

Evie could pick out Andy as he asked a nurse if she'd seen Evie around.

Pushing herself up from the chair, Evie forced another

smile. "I'm glad you're okay. You have Nick's number right? Can I visit again, or at least call?"

Stephen smiled. "Of course. You keep an eye on my library while I'm in here."

Evie smiled back at him, turning away as she tried to fight the emotions welling in the back of her throat. She had to force herself to go to the door and face Andy head-on.

Andy looked up sharply. "There you are." Evie fell into step behind him, twisting around in the hospital before reaching an office Andy walked straight in, nodding toward a chair, which she sank into.

"I need your statement."

"Again? I gave it to the cops at the scene, and we *just* talked at the cabin, Andy."

"I know, I know. But when Chuck called, I dropped everything to get from California to here, including walking out of a debrief." She could see the bags under his eyes, highlighted by the fluorescent lights. "My bosses want to make sure nothing has changed." Andy looked uncomfortable with the admission. "Just tell me again — everything you remember — maybe there's something we missed."

"I *told* you everything."

"Yeah but Nick wasn't there." Andy stopped her, raising a hand. "Okay? Nick admitted to me that he was in his bedroom. He said he called Chuck while this guy talked to you, so it's your word. That's all I've got and I'm going to be honest, Evie, it's not fucking enough for my bosses. The higher ups want to make sure they're not wasting their time on a case that isn't related to Murphy at all."

She sucked in a breath, feeling her hands start to shake. "Do you think I made up the fact he *told* me he was working with Murphy? Who the hell else would hunt me down?"

"I don't know!" Andy threw his hands up in the air, pacing

back and forth. With a heavy sigh, he stopped in front of her. "I don't know. I don't know what answers my bosses want. I don't know the right words to give them." His voice softened. "We don't know who this guy is. We don't think he has a connection to Murphy but we don't know."

"You keep saying *we*. What about *you*, Andy? What do you believe?"

She watched him tug at the tie around his neck. His suit jacket was slung over the edge of the desk, this office of some rural doctor probably curled up in their bed asleep overtaken by the man in front of her.

"I've got my bosses riding my ass. We don't know who Will Bryant is — we have no files on him, we just have a dead body and a story about a break-in. We can't even confirm that name goes with *this* body. What if this was random?"

There it was.

With a small nod, Evie looked away, her eyes unfocusing as she ran over the words.

"You don't believe me."

"I don't have *the evidence* to believe you. You say he admitted to working with Murphy — I don't have any record of a Will Bryant. You say he killed Beck —" At this, Andy's voice broke. "But we can't find footage of him at the motel, I just have a body. I have a body and no proof."

"You have *me*." Tears choked her as Evie looked back at him. "I wouldn't lie to you, Andy. My story isn't changing, regardless of if you think it's trauma or PTSD or fucking female hysteria."

Andy's jaw twitched. "Until biometrics comes back, I have to treat this as a break-in. Right now, according to the FBI, it's unrelated to you or Murphy."

"You're being an asshole, Andy." As hard as she tried, Evie

couldn't stop the tears that overflowed. "And I don't know *why*, I thought you were my friend."

The man in front of her broke. "Evie..."

"I want to go home, Andy." Evie wiped her nose, looking down at her hands.

"Vermont isn't an option right now. You and I both know that."

The weight on her chest crushed her lungs. She let out a breath, afraid to look up at Andy and admit that Vermont wasn't what she meant. She meant Nick's cabin. She meant the warm fireplace just outside of Wells Creek. She meant the well-worn copy of her shitty Scottish bodice ripper on Nick's nightstand.

"Hey, oh —" A young guy poked his head into the office, pausing as he drew up short at the sight of Evie in the chair two seconds from a total breakdown and Andy standing over her. "Uh, coroners want to talk to you, Agent Wilson."

"Yeah." Andy waited for a beat. Evie looked up at him, watching the struggle play out in real time behind his eyes. "I'm coming," he finally whispered, whisking out of the room without another word.

She gave up trying to stop the tears, dropping her head into her hands as her shoulders crumbled inwards, letting the sob finally win the fight out of her chest. It was an ugly sound, a half-wheeze as she pressed her palms into her eyes, shaking.

Stephen could tell her that his heart attack had nothing to do with her until he was blue in the face, but Evie knew better. She had caused this. She had caused all of this. And now Andy didn't believe her when she could still hear Bryant admitting it playing on repeat in her mind.

Point blank, Andy would never take her first-person account at face value as he would with Nick's because of their history. And — she knew Nick wouldn't have intended it to play out like this — admitting that he wasn't in the room when Bryant was taunting her had inadvertently acted against her own statement's validity. His statement couldn't verify her own, because he simply wasn't there.

Nick's words were the hard evidence that Andy trusted. To anyone else, she was just the scared, little librarian who could be making mountains out of molehills — or conflating a break-in with the killer already hunting her down.

Motion in the hall made Evie flinch, choking on another sob as she watched a figure round the doorway.

Nick leaned against the frame, still in his ripped pajama pants, a thick bandage wrapped around his calf. He stared down at her, voice hoarse. "They discharged me. I asked Andy where you were and — what's wrong?"

Evie sniffled, shaking her head and looking down at her hands. "I'm glad you're okay." Her voice shook as she cleared her throat. "Uh, you're okay? Right?"

"Yeah, sweetheart, I'm okay." Nick sank down in front of her on his good leg, reaching out to take her hands in his. "What happened?"

Evie took him in, swallowing the lump in her throat. "Stephen Vogt had a heart attack. I just saw him, he's okay." She hated that word, but she spurred forward anyway. "He told me that Bryant was in the library the other day." It was all out of order, but she was having trouble organizing her thoughts. "I told him about tonight. I know I shouldn't have, Nick, but I was just in there and Andy's been *so*..." She stuttered over the words. "He doesn't *believe* me."

Nick shushed her, touching her cheek. His thumb was rough on her skin as he wiped at the tears. "Look at me. Just breathe."

Evie glanced down at him, breathing in slowly as he wiped under her eyes.

"You shouldn't be on your knee." Evie mumbled the words, clinging to his hand.

Nick flashed her a little smile. "I would break both my legs for you. When are you going to learn that, honey?"

She let out a strangled laugh and dropped her head, crashing her forehead against his as she closed her eyes and just leaned into him. Nick exhaled, cupping her cheek as they sat there for a heartbeat, locked together.

A throat cleared in the doorway.

"There's someone here to take you both home."

Nick pulled back, a line appearing on his brow as he turned his head, but Evie spoke up, giving Nikita a watery smile. "Thank you."

The nurse nodded at the two of them before stepping away. Evie held Nick's hand tightly as he stood up, breathing out harshly once his weight was back on both legs.

"You're sure you don't —"

"No." He held onto her hand, pressing a kiss to her temple. "Let's go home, sweetheart."

Chuck's truck was idling just outside the ER entrance, waiting for them. He offered Evie a hand and she shuffled to the middle seat, leaving Nick room to adjust his leg. Chuck climbed up into the driver's seat after they were both inside, flicking the radio dial until it landed on a station playing 80s rock.

Glancing out the window, Evie turned her torso to stare at the hospital, reaching out blindly to her side. Nick's hand found hers, and her mind raced with questions about Bryant, about Andy, about what would happen when they got back to the cabin.

She shifted when the hospital disappeared behind them, leaning her head on Nick's shoulder. Closing her eyes, Evie clung to his hand, welcoming the lull of exhaustion.

Chapter Twenty-Seven

Evie adjusted the book on the nightstand again, spinning the spine. Sunlight streamed in from the window behind the bare bed, the navy sheets on the floor. One of her cardigans hung on the back of a chair next to the dresser, when she took it off last night before sliding into bed and tucking her head against Nick's warm chest. She'd learned in a few short nights that the quilt often got kicked to the bottom of the bed because the sheer weight of it and the heat of him combined made sleep impossible.

The cabin door squeaked and Evie turned her head, listening as it latched shut again with a small clunk. Chuck *had* fixed it, partially. There was only so much he could do to the split frame and the way the hinges had pulled straight out of the wood. Nick swore up and down the moment it wasn't freezing outside, he would take some time to fiddle with it and make the scraping stop every time the door opened and closed.

Evie didn't have the heart to admit that she liked the noise. She liked being fully aware of the comings and goings from the single entrance and exit. It was less anxiety day to day.

"Got the wood chopped," Nick called down the hall as Evie finished pulling the pillowcases off the bed. "You're still in your pajamas?"

He filled up the doorway, an easy smile on his lips, one hand over his head as he held onto the wood frame. His flannel shirt sleeves were shoved up past his forearms and she could see the sweat on his brow from across the room.

"Yes, I am." She rolled her eyes, unceremoniously dropping the pillowcases to the floor. "Why change?"

"Well..." Nick fidgeted. "I wondered if you wanted to go to town tonight." Evie raised an eyebrow. "Chuck's keeping Adam's open for the New Year. We could ring it in with a bunch of mountain men and off-season lumberjacks."

Evie softened, stepping around the sheets. When she was standing in front of him, she cupped his cold cheeks, feeling the scruff of his beard on the palms of her hands.

"Are you asking me out?"

Nick's lips twitched. "I hope you expect more than that shitty attempt, but yes, sweetheart, I'm asking you if you want to go out tonight."

Something warm blossomed in her chest, but quickly cooled as her mind spun. "What about Andy?"

In the few days since the hospital, she'd tasked herself with helping Nick clean off his leg. It was difficult not to sink into herself, the memory of Andy's anger fueling her nightmares when Murphy didn't.

Nick's expression twisted, reaching out to cup the back of her head. With her hands still on his cheeks, Nick pulled her closer to him and tipped his head down, his nose brushing hers. "I have never listened to him before, I'm not starting now, Evie." Leaning in, he touched his forehead against hers before kissing her jaw. "Go get dressed."

Evie leaned into him, humming. He smelled good, like pine

oil and salt. As quick as Andy had entered her mind, he was gone when Nick's fingers tangled in her hair.

"Can I help you?" Nick chuckled as Evie leaned in closer, turning her head at the last second to inhale and bury her head against his throat.

"You smell nice." She rested there for a moment and Nick took the opportunity to let go of the door frame and wrap his arms around her tightly.

Nick pecked the top of her head as Evie wound her arms around his neck, leaning back just enough so she could see his face. This close she could count the lines next to his eyes, see the sharp lift of the edges of his lips behind his beard, and the tiny scar near his hairline that she always forgot to ask about. She was sure he could see the dark circles under her own eyes, set against a pallor cast across her already pale skin.

His eyes held nothing but adoration in the moment.

He leaned in, pressing a firm kiss to her lips as he squeezed her tighter. "Go, before you distract us both."

Evie laughed, shuffling past him in the doorway. "Fine, I'll get dressed but you have to switch the laundry around."

Nick groaned as she shut the door to the guest room. The only items left in this dresser were the two outfits she wore into town — everything else was in a laundry basket in the corner of Nick's room.

∧ ∧

"You're sure you're okay to drive?"

Nick shot her a look as he climbed into the truck. "Are you offering to drive my manual truck down the side of an ice-covered mountain?"

Evie pressed her lips together and glanced out of the passenger-side window. "Maybe not."

Nick laughed, the deep sound making her toes curl in her boots. After a moment of adjusting the heat and buckling, he reached over and squeezed her thigh. "Yes, I'm sure."

"We could have stayed in tonight."

"You're right." Nick shifted the gears, slinging one arm behind her shoulders as he glanced in the rearview mirror. "We could have." He pointed the truck toward the road. "But we spent Christmas inside, got attacked by an insane man not four days ago, and I really want to listen to shitty rock music with you on Chuck's jukebox because it's just as good of an experience as us playing random CDs on *our* shitty stereo."

Evie's heart fluttered, dangerously close to spontaneously combusting. Nick's hand brushed against her shoulder and she sucked in a little breath when he grinned. The humid air from the truck's old vents ruffled her hair as she stared.

"So yes, we could have stayed in tonight, but *I* wanted to go out. Blame me if you have a shitty time, but I'm going to try my hardest to make sure you don't."

Evie leaned forward in response, turning up the *Kings of Leon* CD that she'd left in the truck for the last few weeks.

The town's main road was quiet as Nick eased his truck past the darkened library. It would have been closed for Christmas anyway, but seeing it made her heart ache. She'd been warring with herself for two days over asking Nick to call the hospital, but this made her decision. Nick could call and Evie could jump on the phone for just a second to make sure Stephen was still recovering okay. Andy would have her head if he ever found out, but Nick's words from earlier echoed in the back of her mind — when had she ever listened to him before? She wasn't starting now.

Nick pulled up to Adam's, parking in a spot farther from the door than normal. There were trucks coated in sheets of ice and cars dusted with salt spray as Evie got out and pulled her coat closer. Noise trickled out from inside the bar as the doors opened, an older man holding it for Evie as she stepped through, Nick just behind her.

She'd never seen Adam's this busy.

The tables normally clustered around the jukebox had all been pulled away, making room for people to mill around and chat. Evie felt Hope before she saw her, taking a hit to the side as Hope threw her arms around Evie and squeaked.

"I hoped you two would come!"

When she pulled back, she gave Evie a wide-eyed look. "Are you okay? Oh my god, hold on." Hope grabbed Evie by the shoulder, steering her away from the door. When Evie shot Nick a panicked look, he just grinned and strode toward Chuck.

Hope clung to Evie's arm. "My dad said he had to fix the cabin door? And that you went to the hospital over in Cascade Valley? And then Stephen Vogt apparently had a heart attack? What the hell happened?"

Evie glanced toward the bar, finding Chuck watching them. Focusing back on Hope, Evie cleared her throat as she fumbled. "Yeah, uh, the wind was really bad. It blew it straight in, just busted the lock. Nick and I went over to the hospital to see Stephen." The lies tasted sour on her tongue. "But Stephen's fine, he's recovering."

A line appeared as Hope's brows drew together. "Are you sure? Are you okay?"

"Yeah." Evie shot her a smile back, motioning around them. "Is it always like this?"

"Oh." Hope laughed, but it didn't quite reach her eyes. Someone from across the room called out the girl's name. Hope brightened and then shot Evie another smile. "I forgot their peanuts again, I'll be right back!"

She was off in a flash, leaving Evie to search for Nick,

finding him at the bar talking to a couple. When the woman turned, she realized it was the waitress from the diner and her husband, Nick's co-worker.

Feeling out of place, Evie took a step toward them, then paused, noticing Chuck lingering near the door to the back. He nodded at her, before disappearing behind it. Evie followed him instead, slipping into the back office.

"Chuck?"

She opened her mouth to ask him what he needed, but her eyes caught on a collection of photos on the wall. Evie moved closer, stopping in front of a photo of a much younger Chuck, his face smooth, holding a cherubic Hope, with both front teeth missing. He had a big grin on his face, but it didn't quite reach his eyes.

The next photo looked slightly older than the first, but what caught Evie off guard was the fact Chuck was standing in front of a church, holding onto a Korean man wearing a matching black tux. Chuck's arms were around the man's waist while the man gazed lovingly up at Chuck, only his side profile captured in the photo. The man looked similar enough to Hope that Evie did a double-take. Next to the man was an unfamiliar woman, also eerily similar to Hope — but *Nick* was by Chuck's other side.

"I thought he would have told you by now."

Nick couldn't have been older than twenty in the photo, his face still round, even though he was in a suit. He looked *happy*, with a brotherly arm slung over Chuck's shoulders. She felt like her world had been knocked off its axis by the image.

"Told me what?" She turned to face Chuck. "That clearly you two have known each other for far longer than he's been here in Wells Creek? I gathered that when you said *you* called Andy."

Chuck sighed. "The reason I came to the cabin the other

night was for him as much as it was for you. Nick and I have a history. It's not a short one, either. We met when he was in the academy and I was a contracted teacher after I was discharged from the army."

Evie resisted crossing her arms over her chest, surveying him.

"It was a different time." Chuck ran a hand over his beard, and for a brief flash Evie got a good look at the age lines marring the older man. It wasn't just the signs of a hard life, it was the haunted look of someone who'd been through too much and was, once again, explaining it. "It wasn't... You couldn't be who you were back then."

Chuck wouldn't meet her eyes. "I met Hope's mother, Amelia, when I was stationed in Germany. That's when she introduced me to her brother, Jonas. Jonas and I couldn't admit what was between us, then Hope's mother got pregnant and the father wasn't in the picture. She had Hope, alone, and I got injured the same year."

Evie couldn't take a full breath as the weight of the words settled. "So Hope..."

"She's my niece, officially." Chuck stared past Evie at the photos. "My injury is what's listed on paperwork for my discharge. They offered to let me do desk work, but being married to another man was something they'd *rather not have to hear about*' so, I opted to leave." His eyes finally pulled away, focusing on Evie. "Hope's mother found out she was terminal — brain tumors — when Hope was three. She knew she could leave this Earth with Hope taken care of by Jonas and me."

Evie's chest smarted, thinking of Hope in the bar not ten feet away.

"So you've known Nick for what? Over a decade? Andy told me Nick moved here to get away from the FBI."

"Andy knows a little, but not everything." Chuck snorted.

"The nature of Nick Barber is that he doesn't often drop every bit of information on every single person. Everyone knows a few puzzle pieces, but never all of them."

Evie swallowed. "I didn't think he would hide things from me."

Chuck held up a hand, shooting her an irritated look. "Now hold on. Before you start panicking on me, I'm not telling you this to make you second-guess Nick. I wasn't going to receive a 911 text from the man who helped me get through both my sister-in-law's and husband's *deaths* without being ready to kill someone for him."

Evie sucked in a breath, leaning back slightly. "I —"

"Evie." Chuck said her name softly, staring at her. "When Jonas died I was a fucking mess. Hope was too young to understand why both her mother and her uncle were gone. I coasted my way through a contract position at Quantico for barely two years and then suddenly I was a single father. I was trying to keep my personal life out of my work life because it was frowned upon to talk about my dead husband and adopted child at home." He stared at her, his eyes narrowing. "Do you really think Nick would put you in any more danger than you're already in? I'm not saying I have bastards after me like the likes of Murphy, but what I did stationed in Germany wasn't paperwork. I worked on some projects that will probably stay classified until the world is nothing but dust."

Her brows pulled together. "I don't understand, Chuck. Why are you telling me all of this? When did —"

His expression softened and she watched his gaze flicker to the photos again. "If I called Nick in the middle of the night asking him to help protect Hope, he would show up. So I showed up for him."

The words punched a hole straight through her chest.

"I'm not going to sit here and pretend there's not *some-

thing going on between the two of you — but I'm also telling you that Adam's is safe for you, Wells Creek is safe for you. I'm just asking that you don't tell my daughter about any of it. I've kept her away from my past this long, I don't want her getting involved in someone else's. What Nick needs from me, he's going to get — and that extends to you."

"Okay." Evie said the word softly, her mind wrapping around the information Chuck had just flooded the room with. She glanced over her shoulder, looking at the photo from his wedding day.

"I just needed you to know that whatever happens with Murphy and that fucker you killed —" Evie flinched, wrapping her arms around herself as she swiveled back to look at Chuck. "You've got me. Nick's got me."

Whatever salve Chuck's protection gave her was washed away with a rush of anxiety that Evie was putting every single person she spoke to in danger. She could picture Hope in a hospital bed just like Stephen, hooked up to IVs and wires, just because she was seen with Evie.

"Thank you for telling me." Evie hesitated at the door. "Chuck?"

He was already looking down at his desk, going over something before his head tilted up slightly. "Hm?"

"Thank you for showing up." Evie knew she'd already thanked him the night Bryant attacked, but the grip around her heart didn't lessen until the words left her lips in a rush. "I... I had to kill him."

"Yeah, you did, Evie. It was you or him. Murphy won't leave this unfinished."

"I know." She turned fully, slipping back out into the bar.

There were even more bodies than before, milling around the bar and taking up booths and tables. Her eyes skimmed the room before she saw Nick again, sitting in the same place as before. The couple he'd been speaking to were occupied with someone else across the room and Evie picked her way over to Nick at the bar.

"Hey." He smiled at her and when she was near enough, Nick's hand snaked out, grabbing onto the side of her cardigan to pull her closer. "Where were you?"

"Bathroom." She tried to give him a small smile back, but it didn't quite land. Shifting slightly, her shoulder brushed his chest. "It's busy in here."

Nick hummed, lifting a beer in his other hand and taking a swig. "Yeah, I'm not surprised. Nowhere else is open this late. Even for New Year's."

"You want a drink?"

Evie turned sharply at the sound of a voice and saw a guy behind the bar that wasn't Chuck. He was looking straight at her and Evie opened her mouth then closed it. Caught off guard, she cleared her throat. "Just a bottle of water."

"It's on Chuck's tab tonight, Jacob." Nick grinned at the guy, his arm sliding around Evie's waist as he spoke. "She's with me."

Jacob nodded, swiveling to grab a bottle of water. He put it on the bar top before stepping away and Evie watched him, confused.

"Hope's..." Nick hesitated, his voice soft in Evie's ear as he leaned closer. "Well, I'm not sure if they're dating. Chuck doesn't want them to be. He's Carol and Jared's son." He used a hand to guide Evie's chin until she was looking at the couple from earlier.

His fingertips on her chin made the hair on the back of her neck stand up straight, goosebumps rising on her skin under her cardigan. "I think Chuck only lets him behind the bar on busy nights because he and Hope can't take care of everyone by themselves. Jacob's not a bad kid, Chuck's just overprotective."

Evie turned her head, her lips nearing the side of Nick's jaw as she whispered back. "You know a lot about these people."

The statement sat between them for a moment before Nick's fingers turned her head slightly so he could press his lips against the side of her cheek. "I do."

The confirmation hurt. "You know I wasn't in the bathroom."

"I do."

Evie's lips twitched. "Are you going to say anything but 'I do'?"

Nick's expression mirrored hers. "What do you want me to say? I know you were back in Chuck's office for ten minutes. Don't know what he said to you but you came out cagey. I was an FBI agent, sweetheart, I think I can read some basic body language."

Evie leaned into his chest, unscrewing the bottle. "He told me enough."

"Okay." Nick took a swig of his beer again, then shot her a look. "He still has those photos on his wall back there?"

"He does."

"You know you can ask me anything, Evie."

Evie glanced back at him, her voice softening. "I do."

They smiled at each other.

The TV behind the bar zoomed in on the Empire State Building as someone shouted, "It's almost midnight!"

Nick picked up Evie's hand. She watched as he pressed his lips to the skin just below her knuckles, before he wrapped an arm around her loosely to pull her close. Evie shifted, pressing her back to his chest, sinking into him as she glanced over at the TVs as the announcers on the multiple stations prepped for the final countdown.

With a kiss to her temple, Nick whispered in her ear again. "Can I kiss you at midnight?"

Evie bit her tongue, nodding. "I think you should."

He chuckled, the low sound making her shiver as the crowd in Adam's screamed, "TEN!"

Evie jumped slightly and Nick abandoned his beer to wrap both his arms around her, sliding his hands over her hips before she turned in his arms to face him.

"Nine." Nick's eyes roved over her face.

His beard was getting unmanageable again and Evie wondered if he'd ever considered shaving it. She hoped not. He'd still be handsome without it, but she liked the way it framed his face and how his long hair brushed the top of it at the sides. It completed the picture of him, a rugged man with laugh lines and a smile that lit up a room.

This was *her* Nick. This was the Nick who sat across from her with a cup of coffee in the mornings, who chopped extra wood just in case, who turned on the stereo first thing so the cabin wasn't silent when she crawled out of bed.

"Five," Evie murmured, standing on her toes to get closer and tangling her fingers in the hair at the nape of his neck.

One of his hands rose, tenderly cupping the back of her head as the crowd around them shouted along with the countdown. Her heartbeat quickened under his intense gaze.

Evie closed her eyes just before the crowd screamed, "one!" as Nick's lips crashed against hers.

"Where there's life there's hope."
J.R.R. Tolkien, *The Hobbit**

꙳ ꙳

*Evie's personal copy of *The Hobbit* was hand-annotated by her brother. This was his favorite quote.

JANUARY

CHAPTER TWENTY-EIGHT

THE FIRE CRACKLED SOFTLY IN THE HEARTH, thawing the January chill settling over the cabin. Even with the front door repaired, Evie swore she still felt a draft every time she walked past.

The days since New Year's blurred.

She returned her library books in the outdoor drop-box because the library hadn't been open in weeks. She'd already tried to read *Wuthering Heights* again, but she could only read about the familial dramatics so many times before even she found her favorite classic boring.

Evie glanced over the back of the couch to see Nick wiping his hands on the hand towel. He caught her eye and winked, causing her to turn back to her book with a slightly disgruntled huff.

"That bad, huh?"

She didn't look up as he neared, leaning over the back of the couch. His hands came into view first, touching the pages and flipping them back and forth.

"How long have you been reading page twenty?"

She groaned, tilting her head back until it collided with his shoulder.

"I'm stir-crazy." She muttered the words, flipping the book closed. "I... I don't know what to do with myself. I keep thinking about Stephen. Then I think about going into town — but I don't want to risk us on the roads tonight —"

"Sweetheart." Nick cut her off, touching her chin and tipping her head back farther.

Evie stared up at him with a little frown. "Sorry."

"You want me to call the hospital again?"

Three days ago she *broke* slightly. She didn't want to ask him to use his personal cell to call the hospital, but she worried about Stephen all alone there. And of course, Nick noticed.

Nick always noticed.

He'd called the hospital and the nurse happily transferred him to Stephen's room. From there, Evie had curled up on the couch and chatted for a solid hour — getting a run-down on an *American Pickers* episode, and then listening to Stephen complain that the doctors still didn't feel he was stable enough to return home alone, especially with the weather as bad as it was.

Evie offered to visit him, but then, realized just as fast that it wasn't a possibility.

Stephen gently told her no — she didn't need to waste her time caring for an old man.

It was a comfort to hear his voice even if it meant she was stuck in the cabin with nothing to read except for hiking guidebooks.

"No, I mean... do I wish I could go up there? Maybe," she admitted softly. "But you and I both know it's a stupid decision."

Nick hummed, voice turning deliciously stern. "Get up."

Evie groaned as he grabbed her book and threw it onto the coffee table. "What? Why?"

"Up."

She stood and soon found herself being wrapped in her own jacket. Nick grabbed her scarf from the coat rack and wound it around her neck. Turning her head, Evie stared morosely out the front window.

" — going on a walk."

"Hm?"

Nick's words garbled, leaving her only to catch the ending fragment before she shifted and reached up, rubbing the left side of her head. Evie blinked at the ringing in her ear, a dullness that had yet to fade since Bryant fired the gun right next to her eardrum. She was beginning to be concerned it would never fully return, but she honestly tried *not* to think about it.

"You and I are going on a walk." Nick touched her chin, moving her head so her right ear was closer, letting her read his lips.

She frowned. "It's cold."

Nick shook his head slowly. "You are a *pain* in the *ass*, Evelyn Morgen."

Her mouth popped open in shock, eliciting a chest-rumbling laugh from the man in front of her. He grabbed his own jacket. "Come *on*."

With a grumble, she zipped up her jacket, whining, "Nick —"

"Hush." He leaned down and kissed her head, opening the door with his free hand and ushering her outside onto the frigid porch. Evie stood in the brisk air for a moment, letting it fill her lungs fully before exhaling in a puff. Shoving her hands into her jacket pockets, she fell into step beside Nick.

They made it around his truck before he motioned toward the tree line. He automatically stepped to walk on her right side, and Evie listened to the snow and gravel crunching underfoot, navigating over rocks and fallen branches.

"So..." She carefully stepped over a branch. "You and Chuck?"

Nick inhaled sharply, looking up at the sky before his shoulders sagged with his exhale. "You want the long story or the short one?"

Evie bumped her hip against his. "We've got time." Wind rustled the trees as Evie stepped closer to him, trudging down the path.

"I met Chuck when I was in the academy. I went in straight out of college." Evie blinked, and Nick caught her eye with a grin. "Yes, I have a *very* useful business degree."

She pulled her jacket tighter. "You can do a lot with a business degree. My library science one on the other hand..." She stared up, squinting for a moment. "I think if I didn't have a librarian job I'd be working at a coffee shop."

"Probably less murderers in a coffee shop."

The statement caught her so off guard that Evie snorted. "That's *awful*."

Nick shrugged, smiling. "I graduated and was given two options by my father — go into the police force, where I'd start as a beat cop, or the FBI. He didn't want me to '*do nothing as a job*' even though that's what my mother's family has done their entire lives."

The sounds of their boots faded as Evie turned her attention to the man next to her. The farther they got from the cabin, the more she felt the tension in her shoulders ease, relieved by the sound of his voice and the distance from the cage behind them.

"I went in knowing that I'd have a hell of a lot of training to do. I was in ROTC as a kid, another familial requirement, but when I went to college I let it slide a little. I didn't... relish the thought of being a cop, wearing blue, the badge — everything with it." Nick's face twisted in her peripheral vision and Evie let him sort through his thoughts for a moment before he continued.

"So I picked the FBI." Nick cleared his throat. "And it was there I met Andy and later on, Chuck. Andy was in the bunk row I was in. We had assigned roommates and both of ours flaked within the first week, leaving us with only each other. Chuck was an interim history lecturer for the FBI — mostly spy work in other countries."

Evie nodded slowly, thinking of the photos in Chuck's office. "Germany, right?"

Nick made a noise of confirmation next to her. "We got close. I was at Chuck's commitment ceremony." He paused, glancing at her. "You know, before marriage equality. Then Jonas died during my final year." His words got a little quieter at the end of the sentence, trailing off in the winter air. "Hope was just a kid."

She looked out at the snow-covered trees. "I can't even imagine."

Nick's voice was barely a whisper. "Neither can I."

They fell into silence, navigating the path for a few minutes until it began to curve around the property. Evie had never been out this far, but there was something peaceful about circling the cabin — still in range of its warmth — but away for the time being.

"I told Chuck when you got here." Nick finally spoke. "I didn't see Andy's call until I pulled up to the house that night." He turned his head, shooting her a little look, his lips twitching. "Imagine my surprise when I saw *you* on my front porch."

Evie huffed. "Imagine my surprise when I was hauled from Vermont to *Washington*, Nick."

He slowed to a stop, shaking his head with a little laugh. "I didn't want you left in the cabin alone with no one else aware of what was going on. I knew I could trust Chuck with my life — and yours." He hesitated, shifting his weight back and forth.

Evie had lost track of where they were in relation to the house, her eyes glued to the man in front of her as he buried his hands deeper into his coat pockets.

"That night..." He looked up at the sky again. "I heard you scream and sent Chuck a text because if I died — I wanted him on his way."

Evie's heart dropped to stomach. "*Nick* —"

"No, let me get this out." His face screwed up in a grimace. "I knew he'd drop everything and come." Nick pulled a hand out of his pocket, cupping her cheek gently. "Evie." He stepped closer, tilting his head down to stare at her. "I just want you to be safe. Your safety is my number one priority — Andy or not. I don't think Wells Creek is safe for you anymore."

"Us," Evie corrected him softly. "It's not safe for *us*. I'm not leaving you. I might be waiting for Andy to call, but if he decides to relocate me, you're coming too."

"I'm not a part of this. The FBI won't relocate me. I'm not an agent anymore —"

"Nick." Evie's voice dropped to a growl. "Shut the fuck up."

His mouth snapped shut, eyes wide as he stared down at her.

She sucked in a ragged breath, her eyes running over him. From his long hair pulled back and hanging down by his ears to the beard covering the lower half of his face. Her eyes committed *this* Nick to memory, the one highlighted by the high sun, slightly tanned skin reflecting the light from the snow.

"Just because you weren't with me that night in the library doesn't mean that you haven't become a target for that psychopath." Her jaw trembled with the effort of keeping her voice even. "I care about you, Nick. I'm not going to walk away, after all we've been through."

Nick's hand slid down, pulling her face toward his. As he bent to kiss her forehead, he muttered, "I care about you too, sweetheart."

"Good." Evie exhaled. "Because it would be weird to go back to the cabin and sleep beside each other if you didn't."

He laughed against her skin, then paused, whispering, "Turn around, *slowly.*"

Evie's heart leapt as he guided her, careful of her footing. There were two deer slowly walking through the snow and snuffing at it. She held her breath, feeling Nick's chest at her back, both of them standing stock-still as the buck and doe moved through the clearing.

Nick's hand slid down, finding hers. Evie wound her fingers with his, crushing his hand as the buck's head rose and stared straight at them.

He huffed, two puffs of steam leaving his nostrils as he looked back down at the snow and cleared a section with his hoof.

They stood there, Nick's hand locked in hers, until both the buck and doe moved on. As Evie watched them retreat, Nick shifted behind her, whispering into her right ear. "Let's go home."

She nodded, letting him pull her back toward the cabin. It only took a few minutes to emerge on the opposite side of the cabin from the front door. They picked their way through the snowy yard and around the house to the front steps, stomping their boots clear of snow as they headed back to the front door.

Nick let Evie step inside first, then dropped down to one knee, patting his leg. "Come here, let me help get those off of you."

Resting a hand on the wall for support, Evie lifted her leg, watching Nick as he braced it on his knee. His hands skimmed over her calves, before he tipped his head up and smiled at her. "Fix us a pot of coffee while I get the fire back up?"

Evie smiled softly, unable to resist combing her fingers through his hair. "Okay."

Nick's eyes creased as he squeezed the side of her leg and began unlacing her boots. When he was finished, she stepped away, feeling his lingering touch on her legs.

Everything in the kitchen was second nature, from filling the coffee pot with water to reaching for the grounds. As her hand wrapped around the tin, Nick slid up behind her, the fire roaring again in the living room. His hands came to rest on her stomach, his warmth crowding her back.

"Make it decaf." He murmured the words in her ear.

She shifted to grab the other tin, laughing a little. "No caffeine this afternoon?"

"I just think we should relax." His left hand sank lower, ghosting over the hem of her sweater. The touch was a distracting hum in the back of her mind as she scooped coffee grounds into the machine. Nick's lips pressed against the side of her head, hot breath fanning her hair. "Let me help relax you, sweetheart."

Evie laughed, but it came out breathy as his fingers found her stomach. The roughened pads of his fingers splayed across her skin as he nipped at her ear. She shivered, turning in his arms when the coffee was finally in the hopper.

He took the opportunity to bend down and kiss her, holding onto the skin of her stomach and pulling her flush against his chest. Nick's lips coaxed hers open before his tongue slid along her lower lip, eliciting a moan that echoed off the kitchen walls.

"*Nick.*" She pulled back just enough to stare up at him. "What are you doing?"

The twinkle in his eye made her heart clench in her chest.

"Winding you up, I thought that much was clear."

She pressed her lips together, trying to hide her smile. His hand crept up, reaching the bottom of her bralette.

"The coffee pot will take *forever* — it's old, you know." Nick leaned in again, kissing her jaw as a finger slid back and forth over the lace covering the bottom swell of her breasts. "And I can think of a few things we can do to kill that time."

She was glad *he* could think — because with his hands on her and his breath on her skin she couldn't form a thought. She couldn't do anything but nod when his hand enveloped her breast and his tongue ran along the curve of her jaw.

"You taste so sweet," he muttered against her skin, voice rough as his lips grazed her cheek. "Can I make you feel good, honey? Will you let me do that for you?"

She nodded, and that was all he needed to pull her away from the counter and jerk her to the living room. Evie let out a startled laugh, cut off by his hands cupping her face, tugging her to his chest in front of the fireplace to kiss her passionately. Evie reached up, tangling her fingers in his hair, squeaking as he nipped at her lips.

"I want to fucking *devour* you," Nick growled, reaching for her sweater. "It never stops, it's a constant. It's like I got one taste and you won't leave my head."

Evie's heart sped up as she lifted her arms for him. "So devour me."

"*Fuck.*" He tore the sweater off, sinking to his knees in front of the fire, tugging her with him. Her bralette was gone in the shuffle of hands and Nick dropped a kiss to the top of each breast. He pushed her shoulders gently until her back collided with the rug, the heat from the flames warming her side as he kissed downward. His lips followed the swell of her chest, leaving wet, open-mouthed kisses in his wake.

She stared as he reached the waistband of her leggings. Nick's eyes darted up, smirking as his hand cupped her through the leggings.

"Is this all for me?"

Evie nodded, worrying her lip between her teeth. "You know it is."

Nick smiled wider, the grin transforming into something wicked as two fingers pressed the seam of the leggings against her, rubbing slowly. Evie's hips jolted, jerking into his touch as she gasped his name.

"That's it," he cooed as his hands grabbed the band of her leggings and tugged them down. "Say my name, sweetheart. Remind yourself who makes you come the hardest."

Her head spun as he threw her leggings toward the couch. She didn't care about them in the slightest as Nick dropped between her legs, his mouth latching onto her pussy through the gusset of her underwear and sucking on the damp fabric.

She arched off the floor, scrambling to grab onto his hair for stability.

"*Evie.*" He chastised her with a chuckle, grabbing her hips to still her frantic movements. His voice was full of emotion, not just lust, but something sweeter and more tempting. His fingers toyed with the top of her underwear before pulling them down slowly, guiding them off her legs and dropping them onto the floor. Nick stared up at her through his lashes as his tongue darted out to run over her slit, whispering, "I want you to suffocate me."

Nick buried his head between her legs, his hands dropping to grasp her ass, hauling her hips up and pulling her legs onto his shoulders. Evie clamped her legs together, holding him in place as she felt his tongue lick over her, circling her clit.

She keened out again, clinging to his hair as he sucked her clit between his lips, teasing her with the barest brush of teeth against her sensitive skin. The warmth of the fire made her feel almost feverish as Nick ate her out, expertly winding her up once, then twice — pulling away each time before the orgasm washed over her flushed skin.

"Nick!" A sob built in her throat, tugging on his hair hard enough his head rose from between her thighs. His mouth and beard were covered in her arousal, a roguish grin on his lips as she panted.

"Yes, sweetheart?" Nick licked his lips.

"Stop teasing me." Evie stared down at him over her heaving chest, her grip tightening on his hair as Nick leaned forward and kissed the lower swell of her stomach, just above her pelvis. His tongue darted out, dragging a cold line down until it circled her clit again, eliciting a whine from the back of her throat. "*Please.*"

Nick smirked. "I like it when you beg, honey. Do it again while you drown me."

Evie sucked in a startled breath, then shoved his head back between her thighs, throwing her head back to the floor. "*Please*, Nick." She repeated the plea like a mantra, screwing her eyes shut as he laughed between her legs.

He dove his tongue back into her, steadily fucking her as one of his hands slid from the back of her hip. His thumb brushed her clit softly, sending her mind reeling. The pressure built in her core, tightening all her muscles as his thumb rhythmically strummed her clit. The slow build became overwhelming in an instant. Her orgasm barreled into her out of nowhere. Her body arched off the rug with a scream as Nick forced her to come so hard that her mind went blissfully blank.

She came back to reality to feel Nick's gentle touch on her inner thighs, kissing her skin. "That is my *favorite* sound." He nosed against her thigh again, glancing up at her as his fingers ghosted over her sensitive clit, making her whimper. "*That* one too."

Evie reached for him, stopped only by his hand on her stomach. "But —"

"Stop." He stared up at her, shaking his head. "I'm not done with you."

She sank back on her elbows, staring at him fully clothed between her legs. "What about you?"

Nick's fingers spread her, before he bent down and blew cold air across her. Evie squeaked, her elbows dropping out from under her as she clenched her thighs in response. He held them open, laughing wickedly before thrusting a finger into her.

She moaned, grabbing onto his shoulder and fisting his shirt in her hand.

"Your pleasure is my pleasure." He worked her up again, mindful of her sensitive clit. Still, it was torturous teasing until she was a begging wreck. Only then did he finally lean in, sucking her clit and adding a second finger to stretch her.

She was caught in an overstimulated loop by his lips, just slow enough to keep her on the edge. He curled the two fingers inside of her, hitting that spot she'd never been able to reach herself and making her gasp his name. He took the sound as an invitation to move faster, the wet sound obscene as he thrust quicker, sucking and flicking her clit with his tongue and teeth.

Evie fell apart, screaming his name into the side of her arm. Her body shook, wrung out and flushed from head to toe as she gasped, her back warm and slick with sweat.

Nick finally pulled away, sucking his fingers into his mouth, grinning from ear to ear.

"I should get our coffees before they go cold."

Evie breathed hard, staring as he raised over her, still fully clothed. His jean-clad hips hovered over her as he leaned in, beard wet. "Unless you've got one more in you."

She grabbed him by the face and kissed him hungrily, wrapping her legs around him. Evie grabbed the bottom of his sweater and started to push it over his shoulders, thanking god that there wasn't anyone else around the cabin to hear her hoarse screams as Nick ravaged her in front of the fire.

CHAPTER TWENTY-NINE

"I SEE."

Murphy squeezed the phone, standing in front of the wide windows that overlooked his family's property. The house in Los Angeles was shuttered for the time being — this was a home his mother purchased years ago, a quiet retreat in San Francisco that Murphy remembered running around as a child.

There weren't many other children around. He did have an older brother — *had* one. The files in his father's office told the gristly story of the fateful car chase and subsequent crash.

Murphy could still picture the devastation on his mother's face and the last shreds of kindness crumbling away from his father's eyes.

It was at that moment that Jonathan Murphy decided if he wanted to live in this family, he was no longer answering to any of the men who lauded themselves above him.

He would rule it.

If his own father couldn't keep Joseph Murphy from sampling the drugs they ferried and then wrapping himself around a guard rail, why should Jonathan listen to him? If he had to go to bed another night as a teen, fully aware of his mother's sobs down the hall, he would have lost it.

So Murphy did what any son would do, he began plotting how to kill his father.

It took him just under a decade. There were men to sway from his father's allegiance. There were business deals to broker, making sure that others saw him as their future. And there were the decisions Murphy made in hopes his mother would be provided for, until the day she held his hand and told him that the cancer had returned.

His plans sped up, but fighting time was a useless battle. He buried his mother. Then, less than eleven months later, he stood over his father's body in the study in LA, his chest heaving as he relieved the older Murphy from his familial duties.

There was a part of him that expected to feel an immediate sense of relief, but the body on the floor was as lifeless as he was. He cleaned up, called his men, and moved on.

Annoyances cropped up — his men didn't want to move east, but Murphy was tired of the hot sun and the constant harassment from the DEA. On the border it was irritating, Murphy knew the men he had entrusted with the cocaine deals were decent *enough* but that didn't stop the visits from agents who thought they had a scrap to go on.

Hawthorne seemed like the logical place to relocate.

His mother's hometown hadn't changed much over the years. Though he'd never been, she regaled him with stories through his childhood of the brief time she spent there, before she met his father — before she was involved with men who had questionable morals and didn't find charm in the simpleness life had to offer.

The first time he visited, it was laughably Hallmark, with its quaint town square and Christmas market. The cheer in the air was downright fucking jolly. He wasn't used to the friendly hellos from strangers, or the bright smiles that greeted him wherever he went.

It became increasingly apparent he could still be close to memories of his mother, while also sinking his claws into a place with less territorial disputes and an easier police force to sway. It was close to the Canadian border, which was far less guarded than he was used to. All the other Murphy business ventures were a mere flight away. His father's fumbled attempts to make the Murphy name mean something in Los Angeles seemed stupid in hindsight, when he could build an empire on a much more manageable scale here.

In Los Angeles, Murphy was only a knight — in Hawthorne, he could be king.

"Call when you get word of his body in a morgue. I want to know the fucking cabinet number before his body is identified, do you hear me?" He hung the phone up, turning away from the windows.

William Bryant was dead.

It was the only reason he'd not heard from Will. It was the reason phone calls had been unanswered for weeks, leaving Murphy questioning what the other man's move was after Colorado. Will was a loose cannon on a good day, often rocking the very tight ship that Murphy liked to keep — but he was *good* at his job. There was a reason he trusted the other man to slaughter a FBI agent and to track down this thorn in his side of a librarian.

Jonathan Murphy's first and only love was Will Bryant.

He stared out at the water, forcing himself to breathe in and out slowly. His eyes burned, throat closing as his hands trembled.

One small woman with a determined set to her jaw had thrown his entire operation into catastrophe in less than two months. It was infuriating, and he couldn't wait to watch that fight leave her eyes with his hands around her throat.

It wasn't just Hawthorne. It wasn't just the FBI breathing down his neck. It wasn't even the knowledge that one woman could put him behind bars to rot for the rest of his life.

Losing Will was different.

Murphy was the one who cleaned up after his father's many drunken mistakes after Joseph's passing. He was the one who buried his mom, who made sure the flowers were set to be placed on her grave until his eventual children's children would be dead.

And he was the idiot who shot Ben Harriet in the school.

He wasn't the beetle on its back under the cat's paw. He was the wolf, haunches raised and teeth exposed, ready to rip the pussycat to pieces.

"Jean, darling." Murphy caught his housekeeper as she walked past the office door. His voice was steady, but his being was unmoored. "I'll be leaving tonight."

What messes Jonathan Murphy made, Jonathan Murphy cleaned up.

CHAPTER THIRTY

"ANDY?" EVIE ANSWERED THE PHONE ON THE SECOND to last ring. She'd barely heard the phone over the sound of the shower, holding a towel to her chest in one hand and as she snagged the burner phone from Nick's nightstand, dripping soap everywhere.

She didn't want to miss a call that might finally give them a crumb of information.

"Hey, Evie." Andy sounded exhausted. "Nick there?"

"He's outside." Evie pulled the towel closer, wrapping it firmly around herself. "He was getting more wood for the fireplace."

Andy's pause was all the information Evie needed.

"I'll go get him."

Evie's mind spun, but just as she reached the kitchen table, the front door creaked open. Nick stepped in with wood balanced in his arms. At her expression, he froze, eyes flickering from her in the towel to the phone.

"It's Andy." She floundered, standing still as Nick moved to shut the door and dump the wood in one quick movement.

Evie pressed the speaker button, handing it over to Nick as he neared. He still had his coat and boots on — something she rarely saw past the entryway, but the warmth radiating off his body made her shift closer, painfully aware of her lack of layers.

"I take it I can finally talk?"

"Go ahead," Nick snapped. "This better be actual news, Andy."

"Wouldn't call if it wasn't, *Nick*."

Evie winced at their tones. "We're listening. Just please — did you find him?"

Silence answered her and Evie felt all the hope in her chest crush with the weight of it. Whatever the news was — it wasn't tied to her freedom from isolation.

"The lab results came back from the body. It matches up with a man named James Green — we have no history of a William Bryant, but the DNA did partially match what was found on Beck's body." Andy's voice hitched, but was gone in an instant. "Which places... Green? Bryant? Whatever you want to call him — as a suspect connected to Murphy."

She turned, staring up at Nick. All the things Bryant said to her in the moment, all the taunts and the smiles and promises — they were *real*. She hadn't imagined any of it.

On the other hand, Andy still didn't believe her from the start.

"We also found the guy's truck." Evie wished she could see Andy's face, to prepare herself for what would likely come from his mouth. "It was a lot of nothing. He'd stolen it, left a backpack inside with a few aliases, none of them Green or Bryant. Nothing suggesting he was working with Murphy. But —"

"But?" Evie leaned in, feeling Nick's arm wrap around her.

"But," Andy continued, "he had a cell phone in his pocket and we're working with forensics to pull the call data from it.

Something must have smashed it to hell during the fight. The internals are busted. He also had a crumpled up photo of you, Evie."

Sudden nausea made her knees buckle and she grabbed onto a kitchen chair, lowering herself into it as Nick looked on, concerned. Something about the way his eyes tightened at the edges told her that this phone call was about to end — and not well.

"So you called to tell her you have nothing." Nick's voice was sharp and loud in the small living room. "You only half believe she was telling the truth about Bryant and only because his DNA barely matches the guy who killed Beck, *which we fucking knew*, Andy. What other evidence do you need? He clearly came here to *find her*."

"Hey," Andy snapped back. "Don't get pissed at me. I'm relaying the information I have. I can't operate on guesses. How can I even believe anything that's recounted to me? How can I move forward in a case this big with that flimsy-ass proof? The photo proves nothing — maybe she just had a stalker that we're only now finding out about."

Evie sucked in a ragged breath, her hands curling into fists as she stared down at the kitchen table. "You believed me the first time, Andy."

"The first time I had cameras — *proof* that Jonathan Murphy was in Hawthorne and killed Ben Harriet. This time? Fucking smoke in the air. I have nothing except for you both insisting a dead man spent his final moments — how did you phrase it?" Each word was like a slap across her cheek. "*Monologuing like a Batman villain?*"

"But he did —"

"I can't *prove* that."

She could see the anger building as Nick's shoulders squared. She reached out and grabbed the phone before he crushed her only connection to Andy — to her parents. Laying it on the kitchen table, Evie stared down at it, her heart in her throat.

"The photo proves he came to the cabin for a reason."

Andy huffed, then softened slightly. "But I can't tell you *why* he was hunting you down. I have nothing that ties this man to Murphy, no sightings together, no suggestion families have worked together, not even a hint that Green or Bryant or *whatever* his name was had any connections. And I probably won't find them."

"Because of the cell phone," Nick supplied, looking down at the one on the table.

"Because of the cell," Andy confirmed. "What I can tell you both is that this isn't done. If this was Murphy, then he sent his best, a motherfucker who killed an *FBI Agent* for him, and he still couldn't kill you, Evie."

All she could think was: *not for lack of trying.*

She didn't say anything as she stared at the cellphone. For days she worried she'd be questioned over Bryant's death. Even Nick's arms around her each night and whispered reassurances against her hair couldn't keep the hair-raising nightmares at bay.

She saw Bryant choking on his own blood, smiling up at her with gore-stained teeth and telling her to deliver the killing blow.

And she saw herself doing it.

"Murphy didn't give up before and he certainly won't now." Andy sounded resigned. "I've got directors breathing down my fucking neck asking me if it's smart to keep you in Wells Creek after the shit-show we just had to deal with."

Evie's heart stuttered. "They want to move me?"

"They'd be stupid not to." Nick finally spoke again, but he shifted to hold onto the back of her chair. Her shoulders relaxed, leaning back into him. "But I'm not going to sit by and watch those idiots take her away. The same shit will happen again and it won't end with Murphy's henchmen in bags."

The room went quiet as Nick's words settled onto Evie's skin like a film. She didn't have to like it, but he was right. The next time Murphy sent someone, they would try even harder to kill her, or drag her back to Murphy to finish the job. And if she didn't have Nick beside her — who's to say the agents she would be left with would care enough to keep her safe over themselves? And who could blame them if they didn't?

"Do you..." Evie trailed off, forcing herself to speak up. "Has there been any movement on spotting him? Anything in Hawthorne? Are my parents okay?"

"I had an agent in Vermont for over a month, there was nothing." Andy paused. "My superior did make me pull the cover, since we had local PD on file to alert us if any of Murphy's known associates were in town. But so far Vermont has seemed to be the safest place possible. Anywhere *you* aren't, he ignores."

Evie let out a half-laugh, hearing it get caught in her throat. "That's *great*, it really is going to come down to him wanting me dead."

"That's what it looks like." The cell crackled before Andy sighed. "For now I've stopped the paperwork from going through with a request to only move you, insisting Nick goes too. And since I didn't do *any* of this by the books, everyone keeps asking *why* Nick would even need to be there —"

"I'm not leaving Wells Creek without Nick, Andy." The words were out of her mouth before she could process them fully. A lump sat in the back of her throat as she looked up at the man beside her, whose hand was pressed against the bare skin of her shoulder, grounding her as she muttered, "I won't do it."

Andy let out a frustrated noise. "No one here understands why he needs to be involved, even if I try to explain it. Washington was a quick fix — now I need to keep my witness safe."

"Great." Evie let silence hang in the air for a beat. "I don't give a shit. I don't seem to have a choice in any of these decisions. I don't get to know the random timetables the FBI seems to be working on, and I'm certainly not being trusted to accurately recount the events that happen to me. So if the FBI wants to move me — *fine*, but Nick is coming with me. I've been patient. I've isolated myself. I've waited for calls from you, Andy, I've had myself poked and prodded at the hospital because someone *broke into the cabin and tried to murder me*. I'm not just a witness, I'm a *person*."

Nick's hand splayed across her skin and from behind her, his voice rumbled out. "Maybe I can make a few calls. I think my dad still talks to the Director — I know my mom is still on that ladies' golf team with his wife."

"Are you threatening to go *above me*?" Andy spat the words and Evie stared at the phone in alarm. "I can't believe what I'm hearing. No, you're not going to pull strings with your military daddy, Nick. I'm the head agent on this case, I'm the one who —"

"Who's going to get the woman I love killed?" Nick cut him off and Evie stopped breathing. "Because that's what this will do. You let them put two agents on her that don't know her and she's dead. The next person Murphy sends won't waste a breath to gloat — he's *made* that mistake. The next man that comes after Evie will kill her and drag her corpse back to Murphy to prove it's done. So either I'm with her every fucking second or I go over your head. It's not just the Barber name that holds weight, and you damn well know it."

"Fine." Andy's voice was clipped. "I'll call when I have

more information. Don't leave the cabin. Don't do anything stupid."

The dial-tone sounded on the other end of the line.

Evie stared down at the phone, leaving it to sit quietly on the kitchen table. Her mind couldn't keep up. Between Andy's anger and Nick's words, she wasn't sure what just happened.

His hand slid up to rest on her neck, squeezing gently. "Hey." Nick leaned down, pressing a kiss against her hair. "Talk to me."

"You love me?"

Nick's breath caught, but she felt him smile against her hair as his fingers rubbed the back of her neck, easing the tension slowly but surely from her body.

"Look at me."

Evie tilted her head back, the weight of it supported by his hand. In his jacket, hair pulled back into a knot at the back of his head, and eyes gentle, she couldn't imagine being stuck here with anyone else. The thought felt wrong. This place was synonymous with Nick. This experience wouldn't be right if he wasn't a part of it. The thought nearly choked her.

She wouldn't go back in time and prevent her encounter with Murphy if it meant she never met the man touching her in this very moment.

"I love you, Evie." He brushed the hair off her forehead before he bent down and kissed her. "I know there were better moments to say it, but I love you. I'm not letting you out of my sight until Murphy is in a bodybag."

Evie's chest ached, she tried to clear her throat but it didn't help how hoarse the words sounded. "I think I love you too."

Nick smiled down at her, the lopsided motion making his beard raise only on the right. "Yeah? You think? You need some convincing?"

She let out a strangled laugh and then grabbed his free

hand, pulling him closer and pressing her lips against the back of it, closing her eyes. "I know I do."

Nick bent down and pressed his cheek against her hair. "We *will* make it through this, but nothing can be done right now except for getting you in the shower that's still running up my water bill and having some supper."

Evie felt her own lips twitch. The shower *was* still running, which meant the hot water was probably all gone by now. But somehow she didn't care as he tugged her up from the kitchen chair and slowly pushed her down the hallway toward the bathroom, unzipping his jacket and kicking his boots off as he stumbled over them to follow her.

He was right. There was nothing that could be done now. And she'd worry about the passion between them fizzling out when Murphy was caught or killed later — if she was even alive to worry after that.

CHAPTER THIRTY-ONE

IN THE DAYS SINCE ANDY'S CALL, ALL EVIE COULD DO was pace like a caged zoo animal. She could tell it was starting to weigh on Nick with the way he insisted on a routine; breakfast, lunch, and dinner. Where she felt aimless, he tried to fill the gaps with something for her to look forward to in the endless bleed of days.

It didn't work.

She went to bed with him each night, pressing her head against his chest, his shoulder, his neck — breathing in his warm scent, but nothing seemed to keep the anxiety at bay anymore.

Evie felt unmoored and *Wuthering Heights* couldn't even help her.

The fire spat embers as she sipped a cup of coffee. Maybe if they finally made it back into town she would pick up some tea from the market — but Andy's voice echoed.

Don't leave, don't risk it.

She stared at the mug, as familiar as the man she slept beside.

That was another thing — the explosive moments between her and Nick, the breakneck speed at which she felt her heart pitching itself off the mountainside for him — they hadn't faded, but there was a film over it. Her brain warred when she couldn't rest. When his steady breath ruffled the top of her head all she could think about was that this was too fast, too much, too soon. She was selfish, he would get hurt.

Evie's chest ached at the thought of leaving him. The threat of Andy moving her to a protection detail and strict rules, was inconceivable

She didn't know what to do anymore and she'd never enjoyed being without a plan.

Evie stared at the stack of books on the coffee table. She'd already read everything in the cabin, including the hiking guide. Maybe Nick could call the hospital tomorrow to see if Stephen was any closer to getting out. It would be a Saturday and she knew they normally waited until a weekday for release — but she would risk going out of town if it meant helping him home.

Uncertainty washed over her. Last night when she couldn't sleep, she'd crept out of the bed and rifled through every kitchen drawer for a notepad. The idea hit her when she remembered the months following her brother's death. There had been a single therapist that looked at her vacant teen self and told her it was okay if she didn't know how to process any of this, but writing it down might help.

So she sat down with the notepad and a pen emblazoned with *GREG'S TRUCK STOP*, pillaged from Nick's junk drawer, and she started to write a letter to her parents.

She didn't know if she'd ever get the chance to tell them everything in person, but she did have words. She always had words to fall back on.

Evie sat her coffee down on a coaster before repositioning

with her legs underneath her. With the fire crackling, she picked the notepad up, staring at the unfinished letter full of mixed emotions, crossed-out words, and thoughts that trailed nowhere.

She started to write again.

There wasn't a good way to explain to them how safe Nick made her feel. It felt like trying to explain the way fresh air felt after being cooped up inside all day, or the way the sun felt after weeks of rainy days. He was a warmth to her, a light that nestled in her chest and made her aware that she didn't *have to be* aware herself. It was a comfort to know he was down the hallway, one movement away from reaching her.

She wondered sometimes if her brother's death had done more damage than she could even process. There was a certain loneliness to knowing that the favorite child was gone and she was all her parents had left. She'd seen the look in her father's eyes when she'd been returned home in the back of a police car, or told, once again, to go to her room even though she and her parents knew she'd just sneak back out.

And then college gave her actual freedom to try to make something of herself. All it did was make her realize that being alone was something she'd known her entire life.

The letter she wrote would never be seen by her parents. She didn't want to hurt them, or reopen old scars with the bluntness of a butter knife — but the past years made her realize that maybe it was okay if she finally found someone she could be alone with.

A door creaked in the hallway and Evie lifted her head. Nick yawned and ruffled his beard, padding barefoot to the bathroom, before making a beeline for her. She pressed her lips together, hiding her smile as the giant man plopped down into the narrow space between the couch and the coffee table and reached back, palming her legs.

"What are you doing?" She felt like she had to whisper, even if they were the only two people in the cabin. It was too early for using her full voice, in case it would break the sleepy spell cast over him.

Nick finally managed to untangle her legs and Evie laughed as he slung them over each of his shoulders and leaned back, his head between her thighs and resting on the couch cushion.

With a sleep-addled smile up at her, Nick grumbled, "Hi, come here often?"

Evie giggled, letting the paper fall to the side in favor of touching his mussed hair.

"This is getting so long," she mused, running her fingers over the dark brown waves. It wasn't curly by any means, but it had a mind of its own. She hoped he never cut it. The Nick she liked best was the one in front of her, a full beard, long hair, and kind, creased eyes.

Nick hummed, his eyes falling shut as she toyed with his hair. The act of moving her fingers through it made her heart rate slow too, a meditation.

"I can't remember the last time I went to a barber." He spoke softly, leaning back into her hands as she ran her nails over his scalp. "I kept it short in my teens because that's what my dad always did with his. It was expected."

Evie pushed it off his forehead, looking down with a little grin. "You know, I think with a half mask we could make you look like Bucky Barnes."

Nick's eyes flew open and a laugh bubbled out of his chest. Evie's heart fluttered as he lifted a hand and laid it on her leg. "Yeah? You want me to wear the tights?"

She laughed, cupping his face. "You know I'm talking about the movies, not the comics. I can't tell you how many of those volumes I've had to stock in my library for the kids." She ran her fingers over his cheeks, split wide from a smile. "I remember I placed such a big order with our distributor that they asked me if I had plans to read them myself. It felt like too much of a task, I like my kid lit. I did have to do research to make sure what I bought was age appropriate."

Nick turned his head, pressing a kiss to one palm then turning to the other side to repeat the action. "It's been so long since I kept up with any of that. When I moved here I got my library card on a whim one afternoon and Stephen and I talked for a good thirty minutes about how I hadn't picked up anything except Ray Bradbury in years."

"You and that book. Did you leave with anything that day you got your card?"

"Oh yeah," Nick assured her, running his hands up and down her calves. "I got..." His brow creased as he leaned back, staring up at her. "Fuck, what did I get? Maybe a book about the area because I thought, 'hey if I'm retired maybe I can take up fishing.' And that clearly didn't work."

"Fishing?" She couldn't imagine Nick sitting in the middle of a lake, waiting for something to swim along and take the bait. "That really doesn't seem like the hobby for you."

"Well —" He slapped her leg lightly. "I had to have some trial and error, sweetheart. There are only so many hobbies old retired men are allowed to have. There's fishing, there's religiously following a sports team of choice, or there's being grumpy to random children on your lawn. I knew the last one wasn't going to happen and I didn't want a TV in the cabin so..."

"So fishing," Evie finished, giggling. "You're not even old, Nick."

He sighed, resting his cheek against her right thigh. The feeling of his breath on her skin made her smile, but it also caused goosebumps. "I'm almost forty, only a couple more years." Nick pressed a kiss to her thigh, burying his face against her skin as he mumbled, "I never thought about age until I left the Bureau. Then, suddenly, all I could think about was the fact that by the time my father was this age, he had a family."

Evie went quiet, stroking his hair gently. "Is that what you want? A family?"

Nick pressed his lips against her leg, then pulled back. "I don't think I do."

There was a pregnant pause, then Nick cleared his throat. "I can't imagine treating a kid how I was treated. How my father treated me when he..."

Evie stayed quiet, her fingers sliding over the crown of Nick's head.

Nick let out a gentle breath. "When he found out I liked men too — that I'm bisexual — it caused a lot of shit."

Her heart clenched, the muscle spasming as she stared down at the man before her. Nick's face was shuttered, closed off as he thought back to something that whispered pain across his features. She opened her mouth, throat dry as she tried to think of the right words to say. She'd never thought much about her own label — but she supposed that did fit — bisexual, pansexual, fluid — it all worked. Whomever she dated had always been *her* business, not anyone else's, and she wasn't entirely certain her parents would care either way. They'd always loved her unconditionally; how could Nick's father not love him in the same way?

The love in her heart choked her. Evie paused the ministrations of her fingers, bending to kiss the crown of his head. Nick stirred under the movement as she whispered, "I'm sorry he made you feel anything less than the perfect man you are."

He turned his chin, letting it rest on her thigh as he looked back at her, unshed moisture shining in his eyes. "I think about my parents, the 'tough love,' the money to show they care instead of actual love and I just... I don't want to raise a kid like that. I want a kid to know they're loved, regardless of who they are."

"You wouldn't," she assured him, touching his cheek. "You'd be an incredible father." She let her fingers trail over his beard. "But it makes a lot of sense why you can't stop touching me all the time. You'd rather show physical affection. I don't mind it — I can't seem to stop touching you either."

He chuckled as she bent, peppering kisses on his face. She wanted him to feel the raw emotion — to drown in the love she was constantly overwhelmed with.

"Do you blame me?" His words were muffed as she kissed his nose. She brushed her lips against his, his words a quiet caress. "It's hard to say no when it's you, honey."

She laughed softly, smiling against his mouth as they kissed. In the quiet of the cabin all Evie could hear was her thumping heart. The moment was the kind she could imagine looking back on, even if everything fell apart.

She would have this moment of Nick close to her and their focus solely on each other.

"You know you're safe right?" He lifted a hand from her leg to touch her chin. "I'm always going to keep you safe. Even if Andy does pull you out. I'll find a way to follow."

"I know." She pulled back slightly, touching his hair again. It was so mussed from the bed that she wanted to run a brush through it and carefully rearrange it for him. The domesticity of the urge made her ache. "I think we did this relationship out of order."

His answering grin made her lips twitch. Nick grabbed her legs again, humming as he fully leaned back into her lap. "Probably, but I wouldn't do it any differently, sweetheart."

Evie smiled, toying with the errant strands of hair around his forehead. "Yeah?"

"Yeah." He patted her thigh. "I guess I can't be too pissed at Andy. It was with *you*. I wouldn't go back on any of it."

She felt her chest warm. Her answer was barely audible. "I can't imagine going through this with anyone but you, Nick."

They fell silent as his eyes shut. She thought he'd lapsed back into sleep when he suddenly let out a tiny sigh. "You know, I think Andy's doing his best. I might not agree with the methods, but I get it. I'm the one who could walk away from the FBI and still be able to do whatever the fuck I wanted. Andy couldn't, and didn't want to."

Evie frowned, touching his jaw and running her thumb over his skin. "You met him during training, right? Just before you met Chuck?"

Nick hummed in affirmation, turning his head so his lips could press against her thumb in a soft kiss. "Andy and I got partnered up pretty quick once we were farther along in the course. No one else wanted me on their side because of my father. I had to perform at double the best — luckily Andy is a competitive bastard."

"You're joking. He wanted you as a partner because he wanted to beat you?"

Nick looked up at her, his eyes sparkling in the firelight. "One hundred percent, I bet if you asked him, he'd tell you that." His hands slid over her calves. "I remember our first few assignments together, desk work, all he kept telling me was that he thought if he got in good with me we'd be off desk in a couple months." He raised his shoulders in a half-shrug. "He was right."

As he hesitated, she took the time to smooth his hair back from his forehead, stroking the strands gently. Nick's eyes fluttered shut before he murmured, "Our first case together was in Vegas. He bought me the keychain that I keep with my truck keys."

She'd seen it multiple times. The keychain was in the style of old hotel room key tags; but a red plastic that had clearly faded over the years. The raised VIVA LAS VEGAS lettering was printed in gold, chipped around the edges. It occurred to her once or twice to ask why it was the only keychain he owned, but in the quiet of the living room, it settled on her that the meaning ran far deeper than a souvenir.

Nick tilted his head, lips against the skin of her knee. "We shared a room — that first case together. We'd grown close through the academy and..." His brow furrowed as he glanced up at her. "And we kissed. Just once. It was a culmination of a lot of moments, and the first time I'd felt truly free away from my father's eye. That little motel room was quiet, it was just four walls and... and —" His throat bobbed.

Evie kissed his temple, whispering, "You don't have to explain it to me, Nick. You cared about each other. You *still* do. Did either of you ever have a conversation?"

"No." He snorted, shaking his head. "That would have made too much sense. It happened. We went back to working together. The needle never moved in either direction — strictly platonic or romantic. It just sat stagnant. We worked a couple more small cases, then I was shot."

Evie reached down, smoothing out the line between his brows. "That's not how Andy told it. He said you *took* the bullet for him. Actually, I think he told me that you seemed like the type to take a bullet for someone. And then you turned around and just took one for me."

Nick's lips lifted. "I didn't take it though, it just grazed me." His palm eased over her thigh, creeping higher. "So, technically, he was wrong. I did take the bullet for *him* though." Evie watched the emotions play across his face for a moment before Nick sucked in a breath. "It hurt, but I didn't want his career to end. I was fine for mine to end — or something worse to happen."

"Oh, Nick." Evie dipped down, pressing her lips against his cheek, wrapping her arms around his torso from the back. After a moment, she realized she'd never asked about the bullet hole she'd felt on his bare skin. It felt small — but she'd never taken much time to turn him around and fully look at where it was on his back. "Did they make you retire?"

He shook his head. "Nah, I did that myself. I found out Chuck officially retired the year before and was living up here. I decided to come up here and bother him."

She rolled her eyes, toying with his beard. "Is that *really* why?"

"No," Nick huffed, readjusting so she was pulled forward against him, almost sitting on his shoulders. "I didn't want to deal with the FBI's shit anymore." He stared at the fireplace. "I was tired of the way they handled everything. It was paperwork and bureaucracy. I felt like the situations we handled needed a faster timetable. You get that." Nick turned his head, glancing back at her. "That's why I got shot."

Evie stared at him, swallowing a lump in her throat. "What happened?"

He turned back to the fire and she felt his shoulders tense slightly under her legs.

"We got put on a case for a small crime group operating outside of Boise. It was a long con, the kind of group that's been around for years and will survive decades more. That night we were supposed to just sit, but one of our undercover guys got made."

Nick's jaw ticked. "It was chaos, the guys in the meeting turned on our guy — Andy and I rushed in. Guns drawn, bullets flying." He shook his head. "I threw myself in front of Andy while he was dragging our guy out the door, got hit in the back and didn't even realize it until we were in the car taking our guy to the hospital."

"Where would it have hit Andy?"

"The bullet?" Nick turned his head, nuzzling her thigh. "From the angle, probably his spine. I knew it had a risk of doing the same to me, but he actually cared. He wanted to help people, do good." Before she could even think of a response, he spoke. "Saved the other guy though, he got out with a broken arm and a gunshot to the shoulder. Nothing major. I turned in my badge the next week, said fuck it to the people and the paperwork. I got hell from my father for not sticking with something, for not helping more people, and moved here. My mom never cared, but she was never one for careers. I guess I could have done more."

Tears burned the back of her throat as she clung to him. This man between her legs, holding onto her just as tightly as she was to him, who had admitted he was willing to do anything to protect her — felt like he didn't do enough.

It broke her fucking heart.

"I love you." She had to say it. Otherwise the emotions would destroy her. "I love you and you do enough, Nick."

She could feel his small smile against her skin as he pressed another kiss to her thigh, his beard scratching as he looked up at her. "I love you too."

Chapter Thirty-Two

THE FLUORESCENT LIGHTS OVERHEAD WERE FAINTLY buzzing as he walked through the automatic doors. The small-town hospital was quiet — any severe patients were often transferred to one of the larger Seattle hospitals only forty minutes away. But Murphy knew that the man he was visiting today was still trapped in a bed somewhere on the second floor. He was too high risk for another heart attack, too stable to take up a bed somewhere else, and too old to go home alone.

He gave the woman at reception a pleasant smile, nodding his head at her as he walked around the circular desk and headed toward the elevators just behind it. Visiting hours would be ending soon, but he didn't plan on lingering long.

Murphy had traveled all night.

First it was to get from San Francisco to Seattle. Then it was from the private airport to a shitty holding cell of a morgue that the cops used for bodies that they still needed for open cases.

It was there he paid someone off to see Bryant.

The elevator doors chimed as they opened — letting

Murphy inside along with a tall doctor who was holding a paper coffee cup, lid half askew to let the steam out. Her focus was on her phone in the palm of her hand, locs pulled back into a ponytail with her lips pursed at the screen. Murphy glanced over at the phone, the text too small for him to read, but it was all the same, none of it really mattered.

William looked so small.

The white sheet the mortician had draped over him was stiff when Murphy tugged it away. Pale, cold skin was firm under his fingertips as he'd touched Will's cheek and felt the first bubble of emotion welling in him. It was hard to argue the facts in front of him last night — Will was dead, a wound so deep in his throat that Murphy's own stomach had churned at the sight.

When he was done clutching onto Will's lifeless body, he'd shot the mortician unfortunate enough to be there. Then he'd taken a phone call.

Trickles of conversation replayed in his mind as he walked down the linoleum hallway. The cop Murphy knew in Washington was a man who had helped the Murphy family out for nearly a decade. He was a beat-cop, more interested in day-drinking in his cruiser than actually defending the public. In essence, he was the kind of man who could be bought, sold, used, and then sold again for the right price. He was a mere tool, a plaything for Murphy to pick up when he needed some extra information.

"Jonathan, how are you, boy?"

Murphy tilted his head as he side-stepped behind the empty nurse's desk. A list of patients and room numbers were easily accessible and he found the name with no problem.

He had, of course, reminded Officer Bernard that he preferred to be called by his last name only — and that the other man better have a very good reason for calling that particular number.

"*I do, I do. I spoke to Karl —*" Bernard chuckled like a mall Santa gearing up to greet a thousand sticky children. "*Heard you were looking for a girl, and I've found her.*"

Wells Creek, Washington — a small town just outside of Seattle, primarily composed of loggers and washed-up retirees who enjoyed eating granola in the dirt. It wasn't Murphy's idea of fun, but it was one hell of a hiding place. Out of sight, out of mind. It was also the current home to Nick Barber, ex-Federal agent and prior partner to Anthony Wilson.

If he'd pulled that thread sooner, maybe Will wouldn't be dead.

"*I got it from the cops that your man's body was transferred from this small town after a chaotic night. Break-in and some old man had a heart attack — he's still in the hospital. They said they're keeping him there, but can't spare a hired cop to watch. He's a local librarian from Wells Creek — no relation to the incident that night but a friend of your girl's.*"

A friend was a dangerous thing to have.

The words *thank you* didn't leave Murphy's lips at the end of the call, but he did send double the amount he normally did for information. Let Bernard buy extra booze and maybe his liquid tongue would get even looser down the line — it didn't matter, because a name, a location, and a place to channel his ire was all Murphy really needed.

The door was partially open to the hospital room, allowing him to easily slip inside. The soft beeping of the heart monitor filled the room as he slowed to a stop, watching the old man's chest rise and fall in the bed.

Murphy reached over and picked up a spare pillow from the cabinets along the wall. In two steps he was next to the bed. In the next second, he had it over the man's face.

Stephen Vogt thrashed — but it wasn't the vicious fighting Murphy expected when he would finally get the chance to watch the light leave Evelyn Morgen's eyes. It was the half-hearted fight of an old man who had seen better days, who had been in a hospital for a month because a heart attack had nearly taken the eighty year old out, and in a pathetically futile moment, Murphy watched a wrinkled hand grasp at his fore-arm, then slide off, dropping back to the hospital bed with a soft, limp, *thump*.

The death of Stephen Vogt would certainly send Jonathan Murphy's message nicely.

He knew where Evelyn Morgen was, and it was only a matter of time before he choked the life out of her as well.

"It had come about exactly in the way things happened in books."
Agatha Christie, *And Then There Were None**

～ ～

*EVIE'S FAVORITE MYSTERY NOVELIST — unfortunately, it'll take her years to pick the genre up again.

FEBRUARY

Chapter Thirty-Three

"Can you hand me the coffee pot?"

Wordlessly, Nick passed it to her, then pushed the drooping sleeves of her cardigan up for her as Evie plunged it into the sink. He kissed her head before walking away, calling back, "What do you want to do today?"

"Same as every day, wait for a phone call!" Evie rolled her eyes as she ran the kitchen sponge over the old glass coffee pot. It had no bells, no whistles — exactly what her grandfather would have preferred. Even if he had secretly enjoyed ordering the fanciest thing on the menu when they found themselves outside of Hawthorne at one of the big coffee shops.

The memory stung as she rinsed the soap off. As she placed it on the kitchen towel to the side, she rolled her neck back and forth. For all the monotony of the past few weeks, Nick had been trying his best to keep her entertained. He'd even asked if Chuck could bring a TV to the cabin. Evie recoiled at the thought of mindless infomercials.

She did, however, tell Chuck that he could bring *any* book to her and she'd read it.

He'd delivered her a stack of five books from Hope two days ago. They were still sitting on the coffee table and Evie couldn't wait to pick up one. Hope's taste was... different to what Evie preferred, but most of the fantasies that Hope sent *did* have aspects of romance — and Evie was on a romance kick. Anything to mentally escape the four walls of the cabin worked.

She and Nick hadn't left the cabin since Andy's call. If this was the way the FBI wanted to play it, Evie would be a sitting duck. It was either play along, or be relocated. And that wasn't something she wanted to risk.

She didn't like staying put — but she hoped that one day Murphy would be miraculously taken into custody and she'd never have to look over her shoulder again.

As she turned the water off, Evie wiped her hands on the spare towel and paused, turning her head. There was a faint ringing sound. It was hard to pinpoint, but it wasn't Andy's cell.

"Nick? Is that your phone?"

The soft ringing cut off and Evie stood in the hall, frowning as Nick stepped out of his bedroom with his phone. Every step he took toward her took a year from her life.

He cleared his throat, making a noise of confirmation to the person on the other end of the line. "Yes, thank you for calling. I'll call in a few days about the arrangements."

Evie's heart stopped. There were tears already welling even though she didn't know why. Her body was reacting before her mind could comprehend the look on Nick's face.

"Evie." Nick cupped her face after he put his phone into his pocket. His voice sounded rough and she could see tears in his eyes. "Sweetheart, that was the hospital."

"No." The word ripped itself from her chest. "*No*, Nick."

His face twisted. "Honey, it was Stephen's nurse."

"No," Evie sobbed, reaching out for him. Her hands wrapped around his forearms as she felt her chest collapse. "No, please don't say what I think you're going to say. Please tell me he's *okay*."

Nick pulled her into his chest, cradling the back of her head. "Stephen died two nights ago. The hospital had to open up an investigation — they think someone suffocated him in his sleep."

"Oh my *god*." The wail that left her throat didn't sound human. His arms were the only things holding her up as all the emotions from the past month hit her like a freight train. She couldn't think straight. She couldn't even breathe, gasping against his t-shirt as she tried to process the words.

Stephen was dead. Someone *killed* him.

The same man who had welcomed her with open arms into Wells Creek was gone and it was her fault.

Evie sucked in a ragged breath, feeling like she was inhaling razors as she pulled away from Nick in a rush. His hands moved away, giving her space and Evie ran her arm over her face, smearing tears and snot as she pushed past him. Nick called her name, but she charged toward the bedroom, slamming the door open as she made a beeline for the nightstand.

"Evie, don't —"

But he wasn't fast enough.

Her fingers wrapped around the emergency phone. For the first time, she pressed the callback button, holding it up to her ear.

"What's wrong? Evie?" Andy sounded frantic and breathless.

"Are you happy, Andy?" she whispered, wishing she sounded as angry as she felt. She fought to get the next sentence out. "Stephen's *dead*."

Andy made a confused noise. "Who?"

Evie's world crumbled with the single question.

"Stephen, my *friend*, Andy, he's dead. Murphy is here and he *killed* him."

"Murphy is in Wells Creek?"

Her eyes caught Nick's, hopeless. What was she supposed to say? What else was she supposed to do? It was clear that everything she did led to people dying.

Nick took a step forward, slowly reaching out for the phone.

On the other end of the line, Andy was asking a thousand questions. "Stephen who? Vogt? The librarian? I have that paperwork somewhere. He had a heart attack. What's to say he didn't die from complications? Hello?"

Nick pressed the button to toggle the call to speaker, his voice low. "Andy."

"Finally, someone who isn't hysterical," Andy answered with a snap.

"This *still* isn't enough?" Evie felt small. Every conversation with Andy sent her brain into a spiral of inadequacy. What else could Stephen's death mean? The librarian had been *fine*, a little tired, but what eighty year old wouldn't be after a heart attack?

Andy cleared his throat. "I'm not sure what you want to hear from me, Evie." Evie recoiled. "This phone is for emergencies only. It is *not* a way for you to tell me every person who coughs in that town is suddenly being choked out by *Jonathan Murphy*."

Evie looked up at Nick, searching his angry features for the right thing to say. It was like pushing herself up against a brick wall, running her hands over the coarse texture in hopes there would be a give somewhere.

But it wasn't budging.

"Andy —"

"I was going to call at the end of the week." He barreled over her. "Murphy is still active in California. Our digital forensics team confirmed it. I have no reason to believe he knows where you are."

"Andy —" She tried again. "Stephen was okay just a week ago, I *talked* to —"

"How?" He cut her off again. "Did you call the hospital?"

"I did." Nick answered this time. He was brief, but there was boiling anger behind them. This was going to get them nowhere again. It would continue to a dead end because regardless of how much she tried, there was no use arguing with someone who had to go through thirteen other barricades before believing her.

Andy sighed and Evie swore she could picture him pinching his eyebrows together.

"We have to go with the facts. The man was old, Evie, old people die."

It hit her suddenly — no matter what she said, what she did — she wouldn't be taken seriously unless there was a gun to her head and the FBI witnessed it firsthand.

The ringing in her ears grew to a roar as Evie turned, sinking down to sit on the edge of the bed.

"I need you to listen to me, Andy." Nick's words were harsh, whispered but still audible as Evie stared at her hands. "I called the hospital and made sure that Stephen Vogt was all right because I'm not going to let Evie isolate herself to the point of insanity. She's *friends* with him — was." The correction was choked. "And when the nurse told me his family was still states away, I knew that we needed to keep in contact. That's what you *do* when you care about people. I'd urge you to believe us when we say that this means Jonathan Murphy knows Evie is here."

"What am I supposed to do? Take flimsy words and impassioned speeches as proof? Do you *want* me to push the paper-work through? Because I can. I have the pages in front of me, a couple signatures and Evelyn Morgen will no longer exist. Her case goes into WITSEC and there's no more input from a retired agent — Barber or Warren. If I do that she can't go back to her old life *ever*. I'm trying *not* to cut her freedom short, but you're telling me that she'll be dead if I don't."

Evie didn't recognize the second name Andy said, but Nick's expression was drawn.

"I need you to look into this, Andy."

There was silence as Nick reached out, covering one of Evie's hands in her lap with his own. She raised her chin, staring up at him as Nick whispered.

"Please, Andy. I'm asking as a friend."

A noncommittal answer was all they got before the line cut. Nick looked down at the phone before tossing it onto the nightstand and sinking down to kneel in front of her, sliding his hands over hers and squeezing.

"We'll figure this out," Nick muttered, keeping his gaze locked on hers. "I swear to you, we will make sure you're safe. *I* can take you somewhere. What Andy doesn't know won't kill him."

Evie's heart shattered — someone would always end up dead because of her. This would end with death, just as it began.

CHAPTER THIRTY-FOUR

Evie woke up to Nick's lips against her jaw.

She loved the way he pulled her into his chest and buried his head in the crook of her neck. For such a large man, he could burrow deep enough that she felt it in her soul. His beard tickled her as he lazily brushed his lips over her pulse-point.

"You awake?"

When she said yes, he didn't speak again until she was giggling and panting against his mouth twenty minutes later.

"I have a surprise for you."

Evie was never really a fan of surprises. Surprises led to too many unknowns, but when Nick's eyes caught hers and she saw how excited *he* was, she relented.

"I'm going to give you something" — he pressed a kiss against her stomach — "and you're going to go get ready, no questions. You're just going to do what I say, okay?"

She crawled out of bed at his beckoning. The garment bag and shoe box wasn't what she *expected*, but she took them into the bathroom, humoring him. Evie unzipped the bag first, staring at the swath of light blue fabric, speechless. It was the same color as his eyes. The shoes were next, a simple pair of black heels that had no practicality, but were stunning and looked expensive.

Hurrying, Evie cobbled together make-up with what she had, using bronzer on her eyes and lipstick as a blush, before getting dressed. Evie slid her hands over her silky hips, her heart in her throat as she stepped out into the hallway.

Nick sucked in a breath, fidgeting in the doorway of his room, in a pair of dark wash jeans and a button up navy blue shirt she'd never seen before.

Evie twirled, letting the skirt flare out for him. "What's all this for?"

"I told you not to ask." His eyes roving over her made her skin heat. "And if you don't behave, you'll get in trouble."

Evie laughed. "Nick, I can't imagine you hurting a fly."

He cocked an eyebrow, smirking. "Get your ass to the truck or we'll be late."

∧ ∧

When the truck bumped past Wells Creek and Nick merged onto the highway, all the breath left her lungs. This was *certainly* not approved in any way, shape, or form. And for the first time in months, Evie was *excited*.

"I wish you'd give me a little hint where we're going."

"We'll be there in..." Nick trailed off. "Maybe ten more minutes? I'm pretty sure I remember the roads."

The *pretty sure* got her, but Evie didn't bother addressing it as she gasped. "Was that a *bookstore*? Nick, oh my god." She turned in the passenger seat, watching the shopping area fade behind them with the hope he was taking her there.

"— go tomorrow." Nick's voice was garbled and Evie

turned back around, making sure her right ear was closer to him.

"Tomorrow?" She whined his name. "*Nick.*" There were *hundreds* of books back there, she'd be entertained for *days* if he let her buy one or two... or ten.

He laughed, his head tipping back as he finally took an exit. Evie's head swiveled again, taking in the small city as they passed through it, opening her mouth to ask again if they were close before the words died.

The city fell away as the view opened up to the bay. The water sparkled in the waning afternoon light, casting rays across the low scattering of buildings. Evie sucked in a breath as the truck rumbled up to the biggest one — a white building that sprawled more than it rose in height. Under the awning, Nick pulled the truck into a stop, glancing over at her with a little smile.

"Surprise, honey."

"I —" Evie looked around, registering a valet approaching them.

Nick opened his door, winking at Evie before jumping out and taking the keys with him. He exchanged a few pleasant words with the valet, chuckling at something before walking around and pulling the passenger door open. Nick held out a hand to Evie.

"Come on, sweetheart, we've got a dinner reservation."

Evie picked up her skirt, sliding her hand into Nick's. When her shoes hit the cobblestones, she swiveled her head back and forth, taking in the extravagant entrance of the hotel. Nick grabbed a bag from the truck and her hand.

"You can look around while I check us in."

"We're *staying*?" Evie was floored as he guided her inside, an employee opening the door for them. She tried not to gape, but it was futile. There was an entire wall of paintings, with little placards denoting the local artists. Her hand slipped from Nick's as she headed for them, glancing over her shoulder to see him at the desk.

"I'll be right over here. Go on, it's okay."

She grinned back at him, hurrying over to the wall to stare up at the multiple paintings. There were a few oil and thick gouache paintings of various perspectives of the bay. Scattered illustrations of boats were sporadically framed around them, but it was the watercolors at the far end that drew Evie close.

The watercolor painting she stopped in front of was vibrantly green and blue, the cerulean water juxtaposed against the pine forest across the bay. There was a single dock on the opposite side of the water with a little lantern, painted yellow to cast light against the rest of the night-scape.

Evie's eyes flickered to the display card. The local artist's information was listed just above the price.

There were *a lot* of zeroes.

She shuffled backwards a step, clearing her throat as she smoothed her hands over the dress Nick had already given her.

How had he planned this? Or funded it?

The last few days since learning about Stephen started to fall into place. Nick had gone into town and picked up groceries *twice*. He hadn't been gone long, but the dress and the slim pair of kitten heels screamed of Hope's input. She couldn't imagine Nick having the time to go any farther than town to get them and wondered briefly if this had been in motion for a while.

Heat warmed her back and Evie turned her head just as a hand slid across her skin past the low back of the dress.

"This one is nice." Nick's voice was gentle in her ear as he bent down and kissed the right side of her head. "I have to admit — I wasn't looking at the paintings when I walked over. I don't think anyone else is either."

Evie flushed, stepping back into his touch. The hotel lobby wasn't bustling — but it wasn't empty. She hadn't even thought to skim it. The urge to look over her shoulder had been overpowered with the sheer novelty of being *away*.

"Where's the bag?" She turned slightly, glancing down at his other hand.

"They're going to put it upstairs for us." Nick smiled down at her, lifting the hand in question up to brush her hair back. "You look beautiful. Have I said that yet? I need to say it again." He leaned closer, his voice a murmur. "You look beautiful, Evie."

His lips brushed hers and she melted, pressing a hand against his navy shirt as he drew her closer. Nick's head tilted, before his hand splayed across her back, fingers grasping at the fabric and sliding under to access bare skin.

Goosebumps erupted and Evie giggled softly, turning her head, feeling his lips fall to kiss the apple of her cheek.

"I've been waiting hours to do that. I hoped you'd like the dress — I picked it out and then asked Hope for approval." His eyes flickered from her face down to the thin straps on her shoulders and across the low dip of the neckline.

A thrum of pleasure jolted up Evie's spine at the way his eyes darkened, his eyelashes lowering as he whispered, "You do like it?"

"I love it." She slid her hand over his chest. "It's pretty. I never..." Evie glanced away from him for a second, her eyes finding the watercolor painting again. "I never really get a chance to dress up. I go for comfort at work and I normally wear the same thing to the upper and lower school graduations every year. It's not like Hawthorne has events. If they do, *I'm* not invited."

"That's a damn shame." Nick pressed a kiss to her jaw, his teeth following with a nip. "Because you look fucking gorgeous." His beard was just coarse enough to send tingles across her skin as she turned into his touch. Nick hummed for a moment, his fingers lingering on her skin. "You ready to go to our reservation?"

Evie turned. "Our reservation?"

"Yeah." His smile was easy, only for her. "Valentine's Day dinner on the bay."

Her heart thumped in her chest at the words, opening her mouth then closing it after another second. She wanted to press her hands against her cheeks, feeling a flame creep up her neck as she realized *that* was why the calendar had 'disappeared' from the kitchen.

Nick's lips twitched. "Is that okay, sweetheart?"

The nickname sent a shiver down her spine. Evie turned her head away, now *absolutely certain* her cheeks were bright red. "Yes, that's okay. That sounds amazing."

He laughed, the sound loud and bright in the lobby as he slid his hand around her and pulled her closer, guiding her away from the wall of paintings. She let herself glance back, lingering on the watercolor painting before turning her attention to the feeling of his touch. Nick's head bent toward hers as he guided her up a couple steps.

"I had plans at the cabin for today." He cleared his throat, humming softly as he helped her up the last step. "But then the last couple weeks happened. It made me think a little breather *away* might serve us both well." The unspoken words were clear. After Andy — and Stephen — he'd orchestrated this to whisk her away without a worry.

It felt like someone had her heart in their fist as she stared at him, holding onto his hand tightly as he walked backwards for a moment, leading her toward a large wall of windows. He was silhouetted by the afternoon sun beaming off the water, the overcast skies providing just enough light to make the glass sparkle.

Nick's smile took her breath away.

"So we're going to have dinner and you're going to see what life is like with me when we're not stuck in a cabin twenty-four seven."

Evie stepped closer, stopping them both just before the entrance to the restaurant. She lifted her free hand and cupped his face, the warmth of his beard on her palm a salve for her anxieties.

"Nick —"

"I love you." He interrupted her, dipping his chin down. "I love you so much, Evie." His eyes twinkled with something deeper than love and Evie's stomach exploded into butterflies. "Happy Valentine's Day."

He closed the distance, kissing her firmly. With a sharp move of his hand against her back, they were chest to chest and she was clinging to him as she smiled into the kiss.

"You didn't even let me say it," she whined.

"We'll have plenty of time to say it a thousand *more* times." He pressed a kiss to her forehead, chuckling. "Come on, I think we're giving the poor *maître d'* a show."

Evie blushed, tucking her head against his side. The glass doors to the restaurant were open, giving a clear view through the dining area to the bay.

The *maître d'* was a kind man who looked a little older than Evie. He motioned for them to follow, but all Evie could do was stare at the way the windows at the back opened up to a small covered patio where a single table sat close to the railing overlooking the water.

Nick's hand on her back fell away as Evie stepped outside, drawn to the railing. She leaned forward, the breeze ruffling her hair as she turned into it, closing her eyes. When she finally turned around, hands gripping the metal rail, it was just her and Nick.

He stood next to the table, his hands in his pockets as he smiled.

"Nick" — she spun around — "where are all the other tables?"

CHAPTER THIRTY-FIVE

"I'M GUESSING THEY PUT THEM IN STORAGE, SINCE I reserved the entire patio." His careful expression flickered, his mouth twitching in a grin as he pulled a chair out for her. "Come sit down, Evie."

She pushed away from the railing, confused but curious. Nick's hands brushed her shoulders as she sat down, letting him push her up to the edge of the table. He stepped away after kissing the crown of her head, taking his own seat.

"I..." Evie glanced across the water, mind racing. "How?"

He laughed, but it was punctuated by him rubbing the back of his head sheepishly. "I wanted you to know how much I love you. I needed you to realize that nothing I've done for you is because of some ulterior motive. It's only been driven by love, Evie."

Nick reached across the table, his hand flat, palm up in offering. "You can ask me whatever questions you need to feel comfortable, but I wanted you to see what life will be like *after* this is over. Your future with me doesn't have to be the cabin, nights at Adam's, and giving up the job you love."

Evie's breath caught in her chest, staring at his hand. She reached out slowly, placing her palm on top of his. "How did you pay for all of this?"

Nick grinned, tilting his head at her as multiple emotions played across his face, ranging from amusement to caution. "I'm... comfortable."

"Nick." She leaned forward, unable to keep her nervous laughter at bay. "That is *exactly* what someone who had more money than sense would say."

It hit her that as much that she *did* know about the man in front of her, there were still secrets. There were years of unknown moments, memories unexplored, and parts of his history that she wasn't privy to.

The memory of arriving at his cabin hit her out of nowhere. His smile as he assured her that she didn't need to worry about anything because he'd take care of it.

Nick's hand shifted, squeezing hers. "My father is a three-star general and the Barber family has been involved in the US Government for generations." He cleared his throat and stared at her seriously. "My mother is a Warren — I'm comfortable."

Evie clung to him as she whispered, "You keep using that word and I don't think it means the same thing to each of us."

She wasn't stupid. She'd heard the Warren name for generations, old money — but when Andy had said it, she had *no* idea it was because Nick was connected to them. One sect of them owned an international hotel chain with resorts across the world — she knew it had an heiress and more money than sense in their collective net worth.

He smiled, his eyes narrowing with the action. "I made good money being a logger, but when I left the FBI I didn't *have* to do anything. I could have relocated to Morocco if I wanted to, but I didn't. I wanted to work." She watched his gaze flicker to look at the water as he spoke. "I don't want you to think I'm doing any of this to suddenly show off, or that all I have to offer is the cabin..." His throat bobbed as he swallowed, looking back at her. "What I do hope is that this will be the start of a future together."

She blinked, the words hitting her as a waiter appeared with drinks they hadn't ordered. Nick kept hold of her hand until she slipped her fingers away from his to pick up the glass, letting the revelation sink into her bones.

Nick hadn't *lied* because she'd never asked. She'd taken him at face value, a retired agent to her school librarian. It was a side-step, and she couldn't blame him for never diving into it — nor blame herself for never asking.

"All of this..." A question sat on the tip of her tongue. "Does it come with strings?"

He frowned. "My parents might be well off, but so am I, thanks to a few careful investments and the guidance of my grandmother." She tried to match this man to the one who compared prices of peanut butter in the market. "I don't speak to my parents much anymore — especially not about this." He motioned at the two of them. "Andy knew when he left you with me that if the need arose, I could have you out of Wells Creek — out of the fucking *country* if needed. There's a reason I go by Barber instead of Warren — though my mother never liked that." Nick made a face, taking a drink. "Money moves faster than the FBI, but so does molasses."

Air entered her lungs as she sat with the words. "Okay."

"Okay?" He gave her a hopeful look, clearing his throat. "Sweetheart, don't tell me I can start spoiling you, I'll never stop. It would be my *honor*."

Evie blushed, pressing her hands against her cheeks at the sudden feeling, a laugh bubbling up. "I don't know what else to say. I understand why you didn't tell me." She couldn't imagine her reaction had Andy dropped her off at a penthouse somewhere — if Nick had been the kind of man to isolate in glamorous settings. She loved the quiet version of him, living off the necessities, and who was both the man in front of her but the same man who bought her CDs for the cabin's two decade old stereo.

She loved him, regardless of circumstance, that would never change.

The first course came out quickly. Evie grinned at Nick as the waiters whisked around their table, interchanging plates. There was an expensive bottle of red wine at the center of the table, nestled in a bucket on ice, that the waiters kept flowing into their glasses. She didn't feel cautious about the way everything was pre-chosen, out of her control — because her heart was settled — she trusted Nick.

The food was better than anything she'd had in years. The salads were so fresh that the lettuce exploded in a burst of moisture in her mouth. Evie ate it all, from fresh shrimp bouillabaisse to elaborately plated steaks that came out as the sun set across the water.

Ships lazily drifted up and down the bay, and Evie's gaze kept being pulled to them. Nick laughed softly. "I considered renting a boat but I thought that might be too much."

"I like this," she answered, cutting another piece of her sirloin. "I'm still wrapping my head around the fact we're here — not listening to the same 80s CD in the cabin."

He grinned at her, shrugging his shoulders. "It *was* part of my plan to take you upstairs when we're finished and blast Marvin Gaye."

Evie laughed loudly, shaking her head at him.

When both their plates were almost empty, her eyes found his. The food and wine mixed together in her stomach, warming her from the inside and leaving her satisfied, full, happy.

"Have I behaved, sir?" she asked the question softly, watching as the words rolled over him, halting his last bite halfway to his mouth. "Or am I still in trouble for asking so many questions earlier?"

Nick's head rose, his voice huskier. "You've behaved, but this is cutting it close, honey."

Evie smiled, turning her head to glance out at the water as their plates were cleared. In the movement of it all, Nick's rough voice sent shivers down her spine as he spoke to their waiter. "We'll be taking dessert in the room. We'll be there shortly."

The waiter bowed out quickly and Evie felt her skin heat under Nick's gaze.

Nick stood, folding his napkin and leaving it on the table. He offered her a hand, helping her stand while looking down at her dress as it rippled over her legs and fell back into place. Evie followed his lead, walking with her hand in his until they were at the railing.

The wind picked up, sending a brisk chill through the otherwise pleasant air. Before she could realize she was shivering, Nick's warm hands were sliding over her exposed arms, standing behind her, resting his chin on her head.

"Thank you for everything, but thank you for today."

He pressed his lips against her jaw. "You're welcome." One of Nick's hands slid off her arm and came to rest at her hip, palm pressing against muscle through the dress. The pressure made her throat bob with a held-back moan as his fingers rubbed back and forth. "Will you keep listening to me, honey?" His words kissed the shell of her ear. "If you listen and behave, I'll give you a reward."

Evie's lashes fluttered, lips parting as she leaned back. His hand sank lower on her leg, stopping at the slit on the side, parting the fabric as his fingers ghosted across her exposed skin.

"Evie," his voice rumbled. "Are you going to listen?"

"Yes," she gasped as his fingers splayed across the front of her thigh, painfully aware they were still in public. Every inch of him pressed against her back, igniting flames across her skin as she tried to control her breathing.

There was a smile in his words as he nipped at her ear. "Yes, what?"

"Yes, sir."

The noise that left him was a low, unrestrained growl as his hand pulled out from under her dress. The loss of the heat of his body was only momentary as he turned her around, pressing her up against the railing and putting their foreheads together.

"Will you come upstairs with me now, sweetheart?"

She nodded, sucking in a breath at his dark eyes.

He pulled them away from the water. Her face felt warm as he led her down a hallway and to a pair of elevators. Nick guided her inside and Evie fidgeted, lifting her hand to adjust the strap on her shoulder. At one look from Nick, she stopped.

He reached out, toying with the thin strap as he grinned. "Don't bother, it won't be on for much longer."

All thought halted as the elevator stopped. Nick grabbed her hand, leading her to one of the few doors on the floor, motioning her inside first. Evie walked past a cracked door to a bathroom, then a closet, before the room opened up.

The bed was huge — centered on the far wall with lamps on each side. One wall was glass, open to the bay as boats drifted, dotting the water. There was a small desk with a silver platter adorned with an arrangement of berries and bite-sized desserts. The small overnight bag Nick had packed for them sat to the side.

She neared the dessert, spotting a piece of hotel stationary with elegant handwriting hoping that *Mr. Warren* would call the front desk if anything else was required. The fact that he'd pulled strings for them to have this *one* night — sent a shiver down her spine.

Nick's footsteps were soft as he neared, glancing from the desserts to her before his lips lifted in a little smile. He nodded toward the bed. "Sit down."

She *liked* this side of him, softly domineering, caring but ravenous for her. Her mind was stupidly blank, all the anxiety leaving her as she listened. Evie lowered to the edge, licking her lips and looking up at him as he stood in front of her.

"Good girl." He flicked the strap on her shoulder, letting it fall to match the other side.

She shivered, her mouth going dry.

Nick dropped down to one knee, taking her breath with him as he lifted up her left leg and placed it on his knee. His fingers deftly moved over her ankle, unclasping her heel, placing it on the floor. His fingers rolled over her skin, massaging briefly before repeating the process with her right shoe, touch loving and gentle but restrained.

Evie's breaths were coming uncomfortably quick as she stared, trying to measure her reaction as his hands grasped her calves and pulled her legs apart, letting the dress rise in the process.

"Eyes on me." He shifted closer, his right hand skirting up to grasp at her hips. Her leg splayed out of the slit in the side of the dress. "I've wanted to get under this dress since this morning. Doesn't *my* patience deserve a reward?"

Evie's eyes were locked on his as she nodded.

"Verbal answers, sweetheart." His fingers paused on her inner thigh, leaning up on his knees to draw closer to her. His eyes focused on hers, making sure this was what she wanted too. "Do I deserve a reward?"

"Yes," she squeaked. Two fingers ghosted over the seam of her underwear, pressing the fabric against her. "*Sir.*"

He groaned, falling forward as his other hand lifted up and dragged her hips past the edge of the bed. Nick's head landed against her thighs, kissing the skin as the dress rode up higher and higher. Supporting her ass, his mouth moved over the sensitive skin of her inner thighs, making her squirm and gasp as he got so *close* but never close enough.

Her hands flew to his hair, holding onto him with a little whine. "*Nick*, please."

He stopped and Evie could feel his hot breath against her skin as she clung to him, biting her tongue. She knew immediately why he was motionless, but she couldn't find it in herself to get annoyed at the fact he was toying with her.

She didn't have much experience with any past partners liking honorifics in bed, but she *loved* the way Nick reacted to being called *sir*. His entire body coiled, like a predator. The burning want scorched her, leaving her aching and wanting.

"What was that?" He kissed down her thigh, reaching her knee, smiling slightly.

Even biting her tongue couldn't keep the stupid grin from twisting her features as she pushed his hair back. "You're killing me."

He laughed, turning to kiss the inside of her knee. "I haven't even *begun*."

Evie gave up, dropping back to the bed with a huff and another laugh as she felt his hands skim over her legs. With a slight shift, Nick was suddenly leaning over her and Evie shivered, victory in her veins as she wrapped her legs around his waist.

"I had mean plans." He kissed her in slow sips. "I was going to keep you on the edge just because I could." His hand slid over her jaw, tangling in her hair as he grinned and glanced down at her. "But now that I have you, I don't want to wait."

Evie pushed errant strands of hair away from his face, her eyes running over his handsome features. His strong brow, slightly crooked nose, the little scar above his eye, and the way his eyes were a fathomless blue that she could get lost in. Emotion gripped her chest, crawling up her throat as she ran her thumb over his beard, feeling the curve of his jaw underneath. "I'm all yours, Nick."

A soft groan left the back of his throat as his kisses grew frantic. His hands shifted, picking her up by the hips and moving them up higher on the bed as he pressed their foreheads together. Between kisses and gasps for air, Nick pushed her dress up around her hips, coaxing it over her stomach before pulling back and guiding it over her head.

He chucked it to the side and kissed her again, interrupting her as she gasped, "Thanks for not destroying it."

"You're welcome, but I could buy you twenty more." Nick peppered kisses along her jaw, glancing down and groaning as his mouth moved lower. "You're so beautiful." The words made her toes curl as his lips skimmed across her chest, tongue running over one of her nipples before his palm slid down to find her underwear. "Absolutely stunning." His fingers slid between her legs, rubbing her through her panties, making her arch off the bed with a little sigh.

Nick chuckled, lavishing each breast and leaving each nipple wet as he pulled back. "Do I have your permission to try something, sweetheart?"

Her head rolled back, half delirious. Evie looked at him, nodding slowly before licking her lips, remembering his request for verbal answers. "Yes, sir."

He muttered a soft *"fuck,"* before pulling away. Evie lifted up onto her elbows, watching wide-eyed as he grabbed their bag, rifling through it. When he pulled out a small, blue bullet vibrator she gaped. The sleeves of his button up were pushed up, exposing his forearms as Nick walked back over to the bed, focused on her, expression shyly cautious.

He bent down, placing a knee on the bed to kneel over her. "Kiss me?"

Evie lurched up, pulling him by the hair to kiss him again. He held back just enough to make her whine against his lips, before one of his hands dropped, ghosting over the side of her hip, touching bare skin. A small click was the only warning her brain had before vibration pressed against the skin of her inner thigh.

A soft noise left her in an exhale as she stared down at his hand holding the toy.

"Is this okay?" He cupped her face with his free hand. "I can put it up — fuck, I'll throw it into the harbor if you don't want it." Nick licked his lips, staring at her with blown-out pupils. "I'm not going to lie, I've been thinking about this. I've had this fantasy of getting you in our bed and using a toy on you." He leaned in, brushing his lips against hers, his voice rougher. "Seeing how far I can push you — until it's too much and you're just limp from it. I like the idea of making you completely boneless from pleasure and pushing for more. I want your idea of an orgasm to be shattered. I want to be the one to make you come until you can't stand it. *That's* what gets me off, honey. Call me *sir* and let me wreck you in the most delicious way."

Evie didn't give a *fuck* what happened to her as long as he made good on the fantasy that he'd just described.

"Do it." She panted the words against his lips, drawing him in for another bruising kiss as his hand and the toy on her thigh jolted with the movement, sending vibrations over her skin. Evie moaned, pressing up against him. "*Nick*, fuck, *please.*"

His responding chuckle made her skin prickle as he pressed her to the bed with the full weight of his body. Pinned under him, Evie squirmed, spreading her legs wider to allow his hand access as he ghosted the toy over her underwear, making her squeal.

"You beg so well for me." Nick pulled it away, a wicked look in his eyes as he caught her startled expression. "But the only time I want to hear you scream like that is when I'm between your thighs."

His free hand rose, grabbing her arms and pinning them above her head. Evie's chest heaved as he caught her gaze, unspoken consent passing between them before his head lowered, kissing down her chest and stomach, joining the toy between her thighs.

If this killed her, it would be a *way* better death than whatever Murphy had planned.

Evie arched off the bed, held in place by his arm while his tongue ran over the gusset of her underwear, sucking on the damp fabric. The toy moved, pressing against the sensitive skin between her thigh and pussy, making her writhe under him.

"I could watch you squirm like this all night."

His voice was sinful, goosebumps rising as he hummed and tortured her with teasing movements. He kept shifting the vibrator, never leaving it on one spot long enough for her body to adjust to the sensation. Nick dragged kisses across her underwear, then pressed the toy against her clit through the fabric.

Evie gasped his name, clinging to him as her thighs instinctively closed.

"Do you want me to keep it on your clit like this?" He pressed the bullet harder against her clit, sending shockwaves up her spine. "You don't want me to move it?"

Before she could even think to reply, the vibrator was gone.

"*No* —" She scrambled to get out of the hold. "Nick, *fuck*, please put it back, please."

He glanced up at her from between her legs, hair mussed and beard scratching her thighs as he grinned. "Ask *nicely*, Evie, and I'll put it back."

Every word in the English language left her brain as she stared down at him.

"*Nick.*"

He kissed her thigh, patiently waiting. "You can do better than that."

Evie licked her lips, breathless as she begged, "*Please*, sir. Please do it again. Put it back. Make me come with just the vibrator and your tongue. *Please.*"

"That's my *very* good girl." Nick dove back in, sucking on her inner thigh as the toy pressed against her clit through her underwear. She grasped at him, trying to hold onto anything as she shuddered, tension coiling in her stomach as she felt an orgasm build.

"Fuck — *look at you* — you're making a mess." His words were gentle, only for her as he kissed across her skin, moving the toy just enough to send the vibrations through her entire body, clenching around nothing as she whined. "I know, I know," Nick cooed, leaning his head back to look at her, breathing out harshly. "Look at how wet you are, sweetheart. Your poor panties; let's get these off you."

He pulled the toy away again and Evie whimpered, on the edge just to feel it slip away again. Her body felt flushed, skin on fire as he let her hands go, leaving the vibrator on the bed. Nick's hands smoothed up her legs, hooking her underwear. "You're such a good girl, letting me pleasure you until you can't think."

The praise sent a shiver up her spine, making her lips part as Nick pulled her underwear down. For as torturous as he was, his movements were gentle as he leaned in to kiss her bare leg, pulling her thighs apart.

"Such a pretty pussy. It's a shame I'm going to have to ruin it tonight."

Evie shrieked as he dove between her legs, his tongue running over her. She clamped her legs around his head, the shriek turning into a breathless laugh, then a moan as he forced her thighs apart just to grab the vibrator and put it directly on her clit.

Evie shook, her mouth opening in a silent scream, vaguely aware of his fingers as they slid against her entrance. He thrust them into her at the exact same moment he turned the vibrator up.

"There she *is*, just like that, sweetheart." His voice was muffled, but it just drove her wilder as he knelt between her legs, broad shoulders keeping her thighs held open even when her muscles fought to close them. "I want you to show me with your cum how much you need my cock. You're going to be a good girl and make that pussy explode all over me, and then I'll fill you and fuck you. Nice and deep with my big cock, just how you like it, honey."

She found her voice, screaming as he curled his fingers, her body bowing in on itself, the orgasm knocking her flat on her back as it hit. Evie gasped, barely feeling the euphoria before Nick replaced his fingers with his tongue, gathering up her release and sucking on her, leaving the vibrator torturing her overly sensitive clit.

"Nick!" She grabbed his hair, unsure if she wanted to jerk him away or pin him between her legs. Before she could decide, he pulled back just enough for her to see his beard, damp with her orgasm, and offered her a wicked grin.

"Are you sensitive?" He licked his lips again, cocking an eyebrow. "I think you've got another orgasm for me before I get inside you. I think this sweet pussy is going to come for me and cover my fingers in your cum. Then I'll fuck you. I'll hit that spot that makes you lose your fucking mind, over and *over* again. Do you understand?"

Evie nodded, her head bobbing up and down before her mind could even catch up to the words. Nick's grin widened, diving back between her thighs and putting the bullet on high, sliding two fingers back into her.

She clung to him, every muscle taut, so worked up that her head started to spin. Nick's wrist twisted, moving his fingers just enough that he could add a third, slipping them in and out of her.

"I —" Evie gasped, her mouth dropping open as her eyes screwed shut, her hips jolting.

"Fuck, just like that —" Nick's breath was warm as he commanded, "Come for me. Right now. Fucking come for me again, Evie."

She saw stars, brilliant bursts of light across the backs of her eyelids. She wasn't aware of anything except the rush of warmth over her body, the roaring in her ears, and the release that came with it, drenching her thighs and the man between them.

Nick's soothing timbre brought her back. His hands ran over her shaking legs. "There you go, let it out. Just like that, you're being so good." He peppered her skin with kisses until she peeled her eyes open, looking down at him, fully clothed between her thighs. His beard was wet as his thumb smoothed over her hip bone. "You okay, sweetheart?"

Evie nodded, licking her dry lips. He leaned back, quiet for a moment, face unreadable as he took her in.

"All mine," he whispered, running his hand over her waist. The expression on his face was almost reverent as he pulled his hands back and tugged his shirt off.

Evie bent forward, watching his hands fall to his belt, unbuckling it with a soft clink and flicking the button open on his jeans. She craved the feeling of his skin on hers and his weight pressing her into the bed.

Dinner had been nice — but she didn't need extravagant dates. She didn't need hotel rooms that probably cost too much for a view of water she could see from the road. She needed the man who loved her. She needed the man who constantly put her pleasure over every iota of his own. She just needed *him*.

Nick leaned forward, his jeans and boxers on the floor. With a small smile that made the skin next to his eyes crinkle, he pressed a light kiss to the tip of her nose. "We can be finished, just say the word."

"I need you." She watched him process her declaration and then found herself flat on her back a moment later as he kissed her again with renewed vigor.

"Gonna give me an ego," Nick muttered against her lips, cupping her thighs with his hands and wrapping her legs around him. The movement shifted them closer together and they both moaned. "With all these compliments?" He bit at her jaw, rolled his hips. "Saying you're mine? Saying you need me? *Fuck*, honey."

One of his hands dropped between them, fingers parting her as his hips thrust forward again. His cock slid through her pussy, grinding and rubbing against it as she gasped. Grabbing onto his biceps, she looked between them, watching as he wrapped a hand around himself. His forehead pressed against hers, chest to chest, breathing the same air.

Her body gave way as he thrust forward, her nails dragging down his arms. She panted against his collarbone as he sank into her, slowing to a stop as she adjusted to the burn and stretch. His arms shook under her palms as he fought to gain an ounce of control back.

Nick pressed a searing kiss to her shoulder, grasping her hips before he pulled back and thrust in again a moment later. His groan was echoed by hers as the weight of him pressed her into the bed, writhing against him. Evie shifted her legs, wrapping them firmly around his waist as she tilted her pelvis up, feeling him move deeper with the action.

"That's it," he grunted, kissing her neck. "Tell me what you need to come again, sweetheart." He nipped at her lips. "I'll do it. I'll do anything."

Her mind spun. He'd been right — she'd never come this much with a partner — he was *breaking* her in the best of ways. Her muscles were tensing already. "I don't. I can't —"

Evie wrapped her arms around his neck, her head dropping back as Nick's mouth landed on her chest. Nick lavished her left nipple before sucking it into his mouth and rolling it between his tongue and teeth. She shattered again, her core clenching as she shrieked. Nick cursed against her skin, hips stuttering with each kiss. It was easy to grab his head and pull it up to hers. She kissed him as they panted against each other and let their bodies ride the aftershocks.

Evie turned her head, pressing her lips against Nick's beard, exhausted but satisfied. His hand rose, cupping her cheek as he slowly rolled over onto his back, pulling her body with his. It took some shifting, but he dragged the blankets over them, kissing the crown of her head with a softly muttered, "Mine."

She dropped her head onto his chest, her heart still echoing in her ears as she curled up. For just a moment she could pretend that nothing else existed but the feeling of his arms around her and the sound of their labored breaths.

Chapter Thirty-Six

Nick did, in fact, take her to the bookstore.

Evie didn't even have to ask. He just pulled the truck off and let her run free the moment the doors were unlocked by a bemused employee the next morning. She was in a pair of leggings and one of his shirts, but Evie didn't care because Nick just let her stack books in his arms until she was giddy.

Even though the trip was less than twenty-four hours, Evie still felt refreshed three days later.

When the cell phone on the coffee table rang, Evie stared at it over the top of her new book. From the other end of the couch, Nick reached over, answering it on speakerphone.

There was a quiet sigh before Andy spoke. "We lost Murphy."

Evie slid her bookmark into place, her grip tightening on the innocent paperback.

"What do you mean?" Nick's voice was clipped. "Did you *have* him, Andy?"

Evie could picture Andy, bags under his eyes, probably running on cheap coffee and two hours of sleep.

"We got a tip and found property registered to Jonathan's mother but when a team got there, he was gone. We're not sure how it was missed when we combed through property records. She's dead, she shouldn't *have* property —"

"Andy," Evie said his name softly, keeping her eyes shut. It was easier if she could just exist in the darkness for a moment, ignoring everything except the call.

He had the good graces to sound sheepish. "Sorry, I... I'm sorry, Evie."

At the apology, she opened her eyes and stared down at the cheap little phone. "Why?"

"Because" — Andy sounded defeated — "I should have made them listen to you. He was there hiding for at least two months. And we were upstate, following smoke trails."

Evie nodded slowly, wrapping her arms around herself. "So you're calling to tell me you have nothing? Again?"

"It looks like he was in San Francisco while he was regrouping," Andy admitted. "We got some intel that he left about a month ago when he received a call from someone. We can't get his housekeeper to talk. We're trying to figure out if he —"

"If he knows where she is." Nick finished the sentence, matter-of-factly.

She let out a strained laugh. "He does. He's just waiting." For what, she didn't know. Murphy could be anywhere. And there was nothing she could do.

The world felt like it was collapsing.

"Evie?" Andy's voice trickled through the phone as Nick picked it up. He pressed it to his ear, standing and walking around the couch. Nick's free hand squeezed her shoulder gently before he stepped outside.

She sucked in a ragged breath the moment the door creaked shut. The air made the jamb stick — ever since Bryant, it refused to shut cleanly. She figured there was a metaphor in that somewhere. Her eyes flickered across the room, coming to land on the ceiling above the kitchen table, searching for the small dent in the beams across it. Just to the left, above the entry to the hall, was a small notch where one of Bryant's bullets pinged off the ceiling. The slug was long gone, but the impression remained.

Jonathan Murphy would find her.

Something about the thought was both terrifying and soothing. Terrifying that she couldn't do anything about it. It was always going to come to this — to Murphy tracking her, fighting his way through every single person she knew just to get to her.

But it was also soothing. She *couldn't* do anything. Evie was powerless, and the lack of control made her stare at the ceiling, eyes glued to the marred wood until the door creaked open and Nick's soft footfalls stopped behind her.

His hands slid over her shoulders and she knew his eyes were following hers, staring at the same place.

"Andy's stubborn, but he's trying to make the Bureau listen." His voice was terse, but gentle. "At least he apologized — I'll ride his ass about the way this has all been handled later."

The way Nick implied there would be a later made her heart clench. He was so certain.

"I don't think I should be here anymore." She said the words softly, trying to ignore the way his hands tightened on her shoulders, then eased just as fast.

"Don't say that." Nick moved around the couch quickly, kneeling in front of her. His pleading tone dragged her eyes from the ceiling to his face. His brow was drawn, lips pursed.

"Evie." He grabbed her hands. "You're staying here with me. Andy is going to pull every string he can until Murphy's entire operation unravels. I told you I didn't think I ever did enough but that was a lie — you're my enough."

Her throat felt like it was on fire, a mixture of bile and emotions choking her. She wanted to run — but she also wanted to freeze on the couch, to sit there until she turned to stone or Murphy barged through the cabin doors and shot her and finally put an end to all of this.

"It was long fucking hours, deadly issues, deadly *people*, and not a single fucking second did I feel like I helped anyone. Not a single second was worth it until I came home one afternoon and saw *you* sitting in my rocking chair, curled up in on yourself, and I knew —" Nick's voice cracked, shifting forward to cling to her. "I *knew* I would do anything to protect you."

"You should be retired." It felt like she was speaking with a mouthful of broken glass. "You should be drinking beers with Chuck, watching football game reruns at the bar, and living your life."

"Fuck that. You want to know why I picked logging, Evie? Ask me."

She floundered, the question catching her off guard.

"Ask me, Evie."

"Why did you pick logging, Nick?"

His face split with a grin, eyes crinkling. "Have you ever seen *X-Men Origins: Wolverine*?"

Evie wasn't sure what sound came out of her mouth. It was a mixture of a gasp and a laugh, fighting past panic and fear to guffaw at the sheer stupidity of the sentence.

"No, you *didn't*."

Nick's grin widened. "You're just lucky I only fled to Washington and not Canada — you know, like Logan did."

"Oh my *god*, Nick, that's so *stupid*."

He laughed, the mirthful sound filling up the cabin as his head tilted back slightly. Her eyes were drawn to one of his hands dropping from hers, pressing against his chest. "I've never told anyone that, not even Chuck. I can hear him now, '*you're a spoiled idiot, Nick Barber.*' But that's why — if Logan could do it, why couldn't I?"

A little laugh bubbled up. "You uprooted your life because of a Hugh Jackman character."

Nick shrugged at her, his smile lopsided. "It was working. Until you."

She sucked in a breath, shaking her head. "Until me?"

"Until you, Evelyn Morgen," Nick cupped her face, his eyes earnest. "However this ends, I'm with you. You're stuck with me. And I'll be with you after it if you'll let me."

CHAPTER THIRTY-SEVEN

THEY STARTED SLEEPING WITH NICK'S GUN ON THE nightstand.

Evie knew that the likelihood of Andy calling again to extract her was just as slim as him calling with concrete information on Murphy's location, but she still woke up every morning with her stomach in knots. To Nick's credit, even when she fidgeted all night, all he did was pull her close and run a soothing hand over the curve of her hip until she sighed and burrowed into his chest.

"Do you want breakfast?" He shifted in the bed, brushing her hair back. "We have eggs."

Evie turned, resting her cheek against his breastbone. The echo of his heartbeat made her breathing regulate — at peace surrounded by him.

"I should get up." She mumbled the words, painfully aware it was late morning. Every day when the sun filtered through the thin curtains, casting light against the wall, Evie thought, *Well, we made it through the night.*

"I didn't ask if you should get up." He gave her a half-smile, tipping her chin up with a finger. "I asked if you wanted breakfast."

She pulled her head away and instead pressed her face into the hollow of his throat. "I don't know."

Nick's hand soothed over her shoulder, rubbing the back of her neck. "I know." So many words were left unspoken. He knew so much about her, from the way she took her coffee to the noises she made when she came. Months with no end in sight and he didn't flinch once at her anxiety, her moods, or her unflinching ability to compartmentalize.

Unbidden, his words from the first weeks in the cabin came back to her.

"I'm gonna be honest with you, this shit will not be easy."

She remembered everything — the way his eyes caught hers after screaming into the woods — telling her to let it all out before it festered.

"This will never be easy, but it doesn't have to be all bad. You may not know me or trust me yet and we may have had a very weird first meeting, but... you ever need to scream at the trees again and I'll be there with you, Evie Morgen."

She wondered if these moments would feel dream-like after this was all over. She didn't want them to. She wanted to remember everything in vivid technicolor, the way the edges of Nick's beard lifted, the smell of his breath after drinking coffee, and the shine of his eyes in dim light.

"I'm going to make eggs. Mostly because I don't think you'll let me have the breakfast I really want." His hand, so gentle on her neck, popped down to smack her on the ass, jolting her out of her thoughts.

"*Nick!*" Evie's eyes jerked up as he cackled and climbed out of their bed, boxers hanging on his hips as he headed toward the bathroom. She shook her head, falling onto her back, staring at the ceiling.

She'd do everything in her power to remember every second of these moments.

Evie got up, technically following her normal routine of making the bed — it was never as neat as when Nick did it. She pulled on her cardigan as the bathroom door opened, watching Nick go into the living room to start the fire.

She smiled softly, glancing over at the small cell phone on the nightstand before pocketing it. She didn't want it — but she also didn't want it far away.

After running a warm washcloth over her face, Evie finally made it into the kitchen in time to watch a half-naked Nick crack eggs into a frying pan, humming under his breath. She picked up the stereo's remote, flicking it on before moving around him to start the coffee pot.

It was easy with him. They had a rhythm in the cabin that she wasn't sure could be replicated anywhere else. She wondered if he would fit in her kitchen — all broad shoulders and big hands opening cabinet doors to find her massive collection of mugs and little to no pantry space.

Her heart fluttered as she watched him plate their eggs and put them on the table. She'd move for him, if he needed a bigger place.

Nick glanced back at her, nodding toward the coffee. "I can finish that. Go sit."

"I've got it." She smiled, filling two mugs. "Are you going to put a shirt on? Maybe pants?"

"I think I might become a nudist." Nick's voice carried a grin as he sat down. "Would you be offended if I just stopped wearing anything?"

"I'd miss how warm your hugs are in a flannel." Evie picked up the mugs, smiling as she walked around the counter and placed one in front of him. His arms snaked out, catching her by the hips the moment she put her mug on the table, carefully making sure she didn't spill anything as he jerked her back onto his lap. Evie laughed, dropping down to sit on his thigh and looking down at him. "How *are* you always so warm?"

Nick beamed at her, his hands running up and down her hips. "I'm hot."

She scoffed, turning away from him. "Let me up, I want my food."

"Hm... no." He pulled her closer, and she felt his stupid smile as he nuzzled her neck, pressing his lips against the concave of her throat. Evie ran her hands over his hair, hiding her smile with a kiss on his head. "Maybe we can just stay in today."

"We stay in every day." The words left her with a laugh as she tugged him away by his hair. "*Behave.*" Evie sucked in a breath at his heated expression, biting her tongue. "But maybe we should."

His eyes sliding over her made her feel untethered. Nick's hands carefully crept up her hips, fingers edging under her sleep shorts, seeking out the junction of her thighs.

Evie's head bowed, their noses bumping as he captured her lips, hooking his hand around her inner thigh and jerking her legs open in his lap. She let out a little breathless moan, the sound swallowed by his lips as she clung to him. Her skin felt like it was on fire as his touch explored every sensitive dip and swell of her body.

A sharp ringing jerked them both from the moment.

Evie's hand went to the pocket of her cardigan, but it wasn't the burner phone. Nick grunted, looking sharply at the hall. "That's mine, I need to get it."

She shifted out of his lap quickly, watching him as he angrily jogged to the bedroom. His voice was sharp when he answered the phone, asking the person to repeat themselves. Pulling the cardigan closer, Evie walked down the hallway, leaning in the doorway to watch as Nick grumbled into the phone. "This afternoon though?" He ran a hand through his hair, catching her eyes. "If you really need me, I'll be there."

He ended the call, chucking the phone onto the bed. She glanced at it and raised an eyebrow.

"Work wants me up so they can put spring teams together. The thaw is coming faster this year." He approached her, sliding his hands over her shoulders and holding her by the upper arms. "Come with me. Don't stay in this cabin all fucking day while I'm gone."

Evie's heart jerked. "I couldn't. How would it look if I just sat in your truck the entire time? Do the other men bring their..." She trailed off, suddenly painfully aware they'd never given this a name.

"Their girlfriends? No." Nick finished her thought, bending down so his face was taking up her entire worldview. "But I don't care. I want to know you're safe."

Evie fidgeted. "Is the phone signal okay up there?"

His face fell. "No, it's spotty at best. If Andy calls, it might not come through."

"I think I should just stay here." She slid her hands over his arms. "I'll be okay, I'll just..." She turned her head, looking around at the mostly clean room. She'd scrubbed the baseboards just last week. "Clean, I guess."

Nick made a strangled noise in the back of his throat. "I'll call my boss back. I'm quitting. I'm not leaving you here by yourself. I don't need the fucking money anyways."

She caught him before he could grab the phone. "Nick, no. Get dressed, go into work. I'll be here when you get home."

His eyes searched her face. "Let me take you to Chuck, you can sit with Hope at Adam's."

"It's not even noon, Nick. Adam's isn't open." She smoothed her hands over his arms. "Honey, just go to work."

Nick sucked in a breath, the motion stuttering as he pulled back and cursed under his breath.

They finished their breakfast in record time. Evie retrieved a t-shirt for him from the laundry and watched as he tugged it on. Every motion was grumpy, down to the way he threw his coat over his shoulders when he eventually made it to the front door.

"Evie." He held her face, pleading. "Come with me."

"No." She put her hands over his. "I'll be okay. You'll be back tonight."

Nick's eyebrows pulled together as he scowled. "Fine. He can give me my damn team in ten minutes. I'm not going to be gone longer than I have to."

"I know." She smiled gently, letting him tug her close just to kiss her. When they parted, Evie squeezed his hands and then pulled away, aware he wouldn't be able to do it himself. "Go."

He cast her one last look. "Call Chuck if *anything* happens. You know where the guns are."

Evie nodded, leaning in the doorway to watch him walk to his truck. The engine roared to life as she raised a hand to wave, and in the next moment, he was gone.

Easing herself away from the door, Evie locked it behind her after stepping back inside the empty cabin. The CD looped on the stereo, clicking to restart the oldies album. She walked over to it first, fishing out the Taylor Swift album Hope had sent up to the cabin last week. The music filled the living room as Evie sucked in a large breath, filling her lungs and letting it all out in the next moment.

Turning toward the kitchen, she surveyed the darker section of floor that marred the rest of the old linoleum. Bending down, Evie stared at the splotches — scrubbed within an inch of their life by both Chuck and Nick. There was still a soft impression where Bryant bled out.

Evie fished the cleaning supplies from the cabinet, filling a bucket with warm water, vinegar, and dish soap. Then she knelt down, pushing her sleeves up to get to work.

As she scrubbed, she couldn't help but think of what her mother would say if she saw her in this moment, held together by a hope and a prayer. Emptiness moved into Evie's chest every time Nick wasn't around, not that he left very often these days. There were too many unknowns for him not to be immediately available.

As much as Evie liked Chuck coming up to the cabin with a few bags of groceries and goodies from Hope, she missed going into Wells Creek herself and walking past the familiar small shops in the town square. She wanted to people watch as hikers flooded the town for early spring hiking excursions and tour groups visited the mountain's fishing spots.

All the thoughts about Wells Creek made her mind drift to Hawthorne — missing the New Year's celebration, the kids putting together Valentine's Day shoeboxes and exchanging candy, and gearing up for little league baseball season. She wondered if her library doors were shuttered. She wondered if someone had stepped in to check out books in her stead.

Evie looked down at the linoleum, the vinegar burning her nose as she sat back on her legs and stared at the stain. The edges were a little more blurred, her cleaning mixture a nice shade of rust in the bucket.

What would she say on the stand if they caught Murphy?

Would she be able to get up there and stare at him in a courtroom? Would they bring him in chains and sit him in front of her while she recounted the moments in her library? Or would Andy let her just write it all out in lieu of a public appearance?

Her heart jolted in her chest, a painful pang that left her sucking in a quick gasp. As angry with Andy as she was — she *understood* him. Unlike Nick, he hadn't grown up with a name that swayed opinion. Nick told her Andy had worked to get where he was, to get onto a case like Murphy's just to have an opportunity to take the other man down. He had worked to make a name for himself in a world that only wanted to take him at face value.

And hadn't she done the same, in her own way? After her brother died — after his body was taken from a wrecked car, put on life support, and the drunk driver carted away only to later be let go on a technicality — Evie spent her entire teen years trying to be more than just the girl who lost a brother. The shadow he cast in life was bad enough, from small-town football stardom to rumors of maybe going pro, cut short in an instant. She was just his sister, and even in the wake of his death too many people still only saw Evie as an extension of the better Morgen, the *talented* and *promising* one. *Poor Evelyn Morgen, has she done anything of note to fill the void her big brother left behind?*

The rag in her hand dripped vinegar onto the floor, a puddle forming from small drops. Wasn't that what life was? Hoping every minuscule action was enough to *finally* reach your own dreams?

Maybe empathy would be the death of her. In Andy's place, she'd be trying to balance safety and policy. In Nick's place, she'd war with love and responsibility. And as much as she didn't want to admit it to herself — Murphy probably found a way to justify his own actions.

Evie squeezed the rag out, hunching to scrub at the stain again.

There was no use misdirecting her rage at Murphy, at Andy, or even at Nick. Her discontent and fear were just byproducts of an entire system that was broken beyond repair. Even if Andy did have to move her, if his higher ups continued to pressure him to take her from Nick, that wasn't his fault. When Murphy came after her, Andy brought her to the one place that — she was certain — he would have gone himself. To him, the safety Nick provided was worth risking the ire of the entire federal government, and maybe even his badge — the very representation of everything he had worked so hard for.

Could she do it? Could she swear to tell the truth in front of her peers, and hope her words were enough to convince a justice system to actually care?

Evie was angry with a world that failed her in so many inconceivable ways that *she*, a children's librarian with her dead brother's ghost hanging over her, was the one to drive a knife into Bryant's neck — because no one else was going to kill him for her. No one else would stop him, or Murphy, or men like them because without men like them, the entire world wouldn't continue to thrive on the pain, fear, and oppression that lined the pockets of so many in power.

This was her life hanging in the balance, and to someone else it was just a pile of paperwork.

No — she couldn't imagine herself taking the stand, because every single moment thus far had proven to her that this case would never and could never end in neatly filed paperwork and handcuffs. It was going to end in the exact same way it always did — with blood and normal, everyday people scrubbing the stain until it was faded enough to ignore.

Taylor Swift crooned about illicit affairs and invisible strings, waxing poetic about mad women while Evie mindlessly tackled the oblong and wobbled edge of the bloodstain. Throwing the rag into the bucket, Evie pushed unsteadily to her feet, realizing the CD had looped yet again. She cleaned up the mess from the floor, pushing her hair back and checking the clock over the stove. Nick would probably be gone until sunset — he'd mentioned briefly that the logging headquarters were pretty far out, somewhere remote where the trucks could come and go without destroying too many residential roads.

As Evie passed the stereo, she turned the volume up even higher, letting Taylor Swift carry her to the shower, turning the hot water on full blast. It would take the water heater forever to recover, but she didn't really care as she stepped under the spray and let out a sigh.

She stayed there until the water cooled. When she wrapped herself up in a towel, she poked her head out cautiously, not a soul in sight. Evie eased herself to Nick's room and rifled through his drawers, stealing a shirt.

The front door slammed and Evie jumped in alarm. She tugged the shirt on with one hand, stumbling into the hallway to see Nick, grinning ear to ear and holding a greasy paper bag.

"I brought us food."

Laughing, Evie found herself rushing down the hallway to him, ignoring the bag in lieu of tackling him. He hummed, head tucking against her wet hair. "You smell so good." He pressed a kiss to her temple, swinging her around to push her toward the kitchen table.

"How are you already home?" She whispered the words as her thighs hit the table.

Nick bent down, dropping the bag before cupping her face. "I was halfway there before I decided — fuck it, they can just call me with the schedule or fire me. I don't care. By the time I turned around, I was already in town, so I stopped for food. I wasn't going to come home empty-handed." He pulled her closer before pressing his lips against hers, his voice a whisper. "And I missed my girl."

CHAPTER THIRTY-EIGHT

THE RUNNING KITCHEN SINK WAS SLIGHTLY MUFFLED as Evie finished scraping off their dinner plates into the scrap bucket. The repetitive motion of making sure the plates were clean enough to hand off to Nick kept her mind off the fact his work had called earlier and told him his start date was only a few weeks out — as soon as the ground thawed.

Nick took the second plate from her and turned to put it in the water as she stared down at the bucket for another moment. She couldn't ask him to stay, even if he wanted to. And she knew the moment she told Andy the news, he would insist that she be relocated.

Their bubble felt ready to burst.

Evie turned her head, frowning at the front door as she slipped the handle of the bucket into her hand. The sounds of the emerging spring wildlife had startled her more than once in the past few weeks. Just yesterday she and Nick had woken up to a buck outside the bedroom window, rubbing his antlers against the side of the cabin.

Nick had damn near shot it through the wall before they'd realized it wasn't an actual threat.

Her eyes scanned the door frame, eyeing the repairs Chuck made over a month ago, then found the small dent in the ceiling. Both spoke to the danger of Nick not being home.

Clearing her throat to be heard over the water, Evie's grip tightened on the food bucket. "I'm just going to take this out."

He turned, flicking water off his hands. "Okay, you good?" He grabbed the towel near the side of the sink and then leaned back onto the cabinets. "You look tense."

"I'm just on edge." She grimaced. "Like always."

Nick dropped the towel and pushed off the cabinet, sliding his hand over her arm and holding onto her forearm for a moment before leaning in and pressing a kiss to her temple. "I know." The words were familiar, washing over her as he muttered against her skin. "Go get some fresh air. I'll see if I can mix us up a mug cake."

Evie laughed, shooting him a wry smile. "I can't believe Hope sent all the supplies up here and *printed out* a recipe. She acts like we're in our eighties. I know how to make a —"

"Shh," he laughed, bending down and cutting her words off with a slight kiss. "She's just young, and Chuck said she misses us being at Adam's and doesn't understand why we can't come to town anymore."

As he pulled back, Evie caught the frown on his expression. The emotions flickered across his face too — the awareness that this wasn't going to last forever. There was no way this entire arrangement had any kind of longevity to it and they'd already played with fire once.

"Go." Nick patted her on the hip. "I love you."

"I love you too." She slipped her boots on, whining a little. "Wait on the cakes though, I'm too full. And text Chuck to bring over that TV, I want to watch stupid 80s movies with you. This is me breaking, I can't exist only on music."

He grinned, glancing over at the crackling fireplace and the stereo. "Yes, dear."

She waved him away, pulling the door shut behind her with a dull thunk as the wood ground against itself from the uneven edges. Evie paused on the porch, sucking in a crisp breath tinted with a hint of smoke from the chimney.

There was nothing out here, it was just her anxiety.

As she walked across the gravel drive, she listened to the dull crunch underfoot, glancing down as she turned her head from side to side, testing her hearing. It was uncomfortable — the sudden awareness that everything was dulled on one side only — a concept that felt foreign to her to suddenly be *without*.

She bet it would make Adam's more bearable.

Evie made her way to the edge of the forest, finding the spot to the side where they normally dumped the scraps. Chuck had asked a couple days ago when he delivered groceries if they'd consider coming to Adam's just one night. She knew from his tone and expression he missed Nick — she missed being out too. She missed the early days when she could bundle up in Nick's truck and go to the library and greet Stephen and —

The emotions choked her as she stood at the forest's edge, holding the bucket upside down, all the food already in the underbrush.

She closed her eyes and breathed in through her nose, paused, then let it out.

This wasn't the time to think of Stephen, or the fact she'd heard from Nick that Stephen's ex-wife had his body cremated, his remains already gone from the state. The library was sitting empty now — probably full of forgotten paperwork and half-shelved books.

Evie righted the bucket as she glanced over the roof of the cabin, the sunset haloing it in red.

Passing by the truck, she swallowed back the lump in her throat and shook her head, clearing her thoughts again. If she strode back in there this distracted, Nick would know something was wrong immediately. He just... knew her.

The top step creaked under her boots as she stepped onto the porch, and stopped short.

The door was partially open.

Time slowed as she glanced up at the corner where the wood ground against itself, where Chuck hadn't sanded it down enough. She always shut it hard so it would latch.

Dread gripped her. It was only seconds, but it felt like years as she processed what it meant. She didn't need to open the door to know something was wrong.

It was always going to end like this.

Evie inhaled sharply and pushed the door open. The wood scraped as it shut behind her.

"Hello, Evelyn."

The bucket fell out of her hand, clattering to the floor hard enough that she heard the plastic crack as she stared at Jonathan Murphy standing in the kitchen next to Nick, gun casually pressed against Nick's side, making a dent in his t-shirt.

Her brain started to catalogue the situation immediately. Murphy was standing on Nick's right, closest to the fridge. Nick's body was partially turned like he'd thought *she* was the one who had entered the cabin, body tense and not close enough to the frontmost cabinet with a gun.

She'd checked the cabinet this morning — staring at the loaded weapon just in case.

The man who had haunted her nightmares for months was smiling.

Her subconscious had remembered him perfectly — he was still tall, but next to Nick she realized they were exactly the same height, matched in ways that felt a little too yin and yang for her tastes. Where Nick's hair was dark brown and tumbled near his shoulders, with a thick beard covering the lower half of his face — Murphy's blond, stringy locks were slicked back, and he was clean shaven and sharp-eyed.

The thing that unnerved her the most were the creases next to Murphy's eyes — light laugh lines that were nowhere near as deep as the ones Nick had... but they were *there.* This monster had once felt joy too, enough that it scarred his face permanently.

Her stomach roiled, threatening to empty the dinner she'd just eaten as she stared at Murphy, unsure what to say or do.

His eyes traced her body, sending another shutter of revulsion through her. "Don't tell me I don't need to do this. I've had *plenty* of time to consider how this evening will go."

From beside him, Evie watched Nick glance from her to the door, once — then twice. He wanted her to run. She didn't have to read his mind to know the clear expression on his face.

She turned her head slightly to the side, a sharp, quick *no.*

"I think..." Murphy raised his free hand, holding up a finger as he stared at her. "I think you don't understand the sheer *trouble* you've fucking caused me. And I've had a lot of time to mull this over. I don't want to monologue, but I'm so *put out* with you, Evelyn."

Her eyes jumped back to Murphy, watching as he stared up at the ceiling and spoke into the air. He had a captive audience, and he knew it.

"I think you got yourself into some of this trouble." Evie

almost didn't recognize her own voice as the words dripped out, icy. "I think this all started because you killed a man —"

"I killed a *fucking cop*. Don't moral high ground me." Murphy's neck snapped down, eyes narrowing. "He was a *cop*, he didn't *care* about you. He didn't give a shit about Hawthorne, the history, the *town*." He waved his free hand again, face twisting. "You should know how much it hurts to have a stranger move into your small town and just... not get it."

Evie swallowed, eyes locked on Murphy as she raised her chin. "I don't think killing a man in the local school is the entrance *you* needed to make before moving in — was it?"

"I lost my temper." Murphy glanced to the side, adjusting his grip on his gun, pressing it a little harder into Nick's side. Evie caught the slight wince at the edges of Nick's eyes as he stared forward, refusing to acknowledge Murphy. "What about you, lumberjack? Agent? Boytoy? Leech on the Warren tit? What do you prefer?"

"Nick," Nick said dryly, his expression guarded.

"You're not fun. At least she's talking to me." He refocused. "I saw Will's body, by the way. That's why I'm here. You did *quite* the number on him, goddamn, Evelyn."

"I did." She glanced at the floor under Murphy's feet. "I still can't get all his blood off the linoleum."

Murphy's face twisted. There was pain — grief, then nothing. "That's why I have cleaners."

"Is there a point to all of this?" Nick looked at Murphy from the side, eyebrow raised. "Because this is the longest fucking stand-off I've ever been in."

"You want me to shoot her?" Murphy looked at him, the gun still. "Because I'm getting there." He paused, and the shift in Murphy's expression made Evie's blood run so cold that even the warmth of the fireplace couldn't thaw it. "I know the longer I'm here the more I risk... but *god* when you have this much time to think, you run through a lot of plans."

Evie forced herself to stay still as she let his words fade to the back of her mind.

They had options too.

She wouldn't risk Nick — it was her own neck on the line. They needed a way for Nick to arm himself. Where Bryant had been brash, Murphy was calculated. She needed to unsettle him.

Her eyes flickered to the kitchen counter near Nick — and the stereo remote within his reach.

"I thought to myself." Murphy's voice came back to her as Evie caught Nick's eye. "Tonight seemed like a *great* night to see you, and then I was outside and I just kept thinking — why let it *only* be tonight? Why let it end quickly?"

"Careful of your hubris, Murphy."

"I know." Murphy smiled at her. "You've driven me to dramatics, Evelyn. I mean look at me. I'm a wreck. You killed someone I care about. It's really only fair that I do the same to you."

Terror flooded her veins, and with it came *rage*.

The fire crackled as Murphy tilted his head and she knew exactly what her only option was.

"Fine." Evie raised an eyebrow. "Regale me, what's your grand revenge plan? You're clearly ready to burst."

His eyes sharpened, sneering, "You're a bit of a cunt, aren't you?"

"Oh, you'll have to be meaner than that, I work with children."

Murphy barked out a laugh, his body jerking with the movement. Evie's eyes didn't stray from him as Nick moved in a flash, grabbing the stereo remote, fingers on the volume.

"Well, funny you mention kids. I had the *great* idea that I take you back to Hawthorne." Murphy smiled. "I thought it would be pretty fucking poetic if I take you back to your little library. I want to watch the light leave your eyes *just* before you hit that big red button."

"Tempting fate." Evie breathed slow, muscles tense. "What if I get away again?"

Murphy raised one shoulder in a shrug. "I'll —"

His words were cut off as Nick held the volume button, making the stereo blare Elvis Presley so loud that even Evie flinched on reflex.

Murphy startled, gun tilting as Nick took his chance and tackled the other man.

Evie refused to watch as she climbed over the couch, jumping the coffee table, and plunged both arms into the roaring fireplace. The flames licked her skin like a lover, burning as she grasped onto the flue chains inside and tugged them, closing the smoke's only escape outside.

The room began to fill almost instantly.

The pain radiating from her arms blinded her, her skin red and tight as she pushed away from the fireplace. She stumbled up, coughing as she inhaled smoke. Blurry figures fought in the entry, both men indistinguishable through the haze.

Evie rounded the couch as the two bodies separated, heading toward the gun cabinet. Someone stumbled toward the front door as the other landed near the fridge. She turned quickly, grabbing onto the cabinet door just to find the holster empty.

It couldn't have been more than a second, but in the haze, she froze.

Hands wrapped around her throat from behind.

"Gotcha." Murphy cut off her air supply with his palms. Evie's response was pure instinct. She slammed her head back into his face with a choked snarl. His hands slipped from around her throat, grasping at her shirt as she twisted, fighting against his grip.

Evie stumbled, pressing against the cabinets as Murphy lunged for her again. She kicked out, her foot connecting with his arm. A *snap* echoed. He howled in pain as she dove for the knife block, her burnt fingers grabbing at the handles as Murphy's hands dragged her backwards.

Evie screamed as she grasped the handle of one of the butcher knives, but her fingers hurt so much she couldn't pull it from the block. A gunshot rang out and the hands on her fell away as Murphy lurched to the side. Through the smoke, she could see the glint of his gun on the floor.

She took her chance and bolted toward the hallway where the only other body in the cabin was standing, holding a gun.

"Did I hit him?" Nick's words were tight as she ran her hands over his shirt and his stomach, making sure he wasn't hurt.

"I think so." She gasped for clean air, dropping lower as the smoke began to cloud the entire area above their torsos. Nick followed her. "Nick we need to go, we need to get out."

"My phone is in the bedroom." He said the words so softly she wasn't sure she heard him correctly. "I need *you* to go, sweetheart. I need you to get out of this cabin."

Evie stared at him, shaking her head as glass crunched, a body rising in the smoke. Murphy rolled his neck from side to side, lifting his gun as he grinned, his arm slightly wavering. Murphy's white shirt was slowly turning red near his left shoulder.

Nick raised his gun, pushing Evie to the side and twisting his torso to have a better shot.

Both guns went off at the same time.

She flinched, the movement drawing her away from Nick and against the wall as she heard him grunt in pain. Evie swung herself around, gasping as blood poured from his collarbone. The gun in Nick's hand shook as he raised his other hand and pressed it against his shoulder.

"Evie, *run*."

She ignored him, grabbing Nick and tugging him into the hallway, pushing him to sit against the wall as Murphy coughed and groaned behind them. Pressing the gun firmer against his hand, she stared at Nick, telling herself the tears welling in her eyes were from the smoke and nothing else.

"I love you," She rushed the words out of her throat before they could choke her. "I love you, Nick Barber. He's not going to kill you, he wants *me. I love you*." She pushed away from him as Murphy shouted her name, firing his gun into the smoke.

If anything happened to her, those had to be her last words to him.

Evie waited to feel a blossom of pain, but nothing came. When she turned her head, she could see Murphy barely visible, gun pointed at the ceiling. She stood, dodging Nick's legs as she grabbed one of the kitchen chairs.

"Murphy!"

He twitched as she got his attention — eyes widening but not fast enough to dodge as she lifted the chair and threw it at him with all her force. From behind, Nick choked out a strangled "*move*," before he fired again. Murphy crumbled in front of her eyes, blood soaking his pants just above his left knee-cap.

"If you want me, you'll have to fucking catch me."

It was a gamble, but Evie darted around Murphy's crumpled form, making for the front door. She threw it open, ignoring the blinding pain in her hands as she stumbled outside with smoke billowing behind her.

Heavy footsteps pounded against the wood of the porch as

she skittered across gravel and dove to hide behind Nick's truck, a gun firing three times behind her.

The tree line was her salvation.

Nick needed time to get help and she intended to give it to him.

CHAPTER THIRTY-NINE

EVIE WONDERED IF THERE WOULD BE A *60 MINUTES* special about her.

The classic Americana sound of the ticking stopwatch echoed in her mind as she ran toward the tree line just past Nick's woodshed. From behind her, Murphy shouted something unintelligible and fired his gun again.

It would be poetic, it was always her grandmother's favorite show to watch before bed. She said she enjoyed learning about new things, new people, even the macabre ones. After her grandfather's death, Evie's grandmother would recount the prior night's episode on the phone to Evie.

All things considered, Evie thought this would make a pretty good special.

She stumbled as she plunged into the forest, the sun no longer overhead. It had set and left the world in a semi-twilight that coated the forest floor in shadows and shrouded anything in front of her that could send her sprawling.

She moved as quickly as she dared, parallel to the cabin's yard. The last thing she needed was to lose her bearings while trying to confuse Murphy. She had to double back and get to Nick —she needed him to be okay. The frantic sounds of cursing and gunshots echoed through the trees as Evie grabbed onto the side of a large oak, going still. She sank into a crouch next to a small cluster of bushes as the ruckus behind her quieted.

"Evelyn." Murphy's voice echoed, giving it a god-like quality as she closed her eyes, willing her breathing to slow enough that she could be silent.

"I'm so tired of games. Aren't you tired of playing them? Cat and mouse, miners and their canaries — don't you feel like you've been prey long enough? Aren't you ready for this to end?"

Her jaw trembled as she kept her mouth shut, inhaling in short bursts through her nose as she heard his footsteps creep forward from somewhere behind her.

He wasn't shooting. There was nothing *to* shoot out here. The sound of them moving through the underbrush had long startled the animals, and the other predators in the forest had too much sense to join their game.

"I want..." Murphy's voice trailed off. "I want to kill you, Evelyn Morgen. You ruined so *fucking* much. You killed *Will* and I'm not going to stop until I get what I want."

Evie opened her eyes, staring at the forest before easing forward on the balls of her feet. Her boots felt restrictive, made for hikes through unknown terrain, not creeping along the forest floor. She slunk forward, keeping herself low to the ground, movement stilted like a baby's first steps, uncertain that the next place her weight settled would be quiet enough.

With time, she eased around another tree, glancing to the right to stare through the darkness, using the smoke from the cabin as her compass.

"Evelyn." Murphy spoke again as she came to a quick stop

near a fallen log, glancing over her shoulder and willing her eyes to adjust to the darkness. The sounds of the forest were already normally disorienting, but her balance was off — her brain fighting to overcompensate for the deafening in her ear to figure out where the danger was.

She eased herself down, her belly brushing dirt, palms smarting, willing herself to be small.

"I saw Will's body." His voice sounded tired, out of breath. "I saw the gash in the side of his throat. You did that — didn't you, Evelyn? You stabbed my — *him* in the throat? With that kitchen knife you tried to put in me earlier? Or maybe a different one — I should have looked at the set, to see if the weapon was wiped off and put back in the block. Are you keeping trophies? Are we more similar than even I thought?"

The sound of a branch breaking cut through her shaking fear. She exhaled, ignoring the searing pain in her burnt arms, not daring to move.

"When I thought about it, I realized why you made me *so* mad. It was that look." Murphy went quiet again, before she heard him in the forest around her. "The look you gave me before you hit the button — you *knew* you were seconds from death but you still stared it in the face. I can't even say that some of my men have done that. My father certainly fucking didn't. He couldn't even meet my eyes when I had my gun pressed to his temple."

Evie swallowed back bile, using the sound of his footsteps to mask her own movements as she pushed away from the log. The smell of smoke grew staunch, souring the once pleasant pine smell she associated with Nick.

"Will told me something on the phone the last time I spoke with him."

Murphy's voice sounded farther away now and Evie refused to stop as she spotted the wood shed — from a slightly askew angle, placing her almost behind the cabin. The change of scenery discombobulated her as she paused, trying to catch her bearings.

"He said you weren't what he expected. I have to agree."

Evie pressed her hands against the forest floor, staring directly at the stump she'd watched Nick stand in front of hundreds of times. Embedded in the top was his wood axe.

She stood up and ran.

Branches cracked behind her as Murphy gave chase. Evie reached the stump first, grasping onto the handle and pulling with every ounce of strength in her body, lifting it just in time to swing herself around. Her entire body flung itself into swinging the axe, Murphy stumbled out of the forest and stopped short of the axe's berth.

He let out a startled laugh, a sound so out of place that it shocked them both.

"What are you going to do with that, Evelyn? An axe against a gun? Is the option to come with me really that bad?" His eyes sparked with the smoky light of the cabin behind her, wild and bright.

The gun in his hand twitched. Evie didn't give him a chance. She stepped forward, screaming as she lifted the axe. "If you kill me, I'm fucking taking you *with me*."

Murphy flinched, lifting his injured arm as she stumbled forward, bringing the axe down hard. The weight forced her off-balance, the axe not as high as she intended and the angle wrong. The blade struck Murphy's hip just as he got the gun level with her side, pulling the trigger.

Blinding pain exploded through her body as Evie gasped, jerking backwards. The axe came with her, leaving Murphy's side with a soft squelch, the other man grunting in horror and pain as he grabbed onto the wound.

She knew the gash wasn't deep enough. She wasn't strong

enough to strike a felling cut from this angle, but it gave her a moment to stumble back. With one hand clutching the axe, she brought the other to her side, warm blood on her palm.

They were mirrored injuries.

The distracted look on Murphy's face faded into sheer rage as he raised the gun again. She lunged forward, half-feral, like she was going to hit him again, and he jerked, the gun firing off to the side and hitting the wood shed.

Evie took a step back, forcing herself to retreat to the cabin at her back, watching as Murphy stumbled on his bad leg, then fell into the grass. She grabbed the axe again with both hands, heaving it up so it wouldn't drag as she stumbled into Nick's truck, pushing herself forward again and again until she dragged herself up the porch steps.

She didn't look back.

CHAPTER FORTY

THE SMOKE SAT IN THE AIR, THE ACRID SMELL lingering. She had to get to a phone before Murphy caught up. Evie rushed past the kitchen table, glancing to the side where she'd left Nick, only seeing blood splatter.

"Nick?"

Her stomach churned as she ran down the hall, snatching Nick's phone from the side of the bed. She mindlessly plugged in *911* before the sound of a grunt made her flinch.

"Evelyn! This is *over*! Get out here before I riddle your little agent with bullet holes."

Evie grasped the phone in her hand, nearly crushing it. In her other hand, the handle of the bloody axe grew slippery with sweat from her palm. Ignoring the pain in her side, she took a step forward, then another.

Murphy stood in front of the couch, the coffee table on its side. With the light of the fire, she could see the blood trail Nick left as he'd crawled toward the fireplace pokers. Murphy's body obscured Nick, who'd only made it to the stereo before he'd stopped.

She could see his chest rising and falling, but she didn't know how much longer that would last. She was keenly aware of her own side on fire, her own breathing labored.

"I'm here." Evie took another step, leaving the safety of the hallway's darkness, holding the phone by her side as she met Murphy's eyes.

He took a step forward, but unlike months ago, she didn't fear him.

Murphy looked like *shit*.

One shoulder drooped as he limped, a hitch in his step, pants bloodied. If this was Hawthorne she'd think he was one of the high schoolers dressing up as a zombie for Halloween, one who'd gotten a little too zealous as they'd applied fake blood from the theater storage closet.

The phone in her hand felt warm. She couldn't remember if she'd actually pressed call.

Murphy shifted the gun before he lifted it and shook his head at her. "I thought I'd kill *him* first." He pointed it at Nick for a brief moment before swiveling his attention back to her. "But I think I'm going to make him watch you die, then I'll let him bleed out next to your *lifeless corpse*."

Evie nodded, pressing her palm down, a button compressing. She hoped it was ringing. She hoped this was the right decision as she let it drop and skitter across the floor to Nick.

The man in front of her didn't blink. They both knew that by the time someone picked up — ambulances were dispatched — Andy was called — this would already be resolved.

It was always going to end like this.

"That sounds great, Murphy." She wrapped her other hand around the axe and used every last shred of strength to lift it, letting the head rest on her shoulder.

They stared at each other. Evie watched as his bloodied lips twitched in a smile. "Are you going to swing at me again,

Evelyn?" His eyes flickered from the axe to the gun pointed at her head. "I think the gun will win this fight."

Evie smiled back. "Try me."

She didn't want to do this in front of Nick. She didn't want the man she loved to watch her body fall to the floor in front of him, just out of reach. But if this was going to happen, she was going to try to take Murphy out with her, to give Nick a fighting chance to stay awake for paramedics to arrive, for *someone* to save him like he'd saved her.

Murphy pulled the trigger.

The empty chamber clicked.

Oh Jonathan, the chamber's empty.

With a feral scream, Evie hauled the axe back and swung it. Murphy dropped the gun, but didn't recoil fast enough. A sickening crunch echoed as Evie struck his wrist and severed his hand clean off his arm. The sound of the body part hitting the floor was muted as she heaved the axe again, slamming it into his injured shoulder, sending Murphy's body stumbling.

They both fell to the hardwood floor.

Evie straddled him, raising the axe above her head and ignoring the pain as he dug his only hand into the gunshot wound on her side, trying to stop her as she swung the axe down at his head again and again. Squelching crunches punctuated each blow as she screamed with the effort of each one.

She only slowed when her muscles screamed in pain, her bloody palms unable to keep hold of the axe. She wasn't sure if it was her own skin weeping from burns or the gore of the man beneath her. With a shuttered sigh, she climbed off the corpse, watching in awe as his forearm twitched, a phantom movement of one limb searching for its missing piece.

Dragging her gaze away, Evie threw herself at Nick. She didn't know where to touch him, so she just put her hands on his chest, staring into his glazed eyes. "It's okay, it's over, we're okay."

There was a din somewhere near them, a muffled sound that drew her attention briefly to the phone on the floor. The sounds registered — someone shouting on the other line.

Evie looked back at Nick and smiled, touching his beard. "Say something, please."

His voice was rough as his hand brushed her side, grabbing onto her shirt as he rasped, "I told you I'd take a bullet for you."

She laughed and dropped her head against his, but the sound turned into a soft keen, fading into heavy sobs as her chest heaved with every unshed emotion from the past months. Nick's hand gripped her tighter, pulling her closer as they clung to each other, lying two feet away from Jonathan Murphy's dead body, unmoving until blue and red lights signaled it was all, finally, over.

"He's more myself than I am. Whatever our souls are made of, his and mine are the same."

Emily Brontë, *Wuthering Heights**

⌄ ⌄

*AFTER REREADING *WUTHERING HEIGHTS* MULTIPLE times while at the cabin, she can't help but think of Nick when she sees this quote.

DECEMBER
TEN MONTHS LATER

Epilogue

THE STACK ON THE CIRCULATION DESK WAS SMALL this year.

She told the kids before every winter break that she didn't mind if they took their books home for the holiday season. Her most voracious readers, of course, always rushed to finish the ones they had, only to take out five more the last day before dismissal.

As Evie scanned the final two books back into the system, she registered a muffled sound coming from the hallway. Her head rose, staring at the double doors just before they were unceremoniously shoved open.

"Excuse me, sweetheart, do you think you could help me find a book?"

The little giggle that bubbled up in her chest was light as Nick stood just inside the doorway, hands on his hips. He was bundled in a huge jacket — a new one her parents had insisted on giving him early for Christmas. But his face was slightly pink from the cold and his beard lifted at the edges of his lips.

"I think I've got a copy of *Fahrenheit 451* somewhere over

— *Nick* —" Evie gasped and then shrieked as he rushed to grab her by the hips, pulling her against him as he moved them back in almost the same motion, pinning her to the circulation desk and dipping his head down to kiss her. The movement made her head spin, and she let it whip her away in the feeling of his hands on her and his nose brushing hers.

"Your mom won't let Andy have any hot chocolate until you come outside." He pressed another kiss to her jaw, murmuring against her skin, "I told her I'd come get you because it's a damn shame if we miss the Christmas market's first cup of the season."

Evie wound her arms around his neck, humming as he paused next to her right ear.

"Plus, if we drink it *now* then we can go home early. We could have a little time to ourselves before the dinner party tonight." He nipped at her earlobe, his tone now teasing. "And I think we should do that, honey. Especially if I can *finally* give you your Christmas gift."

She knew exactly why he was excited. She'd spoiled the surprise for herself two weeks ago when she caught a glimpse of the wrapped watercolor painting in the back of the hall closet. He might have been an ex-FBI agent, but he was *terrible* at hiding presents.

Nick's fingers on her hips shifted and Evie felt his hand creep under her shirt. They were drawn to the divot in her side, a mirror to his own wound. When they were in bed, side by side, bodies wrapped around each other, the two halves were whole.

"Okay." Evie smiled. "I'm done anyway, at least until school reopens in January."

Nick's nose wrinkled. "Three weeks of break, whatever will we do to fill the time?"

She pulled him down again, fingers knotting in the back of

his long hair that was already tangling around the rock on her finger. As she pressed her lips to his, she could already think of a few things to occupy her time until the New Year ahead, and all of them involved her new fiancé.

Because when Nick Barber got down on one knee next to their bedside this morning and presented her a diamond ring resting on top of a worn book cover — one with a couple clad in tartan, a single boob artfully covered — she said yes.

CONTENT WARNINGS

The Felling Cut contains content that might be triggering for some readers.

GRAPHIC (throughout the narrative, on page, explicit):

- Bodily harm (including maiming, violence with a wood axe, violence with a kitchen knife, and gunshot wounds to the body and head)
- Confinement (a character is relocated to a remote cabin and told to remain there indefinitely until the villain is apprehended, though she is not trapped/locked inside)
- Cursing (throughout)
- Death (on page, described in multiple instances, also present in past related to drunk driving and terminal illness)
- Gun violence (some in a school setting, characters are shot, and a character is shot in the head)

- Gore (characters are shot and wounds are described in varying detail)
- Mental Health (characters suffer from anxiety, PTSD, and a character struggles after losing their hearing in one ear)
- Murder (by villains and main characters)
- Injury/Injury detail (gunshot wounds, a character suffers a heart attack off page, a character's hearing is permanently damaged)
- Panic Attack/Anxiety (through narrative, implied PTSD, a character has nightmares)
- Sexual content (on page, Male/Female, kinks/info: praise, dirty talk, soft dominant/pleasure dominant, oral, overstimulation, use of a toy, use of "sir" and "good girl")
- Stalking (by villain)
- Violence (varying degrees, including death, murder, torture)

MODERATE (on page, appears in a few instances):

- Alcohol (scenes set in a bar, characters drink casually)
- Gaslighting (by a side character to the main character)
- Grief (discussed on page)
- Medical content (scenes set in hospital, EMTs/Nurses present, a character is visited in a hospital)
- Misogyny/Sexism (by villain, in thoughts and spoken aloud, also toxic behavior in past related to main characters and masculinity)

- Sexual Harassment/Sexually suggestive taunts (by villain, in thoughts and spoken aloud)
- Suicidal thoughts/references to suicide (by villain)
- Torture (on page, mild violence)
- Vomit/Nausea (brief scene of vomit, characters are nauseous from anxiety)

MINOR (in reference):

- Alcohol abuse (in past, mentioned)
- Biphobia/Homophobia (in past, mentioned regarding family and workplace)
- Death of a sibling (in past, mentioned)

ACKNOWLEDGMENTS

I received over three hundred rejections while querying this manuscript for traditional publishing.

Despite working on it for three years, investing time, money, energy, and tears — and considering setting it on fire — I could never let Nick and Evie's story go. That stubbornness and the endless support from friends who watched my trad pub journey turn to self publishing (three books out in one year!!!) is the reason this book is even here.

All my appreciation and thanks to: Anne-Marie, Kai, Allegra Hall, Amalia, Ana, Ash, Chey, Emily, Isa Agajanian, Jean, Julia, Katie Neel, LJ Kobzina, Michaela, Nikita Navalker, and Robyn. A special thanks to Silvy, who read multiple versions of Nick and still loved him despite the copious errors in those earlier drafts, you'll always be the first Mrs. Nick Barber.

Thank you to my family who heard me talk about a hot lumberjack endlessly, share querying woes, and then ultimately watched me forge my own path.

Thank you to all the readers who picked up *Gold Rush* and *Gold Mine* then decided to stick around for more romantic suspense in a non-omegaverse format. (Nick would totally be an alpha. Evie might just be one too.)

I have a good chunk of gray hair now, but I am **so proud** of this book. I can't wait for everyone to read the other books coming in this world, continuing with the story of a certain Warren heiress and her bodyguard.

Let this be a reminder to never give up — you are stronger than you think.

May your axe strike true.

ABOUT THE AUTHOR

R. L. Randolph is a mildly feral human woman who just wants to write about people kissing for her day job. She lives near the mountains, but, ironically, has grass and tree mold allergies so she never leaves the house.

⋏ ⋏

FOR MORE INFORMATION

You can follow her on Instagram @rlrandolph or join her reader Facebook group.

Also by R. L. Randolph

Golden Omegaverse

June's Duet

Gold Rush (#1)

Gold Mine (#2)

Final Girls

The Felling Cut (#1)

More books coming in 2026